中国农村发展中的能源、环境及适应气候变化问题

林而达　杜丹德　孙　芳等　编著

科学出版社

北京

内 容 简 介

本书首先分析了我国农村发展中的能源问题，即我国农村能源的现状（包括农村能源的种类、消费方式等）；农村能源发展存在的问题；不同用途的农村能源未来的发展趋势以及未来农村能源建设的政策建议。其次研究了由农村能源问题所引发的农村环境问题，如农村能源发展产生的传统污染物（如 SO_2，NO_X，VOCs）增加带来的环境问题；污染物传输引起的环境问题；如臭氧对作物产量的影响；农村能源发展衍生的气候变化问题等，进而研究如何提高我国农村能效、实现能源可持续利用、发展低碳经济的国家机遇与挑战；如何采用市场机制解决农村能源问题引发的环境问题；以及农村能源、适应气候变化与粮食安全的对策。最后根据以上科学研究，提出相关的政策建议：一是发展可再生能源等新型能源开发利用对策；二是发展低碳经济是解决农村能源、环境问题以及气候变化问题的主要途径；三是采用市场机制和国际贸易手段解决农村能源问题的可行性案例研究；四是我国农村能源建设的政策建议。

本书可供广大能源、环境和气候变化研究人员参考使用。

图书在版编目 (CIP) 数据

中国农村发展中的能源、环境及适应气候变化问题/林而达等编著. —北京：科学出版社，2011

ISBN 978-7-03-031047-7

Ⅰ. ①中… Ⅱ. ①林… Ⅲ. ①农村能源-研究-中国 Ⅳ. ①F323.214

中国版本图书馆 CIP 数据核字（2011）第 086462 号

责任编辑：文 杨 朱海燕／责任校对：钟 洋
责任印制：钱玉芬／封面设计：王 浩

科 学 出 版 社 出版
北京东黄城根北街16号
邮政编码：100717
http://www.sciencep.com

北京通州皇家印刷厂印刷

科学出版社发行 各地新华书店经销

*

2011年9月第 一 版 开本：787×1092 1/16
2011年9月第一次印刷 印张：17 1/2
印数：1—3 000 字数：384 000

定价：88.00元

（如有印装质量问题，我社负责调换）

本书编委会

主　　编： 林而达　杜丹德　孙　芳

编　　委（按姓氏拼音排序）：

Anil Markandya　Brian Fisher　董红敏　高庆先

郭　敬　居　辉　李俊清　刘世俊　刘小和

鲁志强　Luis Gomez-Echeverri　Martin Parry

孙学兵　徐华清　徐晋涛　张建宇　赵成义

参编人员（按姓氏拼音排序）：

李　劼　李　勇　马占云　戎　兵　师华定　陶秀萍

王　昊　王　蕾　熊　伟　于胜民　Zach Willey　张玉波

Editorial Board

序

自 1978 年改革开放以来，中国逐步从贫穷、落后走向小康、繁荣。中国确定了以人为本、全面、协调和可持续的科学发展方向，并为建设资源节约型环境友好型社会、提高生态文明水平做出了坚持不懈的努力。在汶川地震、金融危机、国际减排舆论压力的多重影响下，中国更需要加倍关注经济、能源、环境和气候变化以及其他可能的重大问题，减少气候、能源和环境危机对人类的可持续发展和全球生物多样性及生态系统带来的重大威胁，维护人类长期生存和健康发展。实践证明，中国环境与发展国际合作委员会将中国农村能源、环境和气候变化问题作为 2009 年的研究重点课题是正确和及时的。

中国是一个有着悠久历史的农业大国，农村人口众多，布局分散，自然条件和发展水平差异很大，为了促进广大农村地区和广大农民收入增加、生活条件改善和生活质量提高，实现中国经济公平、均衡、可持续的发展，势必要增加对农村能源的需求，从而带来了生态和环境问题，尤其是农村地区的气候变化问题。该书在详细阐述影响中国农村能源发展的关键驱动力和发展趋势的基础上，剖析了建立农村新清洁能源发展、农村环境保护以及农村地区减缓和适应气候变化三者之间的逻辑关系，展望新能源和传统能源资源的开发前景以及可再生和非可再生能源的供应蓝图，并提出了符合中国经济发展趋势的以市场刺激机制为侧重点的政策框架建议，为中国在"十二五"期间全面推动节能减排以及将低碳经济、绿色经济纳入国家发展规划提供了科学的参考。

我相信这部著作的出版，将为我国农村能源、环境和适应气候变化问题的解决和相关政策的制定提供重要的理论支持，并为我国实现建设现代化农业的宏伟目标，加快农村能源建设、促进农村生态环境、减缓温室气体排放以及适应气候变化起到重要推动作用。

感谢中外专家为此做出的辛勤努力。

环境保护部部长

中国环境与发展国际合作委员会

中方执行副主席　周生贤

2010 年 12 月

Foreword

Since its economic reform and opening up in 1978, China has gradually moved from backwardness and poverty to modernization and prosperity. To maintain this trajectory, China has resolved to emphasize comprehensive, coordinated, people-oriented sustainable development. Building a resource-conserving, environmentally friendly society in China and also worldwide will require unremitting effort.

The Wenchuan earthquake occurred in 2008, the global financial crisis, and unmistakable evidence of large-scale climate change have recently spurred China to focus even more relentlessly on curbing threats to ecosystems and biodiversity while building a robust economy and ensuring long-term human survival. China Council for International Cooperation on Environment and Development (CCICED) decision to focus in 2009 on the rural energy supply and environment in China-and the contribution of rural areas to climate change, as well as the impact of global warming on them-is therefore timely.

China is a large agricultural country with an immense rural population, and wide variations in geography and climate as well as economic development. Because development has lagged in rural regions, China has resolved to modernize these regions along with their energy supply. However, as rural incomes, living standards, and quality of life rise, energy demand among rural residents is also growing, and will continue to do so. These shifts will worsen environmental and ecological problems in rural regions-exacerbated by global climate change.

This book analyzes opportunities to develop renewable energy sources and protect the rural environment while also mitigating and adapting to climate change. In so doing, the book provides a blueprint for both modernizing the traditional rural energy supply and promoting renewable alternatives. This blueprint therefore supports the overarching goal of modernizing agriculture, expanding the rural energy supply, and improving the rural environment and ecology while also curbing global warming emissions.

By suggesting market-based policy instruments that can spur these changes, the book provides important solutions to China's energy and environmental challenges as well as global climate change. In fact, this book provides both scientific and policy support for making energy conservation, pollution reduction, and a shift to a low-carbon economy China's foremost priorities in its 12th Five Year Plan.

I appreciate the tremendous effort that both Chinese and foreign scientists and economists have made in analyzing these problems and developing a plan to address them.

Zhou Shengxian

Minister of Environmental Protection

CCICED Executive Vice-Chair, Chinese side

December 2010

前　言

中国是一个有着 8 亿农业人口的农业大国，"农业、农村、农民"问题（"三农"问题）一直是关系到中国经济和社会发展全局的重大问题。

胡锦涛同志在党的"十七大"报告中提出要在 2020 年实现全面建设小康社会的奋斗目标，为了实现这一目标，中国政府必须促进广大农村地区广大农民收入的增加、生活条件的改善和生活质量的提高，以实现中国经济公平、均衡、可持续的发展。而农村发展带动的能源需求增长及其带来的环境问题是中国未来经济发展和社会稳定必须面对的世纪难题。与中国城市用能相比，农村能源消费的增长及结构都呈现出一些独有特点，农村人口众多，布局分散，自然条件和发展水平差异，都大大增加了农村能源问题的复杂性，从而对中国能源体系及能源政策的效能产生了巨大而深远的影响。农村能源状况是解决"农业、农村、农民"问题（"三农"问题）的重要切入点。在中国快速工业化、城市化、市场化的带动下，农业生产方式、农民生活方式和农村社会发展发生了前所未有的进步和巨变，带来前所未有的冲击和震动，为加快农村能源建设、促进农村生态环境改善带来了前所未有的挑战和紧迫性，也为适应气候变化带来巨大的需求和机遇。

当前，中国正处在全面建设小康社会的重要历史时期，应对全球金融危机、建设社会主义新农村、建设生态文明和应对气候变化的客观要求，为加快农村能源建设和促进农村生态环境的改善提供了前所未有的发展机遇。加速农村能源建设既可以帮助提高农业产量，进而提高农民的生活水平，也可以改造农村地区的环境和生态。同时，建立稳定和可持续的农村能源供应体系也是农村地区减缓温室气体排放和适应气候变化的关键所在。

本书主要指出了影响中国农村能源发展的关键驱动力和发展趋势，展示了建立农村新清洁能源发展、农村环境保护以及农村地区减缓和适应气候变化三者之间的逻辑关系，分析了新能源和传能源资源的开发前景以及可再生和非可再生能源的供应蓝图，并在最后提出了符合中国经济发展趋势的以市场刺激机制为侧重点的政策框架建议。

本书是中国环境与发展国际合作委员会和中国-联合国气候变化伙伴框架项目子课题研究成果的汇编，由多位中外专家共同合作完成。第 1 章由林而达编写，第 2 章由徐华清、于胜民、孙芳编写；第 3 章由徐华清、于胜民编写；第 4 章由高庆先、师华定、熊伟、戎兵、马占云编写；第 5 章由 Anil Markandya（英）、杜丹德（美）、Zach Willey（美）编写；第 6 章由赵成义、刘小和、Martin Parry（英）、Brian Fisher（澳）编写；第 7 章由董红敏、陶秀萍、孙芳、王昊、赵成义、徐晋涛、李劼、李俊清、张玉波编写；第 8 章由林而达编写。

Preface

China is a large agricultural country with a rural population of some 800 million. The challenges entailed in ensuring the well-being of "agriculture, countryside, and farmers" — "the three rural issues" —have always been critical to the healthy development of the nation's economy and society.

In 2007, President Hu Jintao pledged in the Communist Party's 17th National Congress that China would build a well-off society by 2020, to build a well-off society in an all-around way and achieve fair, balanced, and sustainable economic development by 2020—the goals of the Chinese Communist Party and government—China must raise the income of its massive peasant population, and improve the living conditions and quality of life in its vast rural areas. However, realizing those goals is especially challenging because rural development is now driving higher energy demand and worsening environmental problems—core problems that China must confront to ensure social stability as well as continued economic development. The large and scattered rural populaces as well as differences in natural conditions and level of economic development between urban and rural regions, make China's rural energy challenges especially complex. An accurate understanding of rural energy supply, demand, management, and use is critical. Such an understanding will not only help the nation solve "the three rural issues" —agriculture, countryside, and farmers—but also help ensure the effectiveness of China's energy policies.

Indeed, China is entering an important historical period in its campaign to build a well-off society in an all-around way. It is necessary to address the effects of the global financial crisis and build a new socialist countryside while also creating an ecological civilization and fighting climate change to provide an unprecedented opportunity. That's because accelerating rural energy construction can help boost crop yields and farmers' living standards while also improving the environment and ecology of the countryside. Creating a stable and sustainable rural energy supply is also critical in enabling rural areas to both adapt to climate change and help slow it down by controlling the release of greenhouse gases.

By identifying the key forces that affect the rural energy supply, we will show the links among developing new sources of clean energy, preserving the rural environment, and mitigating and adapting to climate change. We will also analyze the prospects for both new and conventional energy resources, and renewable and nonrenewable energy supplies. Finally, we will suggest a strategic framework and policy recommendations for capitalizing on those links that emphasize market incentives consistent with China's growing economy.

The book is a conclusion of one of the China Council for International Cooperation on Environment and Development task force and China-UN Climate Change Partnership Framework Project, and it gathers the effort from many Chinese and foreign experts. Chapter one was composed by Lin Erda; Chapter two was composed by Xu Huaqing, Yu Shengmin and Sun Fang; Chapter three was composed by Xu Huaqing and Yu Shengmin; Chapter four was composed by Gao Qingxian, Shi Huading, Xiong Wei, Rong Bing and Ma Zhanyun; Chapter five was composed by Anil Markandya (UK), Dan Dudek (US), Zach Willey (US); Chapter six was composed by Zhao Chengyi, Liu Xiaohe, Martin Parry (UK), Brian Fisher (Australia); Chapter seven was composed by Dong Hongmin, Tao Xiuping, Sun Fang, Wang Hao, Zhao Chengyi, Xu Jintao, Li Jie, Li Junqing, and Zhang Yubo. Chapter eight was composed by Lin Erda.

目　　录

Contents

第1章 绪 论

中国是一个农业大国，大量、分散的农村人口以及各地不同的自然条件和经济发展水平使得农村的能源问题远比城市复杂得多。改革开放以来，中国的农村经济取得了快速发展，同时也在能源环境和气候变化方面面临着巨大挑战。一是农村能源消费快速增长，农村生活用能商品化程度低；二是与能源利用相关的环境问题突出，中国农村燃煤产生的二氧化硫和二氧化碳排放量持续增长，秸秆和薪柴等传统非商品能源燃烧成为农村室内污染的重要来源；三是农村为最容易受气候变化不利影响的地区，同时，从土地管理和森林保护的角度看，农村也是增强碳汇潜力最大的地区。

本研究的目的是通过文献分析与中外案例分析相结合，为中国未来农村发展、解决农村能源环境问题以及农村应对气候变化问题提供政策建议。研究成果表明：中国政府应将解决农村能源环境问题纳入新农村建设的战略任务之中，采取综合措施，强化管理，加大农村清洁和可再生能源开发的力度，建立健全农村可再生能源技术服务体系，发展低碳高效农业，并重视农村适应气候变化的政策措施。

（1）提升农村能源发展在国家能源与应对气候变化战略中的地位。加快对农村电网的改造并提高电网效率；加强对适宜不同农村地区应用的节能技术和新能源技术和产品的研发；研究建立国家农村能源建设资金投入机制，推动农村可持续能源建设。完善农村可再生能源发展规划及配套法律法规体系；因地制宜地大力发展农村生物质能；把农村生物质能利用设施，特别是大中型沼气工程，纳入国家农业基础设施计划。同时，加大对农村环境的整治，减少健康风险。

（2）采取综合措施，加大农村清洁和可再生能源开发的力度。农村煤炭、石油产品和电力等商业能源使用的增长导致了环境污染和温室气体排放的增加。亟待加强清洁的、可再生能源，如沼气、生物质发电等的开发利用，减少能源供给与需求之间的缺口，削减污染，提高农民收入，控制温室气体排放。首先，需要制定农村可再生能源战略和配套法律法规，改善农村环境和应对气候变化。第二，政府应促进可再生能源技术的发展并扩大应用范围，扩大政府在现代生物质能利用设施上的投资，或提供补贴和税收激励措施鼓励私营资本在农村可再生能源技术研发上的投资。只有在政府的强力推动下，中国才有可能充分实现其可再生能源的商业化。农村能源建设基金将会促进可持续能源的发展，而"转移支付"可以为农民用电提供补贴。第三，中国应推广农村沼气应用，将沼气设施纳入农村基础设施建设工作之中，并建立适当的市场机制来鼓励沼气设施的发展。第四，中国应扩大可再生能源利用，为农村建筑供暖和供电。农村建筑的能耗已经占中国能源使用量相当大的一部分，其能源消耗量正在快速增长。为此，在落实农村建筑节能政策的前提下，对节能示范技术、补贴额度和方法进行监测评估，推广节能材料在新农村建设中的应用，同时，依靠可再生能源技术为农村建筑供热能够帮助节约能源。为了实现这一目标，需要推广用太阳能和浅层地热技术为农村建筑供热的做法，并作为建设社会主义新农村的一部分。

（3）优化土地利用，增加碳汇潜力，支持发展低碳高效农业，引入新的农村碳汇补偿机制。中国应维持并增加其森林、农田、草原和湿地的碳汇，引入土壤和生物质固碳的实践，减少温室气体排放。这些实践包括植树造林、改进自然生态系统管理、低耕和非耕农业，改善草原管理，改变牲畜和饲料品种，化肥的高效使用。政府应建立健全农村能源技术服务体系和长效管理机制，在使农民及时获得节能技术和低碳耕作信息的同时，确保有关技术能得到全面推广和长期使用。政府必须为促进这些目标的实现，特别是对那些人口多且生态环境脆弱的地区提供补贴、保险和信贷。恰当的信贷政策和交易机制可以帮助农民通过改变生产实践，在削减温室气体的同时增加收入。低排放、高能效循环农业产业将有助于中国削减污染物排放和农村温室气体排放。中国目前已有很多好的实践。中国应制定综合长期战略，根据各地情况，发展低碳农业，保护生态环境，包括为鼓励新技术投资提供长期的补贴。国家自愿性碳交易机制和为贫困农户削减污染物和温室气体排放提供补贴是促进低碳农业的有效方法，同时也将有助于消除贫困目标的实现。

（4）提高农民和农村地区适应气候变化的能力。加强农民适应气候变化的能力对保持农村经济的持续发展、改善农村生活水平、保护生态系统和生物多样性、确保粮食安全来说至关重要。为此，中国应采取以下措施：①评估潜在的自然灾害的频率和规模，建立区域气候变化监测和早期预警系统；②各级政府机构在制定发展战略时都应考虑适应气候变化，加强社区灾害预防和培训；③调整农业生产和消费结构；④采取灵活方式，确保资金和技术成为支持农村应对气候变化的两大支柱；⑤为保障自身的粮食供应，缓解国内资源与环境的压力，中国应进口资源成本消耗高的农产品；⑥应对气候变化注意加强生物多样性保护，保存国内和国际基因库的生物多样性信息。

（5）加强农村能源使用的统计分析工作。为了保证农村能源成为中国能源系统的组成部分，有关部门需要加强以用户和生产者为统计口径的农村能源终端使用的统计分析。第一，有关部门需要统一农村生产的定义，以确保统计数据能反映乡镇企业的实际能耗。第二，需要加强县级政府组织和管理能源统计数据的能力，然后工业和农林等部门在统计部门的指导下，计算和报告当地能源消费的统计数据。国家统计局收集、检查并发布全面汇总数据，以保证国家农村能源数据的权威性和真实性。

第2章 中国农村能源、环境和气候变化问题概述

农村能源是发展农业生产和保障农民生活的重要资源，其开发和利用与农村环境保护、温室气体减排和应对气候变化等问题之间的联系非常密切，因此农村能源是农村全面建设小康社会和实现可持续发展的物质基础。

2.1 中国农村能源问题的演变

2.1.1 农村能源的基本概念和界定

农村能源的定义分为狭义和广义之分，狭义的农村能源即农村地区的能源，包括外界输入的商品能源，也包括当地的可再生能源；广义的农村能源则是针对第三世界国家农村地区由于经济不发达和很少得到商品能源供应而不得不仅依靠当地可获取的可再生能源而提出的一个概念，其实质是指农村地区的能源问题（王效华，高树铭，2003）。本研究讨论的农村能源问题，涵盖了农村地区的能源供需和管理，以及当地资源的开发利用。所说的农村能源供给，包括了不可再生能源、可再生能源以及新能源在内的所有商品能源和非商品能源。所说的农村能源消费需求，包括了农村范围内居民生活和生产消费两个领域的所有用能：其中的居民生活用能指农民生活中炊事、取暖、制冷、热水、照明及家用电器等用能，农村生产用能包括农、林、牧、渔诸业的作业、运输、初始加工以及在乡村举办的乡镇企业用能。

在过去特定历史条件下，中国在能源问题上实行城乡区别对待和管理，国家能源建设主要侧重于保障工业和城市用能需求，广大农村缺乏基本的商品能源服务，长期以来只能在国家商品能源供给体系之外挖掘当地资源条件自给自足。因此，我国传统的农村能源概念在管理上往往被简单地视同为农村就地开发利用的非商品能源和可再生能源，如作物秸秆、薪柴、沼气、牛粪等生物能源和小型风电、水电、太阳能以及小煤矿等辅助性能源。

经过三十多年的农村经济建设和发展，随着农村生活水平不断提高，中国广大农民的用能品种和方式出现了城镇化趋势，商品能源、可再生能源和新能源不断进入农村视野，农村地区无论能源消费数量和质量都在悄然发生量变或质变，农村能源的管理也在与时俱进地进行调整。

2.1.2 中国农村能源问题的环境影响

中国拥有大量的农村人口，农村地区幅员辽阔，因此农业生产、农民生活和农村发展过程中都要消费大量的能源，而中国农村的能源问题与环境问题总是息息相关。

一方面，农村能源的结构和利用方式不当，会给环境，尤其是农村生态环境，造成极大的压力。在农村能源主要依赖于直接利用生物质能的时代，农村能源利用的低效和能源需求的快速增加曾经是给农村生态环境造成一系列问题的主要原因。1979年全国范围内的调查表明，农村的生活用能和许多农产品加工用能均来自薪柴和秸秆燃料，年耗实物量超过6亿t，其中2.4亿～2.6亿t的薪柴中有30％～40％通过过量采樵掠取，从而加剧了我国的水土流失、土壤肥力下降和荒漠化等生态环境问题（王效华，高树铭，2003）。

改革开放以来，随着农民收入水平的增加，中国农村商品能源消费不断增加。日益增加的化石能源消费大大增加了农村地区各种污染物的排放，包括二氧化硫（SO_2）、氮氧化物（NO_x）、烟尘、粉尘和各种固体废物等，给农村地区环境带来显著的负面影响。由于我国农村地区能源消费分散、利用方式落后，目前农村地区能源消费产生的废弃物和污染物，或未经任何处理过程直接进入环境（例如炊事或采暖等室内燃煤和秸秆燃烧产生的空气污染物直接排放），或长期堆放于农村居民生活环境当中（例如燃煤废渣的就近堆弃），由此带来的环境问题和对居民健康的影响与城市相比更加突出。

另一方面，农村新能源和可再生能源建设，可以促进畜禽粪便、秸秆等农业和农村废弃物的有效利用，对于改善农村环境和促进农村地区的可持续发展有着举足轻重的作用。为了实现这一目标，政府必须建立相应的经济刺激手段和政策框架鼓励开发商和消费者使用新的可再生能源，从而达到控制农村地区污染和改善环境的目的。

2.1.3　中国农村能源问题与气候变化

随着城市化的大力推进、农村经济的飞速发展和农村生活质量的快速提高，农村能源消费结构正不断地发生变化，农村能源的开发和利用与温室气体减排和应对全球气候变化之间的联系也日益密切。

长期以来，中国农民生活用能沿用传统的旧炉灶，热效率不足10％，消耗了大量的秸秆、薪柴和原煤，造成了农村地区的能源短缺和温室气体排放。由于中国城乡二元结构发展，农村和城市生活标准差距巨大，农村人均能源消费和人均碳排放水平均大大低于城市，因此，随着农村社会的结构转型和农民生活水平的提高，中国农村能源消费外延式物理扩张的发展空间十分巨大，并将对温室气体排放产生较大的影响（赵行姝，2003）。

农村新能源和可再生能源的发展可以提高能源效率、替代常规能源，是减少温室气体排放最有效的途径之一。相关研究表明，从1990～2000年中国推动沼气建设、风能等10余项农村可再生能源技术已经使二氧化碳（CO_2）减排15872万t，甲烷（CH_4）减排23.1万t（王革华等，2002）。

根据相关规划，如果中国在农村大力推进沼气等生物质能源的利用，扶持风能、太阳能、地热能和海洋能的开发和利用，以及林业重点生态建设工程和生物质能源林基地建设，预计2010年可以分别减少二氧化碳排放约1亿t和增加碳汇0.5亿t（朱四海，2007）。除了生物质和土壤之外，造林是最好的固碳方式之一。由于中国农村人口众多并具有多样化的特点，通过经济激励政策鼓励供应商和消费者利用以上能源资源，是政府实现预期目标的最佳途径。

2.2 中国农村能源、环境和气候变化问题的政策背景

当前，中国正处于全面建设小康社会的重要历史时期，应对全球金融危机、建设社会主义新农村、建设生态文明和应对气候变化的客观要求，为加快农村能源建设和促进农村生态环境的改善提供了前所未有的发展机遇，也提出了新的任务和挑战。中国已经出台了多项政策应对目前的挑战。

2.2.1 应对全球金融危机

2008 年由美国次贷危机引发的世界金融危机震动了全球。作为全球经济的有机组成部分，中国经济也受到了世界金融危机的严重冲击，外部经济环境日益恶劣，不确定因素显著增多。

中国农村和农民也受到了危机的直接影响。由于出口锐减，国内一些行业产能过剩，部分企业经营困难，首当其冲的就是农民失去就业机会，造成农民工返乡潮，既影响农民收入，又影响农村稳定。

而金融危机也可能导致各级财政收入增幅减缓，致使涉农财政支出受到较大影响，会直接影响农村基础设施和公共物品的供给，从而增加城乡发展差距，加剧农村环境污染程度。

中国抵制金融危机的核心策略在于扩大内需，而中国扩大内需的潜力主要在农村。因此，在当前国际经济形势和中国经济发展形势下，中国农村也面临着一次大的发展机遇。2008 年，在国际金融危机和国内严重自然灾害的双重压力下，中国政府采取了积极的应对策略，加大了"三农"和生态文明建设投资，有效地拉动了内需，保持经济平稳较快发展。

例如，2008 年中央财政增加投资 1 万亿元人民币，重点投向民生工程、基础设施、生态环境建设和灾后重建，预计带动社会总投资规模 4 万亿元人民币。在带动的 4 万亿元总投资中，用于农村水、电、路、气、房等民生工程和基础设施投资约 3700 亿元、节能减排和生态工程投资约 2100 亿元、灾后恢复重建投资约 1 万亿元。同时，为了拉动农村地区的消费需求，财政部、商务部下发《家电下乡推广工作方案》，对实施地区农民购买家电产品实行直接补贴。

这些重大的政策和措施，对中国农村能源的利用和结构的改善、对中国农村地区的节能减排、对中国农村环境的改善和中国农村地区适应气候变化问题能力的增强都将产生极其深远的影响。但只有有了相应的新能源和环境定价政策的支持，这些重大措施才能真正起到鼓励可再生能源的发展和减少温室气体和其他污染排放的作用。

2.2.2 建设社会主义新农村

为防止出现贫富悬殊、城乡和地区差距拉大、经济社会长期徘徊不前等问题，中国

共产党在十六届五中全会上提出"生产发展、生活宽裕、乡风文明、村容整洁、管理民主"的建设社会主义新农村建设的总体要求,作为新形势下加强"三农"工作、大力推进全面建设小康社会和现代化建设的战略举措。

发展新的农村能源是社会主义新农村建设的重要内容。通过经济激励措施和市场定价,新能源的开发可以繁荣农村经济、增加农民收入、促进农民生活方式的转变,并对资源的循环利用、农村环境的优化和城乡一体化的发展具有重要意义。

2.2.3　生态文明建设

中国共产党的十七大把生态文明建设提高到了发展的战略高度。胡锦涛同志在十七大报告中指出,2020 年实现全面建设小康社会奋斗目标的新要求之一是建设生态文明,基本形成节约能源资源和保护生态环境的产业结构、增长方式、消费模式;循环经济形成较大规模,可再生能源比重显著上升;主要污染物排放得到有效控制,生态环境质量明显改善;生态文明观念在全社会牢固树立。

随着农村经济的不断发展,农村的生态与环境问题不断突出,乡镇企业"三废"排放量不断增加、农业废弃物无法有效利用、化肥农药大量流失、生活污染大量排放、生活垃圾大量堆积、大气环境和水环境质量不断恶化等。因此,农村生态文明建设是实现农业可持续发展,农村和谐发展,农民物质生活与精神生活丰富、健康、幸福的重要保障与措施,是解决我国"三农"问题的最终出路。

在生态文明建设的指导下,中国"三农"问题的解决出现了许多新的发展思路,这些发展思路强调了以市场定价为核心的政策机制在综合解决中国农村的能源、环境和气候变化适应能力建设等问题上的重要作用。

2.2.4　控制温室气体排放和增强适应气候变化能力

气候变化是人类社会发展面临的巨大挑战。尽管气候变暖问题仍然存在科学上的不确定性,但是减少温室气体排放和增强社会经济系统对气候变化的适应能力已经成为世界各国积极推动的"无悔行动"。

中国一直是全球气候变化和相关国际环境政策制定和执行的积极参与者。2007 年,中国政府发布了《中国应对气候变化国家方案》,提出了以下目标:

到 2010 年单位国内生产总值(GDP)能耗要在 2005 年基础上减少 20％左右;

到 2010 年单位国内生产总值主要污染物排放要在 2005 年基础上减少 10％;

到 2010 年再生能源开发利用总量(包括大水电)在一次能源供应结构中的比重提高至 10％左右;

到 2010 年森林覆盖率达到 20％,力争实现碳汇数量比 2005 年增加约 0.5 亿 t 二氧化碳。

为了实现上述目标,中国的能源结构、经济结构和消费结构都要进行大范围深层次的调整。这也为中国农村经济发展、农业生产方式变革、农村能源开发利用、农村废物处理以及农村环境保护提供了机遇。大力发展可再生能源、发展循环经济、强化对农业和农村废弃物的综合利用和处理、继续实施植树造林等碳汇工程成为中国农村能源开发利用和农村发展的必然要求。

另一方面，气候变化导致的极端天气事件增加、旱涝等灾害频率和强度加大等问题增加了中国农业生产的不稳定性和农业生产系统的脆弱性，对中国农业和农村的可持续发展构成了挑战和威胁。因此，中国农业和农村必须增强自身对气候变化的适应能力，以确保农业生产持续稳定发展和农村生态系统的良性循环。国家必须出台相应的激励措施，鼓励农民采用新的技术和耕作方式，在适应气候变化的同时减少自身的排放。

第3章 中国农村能源利用的趋势与挑战

改革开放以来，我国按照因地制宜、多元发展的方针，加强农村能源建设，积极发展农村沼气、秸秆发电、小水电、风能、太阳能等可再生能源，改造和完善农村电网，改善了农村生产生活用能条件，解决了3000多万农村无电人口及偏远地区的用电问题（罗国亮，张媛敏，2008）。同时，在联合国开发计划署（UNDP）等国际组织的大力支持与配合下，一些旨在解决农村贫困问题的能源项目陆续实施[①]，对缓解民族地区、边远山区、贫困地区的能源短缺状况发挥了积极作用。

然而，中国是一个有近8亿农村人口的农业大国，农村能源系统投入和统筹规划方面相对滞后，农村能源基础设施薄弱、农村能源消费水平低、用能方式粗放、利用效率低等问题大量存在。由于未来相当长时期内农村能源需求增长将高于城市能源需求增长，依靠传统能源很难满足农村经济社会发展的需求，农村能源紧缺的矛盾将逐步显现。如果不能很好地解决这些问题，将严重影响农民生活质量提高、农村经济的可持续发展和社会的稳定。

3.1 中国农村能源利用的现状

3.1.1 农村能源消费总量

自改革开放以来，中国农村经济发展迅速，农村能源消费的数量、品种和结构也随之发生了巨大的变化。

从总量来看，农村能源消费总量（包括生产耗能和生活耗能）由1980年的3.28亿t标准煤上升到2006年的9.565亿t标准煤，增加了将近两倍。从消费部门来看，农村能源消费主要用于农业生产和居民生活，农业生产用能占农村能源消费的比重由1980年的20.4%上升至2006年的47.6%，呈逐年上升的趋势。

农村生产用能总量仍保持增加趋势，但增速放缓；而在国家农业政策导向的作用下，农村居民人均收入增加明显，生活水平迅速提高，生活用能增加明显，与生产用能增速保持基本一致（表3.1）。

工业化发达国家已经基本消除了城乡差别，农村与城市能源消费相比几乎没有什么差别，均处于较高水平，其终端消费的能源品种基本上是天然气、电力和石油制品，只有极少量的煤炭和薪柴。对于中国农村地区，一方面受传统能源消费模式的影响，另一方面受到经济发展水平的制约，秸秆、薪柴等传统能源仍然是农村能源消费的主要来源之一。农村能源消费结构明显变化，商品能源消费比例增加。商品能源消费从1980年

---

① 先后实施"光明工程"、"农网改造"、"水电农村电气化"和"送电下乡"等。

表 3.1　2000～2005 年农村生活、生产用能消费量

年份	生产用能/万 t 标准煤	比例/%	生活用能/万 t 标准煤	比例/%
2000	300.48	44.8	369.99	55.2
2001	311.75	42.9	414.28	57.1
2002	329.33	42.1	453.47	57.9
2003	350.37	43.2	461.27	56.8
2004	359.65	42.9	479.32	57.1
2005	382.86	44.0	483.97	56.0

数据来源：农业部

占总消费量的 30%，增加到 2006 年的 67.3%（表 3.2 和图 3.1）。农村商品能源以煤炭、电力和成品油（含天然气）为主，其中煤炭消费量占到商品能源消费总量的 2/3 左右，这与我国以煤炭为主的能源结构基本一致。非商品能源消费总量年际间略有波动，总体保持稳定。

表 3.2　1991 年与 2004 年中国农村能源消费情况

项目	1991 年消费量/万 t 标准煤	2004 年消费量/万 t 标准煤
能源消费总量	56 822	83 879
生活用能	36 004	47 932
秸秆	16 213	14 580
薪柴	10 303	12 043
煤炭	7752	16 283
电力	1163	2934
成品油	133	1136
沼气	—	399
其他*	4.04	567
生产用能	20 818	35 947
煤炭	11 996	19 128
成品油	3834	6415
电力	2926	5623
薪柴	2062	3276

* 其他包括液化石油气、煤气和太阳能热水器等

数据来源：农村能源统计年鉴 1997；农业部科技教育司

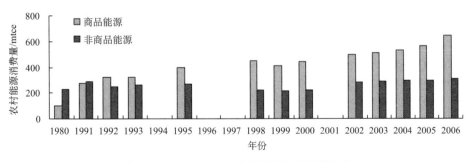

图 3.1　1980～2006 年农村能源年消费量变化

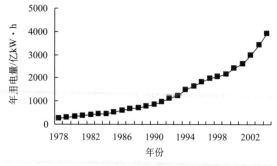

图 3.2　1978~2004 年中国农村用电量变化

以农村用电量为例（图 3.2），改革开放初期的 1978 年为 253.1 亿 kW·h，2004 年达到 3933.0 亿 kW·h，为前者的 15.5 倍，年均增速 11.2%，超过同期 GDP 增长速度，也高于同期全社会用电量增长速度。

以 2006 年各省数据为例，得到不同省区农村居民人均年生活用电量与收入的关系（图 3.3），农村居民人均年收入水平与用电量呈明显正相关，经济发达地区农村居民用电量明显高于落后地区。综合分析 1978 年以来农村用电量增加趋势，表明农村经济水平的不断提高是推动用电量增加的主要驱动因素，一方面用电量的增加来自于乡镇企业生产规模不断扩大的需求，另一方面，来自于农村居民不断提高的生活质量和家用电器的增加，以上两方面都直接表现为农村经济规模的扩大和人均收入的增加。

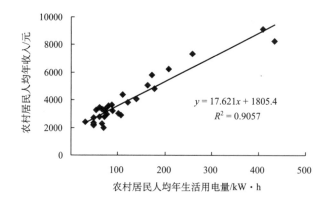

图 3.3　农村居民人均收入与年生活用电量的相关性分析

随着农村经济结构的变化，农村用电由以排灌用电和照明用电为主，转变为以农村工业用电和农村生活（电器）用电为主的局面。农村地区排灌、副业及生产、乡镇企业、居民生活所占用电比重由 1978 年的 44.3%、22.1%、16.1%、17.5% 变为 2000 年的 13.3%、12%、45.1%、24.2%，乡镇企业与居民生活用电所占比重超过了排灌与农副业生产所占比重。

煤炭、电力、成品油等优质商品能源消费增加迅速，液化石油气（LPG）等具有城市属性的能源也出现在农村能源消费中。

以 1991 年和 2004 年农村能源消费数据为例，通过比较能源消费总量数据和能源类型构成（图 3.4）。可以看出，农村生活耗能中的煤炭、电力和成品油消费快速增加，秸秆的消费大幅减少；而农村生产用能结构变化相对缓慢，其中电力和成品油消费稍有增加，煤炭消费量减少。

根据农业部科技教育司《2008 年全国农村可再生能源统计资料》，2007 年全国农村生活终端能源消费量总计为 34575.74 万 t 标准煤（按电热当量法计算，下同），其中商

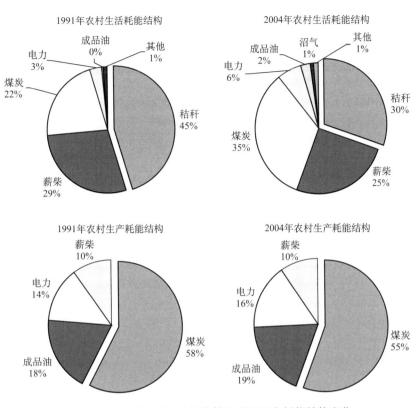

图 3.4 1991 年和 2004 年农村生活和生产耗能结构变化

品能源折合 8015.1 万 t 标准煤,非商品能源折合 26560.65 万 t 标准煤。农村生活用能结构仍以非商品能源为主(76.8%),其中秸秆和薪柴对非商品能源的贡献率分别为60%和35%;商品能源则以煤炭为主,电力次之,两者对商品能源的贡献率分别为62.6%和22.4%(表 3.3)。

表 3.3 2007 年我国农村生活终端能源消费情况

品种	实物量	标准量/万 t 标准煤	人均用能	贡献率/%
商品能源小计	—	8015.10	110kgce	23.2
煤炭	7172.72 万 t	5013.86	69kg	14.5
电力	1459.42 亿 kW·h	1792.68	201kW·h	5.2
成品油	363.12 万 t	532.79	5.0kg	1.5
LPG	378.71 万 t	649.22	5.2kg	1.9
天然气	1.61 亿 m³	21.57	0.2m³	0.1
煤气	1.73 亿 m³	4.98	0.2m³	0.0
非商品能源小计	—	26 560.64	365kgce	76.8
秸秆	33 997.52 万 t	15 978.83	467kg	46.2
薪柴	18 216.89 万 t	9290.62	250kg	26.9
沼气	1 023 962.60 万 m³	731.11	14.1m³	2.1
太阳能	5810.09 万 m³	560.08	0.08m³	1.6
合计	—	34 575.74	475kgce	100

随着经济水平的提高，农村居民人均能源消费量持续增加，传统的以生物质能直接利用为主的能源消费模式被破坏，秸秆、薪柴供给不足的直接生态后果是导致农村周边植被的破坏，改革开放初期因多种经营和生活需要导致的能源消耗增加带来的环境破坏主要是以植被破坏为主；然而，在农村居民经济条件进一步改善后，其生活模式和能源消费方式积极向城市靠拢，传统的生物质直接燃烧的能源利用模式被抛弃，大量的秸秆得不到利用，或被直接焚烧，或被弃置不顾。

传统的、以生物质能消费为主的模式，其物质循环过程是合理的，主要问题在于能效低，以及落后的直接燃烧方式对环境卫生和农村居民生活条件改善的限制，因此无法满足收入水平提高后，农村居民对生活质量提高的需求（表3.4）。煤炭等商品能源消费增加，从环境的角度看是不合理的，导致了农村环境污染负荷的增加，但其转变却是必然的，因为对于农村居民来说，煤炭相对方便、高效，费用在可承受的水平，更重要的是，煤炭消费的灶具以及使用方式对于农村居民来说是容易获得和掌握的。

表 3.4 农村商品能源与传统非商品能源消费特点对比

项目	煤炭	秸秆/薪柴
消费成本	商品能源，价格较高，需现金购买；但与其他优质商品能源比较，价格低	非商品能源，主要来自于农业生产的废弃物；农户分散利用条件下，主要成本是收集、运输和储存，基本不需要现金购买
属性	化石能源	生物质能
使用特点	相对方便、高效	使用方式落后，导致居住环境卫生条件差，能效低
温室气体	高 CO_2 排放	少 CO_2 排放，微量 CH_4 排放
污染物	高排放	排放较低，但落后的直接燃烧利用方式造成较严重的室内空气质量问题
固体废弃物	燃煤废渣数量较多，无资源化利用价值，处理成本高，多数被直接抛弃，导致严重的农村居民点环境问题	草木灰等燃烧残余数量较少，可以作为肥料使用
物质循环	单次使用，需不断购买	可实现在农业生产过程中的物质循环

以煤炭为主的化石燃料消费，给农村环境带来极大破坏，特别在我国北方地区，农村冬季采暖的燃料已经由过去的秸秆、薪柴为主，向以煤炭为主转变。一方面，煤炭燃烧后的固体废弃物无法利用，也缺少集中处理能力，导致环境污染；另一方面，目前农村煤炭利用效率低，单位有效发热值的 CO_2 排放水平远高于城市。

3.1.2 农村生活用能

长期以来，中国农村处于半自给自足的小农经济模式下，秸秆和薪柴等生物质资源为主的非商品能源消费占据主要地位，特别是在生活耗能方面。虽然非商品能源消费比例不断下降，但从消费总量来看，仍然是重要的能源组成部分。非商品能源消费主要用于农村居民家庭炊事和冬季采暖，以直接燃烧为最主要的方式。

改革开放初期，非商品能源消费占到农村生活耗能的 85% 以上，随着经济水平的提高和生活模式的改变，农村生活能源消费中非商品能源比例不断下降，2000 年之后，相对稳定在 50％左右（图 3.5），秸秆消费的变化趋势与非商品能源一致。

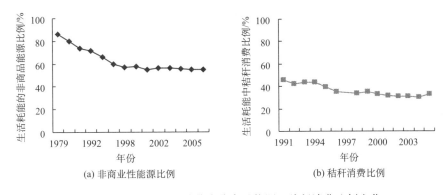

图 3.5　农村生活能源消费中非商品能源、秸秆消费比例变化

　　我国农村人均生活用能的增长趋势与生活用能大体相似，1995～2007 年，我国农村人均生活用能呈现波动性增长，从终端用能的结构变化来看，从 1995～2007 年，我国农村生活用能煤炭和薪柴的使用量分别下降了 10.7％和 7.2％，而秸秆、沼气、太阳能、电力、成品油、液化石油气分别增长了 5.9％、575％、865％、241％、343％、1246％，是我国农村生活用能的主要增量来源（图 3.6）。然而，由于基数小，沼气、太阳能、成品油和液化石油气等优质能源对农村生活用能的贡献度仍非常有限。此外，天然气近三年在农村从无到有发展迅速，目前主要集中在北京和上海等大城市的郊区乡村。

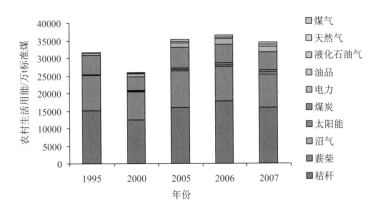

图 3.6　1995～2007 年中国农村生活用能分品种及总量的变化趋势

　　在此期间，商品能源快于非商品能源的增长，两者增长率分别为 3.4％和 1.8％。1995～2006 年我国农村人均生活用能总体上呈稳步增长态势，至于最近两年是否属于触顶下降尚缺乏足够的证据（图 3.7）。
　　从农村生活用能的区域分布来看，由于不同区域农村居民的能源消费水平和结构同地区经济发展水平、资源、气候、住宅类型以及生活习惯密切相关，我国分地区的农村生活用能及结构存在着鲜明的地区特征。中国的农村生活用能总量和人均生活用能，都

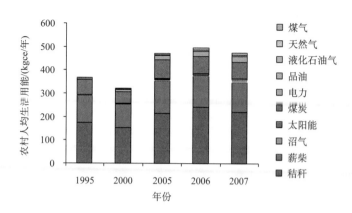

图 3.7　1995～2007 年全国农村人均生活用能分品种变化趋势

由东向西呈现阶梯性增长，西部地区的农村生活用能总量和人均生活用能都高于中东部地区（表 3.5）。从非商品能源和商品能源的分布来看，西部地区非商品能源的总量、人均量和占整个生活用能的比重也远远高于中东部地区，这表明西部农村生活用能以非商品用能为主、效率低下是西部地区人均生活用能高于全国平均水平和中东部地区水平的主要原因。

表 3.5　2007 年分地区农村生活用能状况

地区	生活用能		非商品能源			商品能源		
	总量/万 t 标准煤	人均量/kgce	总量/万 t 标准煤	人均量/kgce	比重/%	总量/万 t 标准煤	人均量/kgce	比重/%
全国	34 575.7	475	26 560.6	365	76.8	8015.1	110	23.2
东部	10 709.5	463	7597.6	329	71.1	3111.9	135	29.5
中部	11 354.2	465	8922.2	365	78.5	2432.0	100	21.5
西部	12 512.0	547	10 040.8	439	80.3	2471.2	108	19.7

注：1. 商品能源包括煤炭、电力、成品油、液化石油气、天然气、煤气；非商品能源包括秸秆、薪柴、沼气和太阳能。2. 东部地区包括北京、天津、河北、辽宁、上海、江苏、浙江、福建、山东、广东和海南；西部地区包括重庆、四川、贵州、西藏、甘肃、青海、宁夏、新疆、陕西、云南、内蒙古和广西；中部地区包括山西、安徽、江西、河南、湖北、湖南、吉林和黑龙江。

中国农村各地区人均生活用电量水平发展同样不均衡，主要表现为东部地区高、西部地区低。从 2006 年中国农村居民人均生活用电量来看，北京地区达到 434.38kW·h，上海地区为 408.59kW·h；超过 100kW·h 的地区还有浙江、天津、福建、江苏、广东、辽宁、河北、山东、重庆、四川，主要为东部地区省份。而人均生活用电低于 50kW·h 的地区有新疆、甘肃、青海、云南和西藏（图 3.8）。

从能源结构的区域分布（图 3.9）来看，西部地区秸秆和薪柴对生活用能的总贡献率高于中东部地区，但是电力、成品油和液化石油气等优质能源的贡献率大大低于中东部地区。另外，图中还显示我国东部地区太阳能使用比例较高，太阳能热水器渗透率估计已达到农村户数的 16%；西部地区户用沼气发展相对较好，渗透率已达到农村户数的 16%。

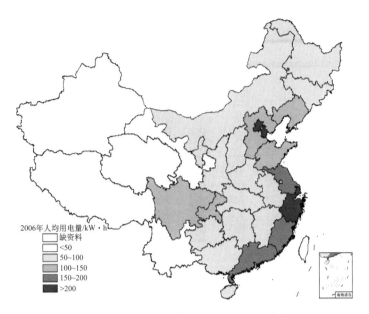

图 3.8　2006 年农村居民人均生活用电量

数据来源：中国农村住户调查资料 2007

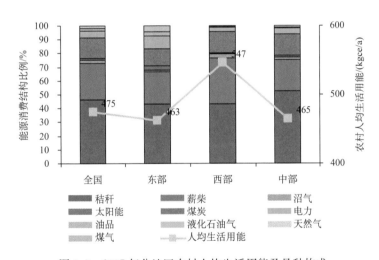

图 3.9　2007 年分地区农村人均生活用能及品种构成

　　一般而言，当地资源状况是农村生活用能的主要决定因素，因此农区倾向于使用秸秆，山地和林区主要使用薪柴，牧区主要使用牲畜粪便，煤炭产区则主要使用煤炭，而经济发达的农村地区能源消费水平和类型更早出现多样化、商品化和城市化特征。我国东部地区经济发达，电力、液化石油气等优质商品能源比例较高，农村能源向商品化、优质化、城市化方向发展，因此大幅提高了能源利用效率，农村人均生活用能低于其他地区。中西部地区煤炭资源比较丰富廉价，煤炭在生活用能中占据了较大比例，但由于经济相对落后，这些地区农村生活用能更多地倾向于使用生物质能，即中部偏重秸秆而西部偏重薪柴。

由于气候或生活习惯等方面的原因，西部地区冬季需采暖、且采暖期相对较长，我国西部地区农村人均生活用能，尤其是人均生物质能源使用量显著高于中东部地区。（图 3.10～图 3.12）

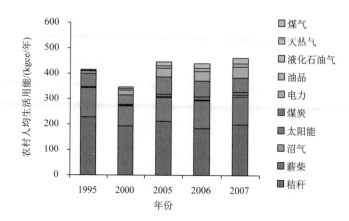

图 3.10　1995～2007 年东部地区农村人均生活用能分品种变化趋势

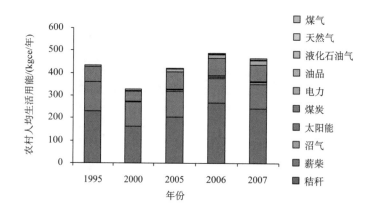

图 3.11　1995～2007 年中部地区农村人均生活用能分品种变化趋势

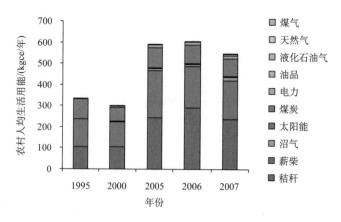

图 3.12　1995～2007 年西部地区农村人均生活用能分品种变化趋势

受资源总量和生活习惯的影响，非商品能源消费存在明显的地区差异，以 2006 年数据为例，各省市秸秆消费量差异明显，最低的西藏自治区仅为 10.34 万 t 标准煤，最高的四川省为 2123.21 万 t 标准煤；薪柴消费量也是西藏自治区最少，仅 11.22 万 t 标准煤，贵州省最高，为 1056.81 万 t 标准煤。华北地区和四川、重庆、黑龙江的秸秆消费量最大，与这些省区是我国主要的粮食产区有关（图 3.13）；西南地区的四川、贵州、云南、广西和广东得益于该地区丰富的林地资源，薪柴消费高于其他地区。

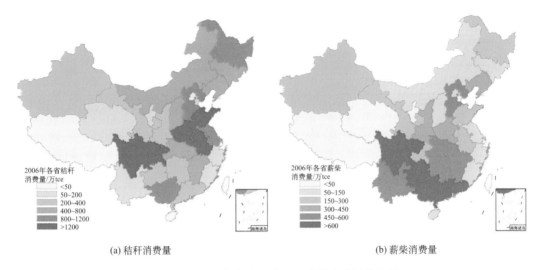

(a) 秸秆消费量　　　　　　　　　　　　　　(b) 薪柴消费量

图 3.13　2006 年各省市秸秆、薪柴消费量分布图

数据来源：《中国能源统计年鉴 2007》

3.1.3　农业生产用能

一般认为，农村经济主要包括农业生产，即农、林、牧、渔业生产和乡镇企业两个部分。因此，我国农村生产用能也可以分为农林牧渔业生产用能和乡镇企业用能两部分。

以 2000 年不变价格计算，我国农林牧渔业增加值已经从 1995 年的 12513 亿元增加到 2006 年的 19028 亿元，年均增长 3.8%。

我国乡镇企业增加值已经从 1995 年的 14405 亿元（根据工业品出厂价格指数 1985 年＝100 折算成 2000 年不变价，下同）增加到 2006 年的 51184 亿元，年均增长达到 11.5%，2006 年对国内生产总值的贡献已经达到 29.2%[1]。

2007 年我国农村生产终端用能总计 38098.2 万 t 标准煤[2]（按电热当量法计算，下

---

[1]　相当多乡镇企业已经向城镇化、工业化转型发展，虽然其增加值被人为地全部计入农村经济的范畴，现实情况很可能有很大比例的能源消费量发生在农村能源的统计范围之外。未来 20 年，乡镇企业将继续大规模城镇化、工业化，其能源消费应该逐步从农村能源的范畴划出，因此下文关于未来 20 年农村能源的需求分析不再讨论我国乡镇企业的能源供需问题。

[2]　其中，农村生产终端用能的分品种数据来自农业部科技教育司的"全国农村可再生能源统计资料"，农林牧渔业终端用能数据来自国家能源统计年鉴全国能源平衡表，结合历年乡镇企业增加值中农林牧渔业的比例，可以推算当年我国农村乡镇企业的终端用能情况。

同），主要来源于商品能源，包括煤炭、焦炭、电力、油品，贡献率分别为 62.4％、5.9％、5.4％、17.3％（表 3.6）。

表 3.6 2007 年农村生产用能及品种构成

项目	生产用能/万 t 标准煤	结构/％	农林牧渔业用能/万 t 标准煤	结构/％	乡镇企业用能/万 t 标准煤	结构/％
煤炭	23 788.2	62.4	1688.0	27.8	22 145.4	68.8
焦炭	2229.9	5.9	79.4	1.3	2152.6	6.7
油品	6581.2	17.3	3109.2	51.1	3555.0	11.0
电力	2047.3	5.4	1203.1	19.8	876.3	2.8
薪柴	3451.6	9.0	0		3451.6	10.7
合计	38 098.2	100	6079.7	100	32 180.9	100

数据来源：《2008 年全国农村可再生能源统计资料》，《2008 年中国能源统计年鉴》；作者推算。

从生产用能的服务对象看，乡镇企业是主要的用能单位，其生产用能占 2007 年生产用能的 84.5％。乡镇企业用能则主要来自商品用能，其中对乡镇企业用能贡献率最大的为煤炭（68.8％），其次为油品（11.0％），非商品能源全部为薪柴，它对乡镇企业用能的贡献率为 10.7％。

从 1995~2006 年，农林牧渔业终端用能的增长率超出了其产量增加值的增长率，达到 4.1％，其中油品和电力的增长率大于 5％。这是由于我国农业生产机械化的广度和深度在不断提升，大幅度促进了农业生产对电力和成品油等商品能源的消费需求，2007 年我国农用机械总动力达到 7.66 亿 kW，农业机械化发展已经跨入中级阶段。

从 1995~2007 年，中国农林牧渔业的终端用能总量稳步增长，年均增长 4.1％，其中以油品和电力的增长为主，两者均保持 5％以上的增长率（图 3.14）。

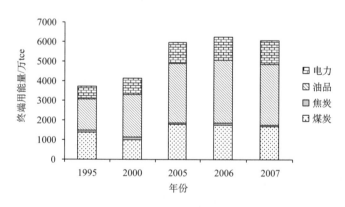

图 3.14 1995~2007 年中国农林牧渔业终端用能分品种及总量的变化趋势

从能源消费强度变化趋势来看，由于我国农业生产机械化水平不断提高，农林牧渔业每百万元增加值（以 2000 年不变价计）的终端能源消费强度从 1995 年的 29.8t 标准煤增加到 2006 年的 32.8t 标准煤（图 3.15），年均增长 0.9％左右。我国乡镇企业每百万元增加值（根据工业品出厂价格指数 1985 年＝100 折算成 2000 年不变价）的终端能源消费强度从 1995 年的 142.4t 标准煤持续下降到 2006 年的 69.3t 标准煤（图 3.15），年均下降 6.6%，到 2006 年甚至低于当年工业增加值的终端能源消费强度（148.3t 标准煤/百万元人民币 2000 年不变价）。由于乡镇企业生产规模的增加，虽然其工业生产总值仍统计进入农村经济的范畴，但其能源消费量并没有在农村生产用能的统计中得到完全反映，因此造成了乡镇企业终端能源消费强度的低估。

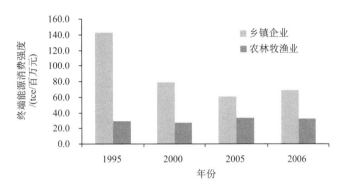

图 3.15　1995～2006 年农林牧渔业和乡镇企业单位增加值终端能源消费强度

　　1995～2007 年，我国乡镇企业的终端用能总量前 11 年呈现增长势头，年均稳步增长 5.0%，但 2007 年比 2006 年降低了 9.2%（图 3.16）。与农林牧渔业能源增长特征不同，我国乡镇企业终端用能增量主要来自煤炭，其次为薪柴、油品和焦炭。

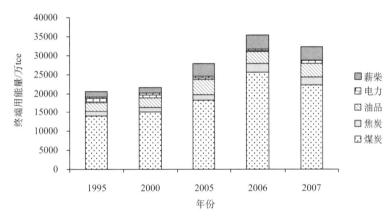

图 3.16　1995～2007 年中国乡镇企业终端用能分品种及总量的变化趋势

3.2　农村能源消费存在的问题

　　在农村能源消费总量快速增加，能源结构明显变化，以及商品能源消费比例不断提高的情景下，农村能源消费存在的各类问题愈发突出。传统的秸秆、薪柴的热效率仅为 10%～15%，家庭炉灶的燃煤热效率也在 20% 左右；到 2006 年，北方地区超过 50% 农户使用地炕和土暖气供暖，然而其热效率也仅有 40% 左右。低能效导致燃料消费量增加，大量的热能得不到充分利用。

商品能源消费，特别是煤炭的消费，导致了严重的农村环境问题，一方面是燃煤产生大量废渣。我国煤炭的平均灰分含量高达23%，农村居民燃煤质量较差，其灰分含量可能高于全国的平均水平。此外，蜂窝煤、煤球等在农村地区普遍被使用，其中掺入的黏土高达40%以上，加之燃烧效率较低，几乎每燃烧一个当量的标准煤，就会产生等量的固体废渣。另一方面，由于农村居民生活燃煤主要在室内进行，悬浮颗粒物（TSP）、二氧化硫（SO_2）、一氧化碳（CO）等污染物，导致了严重的室内环境问题（李智文等，2006）；部分地区由于煤炭中氟含量超标，导致的农村居民燃煤型氟中毒依然严重（李永华等，2002）。不仅煤炭等商品能源消费导致污染物排放的增加，传统的秸秆、薪柴直接燃烧也导致一定的环境问题，主要污染物包括悬浮颗粒物（TSP）、二氧化硫（SO_2）、甲烷（CH_4）、氮氧化物（NO_x）等（王效华，冯祯民，2004）。

农村能源的开发缺乏长期稳定的资金支持渠道。目前中国农村可再生能源的开发和利用最主要的资金渠道为财政资金，但是财政资金与农村能源开发与利用需求之间的缺口正在日益增加。以沼气为例，中央政府每年安排10亿元国债资金用于农村沼气建设工作，但每年也仅能安排建设100万户农村沼气，与各地的建设需求差距较大。农户缺乏农村能源建设的启动资金大大制约了农村能源的开发和利用。仍以沼气为例，调查表明，一口标准（按规定规格）小型沼气池，包括材料费、专业人工费投资大约需要1600元，其中国家财政补贴1200元/口，其余400元的资金缺口则由农户自己负担。由于国家实际拨付给农户的启动资金只有360元，其余补贴资金在工程完工验收合格之后拨付，因此每口沼气池需要农户1240元的初期资金投入。在这种情况下，即使有国家补贴，家境困难的农户也有可能选择放弃沼气池建设。农民贷款难是制约农村能源建设的一个重要原因。在土地集体所有制下，农户拥有的宅基地、房产、耕地使用权等无法流通和转让，农民缺乏信用工具。因此，在农村能源建设中，大多数农民会因"找不到担保人"或"没有合适的抵押物"而难以得到金融支持。

3.3　中国未来农村能源需求

我国要在2050年达到世界中等发达国家的经济水平的目标要求，中国农村人口占总人口的70%，没有农村的现代化就没有国家的现代化。从西方发达国家的经验和规律看，农村用能的历史演变过程与社会生产力的发展过程是相对应的（赵行姝，2003）。从现在至2020年，被认为是我国农村经济水平跳跃式增长的重要时期，因此，农村能源消费总量的迅速增长是无法避免的问题。

农村能源需求与农村人口、收入和生活水平以及能源利用效率等有关。根据目前我国经济发展战略和农村能源政策，预计今后影响农村能源消费的主要因素将发生如下变化。

3.3.1　乡村人口

乡村人口主要受人口自然增长率和城镇化率两个因素影响。从过去的趋势看，人口城镇化的速度高于人口自然增长的速度，我国乡村人口数呈稳步下降趋势。预计到2010年全国乡村人口约7.0亿，占全国总人口的51%左右；到2020年全国乡村人口

6.1 亿，占全国总人口的 42% 左右；到 2030 年全国乡村人口约 5.3 亿，占全国总人口的 36% 左右。农村能源必须满足这部分人口的生活用能需求。

3.3.2　收入、生活水平和能源价格

农户的收入越高，对能源的舒适性、便利性、卫生特性的要求越高，商品能源消费需求越高（陆慧，卢黎，2006）。因此，能源消费与经济收入有密切关系。按当年价格计算，全国农村居民家庭人均纯收入已从 2000 年的 2253 元增加到 2007 年的 4140 元，其中东部从 3137 元增加到 5626 元，中部从 2071 元增加到 3878 元，西部从 1685 元增加到 3033 元。收入增加促进农村居民改善生活质量，提高对电器、机动车耐用消费品的需求，并且使农村居民倾向于购买高效率的农用机械以替代部分劳动。这两方面因素都会刺激农村商品能源需求。

根据我国全面建设小康社会的目标，未来 20 年我国农民人均纯收入仍将保持 5%～6% 左右的增长率，实现从基本小康向宽裕型小康生活的跨越，物质生活水平和环境将会得到较大改善。收入增加和生活水平的提高将极大地刺激对商品能源和优质能源的需求，毫无疑问，生物质能的传统利用方式将逐步消失。

3.3.3　国家的农村能源政策

进入 21 世纪以来，随着国民经济的发展和国家财力的增强，按照工业反哺农业、城市支持农村的要求，国家进一步加强了农村能源建设和管理工作，实施了全国农村电网改造和无电地区电力建设工作，加大了对农户沼气工程建设的支持力度，开展了以电代燃料试点工程建设，农村能源建设取得了更大的进步。

在当前统筹城乡发展、建设社会主义新农村的政策环境下，农村能源也将"统筹城乡发展"，逐步融入国家能源体系。农村最终将获得国家正常的、公平的商品能源服务，同时又将利用与可再生能源的天然联系，为国家能源安全、保护生态环境以及减缓全球气候变化做出自己特有的贡献。为了实现这些目标，需制定新的能源和环境价格政策，鼓励清洁可再生能源的发展，对减排（包括削减温室气体排放）进行奖励。

3.3.4　农村地区的可再生能源

我国农村可供利用的能源资源，除常规商品能源外，还有生物质能以及小水电、风能、太阳能、地热能等。中国农村生物质能资源主要有农作物秸秆、树木枝丫、畜禽粪便、能源作物（植物）等。

根据我国主要农作物产量及谷草比，农作物秸秆理论资源量可达 6 亿 t，扣除收集损失以及直接还田、畜牧饲料、造纸原料等方式利用外，可能源化的利用量在 3 亿 t 以上，折合约 1.5 亿 t 标准煤。

林木枝丫和林业废弃物年可获得量约 9 亿 t，其中 3 亿 t 可作为能源利用，折合约 2 亿 t 标准煤。

畜禽粪便资源理论上可年产沼气约 700 亿 m³。甘蔗、甜高粱、木薯、甘薯、小桐子、黄连木、油桐等能源作物（植物）可种植面积达 2000 多万 hm²，可满足年产量约 5000 万 t 生物液体燃料的原料需求，约相当于 0.7 亿 t 标准煤。

初步估算，中国现在每年可以作为能源利用的生物质能资源大约相当于 6 亿 t 标准煤。

另外，全国农村小水电资源（100kW≤单站装机容量＜5 万 kW）可开发量约为 1.28 亿 kW，主要分布在湖南、湖北、广东、广西、河南、浙江、福建、江西、云南、四川、新疆和西藏等，约占全国小水电可开发资源量的 90%。

我国是世界上季风最为显著的国家之一，风能资源比较丰富，东南沿海及岛屿、内蒙古、西北地区、东北部分地区风能最为丰富，风速 3m/s 以上的时间全年均在 5000 小时以上，这些地区的农村具有较好的风能开发利用条件，可以解决当地的生活或生产用电问题。

我国大部分地区位于北纬 45°以南，太阳能资源十分丰富，其中新疆、西藏、青海、甘肃、内蒙古、山西、河北等地年日照时数超过 2200 小时，具有较好的太阳能利用条件，尤其在西北、青藏等秸秆数量少、薪柴生长慢的地区，太阳能开发利用已有了较好的发展。

3.3.5 满足中国未来农村能源需求的方案

邓可蕴等（2000）通过分析测算，设计了中国农村地区中长期能源需求的常规情景和加强可再生能源开发利用情景。该预测的基本假设包括：①农村能源需求增长迅速，在全国能源消耗中的比重逐步增大；②农业现代化进程需要增加优质商品能源的消耗，增大优质能源的比例；③乡镇工业注重提高用能效率，在生产规模扩大的同时，实现节能减排，降低能源消耗的增长速度；④农村居民生活用能结构优化，优质能源消费比例提高。

该研究的预测结果表明，2010 年、2020 年和 2050 年中国农村地区常规情景下的能源需求分别为 126248 万 t、157417 万 t 和 199320 万 t 标准煤，加强情景下 2010 年、2020 年和 2050 年的能源需求分别比常规情景高 655 万 t、354 万 t 和 10482 万 t 标准煤（表 3.7）。

表 3.7　中国农村地区能源需求预测（单位：万 t 标准煤）

年份	1995	2010	2020	2050
常规情景	68 989	126 248	157 417	199 320
加强情景	68 989	126 903	157 771	209 802

利用"长期能源替代规划（LEAP）"模型对我国农村未来 20 年的能源需求及其碳排放进行情景分析，LEAP 模型分析以 2005 年为农村能源消费分析数据的基年，预测年份分别为 2010 年、2020 年和 2030 年，设置常规和强化可再生能源两个情景。LEAP 模型的宏观驱动因子，如人口、收入水平、粮食产量以及农林牧渔业增加值等，通过定

性定量分析历史趋势和我国相关国家发展规划进行设定，见表 3.8。

表 3.8 未来农村人口及其收入水平的预估

年份	农村人口/万人				年人均纯收入/元 (2005 年不变价)				农林牧渔业增加值 /亿元	农林牧渔业增长率/%	粮食产量 /万 t	粮食产量年均增长率 /%
	全国	东部	西部	中部	全国	东部	西部	中部				
2005	74 544	24 256	24 179	26 109	3255	4523	2389	2977	23 070	4	48 402.2	1
2010	70 695	22 855	23 162	24 679	4333	5911	3197	3984	28 069	4	50 871	1
2020	62 997	20 052	21 127	21 818	7375	10 097	5725	7135	41 548	4	56 193	1
2030	52 298	17 249	19 092	18 957	12 032	16 448	9780	12 187	61 502	4	62 073	1

考虑到未来二、三十年可能出现的产业结构调整、能源技术演变趋势，以及社会、经济、环境等种种不确定性因素对农村能源需求和温室气体排放产生的影响，可以得到常规情景以及强化可再生能源情景下未来农村生活和农业生产终端能源需求（表 3.9，表 3.10）。

常规情景下的计算结果显示，今后我国农林牧渔业的终端生产能耗将随着生产方式的不断现代化和机械化而加大，到 2030 年达到 1.2 亿 t 标准煤（以电热当量法核算，下同），低于邓可蕴等（2000）的研究（表 3.9）。从能源结构看，随着机械化和集约化生产程度大幅度上升，农业生产各环节的能耗都将增加，主要表现为油品和电力快速增长，而煤炭的比重将下降到 10% 左右。

在生活用能方面，随着新农村建设的开展和生活水平的提高，农民将逐步拓展对取暖、制冷、热水以及家用电器和交通等终端用能目的的能源需求，同时由于未来农村每户人口数的下降以及居住面积的增加，农村居民在炊事、照明等方面的人均能耗将有所增长。

依照常规情景，今后 20 年农村生活用的传统生物质能无论绝对量还是消费比重都将在现有的基础上进一步下降，部分秸秆和薪柴资源利用将转向现代化的可再生能源，到 2030 年秸秆的传统能源利用方式和现代化能源利用方式基本达到 1∶1 的比例。

小水电、小风电、沼气和太阳能等其他现代化可再生能源的贡献率也将逐步扩大。农民对优质商品能源的生活用能需求将不断扩大，主要表现为对电力、油品和 LPG 的需求，天然气和煤气将逐步出现在部分发达的农村，但对全国农民的用能贡献仍然可以忽略。由于现代化可再生能源的发展和其他优质商品能源对农民生活用能的贡献率在不断扩大，农村生活用煤量将保持过去三年来的缓慢下降趋势。

在强化可再生能源情景下，为了满足农民对优质生活用能的需求，可以充分利用广泛分布在我国农村的可再生能源资源，采用现代能源技术加强农村可再生能源的开发利用，不仅农村小水电、小风电、沼气和太阳能的发展要快于常规情景，更主要的表现是农村对生物质能源的现代化利用方式得到飞跃式发展，到 2030 年秸秆的传统能源利用方式和现代化能源利用方式基本达到 1∶2 的比例（表 3.10）。秸秆和薪柴的现代化能源开发不仅减少了传统生物质燃烧，还以替代的方式降低对煤炭的需求，最终农村生活用煤量在强化可再生能源情景下较常规情景有明显下降。这是值得我们推荐的方案。

表 3.9 农村生产生活能源需求预测——常规情景（单位：万 t 标准煤）

| 年度 | 农林牧渔生产用能 | | | | | 农村生活用能 | | | | | | | | | | | | | | | | | | 生活用能 | 农村能源 |
| | 煤炭 | 焦炭 | 成品油 | 电力 | 生产用能小计 | 商品能源 | | | | | | | 传统生物质能 | | | 现代可再生能源 | | | | | | | 小计 | 总计 |
						煤炭	电力	成品油	LPG	天然气	煤气	小计	秸秆	薪柴	小计	秸秆	薪柴	小水电	小风电	沼气	太阳能	小计		
2005	1809.4	59.2	3024.9	1077	5970.5	5814.1	912.5	377.6	490.5	3.2	3.4	7601.3	15959.6	10309.5	26269.1	0	0	428	28	492.7	416	1364.7	35235.1	41205.6
2010	1751	109	3543	1436	6839	5717	1629	673	820	27	5.2	8871.6	15407	8892	24299	1020	695	565	45	881	686	3892	37062.2	43901.2
2020	1756	174	5306	2412	9648	5390	2867	1048	1205	47	8.7	10565.5	11923	7493	19416	3422	1577	840	117	1330	1103	8389	38370.7	48018.7
2030	2223	247	6792	3087	12349	4788	3994	1319	1554	66	12.3	11733.3	6875	5386	12261	6009	2148	1114	303	1781	1520	12375	36869.3	49218.3

注：这里假设农村小水电和风电全部用于当地生活用电，表下同。

表 3.10 农村生产生活能源需求预测——强化可再生能情景（单位：万 t 标准煤）

| 年度 | 农林牧渔生产用能 | | | | | 农村生活用能 | | | | | | | | | | | | | | | | | | 生活用能 | 农村能源 |
| | 煤炭 | 焦炭 | 成品油 | 电力 | 生产用能小计 | 商品能源 | | | | | | | 传统生物质能 | | | 现代可再生能源 | | | | | | | 小计 | 总计 |
						煤炭	电力	成品油	LPG	天然气	煤气	小计	秸秆	薪柴	小计	秸秆	薪柴	小水电	小风电	沼气	太阳能	小计		
2005	1809.4	59.2	3024.9	1077	5970.5	5814.1	912.5	377.6	490.5	3.2	3.4	7601.3	15959.6	10309.5	26269.1	0	0	428	28	492.7	416	1364.7	35235.1	41205.6
2010	1751	109	3543	1436	6839	5450	1577	673	820	27	5.2	8552.2	15341	8761	24102	1361	772	606	56	980	709	4484	37138.2	43977.2
2020	1756	174	5306	2412	9648	4757	2653	1048	1205	47	8.7	9718.7	10763	6765	17517	5147	2020	1025	146	1812	1205	11355	38590.7	48238.7
2030	2223	247	6792	3087	12349	3177	3583	1319	1554	66	12.3	9711.3	4813	3735	8548	9645	3114	1449	379	2643	1680	18910	37169.3	49518.3

综合以上两个情景的研究结果，今后 20 年我国农民人均生活用能将进一步增加，到 2030 年可能达到 700kg 标准煤左右，但由于农村人口的持续下降，我国农村生活用能总量将先缓慢上升然后逐步下降。未来的农村生活用能需求增量将主要依靠外部商品能源来满足，但农村内部的能源（非商品能源），包括传统和现代化利用的生物质能以及水电、风电、太阳能仍然是农村生活用能的主要来源，2030 年两者的比例在 1∶2 左右。

第4章 农村能源消费的环境效应分析

煤炭、石油产品等化石燃料为主的商品能源的大量使用产生的废弃物无法同传统生物质燃料那样被循环利用，而且农村居民能源消费的分散性和农村基础设施的落后，导致此类废弃物无法像城市一样进行集中处理，产生严重的农村环境问题。另外，由于农村居民生活燃煤主要在室内进行，各种污染物的排放也导致了严重的室内环境污染。如果这些环境问题得不到重视，必将严重制约农村经济社会发展。

4.1 使用商品能源对环境的影响

改革开放以来，我国农村能源消费中煤炭、电力、成品油等商品能源的比例不断提高，其中煤炭是最主要的商品能源消费类型。煤炭燃烧排放的污染物主要有：二氧化硫（SO_2）、氮氧化物（NO_x）、粉尘和固体废渣。受我国以煤为主的能源结构影响，燃煤排放的各种废弃物数量十分巨大。与城市和工业的煤炭消费相比较，农村缺少必要的污染排放控制技术，燃煤污染物多数直接排放，给农村环境带来显著影响。

4.1.1 农村燃煤的 SO_2 排放

SO_2 是造成呼吸道疾病的重要原因，也是导致酸雨的重要污染物。由于我国高硫煤炭储量较大，城市里的煤电厂必须要安装脱硫设施，以减少 SO_2 的排放。但是，农村燃煤很少安装脱硫设备。

中国 SO_2 排放清单中 SO_2 排放量的计算公式为

$$SO_2 排放量 = 煤炭消耗量 \times f \tag{4-1}$$

$$f = T \times S \times R \tag{4-2}$$

其中，f 为排放因子，T 是 SO_2 的转换系数，为 2.0；S 是平均的煤炭含硫量，为 1.1%；R 为煤的未脱硫率，取值为 1—脱硫率，农村煤炭燃烧的脱硫率为 0，因此 R 取值为 1。

2004 年我国农村煤炭消费产生 SO_2 1091 万 t，其中农业生产过程中的煤炭燃烧排放 589 万 t，农村生活过程中煤炭燃烧排放 502 万 t（表 4.1）（虞江萍等，2008）。我国农村煤炭消费产生的 SO_2 呈现迅速增长的趋势，1980 年我国农村煤炭消费产生的 SO_2 仅为 201 万 t，到 2004 年增长了 4 倍多。

根据各省确定的煤炭 SO_2 排放因子（表 4.2），可以得到中国各个地区农村生活煤炭消费导致的 SO_2 排放量。

表 4.1 1980～2004 年农村煤炭消费产生的 SO₂ 排放量（单位：万 t）

年份	生产过程排放量	生活过程排放量	总计
1980	86	114	201
1991	347	239	586
1995	466	265	731
2000	494	364	858
2002	557	485	1041
2004	589	502	1091

表 4.2 2004 年各省确定的煤炭 SO₂ 排放因子 [*]

省区	农村生活煤炭消费 /万 t	SO₂ 排放因子	SO₂ 排放量 /万 t	省区	农村生活煤炭消费 /万 t	SO₂ 排放因子	SO₂ 排放量 /万 t
北京	189.53	0.0352	6.67	湖北	254.82	0.0352	8.97
天津	39.88	0.0318	1.27	湖南	210.00	0.0352	7.39
河北	947.09	0.0318	30.12	广东	49.57	0.0352	1.74
山西	600.42	0.0318	19.09	广西	4.89	0.0352	0.17
内蒙古	393.52	0.0188	7.40	海南	0.00	0.0222	0.00
辽宁	120.67	0.0188	2.27	重庆	170.02	0.0352	5.98
吉林	64.22	0.0222	1.43	四川	657.61	0.0352	23.15
黑龙江	18.38	0.0222	0.41	贵州	947.10	0.0352	33.34
上海	39.13	0.0318	1.24	云南	333.40	0.0222	7.40
江苏	48.02	0.0318	1.53	陕西	120.73	0.0188	2.27
浙江	13.68	0.0318	0.44	甘肃	311.22	0.0188	5.85
安徽	251.00	0.0318	7.98	青海	61.40	0.0318	1.95
福建	46.68	0.0352	1.64	宁夏	65.00	0.0188	1.22
江西	162.56	0.0352	5.72	新疆	335.00	0.0188	6.30
山东	220.00	0.0318	7.00	西藏	—	—	—
河南	510.50	0.0352	17.97				

[*] 缺香港、澳门、台湾地区资料。

我国农村生活煤炭消费产生的 SO₂ 排放存在明显的地区差异（图 4.1）。由于煤炭产区的农村居民更容易以较低的价格和更方便的途径获得煤炭，所以农村煤炭消费量高的地区，例如河北、山西、河南、四川、贵州，农村生活煤炭消费排放的 SO₂ 较高。人均 SO₂ 排放量最高的地区为北京，其 2004 年农村居民煤炭消费的人均 SO₂ 排放量高达 26.47kg，列第二位的是贵州省（12.24kg/人）。

4.1.2 农村燃煤氮氧化物（NO$_x$）与总悬浮物（TSP）排放

燃煤产生的 NO$_x$ 和 TSP 是重要的污染物。根据虞江萍等（2008）的分析，NO$_x$ 的排放因子为 1.88g/kg，TSP 的排放因子为 1.3g/kg。

估算结果表明，2004 年我国农村煤炭消费产生的 NO$_x$ 和 TSP 排放量分别为 93.20 万 t 和 64.44 万 t，其中农业生产过程中排放的 NO$_x$ 和 TSP 分别为 50.34 万 t 和 34.81 万 t，农村生活过程中排放 NO$_x$ 和 TSP 分别为 42.86 和 29.63 万 t（表 4.3）。

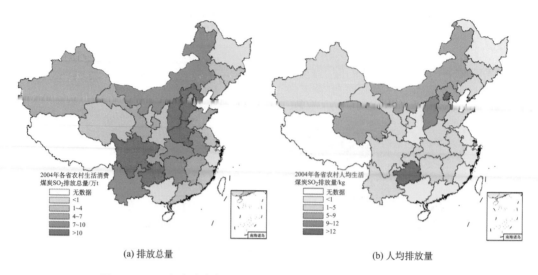

(a) 排放总量   (b) 人均排放量

图 4.1 2004 年各省农村生活消费煤炭 SO$_2$ 排放总量与人均排放量

表 4.3 1980～2004 年农村煤炭消费产生的 NO$_x$ 和 TSP 排放量（单位：万 t）

年份	生产过程 NO$_x$ 排放量	生活过程 NO$_x$ 排放量	总计	生产过程 TSP 排放量	生活过程 TSP 排放量	总计
1980	7.37	9.74	17.11	5.10	6.73	11.83
1991	29.65	20.42	50.07	20.50	14.12	34.62
1995	39.78	22.65	62.43	27.51	15.67	43.18
2000	42.22	31.08	73.30	29.20	21.49	50.69
2002	47.56	41.44	89.00	32.89	28.65	61.54
2004	50.34	42.86	93.20	34.81	29.63	64.44

我国农村煤炭消费产生的 SO$_2$、NO$_x$ 和 TSP 都呈现迅速增长的趋势，并且生活过程中煤炭产生的污染物增长速度慢于生产过程。

4.1.3 农村燃煤的固体废弃物排放

煤炭燃烧产生大量的固体废弃物，原煤中不可燃烧的灰分（我国煤炭的平均灰分为 23％）和未燃烧的碳（我国农村煤炭氧化率约为 80％，即有 20％的碳未被燃烧）以固体形式存在于燃煤废渣中。绝大部分燃煤产生的固体废弃物都得不到处理，而是被随意与其他农村生活垃圾一样，堆弃在农村居民点内部和邻近地点，造成极大的环境污染（图 4.2）。

燃煤的固体废弃物总量可用下面的公式计算

固体废弃物总量 = 煤炭消费量×平均灰分＋平均含碳量×未氧化率   (4-3)

估算结果表明，2004 年我国农村煤炭消费产生的固态废弃物共排放 18485 万 t，其中来自农业生产过程 9985 万 t，来自农村生活过程 8500 万 t（表 4.4）。

图 4.2　农村居民点的燃煤废渣与其他生活垃圾

表 4.4　1980~2004 年农村煤炭消费产生的固体废弃物排放量（单位：万 t）

年份	生产过程排放量	生活过程排放量	总计
1980	1462	1931	3398
1991	5880	4049	9929
1995	7890	4493	12 383
2000	8374	6163	14 537
2002	9433	8218	17 651
2004	9985	8500	18 485

实际上，农村居民煤炭的生活消费中一部分是以蜂窝煤、煤球等形式使用的，这一部分煤炭使用量并没有在上述计算中得到体现。蜂窝煤、煤球在制作过程中掺入了黏土，因此，使用蜂窝煤等产生的固体废弃物远高于直接使用煤炭，从而成倍于增加煤炭使用导致的固体废弃物排放量。

4.1.4　农村燃煤的其他污染物排放

燃煤过程还会产生一氧化碳（CO）、苯并芘（BaP）等污染物和有毒物质，长期接触此类物质，会导致呼吸系统疾病，诱发癌症，以及造成新生儿出生缺陷。

煤炭消费量较大地区的空气污染，特别是燃煤做饭或冬季采暖，会对人体健康造成严重影响。山西省平定县和太谷县农村居民家庭的卧室、厨房和室外空气采样分析结果表明，燃煤污染物一氧化碳（CO）、二氧化硫（SO_2）、苯并芘（BaP）含量，厨房高于卧室和室外，冬季高于夏季，3 种污染物超标情况以冬季厨房和卧室中的 BaP 超标最为严重，最大值超标近 558 倍（李智文等，2006）。

燃煤还会在我国很多地区，尤其是西南地区，造成严重的燃煤型氟中毒问题。煤炭燃烧时，50％的煤炭氟可气化成各种含氟气体，污染室内空气。这些氟化物长时间滞留在室内，或通过呼吸道直接进入人体，或通过飘尘富集于食物经食物链进入人体，导致居民氟骨症患病率上升。

流行病学调查结果表明，因食用煤烟熏烤的高氟粮食而引起的饮食型氟中毒和因吸入燃煤污染空气所致的吸气型氟中毒已成为燃烧高氟煤炭所引起的主要氟中毒类型。在我国西南地区，当地居民习惯于原煤敞烧烘烤粮食或取暖，居民氟骨症患病率与燃煤时间和燃煤量都呈极显著正相关关系（李永华等，2002）。

4.2　传统能源的环境效应分析

农村传统的非商品能源利用以秸秆和薪柴等生物质能直接燃烧为主，排放的主要污染物包括悬浮颗粒物、SO_2、CH_4、NO_x 等（虞江萍等，2008；王效华，冯祯民，2004；曹国良等，2005）。与煤炭等商品能源不同，秸秆、薪柴等生物质燃料中的碳来自于植物光合作用固定的大气中的二氧化碳（CO_2），生物质燃烧排放的 CO_2 不会增加大气中 CO_2 的浓度。

根据"气候变化初始国家信息通报"，1994 年生物质燃烧造成的甲烷排放占到我国甲烷总排放的 6.26％（214.7 万 t），其中很重要的一部分来自于农村对秸秆、薪柴的能源利用。

曹国良等（2005）根据 2000 年中各省市生物质的消耗资料，结合排放因子，计算了中国大陆生物质燃烧所排放的 SO_2、NO_x、NH_3、CH_4、EC、OC、VOC、CO 的总量及各省市的排放清单（表 4.5）。由于地理位置、气候条件、经济发展状况，以及农村人口的差异，各省的污染物排放具有很大差别，由于人口密度大，我国的东、南和中部地区煤炭的商业供给不足。因此，生物质燃料在这些地区的比例较高，污染物的排放量也相应较大。山东列第一位，江苏和黑龙江列第二、三位。

表 4.5　2000 年中国各省市生物质燃烧各污染物的排放量[*]（单位：t）

地区	SO_2	NO_x	NH_3	CH_4	EC	OC	VOC	CO
北京	550	2860	2420	7280	880	3550	13 110	112 430
天津	770	3160	2800	9360	1090	4720	6170	129 190
河北	10 560	66 390	46 690	114 260	18 660	77 880	420 140	2 321 030
山西	2430	14 200	9320	22 160	4090	18 140	81 190	478 360
内蒙古	3600	18 600	14 680	43 720	6190	26 920	87 850	703 520
辽宁	6810	41 600	30 560	78 530	11 870	48 850	253 480	1 493 160
吉林	11 290	67 670	42 520	95 460	19 220	86 160	401 070	2 223 560
黑龙江	17 130	93 170	62 300	156 610	28 200	126 880	483 780	3 176 730
上海	0	0	0	0	0	0	0	0
江苏	17 400	88 650	63 720	174 500	27 170	120 740	391 250	3 164 900
浙江	4000	35 120	24 120	50 250	8880	33 440	306 580	1 196 920
安徽	10 650	61 830	46 430	123 930	18 020	74 660	349 600	2 252 720
福建	1800	10 960	5980	11 080	3560	16 590	80 520	326 690

地区	SO₂	NOₓ	NH₃	CH₄	EC	OC	VOC	CO
江西	3160	26 680	18 890	41 390	6900	25 820	227 930	926 020
山东	24 890	138 040	91 680	226 400	40 600	181 940	722 570	4 693 340
河南	11 800	67 760	46 730	117 210	19 710	85 750	375 950	2 350 220
湖北	8510	57 710	42 740	106 140	15 880	62 550	400 690	2 073 490
湖南	4960	53 180	38 070	78 060	12 650	43 040	517 500	1 849 920
广东	5280	41 330	28 390	61 900	10 800	42 300	330 000	1 414 120
广西	4660	42 380	30 950	68 390	10 610	37 780	376 890	1 497 220
海南	3590	20 510	16 610	46 970	6070	24 210	113 090	782 400
重庆	2850	20 690	15 800	39 300	5570	20 930	154 120	755 550
四川	7050	51 700	38 940	95 580	13 850	52 480	386 720	1 873 330
贵州	1640	21 900	15 860	31 100	4970	15 530	234 400	763 510
云南	1810	26 400	18 890	35 630	5830	17 800	290 230	912 900
西藏	0	10	0	0	0	10	50	120
陕西	3440	25 260	17 650	40 200	6720	26 650	190 110	874 690
甘肃	2590	15 440	11 980	32 410	4470	17 980	90 560	573 020
青海	440	2320	1960	5880	710	2870	10 870	91 320
宁夏	430	2080	1520	4310	660	2960	7890	75 100
新疆	1350	7230	5000	13 180	2210	9960	35 490	252 670
总计	175 420	1 124 820	793 190	1 931 190	316 030	1 309 080	7 339 770	39 338 120

＊缺香港、澳门、台湾地区资料。

曹国良等（2005）的研究涉及的生物质燃烧包括：农村居民使用秸秆和薪柴作为炊事及采暖的燃料；农村在收获季节农田废弃秸秆的露天焚烧；森林火灾；草原火灾。表4.6给出了以全国总量计算的不同生物质燃烧对不同污染物的贡献率，其中秸秆和薪柴的贡献率最主要，约占总量的98%，森林火灾和草原火灾所占的份额很小（曹国良等，2005）。

表4.6　不同生物质对污染物排放的贡献率（%）

污染物	秸秆	薪柴	森林火灾	草原火灾
SO₂	97.98	0.78	1.08	0.16
NOₓ	75.29	23.65	0.86	0.19
NH₃	75.20	24.08	0.61	0.11
CH₄	84.78	14.62	0.47	0.12
EC	83.21	15.00	1.53	0.25
OC	91.18	6.67	1.76	0.39
VOC	46.93	51.66	1.31	0.11
CO	76.08	23.10	0.65	0.17

虞江萍等（2008）应用这些信息计算了我国农村能源消费中秸秆和薪柴燃烧的主要污染物排放因子（表4.7）。

表 4.7　秸秆、薪柴燃烧的污染物排放因子（单位：g/kg）

项目	SO_2	CH_4	NO_x
秸秆	0.53	3.28	1.29
薪柴	0.63	2.07	0.7

这些因子可以被用来计算我国秸秆燃烧产生的 SO_2、CH_4 和 NO_x 的排放量（表 4.8）。

表 4.8　2004 年农村秸秆、薪柴燃烧的污染物排放量（单位：万 t）

项目	实物消费量	SO_2 排放量	CH_4 排放量	NO_x 排放量
秸秆	29 160	15.45	95.64	37.62
薪柴	26 830	18.37	60.36	20.41

不同地区各类型污染物排放量与秸秆消费量正相关。四川、江苏、山东、安徽四省排放总量最高，北京、青海、福建、海南四地排放量较低（表 4.9）。

表 4.9　2004 年各省区农村生活能源消费中秸秆燃烧的污染物排放量[*]

地区	秸秆实物/万 t	SO_2 排放量/t	CH_4 排放量/t	NO_x 排放量/t
北京	138	730	4520	1780
天津	183	970	6010	2360
河北	1742	9230	57 140	22 470
山西	447	2370	14 670	5770
内蒙古	1519	8050	49 810	19 590
辽宁	1314	6960	43 100	16 950
吉林	1279	6780	41 950	16 500
黑龙江	2367	12 550	77 640	30 540
江苏	3279	17 380	107 540	42 300
浙江	302	1600	9900	3890
安徽	2607	13 820	85 520	33 630
福建	202	1070	6620	2600
江西	562	2980	18 420	7250
山东	2882	15 270	94 520	37 170
河南	2366	12 540	77 600	30 520
湖北	1474	7810	48 340	19 010
湖南	729	3860	23 910	9400
广东	1491	7900	48 900	19 230
广西	835	4430	27 390	10 770
海南	216	1150	7090	2790
重庆	824	4370	27 030	10 630
四川	3543	18 780	116 200	45 700
贵州	844	4470	27 670	10 880
云南	518	2740	16 980	6680
陕西	737	3910	24 180	9510
甘肃	648	3440	21 260	8360
青海	128	680	4180	1640
宁夏	301	1590	9860	3880
新疆	511	2710	16 750	6590

＊缺香港、澳门、台湾地区资料。

4.3 农村可再生能源的环境效应分析

可再生能源包括：风能、太阳能、水能、生物质能、地热能、海洋能等。对我国农村地区而言，适合发展的可再生能源主要为生物质能高效利用、太阳能、微水电等。

可再生能源大多属于清洁能源，在消费中不产生或很少产生污染。2005年，中国可再生能源开发利用总量（不包括传统方式利用生物质能）为1.66亿t标准煤，约为2005年全国一次能源消费总量的7.5%，相应减少二氧化硫（SO_2）年排放量300万t，减少二氧化碳（CO_2）年排放量4亿多吨。

大力使用发展可再生能源已成为缓解能源供需矛盾、减少环境污染、增加农民收入的重要途径。因此，政府应该提供经济刺激，确保全面及时的使用可再生能源。这些刺激包括：农民通过可再生能源项目获得的温室气体减排指标可被用来市场交易，为可再生能源直接使用者提供补贴，确保可再生能源，如生物质和风能发电的低上网电价。

4.3.1 沼气的发展趋势及其环境效应分析

我国农村沼气建设起步于20世纪70年代，初期阶段主要是解决农村地区严重的能源短缺问题。80年代中后期，为满足广大农民对清洁、方便和低成本能源的需求，沼气建设以燃料改进和优质化能源开发为主要目标，并逐渐确定为我国农村能源建设和环境整治中重点推广的新型能源技术。

沼气开发的基础资料以秸秆、养殖业畜禽粪便和农村居民生活有机垃圾为主，副产品沼液和沼渣均可作为有机肥使用，其整个物质循环流程可以与我国传统的农业生产模式相结合。

农村传统的秸秆和薪柴燃烧效率很低，秸秆的热转换效率不到10%，薪柴不到15%，而秸秆加上人和牲畜的粪便制成沼气，热效率可提高到60%。

鼓励使用沼气的激励机制包括为修建沼气池提供贷款或补贴，通过使用沼气发电减少温室气体排放的费用，以及确保沼气发电能低价上网。采用更多的手段鼓励农户使用以沼气为原料的高效炉具也非常重要。

相对于其他可再生能源利用技术，沼气发展较早，技术成熟度高，生产成本低，因此得到了迅速的发展。中国农村户用沼气气产量从1991年的11.1亿m^3快速增加到2007年的98.8亿m^3，17年间增长了8倍（图4.3）。据估计，我国沼气产气量将在2010年与2020年分别达到156亿m^3和385亿m^3。

沼气比化石能源廉价，比秸秆、薪柴等传统非商品能源清洁、高效。沼气能大量使用农业生产废弃物和生活废物，并减少温室气体排放（图4.4）。

使用沼气能减少使用煤、秸秆和薪材产生的污染。张培栋等（2005）的估算表明：假设以1996～2003年每年所产的全部沼气分别替代秸秆、薪柴和煤炭作为日常生活用能，则年均净替代秸秆、薪柴和煤炭的实物量分别为423.94万t、318.41万t和254.73万t，分别占年均能源消费量的1.43%、1.93%和1.43%，替代后的SO_2年减排量为每年2.13万～6.20万t。

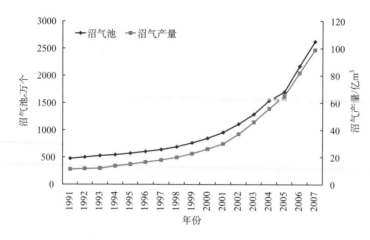

图 4.3　1991～2007 年农村户用沼气发展情况

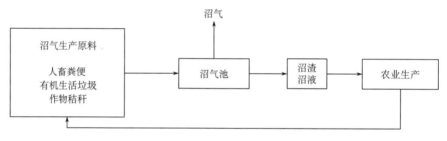

图 4.4　沼气生产的物质循环示意图

4.3.2　秸秆的综合利用与环境效应分析

秸秆是农业生产最主要的副产品，也是主要的传统能源之一。据估算，我国农业生产可利用的各类作物秸秆年产量约 6 亿～7 亿 t，资源量巨大。

秸秆资源具有较大的能源开发潜力，但目前开发比例非常低，2005 年秸秆总产量中仅有 28% 作为燃料使用，主要用于农村居民炊事和采暖的直接燃烧；高达 17% 的秸秆被直接在田间焚烧，总量接近 1 亿 t（图 4.5），导致大量的资源浪费和严重的空气污染。

秸秆是一种很好的清洁可再生能源，每两吨秸秆的热值就相当于一吨标准煤，其平均含硫量只有 3.8‰，而煤的平均含硫量约达 1%。

传统的秸秆燃烧效率十分低下。高效的秸秆能源化利用技术主要包括秸秆沼气、秸秆固化成型燃料、秸秆热解气化、直燃发电和秸秆干馏等方式。

秸秆固化成型燃料是指在一定温度和压力作用下，将农作物秸秆压缩为棒状、块状或颗粒状等成型燃料，从而提高运输和贮存能力，改善秸秆燃烧性能，提高利用效率，扩大应用范围。秸秆成型后，体积缩小 6～8 倍，密度为 1.1～1.4 t/m³，能源密度相当于中质烟煤，使用时火力持久，炉膛温度高，燃烧特性明显得到改善，可以代替木材、

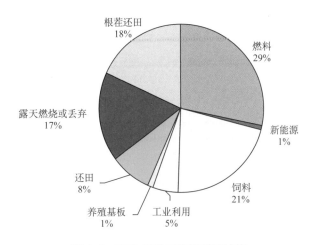

图 4.5　2005 年我国秸秆利用结构

煤炭为农村居民提供炊事或取暖用能，也可以在城市作为锅炉燃料，替代天然气、燃油。使用秸秆固化成型燃料的家庭用生物质颗粒燃料炉灶的热效率可达 80％以上（田宜水，2009）。

　　秸秆热解气化是以农作物秸秆、稻壳、木屑、树枝以及农村有机废弃物等为原料，在气化炉中进行缺氧燃烧，通过控制燃烧过程，使之产生含一氧化碳、氢气、甲烷等可燃气体作为农户的生活用能。秸秆热解气化的热效率能达到 80％。

　　秸秆直接燃烧发电技术是指秸秆在锅炉中直接燃烧，释放出来的热量通常用来产生高压蒸汽，蒸汽在汽轮机中膨胀做功，转化为机械能驱动发电机发电。该技术基本成熟，已经进入商业化应用阶段，适用于农场以及我国北方平原地区等粮食主产区，便于原料的大规模收集。

　　这些新型秸秆利用技术可减少秸秆使用量 50％以上，同时使秸秆燃烧导致的污染物排放相应减少。此外，新型秸秆利用技术的配套炉灶也相应改进，提高能效的同时，改善了使用过程中的环境卫生条件以及室内空气污染问题，有利于提高农村居民的生活质量。

　　政府需要建立额外的经济激励机制，鼓励使用这些新技术。政府应为农民和其他的生产者提供原材料，以减少区域空气污染。相对于燃烧化石燃料，这些技术可以减少温室气体排放，所获得的减排指标也可以在国内外市场进行交易。

4.3.3　其他可再生能源消费及环境效应分析

　　微水电、风能、太阳能等其他农村可再生能源实用性具有明显的区域特点。微水电主要集中于水能资源丰富的西南山区。风能则集中于西北、内蒙古以及沿海地区。太阳能的利用相对普遍，除四川盆地等少数辐射资源条件差的地区外，大部分农村地区均可利用太阳能，尤其是华北和西北干旱地区。

　　微水电、风能、太阳能在使用过程中产生很少的废物和温室气体排放，是最清洁的能源资源。但是这些能源在农村地区应用还面临着技术尚未完全成熟，成本高以及供能不稳定等主要问题。为了减少开发商和消费者的成本，政府可以提供优惠的财税政策，例如，税收减免、补贴、低息贷款和其他经济激励型政策。而且开发商和消费者可以通过能源使用过程中减少的温室气体排放获得资金收益。

4.3.4　可再生能源的根本问题

我国已经将发展可再生能源作为满足农村能源需求、减少环境污染、促进经济发展的重要途径。根据国家发展和改革委员会（2007）制定的《可再生能源中长期发展规划》（以下简称《规划》）估算，到 2010 年和 2020 年，全国可再生能源开发利用量分别相当于 3 亿 t 标准煤和 6 亿 t 标准煤。这一巨大产能可显著减少煤炭消耗，弥补天然气和石油资源的不足。

沼气年利用量相当于 240 亿 m^3 天然气，燃料乙醇和生物柴油年燃烧量相当于替代石油约 1000 万 t。太阳能和地热能的利用对改善能源结构和节约能源资源起到了重大的作用。在满足能源需求的同时，可再生能源的开发利用将带来显著的环境效益。

如果达到《规划》2010 年发展目标，可再生能源使用可减少二氧化硫年排放量 400 万 t，减少氮氧化物年排放量 150 万 t，减少烟尘年排放量 200 万 t，减少二氧化碳年排放量约 6 亿 t，同时，实现年节约用水 15 亿 m^3，保护 1.5 亿亩[①]林地免遭破坏。如果达到《规划》2020 年发展目标时，可再生能源使用可减少二氧化硫年排放量 800 万 t，减少氮氧化物年排放量 300 万 t，减少烟尘年排放量 400 万 t，减少二氧化碳年排放量 12 亿 t，同时，实现年节约用水 20 亿 m^3，保护 3 亿亩林地免遭破坏。

为了达到《规划》的发展目标，政府需要同时对可再生能源的供应商和消费者给予额外的经济刺激。而这些经济刺激机制可分为两大类。第一类为政府支出、低息贷款、减免税收，这些措施可以帮助减少可再生能源的成本；第二类是使用这些能源相对于化石能源的使用减少了污染，因此，供应商和消费者可以通过减排获得经济收益。这些环境收益包括减少区域大气污染物和温室气体排放、减少水污染和提高水利用效率，同时通过减少化石能源开采保护陆地资源。

4.4　农村能源消费与气候变化

随着农村经济的飞速发展和农村生活质量的快速提高，农村能源消费正在发生着变化。农村能源的开发、利用与温室气体减排和应对全球气候变化之间的关系也日益密切。

4.4.1　农村能源消费和温室气体排放

虽然秸秆和薪柴的直接燃烧存在热效率低以及危害生活环境、健康等问题，而且秸秆和薪柴燃烧产生的二氧化碳（CO_2）又来自于光合作用过程中储存在生物质中的碳，这些 CO_2 排放并不计入国家温室气体排放清单中。当农村传统的秸秆（薪柴）为主的

---

① 1 亩≈0.067hm²。

生物质能源消费模式向以煤炭、石油产品等化石燃料为主的商品能源消费转变时，农村地区符合联合国政府间气候变化专门委员会（IPCC）标准的温室气体排放量将显著增加。同时，化石燃料消耗将对传统生物质燃料产生挤出效应，大量的作物秸秆由燃料转变为废弃物，对其进行无害化或资源化处理也需要投入额外的能源。

新能源和可再生能源技术也可以产生温室气体的排放。以沼气为例，其主要成分是甲烷（CH_4），温室效应为 21 个 CO_2 当量。根据能源研究所专家研究，2004 年农村生物质燃烧导致的温室气体排放达到 4.5 亿 tCO_2e。

4.4.2 农村燃煤的 CO_2 排放

农村燃煤目前是我国农村能源使用过程中 CO_2 排放的最主要来源。参考"2006 年 IPCC 国家温室气体清单指南"中有关能源利用过程温室气体排放量的计算方法（IPCC，2006），农村煤炭消费产生的 CO_2 排放量可用以下公式计算

$$CO_2 \text{ 排放量} = 原煤消费量 \times 平均含碳量 \times 平均氧化系数 \times 44/12 \quad (4\text{-}4)$$

其中，平均含碳量以我国原煤折算标准煤的参考系数（0.7143kg 标准煤/kg）换算得到，为 71.43%。煤炭燃烧的氧化系数主要由炉具类型、燃烧过程和居民使用习惯所决定。

我国农村煤炭消费以直接燃烧为主。燃烧通常都不充分，氧化系数较低（普通炊事灶具的氧化系数一般低于 80%，而北方农村使用的燃煤采暖锅炉氧化系数较高，一般在 90% 以上）。一般来说，农村生产活动的煤炭燃烧比农村生活的煤炭燃烧效率高。但是，综合农村煤炭消费的整体情况，本研究将农村煤炭消费的平均氧化系数定为 80%。

研究结果表明，2004 年我国农村煤炭消费过程产生的 CO_2 排放量为 103872 万 t，其中来自农业生产过程 56109 万 t，来自农村生活过程 47763 万 t（表 4.10）。从历史趋势看，我国农村煤炭消费过程排放的 CO_2 一直呈现增长趋势。

表 4.10　1980~2004 年农村煤炭消费的 CO_2 排放量（单位：万 t）

年份	生产过程排放	生活过程排放	总计
1980	8213	10 853	19 096
1991	33 043	22 755	55 798
1995	44 336	25 248	69 584
2000	47 060	34 635	81 695
2002	53 011	46 180	99 191
2004	56 109	47 763	103 872

4.4.3 沼气的减排效果

农村地区沼气的使用不仅对温室气体和其他污染物减排具有重要意义，同时还节省了大量能源资源。因此，大力推广沼气的使用能大力改善农村环境并加强新农村建设。研究

表明，单位沼气产量的年平均净减排量为 1.88kg/m³，变化范围为 1.76～2.11kg/m³（刘宇等，2008）。

从 1991 年至 2005 年，中国沼气为农业生产和农民生活共提供了 2840 万 t 标准煤的热量，净减少温室气体排放量约 7315.8 万 t 二氧化碳当量（CO_2e），年均减排量为 487.7 万 t，相当于全国总排放量的 0.07%～0.16%。沼气的使用可以避免二氧化碳、甲烷和氧化亚氮（N_2O）的排放，分别为 8424.3 万 tCO_2e，356.0 万 tCO_2e 和 26.0 万 tCO_2e。

从 1991 年到 2005 年的发展趋势来看，1998 年以前沼气利用导致的温室气体净减排量增速比较缓慢，1998 年到 2001 年增加幅度加大，2001 年以后迅速增加，到 2005 年达到 1153.8 万 t（图 4.6）（刘宇等，2008）。

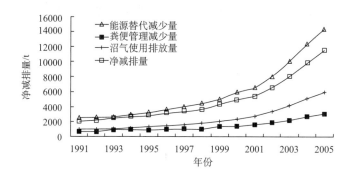

图 4.6　1991～2005 年温室气体减排量

依照我国沼气发展的中长期规划，到 2010 年与 2020 年的沼气产气量将分别达到 156 亿 m³ 和 385 亿 m³，可分别减少温室气体排放 2932.8 万 tCO_2e 和 7938.0 万 tCO_2e。这不仅可以满足农村不断增长的能源需求，还对改善农村环境、国家应对气候变化具有重要意义。

从长期趋势看，中国农村未来温室气体排放增长主要有两个来源：一是生物质能消费转向商品能源消费导致的温室气体排放。目前，生物质能约占中国农村能源消费总量的 1/3，主要用于家庭炊事和取暖。但是，随着农村居民生活质量的不断提高，农村家庭越来越多地使用商品能源替代直接燃烧秸秆和薪柴。二是城市化带动的能源需求导致农村温室气体排放的增加。城乡能源消费差别巨大是我国能源消费的一大特点，农村人均能源消费和人均温室气体排放均大大低于城市地区。2000 年，农村人均能源消费为 0.77t 标准煤，远远低于城市人均能源消费 2.58t 标准煤的水平。因此，城市化将缩小城乡能源消费的差距，刺激能源消费总量增长，而这些额外的需求增量将主要通过外部商品能源来满足。这样将必然增加农村温室气体的排放量，危害农村环境。

根据 LEAP 模型的估算结果，无论是在常规情景或者在强化可再生能源情景下，未来 20 年内我国农村生产生活用能终端所产生的二氧化碳气体的直接排放量都将持续增加（表 4.11）。其中在常规情景下，我国 2010 年、2020 年和 2030 年农村生产生活用能导致的碳排放量将分别为 7870 万 t、9156 万 t 和 10331 万 t，分别比 2005 年增长 8.1%、25.7% 和 41.9%。

在强化可再生能源情景下，我国 2010 年、2020 年和 2030 年农村生产生活用能导致的碳排放量将分别为 7695 万 t、8739 万 t 和 9272 万 t，分别比 2005 年增长 5.7%、20.0% 和 27.3%。

表 4.11　不同情景下的农村生产生活用能终端所产生的直接碳排放（单位：万 t）

年份	2005	2010	2020	2030
常规情景	7283	7870	9156	10 331
其中生活用能	4289	4572	4777	4722
强化可再生能源情景	7283	7695	8739	9272
其中生活用能	4289	4396	4361	3663

中国未来农村用能碳排放的增加主要来自农业生产过程。在常规情景下，农村生活用能所导致的温室气体排放将在 2020 年达到峰值，随后开始下降，到 2030 年排放将达到 4722 万 t，比 2005 年增长了 10%。在强化可再生能源情景下，农村生活用能所导致的温室气体排放将在 2010 年达到峰值，随后开始下降，到 2030 年排放将达到 3663 万 t，比 2005 年增长了 14.6%。

因此，大力发展农村可再生能源将大大减缓温室气体的排放。为了实现这一愿景，需要对可再生能源开发商和消费者提供额外的经济激励措施。无论是在常规情景还是强化可再生能源情景下，农村生产生活能耗所导致的人均碳排放都保持了增长的趋势，而这一现象的前提是不断缩小的城乡能源消费差距。但是，未来农村的人均商品能源消费量和人均碳排放量基本上不可能超过城市居民的水平。

4.4.4　依靠可再生能源应对气候变化

可再生能源的开发利用可以减少温室气体排放，将从三个关键方面帮助我国应对气候变化：一是提高能源效率，控制能源消费的过快增长；二是大力发展可再生能源技术，替代常规能源，满足能源需求的增加；三是建立综合利用的能源生态模式，在取得能源和经济效益的同时，减少农业温室气体和其他污染物的排放。

发展可再生能源和能源的高效转化技术，包括传统的生物质使用向沼气使用技术的转化、太阳能采暖（热水）技术，微水电、风能利用技术和新型节能灶具等，将具有重大的意义。但是，对于新能源、新技术的环境效应进行准确评估尚未系统开展。

在不同情景下可再生能源总量及其对农村能源结构的影响，目前还缺少有说服力的研究成果。一些学者对地区级能源消耗未来趋势的研究中明显忽视了农村迅速发展过程对能源消耗总量的推动作用。此外，从保障能源供给、提高能源利用效率的角度看，积极发展节能技术，对改善农村环境，达到"应对气候变化策略"制订的温室气体减排目标，具有重要的现实意义。

4.5　增强农村地区适应气候变化的能力

中国仅以全球约 10% 的农田和 6% 左右的水资源，供养着全球 20% 的人口。由于严重依赖众多小规模农户人口，中国农业面临严峻的挑战：农田土地数量不断萎缩以及土地质量不断恶化。

温室气体浓度的增加，尤其是CO_2，及其导致的气候变化已经危害到农村发展和农业生产的稳定性。因此，增强农村地区适应气候变化的能力对保障食品安全、维护农村经济的稳定性以及保证农民增收和改善农民生活水平都具有十分重要的意义。

从全球尺度看，CO_2为主的温室气体增加导致的全球变暖，对农业生产的稳定性和农村社会发展带来诸多负面影响，因此增强农村地区对气候变化的适应能力对于确保粮食安全、维护农村经济稳定、保证农民增收和生活水平的提高都有着非同寻常的积极意义。

在过去100年间，中国全国平均气温上升了1.1℃，近50年间增暖尤其明显。伴随着气温升高，降水的时空分布及极端气候事件也发生着变化。

（1）气温增高对农业生产的影响利弊兼有。一定范围内的增温为中高纬度地区和高原区调整种植业结构带来了可能，使我国粮食生产潜力增大，复种比重加大，水稻面积及冬小麦播种面积北扩。但是，温度升高也使我国长期形成的农业生产格局和种植模式受到冲击，特别是低纬度地区，农业需水增加，病虫害危害加重。

（2）一定范围内的大气CO_2浓度的增加，可以通过改善光合作用效率，提高作物产量。但是，其限制条件和长期影响科学上仍未定论，还有待于深入的研究。

（3）极端气候是造成我国农业大幅度减产和粮食产量波动的重要因素。据民政部统计，过去20年干旱造成的损失占GDP的1.2%，洪涝造成的损失占GDP的0.8%。

受2008年冰冻雨雪灾害影响的受灾人口多达1亿多人，直接经济损失超过1500亿元。未来，高温将成为农业生产的重要限制因素，导致缺水区严重干旱、农业生态环境更加脆弱。干旱或强降水的发生将直接影响或终止农业生产进程，导致一些作物受灾减产或绝收。

华北地区目前普遍的干旱、洪涝、病虫害等也将发生在其他地区。这已经在东北地区发生，该地区的干旱和黑茎病已经导致油菜作物大规模减产。但是，我国目前还没有定量的研究结果表明未来农业损失的规模和程度。

Xiong等（2007）研究指出，如果不考虑CO_2的肥效作用和适应措施，全国平均温度升高幅度小于2.5～3℃，我国三大主要粮食作物的单产水平有增有减，这意味着未来的粮食总产水平还可以通过种植结构的调整而得以保持稳定。然而，当平均温度升高幅度大于2.5～3℃时，我国这三种主要粮食的单产水平将会持续下降（图4.7）。

从人均粮食占有量的角度分析，如果以人均粮食300kg（社会发展的基础粮食供给）和400kg（社会可持续发展的粮食供给）两个指标来评估，高排放情景下中国将在2030年前后出现粮食缺口，出现基础粮食供给问题；中低排放情景下中国的粮食基础供给不存在问题，但社会可持续发展的粮食需求将无法得到满足；此外，如果考虑CO_2的肥效作用，目前预测的气温升高将不会对我国未来粮食生产造成负面影响（图4.8）（Xiong et al，2007）。

结合水资源、土地利用变化、社会经济发展和适应措施的最新研究，本研究结果显示升温、农业用水的减少和耕地面积的下降会使我国2050年左右的粮食生产水平下降14%～23%（与2000年5亿t的生产水平相比）。但如果CO_2的正肥效作用能够得到完

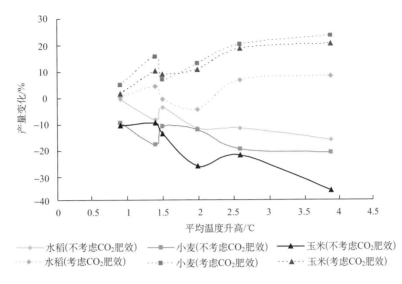

图 4.7　未来我国粮食作物单产的温度阈值

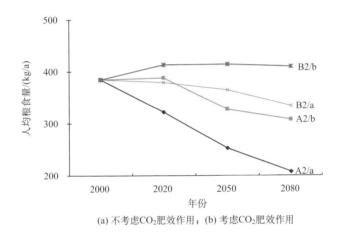

(a) 不考虑CO_2肥效作用；(b) 考虑CO_2肥效作用

图 4.8　未来我国各个时段人均粮食供给量变化

全发挥，上述三个因素对我国 2050 年粮食生产的影响将维持在 $-7\%\pm2\%$。因此，未来 30～50 年的气候变化将不会对中国的粮食供应产量重大影响（Xiong et al，2007；蔡承智等，2008）。但是，也有研究表明，21 世纪后半叶，小麦、水稻和玉米产量将减少 24%～37%（Lin et al，2005）。

　　随着中国的气温持续升高，极端气候事件发生的频率和强度也会不断增强。农业灾害区域和温度持续上升之间的关联已日渐明确。因此，尽管大气中的 CO_2 高浓度可以增加部分作物的产量，但是，持续缩减的水资源和可耕田面积将需要更多的投入来保障食品安全，以应对 2030 年到来的人口高峰。这些投入将包括增加对农业和农业技术的国家投资、控制农田流失和保障农业用水供应。

　　另外，气候变化与粮食安全的研究是一项挑战性极强的探索性工作。目前国内外尚没有通用的研究方法，不同的研究结果之间也存在较大差异，尤其对适应措施和适应效果评价的研究更少，仅仅停留在田间水平的农户自发适应层面，如播种日期的调整、品种的更替等。而意义更加重大的是，为解决国家粮食安全而制定和开展的宏观政策的适应措施对粮食安全的影响，如南水北调、基本农田保护等，以及适应措施与气候变化的交互作用，目前的相关研究还非常少，还需要进一步加强。

考虑到这些不确定性，我国未来的粮食安全将在很大程度上取决于适应措施的有效性，如生态农业的推广、农业技术的进步等。农民使用这些措施的积极性也将十分关键，而这一问题将很大程度上依赖于这些措施对他们收入的影响。如果农民确信他们的收入会实现增加，那么他们就会积极采取这些措施。因此，政府提供财政支持帮助农民使用这些措施的相关政策将十分重要。

4.5.1　温室气体减排和粮食安全

应对全球气候变化，我国农业温室气体减排面临着巨大的压力和挑战，并将对我国保障粮食安全带来深远影响。

为了减少温室气体的排放，我国未来需要在一定程度上控制农村商品能源的消费量。目前，我国农村商品能源主要用于农业生产，并集中在灌溉、化肥施用和农业机械使用等生产环节。这些高能耗的主要环节是改革开放以来促进我国粮食产量大幅度提高和确保我国粮食安全的主要原因。我国农业近20年来相关资料表明，我国灌溉面积与粮食产量的关联度高达0.92，对提高粮食产量贡献率最大；化肥用量、机械使用与粮食产量的关联度则分别是0.59和0.55。

另一方面，受气候变化的影响，我国未来北方地区暖干旱化趋势将更加明显，粮食产量对灌溉的依赖将进一步加大。而受温度升高的影响，土壤有机质分解加快，化肥释放周期缩短，若要达到原有肥效，化肥每次使用量需要进一步增加。

因此，未来我国粮食安全的保障需要加大能耗和化肥使用，从而增加农村实施节能减排的障碍。通过农业耕作方式改变、增加技术投入、提高化肥和水资源等的使用效率可以抵消这一趋势，降低生产成本、减少排放、节约能源并提高农民的收入。但是，如果没有政府的支持，农民是无法广泛采取这些措施的。

4.5.2　生物质能与粮食安全

粮食安全是关系国计民生以及世界和平与稳定的大问题。世界各国普遍认为"新的粮食危机正在形成"，粮食安全问题已经成为一项全球的挑战。

(1) 全球"新粮食危机"的产生与气候变化之间的关系日益密切。全球粮食总产量因严重自然灾害而降低。近年来，受气候变化的影响，全球气候异常带来极端天气事件增加，灾害频繁而严重。为保证本国的供给，一些国家开始限制或禁止粮食出口，从而引起国际市场的粮食供给进一步紧张。

(2) 能源价格增长推高农产品价格。2007年年初至今，国际石油价格一路攀升，同2002年相比，国际石油价格已增长了4倍。受其影响，最近5年，国际化肥价格增长了近两倍。同时，石油价格的提高也增加了农业生产的运输成本。此外，能源价格不仅通过生产成本影响农产品价格，而且直接影响农产品的用途，增加了市场对农产品的非传统、非食品需求，从而推高农产品价格。

（3）燃料乙醇异军突起和生物柴油迅猛发展消耗了大批粮食资源和植物油资源。为了应对"石油价格暴涨"和实现保护生态环境的战略目标，替代性生物清洁能源备受青睐。随着未来石油价格的持续走高，对生物原料的需求还会加剧，这必将对粮食价格产生更大影响。

例如，目前全球玉米产量的12%，美国玉米产量的20%和巴西甘蔗产量的50%被用来生产燃料乙醇。全球菜籽油产量的20%，欧盟菜籽油产量的65%，全球豆油产量的20%和东南亚棕榈油产量的30%都用来生产生物柴油。

根据联合国亚洲经济与社会委员会和联合国粮食及农业组织（Food and Agriculture Organization，FAO）的统计，自2005年以来，世界主要粮食作物的价格已经增长了80%。2007年，大豆价格创34年来的新高，玉米价格为11年以来的最高水平，大米价格成为19年以来的最高价格，而且小麦和菜籽油也分别达到了历史高位价格。

在仅仅几年时间内，大量的粮食作物进入到能源产业，并推高了粮食价格。未来为满足生物燃料的需求只会加剧增长，因此会极大地影响粮食价格。

主要大宗商品的价格持续走高已经在许多低收入国家中引发了社会动荡，尤其是在非洲和南美洲国家。为了稳定国内粮食价格，传统的粮食出口国如越南、泰国和乌克兰已经开始限制或禁止粮食出口。

（4）发展中国家消费结构升级使粮食消费量快速增长。近年来，发展中国家食物消费结构明显升级，主要为食用油、肉禽蛋奶和精加工食品消费需求迅速增长，由此导致生产食用油的油料作物和生产肉禽蛋奶的饲料原粮需求大幅增加。据联合国粮农组织发布的数据，2006年世界谷物消费总量增长到20.43亿t，这些都增大了世界粮食市场的压力。

只有如实认清和承认这些客观存在的实际原因，才能有针对性地采取必要措施，恢复世界粮食价格的正常水平。

大量研究认为，较高的CO_2浓度可以提高作物的水分利用效率和光合作用效率，从而促进农业生产。有估计表明，大气中CO_2浓度增加一倍可致使全球粮食增产10%～30%。

然而，CO_2浓度升高导致气温升高将对作物产量产生不可忽视的负面影响。平均气温的升高会加速作物的生长发育过程，缩短生殖生长期、特别是灌浆期的长短，从而降低作物的产量，如果温度超过40℃时，作物的部分生理过程将发生崩溃（Alexandrov et al，2002；Hulme，1996）。

温度升高也会带来作物病、虫、草害的增加，从而间接影响作物生长（Chen et al，2004；Fuhrer，2003）。气候变化导致的降雨量变化也会对作物产量产生影响。很多研究表明，未来降水量的总量和时空分布将是决定气候变化对农业影响的首要因素（Hulme，1996；Fischer，1996；Strzepek，Smith，1995）。综合各种气象因素，气候变化对作物产量的影响因地区而异，一般来说高纬度地区作物产量将会增加，而低纬度地区将会导致产量降低，但各地的影响程度不尽相同（表4.12）（林而达，1997）。

表 4.12　CO₂ 倍增平衡态 GCM 情景下若干作物受影响的最新研究结果

地区	作物产量变化的百分率/%				
	玉米	小麦	大豆	水稻	其他
拉美	$-61 \sim$ Incr.	$-50 \sim -5$	$10 \sim 40$		
前苏联		$-10 \sim 11$			$-10 \sim 13$ (G)
欧洲	$-30 \sim$ incr.	decr. /incr.			Incr. (V)
北美	$-55 \sim 62$	$-100 \sim 234$	$-96 \sim 58$		
非洲	$-65 \sim 6$				$-79 \sim -63$ (M)
南亚	$-62 \sim 10$	$-61 \sim 67$		$-22 \sim 28$	
中国	$-19 \sim 5$	$-21 \sim 54$	$-44 \sim 83$	$-21 \sim 28$	$15 \sim 49$ (C)
亚洲其他地区及大洋洲		$-41 \sim 5$		$-45 \sim 30$	$-1 \sim 35$ (P)

注：G—谷物，V—蔬菜，M—谷子，C—棉花，P—牧草，incr.—增加，decr.—减少。

4.5.3　农业开发政策与气候变化

我国是人口大国，也是农业大国，确保粮食安全是农业生产的首要任务。但是，以粮食产量为单一目标的农业开发政策与行动如果行为不当将带来潜在的或直接的适应气候变化影响风险。

例如，根据《国家粮食安全中长期规划（2008）》的目标，2020 年我国需增产粮食 500 亿 kg，其中东北地区承担着 1/3 的增量任务。粮食增产的巨大压力增加了该地区的生态压力，同时增加该地区对适应气候变化影响的脆弱性。

过去的农业开发政策大多依靠和利用科学技术，易于引发技术的单一化和异化。然而，由于气候变化使得环境因素发生了改变，原有的技术储备已经不能满足现有的条件和需要，同样的作物品种在现在的气候条件下不能发挥其最大生产潜力和优势。相应地，作物田间管理和机械化现代化也需要进一步考虑气候变化的影响。大量使用化肥、农药的农业生产模式在资源不断减少、环境日益恶化的今天，已经完全不能适应现代农业的发展。

为了确保粮食产量，黑龙江省近年来不断扩大水稻种植面积，到 2008 年黑龙江水稻播种面积为 244.67 万 hm²。但是，黑龙江的水稻生产中面临着一系列的气候灾害问题，大大增加了其粮食产量的不稳定性。例如，2000～2001 年的干旱导致黑龙江省水稻种植大面积缩减，很多地区把水田改成旱田，不得不增加灌溉频率，从而加大了当地减少能源消耗和农业温室气体排放的压力。随后，2006 年 7 月下旬，黑龙江省出现了严重阶段性低温，致使水稻减产 10%。

这一事例表明，在气候变化的背景下，如何调整区域农业开发政策、增强区域对气候变化的适应能力，对于保障区域的农业生产的持续性和稳定性有着积极意义。近年来，我国政府加大了基础设施的投入，重点投入农业领域，主要用于农田基本建设，农田水利设施的改善，农村环境改善和沼气工程等项目。最近，针对全球金融危机而采取的新的经济刺激计划也针对农业基础设施建设提出了一系列的刺激计划和投资计划。基础设施的建设和经济刺激计划能从不同程度上减少温室气体排放，提高粮食产量，改善居住环境，提高生活质量，减缓气候变化给农业造成的不利影响。

例如，改善水利设施有利于提高水利设施的调蓄能力，抵御干旱和洪涝灾害的发生。改善农田配套工程设施，拦蓄降雨，减少地表径流和土壤渗漏，增加降水就地入渗量，可以提高农田保水保土保肥能力。发展节水农业新技术，可以提高农业水资源的利用效率。气候变暖会加重病虫害发生程度，病虫越冬存活量将增加，发生期会提前，发生程度加重，因此病虫测报及防治工作的强化有利于增强农业的抗虫害能力。

第5章 农村能源、环境和适应气候变化的国际经验

5.1 国外能源研究的经验启示

随着经济的发展，使用现代型化石能源（如电、石油产品与天然气）的人越来越多，而使用传统型生物质能源（如燃材与动物粪便等）的人越来越少。很明显，上述两种能源类型常常混合在一起使用，但是能够促进发展的现代型能源的供应能否持续增加，或者此种能源供应的增加是否与其发展要求相适应却难以做出明确判断。

当然，大多数国家（包括当今的发展中国家与20世纪上半叶发展起来的发达国家）已经开始试图通过各种各样的方式鼓励农村地区发展现代能源。如此行动的原因一方面是缘于社会效益而另一方面则由于经济效益的原因。例如，在没有自然光的情况下，人们可以利用电来学习与工作，而且家长们还可以为他们的孩子提供便利的学习条件。妇女们也因此受益匪浅，因为她们不再需要在烹饪以及收集燃料和其他传统的能源上花费大量时间。此外，有明显的证据表明，在室内使用传统的能源烹饪与供暖会导致严重的健康问题（Markandya，2008）。

除了使用现代能源带来的社会效益之外，"使用现代能源还可以提高生产力"这种坚定的信念也已经在大大推动农村能源现代化的进程。例如，相对于手工或畜力操作，使用电力进行操作的效率非常显著，且有助于降低成本。此外，如果可以提供电力，还可以在农村地区发展农业加工业。通过这些方法和手段，可以改善农民的生活水平和促进经济发展。

促进农村地区能源现代化的最主要阻力是客户的需求、客户的支付能力与供应成本三者之间的差异。人们普遍认为，促进农村电气化发展需要向供应商或用户提供一定的补贴。补贴金额将根据所使用的系统（如电网连接会比小型电网或家用太阳能系统更贵，但是不容易出现维护问题）和与电网连接的社区居民的收入水平而定。但是，补贴并不总是持续的，如果以低于成本价提供电力，并且未对此给予相应补偿，则在系统压力较大时，供应商会降低供电量，甚至断开农村用户与电网的连接。有时补贴还来源于捐赠人的捐款，但是当这些捐款停止后，项目也由此而中止。

回顾农村电气化的经验，可以看到一些国家已经采用了一系列的措施来解决该问题。有时补贴会直接拨给"应受补偿的用户"，而另外一部分补贴则直接拨给供应商以弥补由于向农村用户低成本供电带来的损失。另外，是否应该为投资成本或经营成本提供补贴也成为一个问题。再者，还存在一些体制方面的问题，例如应由哪些实体提供这样的服务，以及如何组织这些实体（Barnes，Foley，2004；Barnes，2007）。

以下国家的例子可以描述现代型能源供应与农村发展之间的关系，并识别能源发展过程中存在的障碍，从而给予中国一些经验和教训。

5.1.1 发达国家的经验和启示

5.1.1.1 美国的案例和经验

二战之前，美国农村地区主要依赖传统能源。直到 20 世纪 30 年代中期，约 90% 的美国家庭还没有使用电力。农民在微弱的煤油灯下用手挤奶，妻子们则像奴隶一样忙于伐木和洗衣。因为农村地区没有电力可用，所以种植收入是他们唯一的经济支柱。当然，工厂和公司会更愿意到那些易于获得电力的城市地区发展。

尽管电力在城市地区能够得到广泛地供应，但是私营企业认为将电力供应延伸到农村是无利可图的，原因在于农村用户密度小且离主要的生产中心相对较远。而以下两个条件则促成了电力使用范围向农村扩展。

首先，为了吸引电力公司向农村地区供电，美国总统富兰克林·罗斯福决定向那些愿意向农村地区提供电力的电力公司提供低息贷款。1935 年 5 月 11 日，罗斯福总统在 7037 号行政命令中规定设立美国农村电气化管理局（Rural Electrification Administration，REA）作为紧急事件处理机构。一年以后，国会通过 1936 号农村电气化法案并将此机构迁至一个比较固定的地址。此法案授予该机构通过 4.1 亿美元的优惠贷款来推动实现农村电气化。

但只靠这项计划自身并不能获得成功。美国农村电气化管理局第一任行政长官也的确未能使这些电力公司相信农场主们愿意参与此项计划。这些电力公司声称，因为农场的数目太少，即使有低息贷款投资于输变电及配电设施也并不划算。而农场主自身的积极态度使得这一问题得以解决。在美国农村电气化管理局的鼓励下，他们成立了合作社，这些合作社大批量购电并承担本地电力分配的任务。美国农村电气化管理局在 1938 年审批通过将 0.88 亿美元的贷款给农村合作社。而此金额到 1939 年则高达 2.27 亿美元。农村电气化建设由此发展起来了。

合作社对美国农村电气化项目的成功起了关键作用。美国农村电气化管理局官员不分昼夜开会讨论，终于为合作社领导制订出工作流程及操作方法。这些尽责的工作人员付出了惊人的努力、巨大的耐心和艰苦的劳动，他们不辞辛劳地往返于乡村小路，奔波于农场之间，为的是获取成为新会员所需的签名，还有来之不易的 5 美元"注册费"。"注册费"的金额要确保社区有足够的收入来支付供应商采购与分配电力的成本。

随着越来越多的社区联网，每家生活用电需求量开始增加。农场主和牧场主开始意识到电力在他们的日常工作中所发挥的潜力。应用电力可以研磨饲料、脱玉米皮、抽水和锯木材。应用电力可以给挤奶机提供动力，还可以将干草抬升到粮仓中。用电力提供明亮的灯光，可以给庄稼的收获带来额外的宝贵时间。减轻劳动者负担和提供生产力的核心是电机——新的"雇员"。当然，随之而来的结果是用电量的激增。早在 1939 年，合作社曾想过如果每家生活用电需求量达到 40kW·h/月，供电量会比较充足。到 1948 年，每家生活用电需求量达到 120kW·h/月，是 1939 年的 3 倍，在此之后的 20 年，每家生活用电需求量继续攀升。

农场内的用电增长广泛，延伸到了农场外的社区。学校、教堂和会议场所第一次有了灯光以及其他电力便利设施。在主要的街道两侧，电力设施的所有改进催生了新的经济活动。开始出现新业务与新商业形式，商场里出现了电线、铅管和一些新的电器用品。另外，电力的发展引入了新行业。有了生活合作社供应的电力，工厂也可以将地址设在农村地区，这可以提供大量就业机会。这些新的就业机会（农村就业机会）为美国农村地区年轻一代带来了希望、保障和前途。

现在，农村能源合作运动已经在美国成为能源供应的一个特色，它涉及发电、输电与配电等各个方面。1997 年，农村有 3190 个公共电力设备。其中有 935 个（占 29%）公共电力设备归集体所有，这些设备可以为 46 个州、3200 万人供电，占所有配电线路供电量的 45%。但农村电网的集中度相对来说还是比较低。现在，合作社每公里电线供电量可满足 3.6 个用户（Griffiths，2000）。

合作运动的作用是在有竞争力的环境内，以有竞争力的价格为农村用户群提供电力，目前此种方式运作很成功。同时，农村能源用户接受很多补贴，这样能提高能源利用效率与减少矿物燃料的使用。2008 年农业法案出台了许多有关可再生能源的规定，为各类可再生能源项目提供资金支持、建立生物提炼厂、开发高级生物燃料、提高水利发电站的使用效率及激励农村社区加强能源自给自足。可再生资源项目拨款金额范围是从 2500 美元至 50 万美元，但是拨款金额不能超过总项目成本的 25%。除此之外，贷款担保的有效范围最多为合格成本的 50%，范围从 5000 美元到 1000 万美元不等。

5.1.1.2　爱尔兰的案例和经验

直到 20 世纪 40 年代后期，爱尔兰农村地区还非常依赖传统能源，依赖程度比美国还要严重。1946 年启动农村电气化项目时，几乎还没有农户能用上电。而 30 年后，几乎所有的农村人口都能用上了电。爱尔兰政府如此行动的动机有社会效益方面的原因，还有经济效益方面的原因（Shiel，2007）。

1946 年该项目正式启动，而对项目的精心筹备工作早在 5 年前就已经开始了，工作中特别研究了美国、加拿大和斯堪的纳维亚半岛的案例。项目所面临的最大问题是财务问题：如何确保有足够多的用户愿意联网，从而确保此项目进行下去，以及如何确保利用提供的补贴来实现其目标。若要支付农村电气化改造所需的全部资金成本，所需的高额收费远远超过大多数农村用户的收入水平。

政府部门一开始就制定了一系列措施。第一，首先在计划中排除居住在最偏僻区域的 30% 的农村用户，以此节省整体成本；第二，不提供从城市到农村的交叉补贴，原因是城市用户群太小以至于交叉补贴不可行；第三，决定为供电局提供资金补贴，金额视可用资金情况而定。公司必须设定价格来支付其余的成本费用。几年中的账目表明公司起初在农村经营中有少量盈利，但最终还是从盈利转为亏损。

此项目在体制方面的许多特征是非常重要的。如果某个区域联网签约用户的数目足以确保项目的实施，那么将会选择这个区域。当地社区负责确保上述情况属实，因此该系统有当地参与的特点，这点与美国类似，只是系统结构与美国不同。无论如何，当地支持以及与通电地区居民的交流是需要强调的重点。

电费由两部分费用组成，一个是固定收费，另外一个是可变收费。可变收费是相当高的：按照现在的价格计算，每个月的用电量为 80kW·h 的费率大概为 18 美分/(kW·h)。随着用电量的增加，边际费率会降低，如果单位用电量超过 360kW·h，则费率只有 5.4 美分/(kW·h)（Shiel，2007）。

寻求当地支持是非常重要的，当地支持工作不仅包括吸收新用户，还包括对社区进行有关电力使用益处的教育。

有关当局所面临的最大问题是固定费用，此项费用类似于英国地主地租。因为成本增加而调整此部分收费会更加困难。

然而最终可以证明，此项目是成功的，电气化已经实现。因为有许多新的行业开始在农村落户，所以农业生产率显著增加。但是，要实现用电需求与用电量的大幅度增加，还需要花 15～20 年的时间。

5.1.1.3 对中国的启示

对中国来说，可以从上述两个有关农村能源与能源开发的案例分析中吸取重要的经验。需要在此说明，中国在农村地区开展的项目已经进展非常顺利。自 1949 年以来，已有超过 9 亿的农村居民联网，总体联网率约 99％。现在约有分布于 9300 个村庄和 608 个城镇的 460 万户农户没有用电。他们大多数居住于偏远地区，为他们供电的难度会逐渐加大。因此，中国的农村电气化项目计划是向 350 万户农户提供再生电（2010年）；到 2015 年，实现全面使用再生电的农村电气化。

中国农村能源利用的另外一个特点是现代能源消耗只占总能耗的很小一部分。2000年有 1/3 的农村能源使用来自"非现代"资源（即木材、秸秆等）。并且，电力只占总能耗量的 11％，煤在家庭使用时是一种污染源，其使用量约占总量的 45％。因此，我们需要努力增加电力的使用量。

根据美国与爱尔兰的经验，在实现此目标过程中，合作社应起到一定作用。合作社的主要作用是帮助实现低成本配电，以便降低农村用户的电价。他们甚至还能部分承担发电和输电的责任。现在，农村用户用电所支付的费用约为城市用户的两倍，因此他们的耗电量这么低并不令人惊讶。随着合作社对当地配电网的建设，农户用电成本会降低。合作社还可以帮助向其余的 460 万用户提供便利的入网服务。

另外一个经验：地方社区宣传电力的好处，可以帮助扩展电力应用范围，使其应用不仅局限于照明。这在美国和爱尔兰就起到过重要的作用，一旦人们认识到电力能够帮助降低成本和增加商业机会，电力需求就会快速增长。

当然，在发展电气化的最初几年当中，合作运动确实需要来自政府部门的支持；如果没有中央政府的资金支持，爱尔兰的电气化项目也同样不会成功。尽管这些资金是必需的，但只有这些资金是不够的，所以当地参与是成败与否的关键条件。

最后，随着中国市区外围地带的扩大与本地革新能力的增加，也可以在中国发展类似于美国的可再生能源项目，从而发展可再生资源并提高能源效率。然而，必须确保补贴分配到的项目都是经过精心规划及认真审查的。例如在美国只提供联合基金，我们要研究这些项目，看看我们能得到什么经验。

5.1.2 发展中国家的经验和启示

5.1.2.1 发展中国家的经验

从发展中国家的经验中，我们发现的最突出的事实是电气化率太低。在许多非洲和亚洲国家，电气化率比人口增长率还要低。

国家项目经常会遇到财政方面的困难。例如，印度的高额资助项目已经耗尽许多国有电力公司的财力，这极大地破坏了这些公司的总体绩效和服务质量。财政困难产生的原因有三个因素。

第一，过于相信能够得到项目补贴所需的资源。一旦那些资源停止供应，项目便会遇到困难。第二，从居民支付电费的能力和意愿，以及现有的资源方面来说，所选的要进行电气化的区域不是最合适的。政治家干涉有序的计划与项目运转，坚持特权用户优先联网，并阻止断开不付费用户的网络。第三，在某些情况下未充分保证用电农户有支付电费的能力和意愿。由此产生的结果是，收入确实能达到期望值，而在回收电费违约者的款项方面出现问题。

然而，尽管这些问题都存在，许多国家已经悄无生息地为他们的农村地区成功提供了电力。在泰国，已有超过80％的农村人口能够使用电力。在哥斯达黎加，电力公司和政府合作已经为95％的农村人口提供电力。在突尼斯，75％的农村用户已经用上电，国家电力公司信心十足地预计，此比例到2001年会超过80％。

巴恩斯和弗勒总结了从发展中国家吸取的经验（Barnes，2007）。要成功发展电气化项目，必须满足以下条件。

1）建立有效的体制结构

基于大型网络的农村电气化是一个相对较复杂的工程，建立一个有效的执行机构是其最基本的要求之一。然而，体制结构并不拘泥于十分具体的形式，因为已有很多种机构的设置方法已经获得成功，其中包括独立的农村电气化管理局（孟加拉国）、设立农村电力合作社（哥斯达黎加，部分是吸取美国的经验）、将农村电气化分派到国家配气公司（泰国）某部门或将农村电气化委派给区域电力公用设施办公室（突尼斯）。

尽管没有一个体制模式是最完善的，但运行完好的体制模式都存在共同的因素。一个高度自治的操作体制（执行机构把农村电气化作为其首要目标）似乎很重要，但责任与自治同样重要。举一个典型的例子，爱尔兰的农村电气化代理机构有其自己的预算，并拥有对材料与劳工的控制权，能根据实际情况及成本制订工作计划，但该机构还是对实现目标非常负责任。

另一个无形的但更重要的要素就是执行机构需要精力充沛的领导，他应有激发全体员工积极性的才能，并专注于农村电气化任务。在泰国和其他有成功项目经验的国家，执行机构工作人员认为自己在为国家的发展和进步奠定基础，且这种感觉非常强烈。

2）政治事务处理

农村电气化项目使用公共资金时常遭到国家和地方政治干预。政治家认为他们有干预使用公共资金的权利，但是以往经验表明，这正是最糟糕的一点。

一旦执行机构屈从于政治压力做出技术与财政决策，就会摧毁职业纪律，破坏组织结构。在那些遭受高度政治干预的地区，农村电气化项目建设中资源会被浪费，员工士气较低，操作效率也较低。

有时，政治干预也会转化成积极作用，例如，泰国鼓励当地政治家筹措资金，这样当地的农民就能够在规定时间之前开始用电。农村电气化规划的开放和客观似乎更为重要。成功的项目使用明确规定的排列农村电气化区域的优先排序，以便保证所有决策的公平和透明。

3）农村电气化标准

无数失败的案例表明，过早进行农村电气化是毫无价值的。只有当其他必要条件都具备时，供电项目才会对农村的可持续发展做出重要贡献。

实施农村电气化的必要条件是：农民具有土地所有权，可以进行农业投入，能够获得医疗和教育服务，拥有可靠水源以及有足够数量的常住居民。农户们要增加农业生产投资，必须能够打入市场，只有进入市场后，他们的高产出才能获得公平的价格，从而获得较高的收入，当农户们的可支配收入达到一定水平，他们才愿意安装先进的电灯，购买电视机和其他家用电器，也才会支付电费。

成功的农村电气化项目都已经全面开发了自己的系统，目的是对通电区域进行分级排序。通常情况下，资金投资成本、本地出资水平、用户数目与密度以及可能的用电需求都是需要考虑的因素。在哥斯达黎加，对社区进行排序的依据是人口密度、商业发展水平和潜在的用电负荷。泰国开发的数字排序系统则考虑到了各种因素，例如收入水平、现有商业企业数目以及政府在此区域对其他基础设施的投资计划。

4）成本回收的重要性

成本回收可能是决定农村电气化项目长期经济效益的最重要的因素。当追求成本回收时，项目中的大部分其他因素就很容易依次排序。尽管实现成本回收的方法有很大的差异，但案例中研究的所有成功项目都强调成本回收。

与此相反，依靠经营补贴的供电机构很容易受到补贴金减少的影响。当补贴减少时（这种情况的发生是不可避免的），销售量的增加就会转变成更大的亏损，优点也就变成了缺点，这样会对新电力用户（尤其是贫困用户）的开发造成非常不利的影响。这些与经营管理相矛盾的因素会使机构无法正常运营。

例如在肯尼亚，依靠捐赠人的补贴金开展农村电气化项目，项目的进展情况很慢，并且时断时续。在马拉维，国家电力公司明确声明其对农村电气化不感兴趣，因为政府规定的电价太低以至于连经营成本都无法支付。

资本投资补贴会引发各种各样的问题。在大多数的成功项目中，相当大比例的资本是通过优惠利率贷款或以拨款的形式获得的。如果大部分资本是通过商业利率获得的，那么农村永远实现不了电气化。哥斯达黎加的一个项目，其启动资金就是从美国国际开发署（United States Agency for International Development，USAID）低息贷款获得的。在爱尔兰，部分投资成本是通过政府拨款获得的，其比例将视国库的资金状况而定。

如果广泛使用资本投资补贴，并且可以支付经营成本，那么这种优惠利率资本对执行机构或农村电气化项目应该不会有不利影响。但是，优惠利率资本绝不能提供给没有能力支付经营成本与维护费用的组织机构。这样只会使他们的财务状况恶化。

5) 合理收取电费

大家普遍认为，如果想让农民受益于农村电气化，那么电价就要非常低，比实际供电成本还要低。但事实并非如此。农村电气化只有在对用电服务（诸如电灯、电视机、电冰箱和动力应用）有需求的地方实施才有意义。由于没有电网，用电需求是通过购买煤油、液化石油气（LPG）、干电池、车用蓄电池和小型发电机等来实现的，这些能源的电费单价都非常贵。最近对乌干达和老挝未供电地区的调查表明，当地居民使用这些能源大概每个月要花费 5 美元。民营供应商发现供电市场前景很好，其供电价高于 1 美元/（kW·h）。

根据当地农民的实际经济条件来设定农村电力价格，仍然可以大大节约农民的用电成本，并且还能让他们享受到许多改进后的电力设施服务。合理的收费可使供应商以更加高效、可靠和持续的方式为越来越多的满意用户供电。在哥斯达黎加，虽然电价是通过一套标准化的程序来设定的，但是电价仍足以让合作社从中获得适度的利润。1996年，住宅用电的电价标准是：前 30kW·h 的固定电费为 2.59 美元；对每月耗电量超过 150kW·h 的用户，其可变电费稳步增加并超过 25 美分/（kW·h）。

6) 降低门槛，供应电力

对农村家庭来说，支付供电机构要求的首次入网费往往比支付每月电费更困难。即使降低首次入网费标准，或将这些费用分摊到几年来收取都会提高电费单价，从而让更多的农村低收入家庭获得电力供应。

例如在玻利维亚的一家小型本地电网公司，其电费仅为 25～30 美分/（kW·h）。但是当该公司允许用户在 5 年内付清连网成本费后，其用户数目迅速增加到原来的两倍。相比之下，马拉维的一家电力公司向新用户全额收取 30 年的布线成本费，其农村电气化率仅仅为 2%。

7) 社区参与的好处

按照传统的思维方式，许多公用事业单位往往意识不到本地社区参与所起到的作用。农村电气化常常被简单地认为是一个技术问题，即将电线延伸到充满感激的客户那里。上述案例分析明确表明农村电气化项目可从本地社区参与中受益匪浅——如果没有社区的参与，公用事业单位就会蒙受损失。

设立农村电气化管理委员会来代表本地社区行使职权，这样做可使此项目的实施更加顺利。农村电气化管理委员会可以在帮助评估需求水平、预先培训用户、鼓励用户签订供电协议与促进电力广泛应用等方面发挥重要的作用。

在孟加拉国，用户在通电之前曾举办过多次会议，这样做有助于避免在通行权和道路、建筑损坏发生的纠纷，因为解决这些纠纷需要耗费大量的金钱与时间。在泰国，社区出资（以现金或实物的形式）往往成为将此区域纳入农村电气化项目范围内的关键因素。爱尔兰教区农村电气化管理委员会为了增加电力用户付出了很多努力，确保了公用事业单位收到足够的投资回报，这样做有助于快速实施国家农村电气化项目。

8）减少建筑与经营成本

在大多数国家，有很多机会可以减少农村电气化建设与经营成本。在众多案例中，增加对系统设计方案的重视可以减少多达 30% 的建筑成本，这样做更有利于促进农村电气化项目的建设进度与规模。

在那些主要用电力照明或使用小家用电器（许多农村地区的典型特征）的地区，不需要采用负荷较重的城市系统所应用的设计标准。可以根据实际的用电负荷设计农村配电系统，通常月用电量不超过 15kW·h。尽管耗电量一般会增加，但在通常情况下增长速度非常慢。如果已进行了必要的设计，将来配电系统升级也相对较便宜。

每个国家的农村电气化规划者都有自己节约成本的方法。在泰国，所有原材料都是标准化的且都在本地生产制造，这样会减少调配、物料搬运与采购费用。在哥斯达黎加、菲律宾和孟加拉国，采用 20 世纪 30 年代美国农村电气化项目中曾经使用且经过验证的单相配电系统，该系统比非洲和其他地区广泛应用的三相配电系统可以节省大量成本。案例研究表明，对设计假定和操作实践的认真的批判性分析都具有减少成本的潜力。

9）电网替代方案

人们常常认为基于电网的农村电气化与其他形式的能源（尤其是光电系统）之间存在竞争，这种想法是错误的，因为两者之间几乎没有冲突。

农村电网允许用户使用标准的电器设备和家用电器，而对消耗的电量没有任何实际约束。电网可以提供的服务水平是其他替补能源所不能给予的，在技术和经济条件允许的情况下，电力始终是用户的首选。

考虑到成本、技术或机构因素，在偏远地区或难以到达的地区通电是不切实际的。在通常情况下，农民满足用电需求的方式是使用煤油、液化石油气、干电池和车用蓄电池，偶尔还会使用小型柴油或汽油发电机。光电系统越来越能证明其在成本与服务方面比常规能源更有竞争力。

5.1.2.2 发展中国家的经验对中国的启示

总的来说，中国在农村电气化进程中避免了许多令其他发展中国家头疼的问题。这些发展中国家的经验教训总结如下：

（1）如果一个国家将电气化项目扩展到更偏远且条件更困难的地区，那就需要考虑成功实现农村电气化所必须要满足的条件。其中最主要的条件是农民可以承受的电费支付能力。

（2）因为这些地区相对来说比较贫穷，如果首次入网费是通过分期付款的方式收回，那么将会有更多的农户愿意联网。

（3）社区积极参与的好处是不言而喻的，其中包括动员本地团队这种基础工作，甚至可能会组织本地配电协会，以及其他好处。

（4）减少成本所采取的措施和对需求水平低这一事实的利用都有助于保持较低的电费和维护电气化项目的可持续发展。

（5）已经在中国使用的电网替代方案会在偏远地区发挥更大的作用。

5.2 国外农村地区适应气候变化的经验

改变土地的使用和管理习惯可以达到减缓和适应气候变化的双重效果。同时，通过这些改变获得的温室气体减排额还可以带来经济效益，有助于农村地区的扶贫和创收工作。本章着重介绍美国的农业和林业温室气体减排项目及经验，列举此类项目的定义和评估体系中的主导因素，并通过案例详细介绍如何定义和测量温室气体减排额使之真实、可信并具有较高的成本效益。美国的经验将有助于中国农村地区能源和环境的可持续发展。

5.2.1 农业温室气体减排的经济刺激手段

基于土地活动的温室气体减排项目需要在技术上和实践中做出相应的改变。这些改变可以通过土壤和生物的固碳作用实现可测量的减排，也可以直接减少温室气体排放。技术和实践上的改变需要一定的经济成本。通过适当的机制为土地经营者提供相应的资金是必要的。生态补偿的概念让实现农业温室气体减排成为可能。

中国的农村地区已经建立了实现温室气体减排的经济刺激框架。根据中国环境与发展国际合作委员会（简称"国合会"）的定义，生态补偿是"以保护和可持续利用生态系统服务为目的，以经济手段为主调节相关者利益关系的制度安排"。强调生态补偿的生态系统管理的关键概念是：生态保护的经济成本；生态系统退化的机会成本；生态系统服务的经济价值。为了平衡成本与收益，政府和市场必须为生态保护行为提供经济奖励，并向生态和自然资源的破坏者征收修复成本。国合会提出了生态补偿机制的基本原则：

破坏者付费——破坏者应当就其行为对生态系统造成的负面影响负责。

使用者付费——环境资源的使用者应当就使用的稀缺资源向政府提供补偿。

受益方付费——受益方应当补偿生态服务的供应方。

对保护者的补偿——对生态建设做出贡献的群体或个人应当按照其投资和机会成本得到补偿。

国际上已经有许多国家，包括美国，采用了生态补偿政策。具体措施包括以下几个方面。

直接私人付费：由私营机构向土地管理者支付生态系统服务的费用。

直接公共付费：由政府直接向土地经营者及生态服务的其他供应者付费。

生态认证计划：通过产品标签和绿色认证为生态友好产品及服务支付较高价格。

财税激励措施：由政府为提供生态系统服务的土地管理者提供优惠的财税政策。

配额交易计划：由政府确定某一特定地区生态系统退化或污染程度的限额，使用者和污染者或直接遵从限额，或出资由他人开展保护活动以完全抵消其产生的损害。此类项目在控制温室气体排放中起到了至关重要的作用，欧盟、日本等国家正力图通过这一体系实现京都议定书目标。

5.2.2　农业温室气体减排

改善土地管理的措施和技术有利于降低大气中的温室气体含量。农田和林地中的生物质及土壤能够储存碳，称为"汇"。森林在生长的过程中从大气中吸收二氧化碳，并将碳储存（或埋存）在植物的枝干、叶子、根和土壤里。免耕和少耕，草地恢复以及种植覆盖植被等土地管理措施也可以将碳存储在土壤里。通过保护和再造森林，恢复草场植被，改善农田的管理方式，土地使用者可以减少大气中的温室气体含量。良好的土地使用方式也可以降低温室气体，尤其是甲烷和氮氧化物的排放。例如，精确地使用化肥可以降低土壤的氮氧化物的释放量；减少水对土壤的浸淹（尤其是水稻田）以及收集和燃烧粪肥等措施可以控制甲烷的排放。

5.2.2.1　改善土地管理措施和技术实现温室气体减排和抵消潜力

改善土地管理措施具有巨大的减排潜力，可以通过研究项目来评估其效果。美国已经完成了相应的研究，结果令人振奋。美国目前每年仅二氧化碳的排量就达到 60 亿 t以上，其他温室气体，包括甲烷、氮氧化物和氟化物，年释放量也相当于 10 亿 tCO_2e。1990 年美国的年平均温室气体排放约为 61 亿 tCO_2e，到 2004 年则接近 71 亿 tCO_2e，平均每年增长 1%。如果没有限排措施，这 1% 的年增长率就意味着到 2025 年美国每年将多排放 16 亿 tCO_2e 的温室气体，即年排放总量达到 87 亿 tCO_2e。

目前一个可能的目标是，美国在 2025 年之前将其温室气体排放在现有的基础上减少 15%。这意味着美国每年需要减少 10 亿 tCO_2e 的排放量[①]。加上预计的每年 16 亿 tCO_2e 的增长，美国每年实际需要减排约 26 亿 tCO_2e。

土地管理实践和技术的改善将为美国实现其年减排 26 亿 t 的目标做出巨大的贡献。减排和抵消额的市场价格是决定土地管理者能否大规模提供减排和抵消额度的主要因素。价格越高，农民和土地管理者参与市场的积极性就越高（图 5.1），所创造的温室气体抵消额也就越多。若价格维持在每吨 CO_2 为 15 美元，在 2025 年之前，土地管理项目每年可以创造 15 亿 t 的抵消额度，即美国完成其 15% 目标的 60%。若价格达到 50 美元/t，土地部门可以创造 20 亿 t 的年抵消量，这几乎相当于美国需要实现的所有减排量。

从现实的情况看，碳市场上价格可以激励土地管理部门创造大量的减排额或抵消额。美国目前的碳市场是一个基于自愿交易的市场，需求量相对较弱，价格在 1~10 美元/t。欧盟根据《京都议定书》的要求建立了强制性的排放限额，碳市场的价格在近几年曾经达到 35 美元/t。如果美国近期内有关气候变化的法案得以实施，其强制性的温室气体排放限额将大大提高市场上碳的价格，使其足够激励土地部门成为主要的抵消额提供者。

---

① 二氧化碳当量是衡量所有温室气体全球变暖潜能（GWP）的指标，一吨二氧化碳具有一个单位的全球变暖潜能，即一个二氧化碳当量。其他温室气体的全球变暖潜能各异。如，一吨甲烷具有 23 个二氧化碳当量的全球变暖潜能。

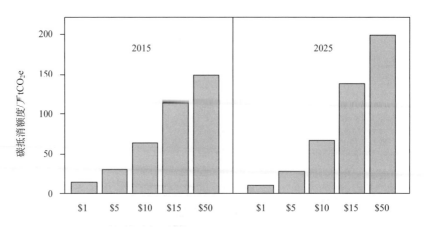

图 5.1　预期美国土地部门创造的碳抵消额度随年份和碳价（万 tCO_2e）的变化

注：随着抵消额价格的升高，农民和土地管理者参与市场的积极性提高，导致市场上的
抵消额总量上升（来源：美国环境保护总署，2005）

5.2.2.2　农业减排项目的种类

土地管理者，农民和碳抵消项目开发商可以通过多种方式减少农业碳排放。主要的项目类型如下：

生物质储碳项目。造林和种草，或延迟森林砍伐减少碳流失的项目。

土壤储碳项目。改善耕作习惯，如免耕农作、改种多年生植物或改善草场状况等项目。

改善耕作习惯减少甲烷和氮氧化物排放的项目，如减少氮肥的使用、改变化肥的成分、改变水稻田秸秆残渣的管理方式等项目。

改变粪肥处理和利用方式减少甲烷排放的项目，如收集粪肥并进行厌氧消化处理等项目。

尽管不同类型土地项目的成本有很大差异，总体上讲这类项目能够用低成本在单位面积的土地上创造大量的抵消额（图 5.2），美国各类土地项目固碳潜力评估。每个项目往往包含有多种不同的减排方式，例如，把使用氮肥并种植一年生农作物的土地退耕还林，可以通过树木和土壤的固碳作用、减少农业机械使用的化石燃料、减少化肥的使用等降低温室气体排放。所有这些都将计入项目的总抵消额。

5.2.2.3　温室气体减排和抵消交易类型

土地利用减排项目通常可以通过两种合同形式出售——一次性永久销售和有条件短期租售。永久销售一般用于直接减排的项目，包括减少甲烷排放的粪肥管理项目、通过减少化肥的使用减排氮氧化物的项目、通过免耕降低燃料的使用从而实现的 CO_2 减排项目等。另外，一次性永久销售的合同也可以用于能够实现温室气体在生物质和土地中永久储存的固碳项目。尽管此类项目理论上可以实现永久性固碳，合同中有必要加入防止碳泄漏的违约条款。

非永久性土壤和生物质固碳的项目可以通过短期合同购买。此类合同要求土地管理者/碳抵消额的卖方同意在一定的时间内贮存温室气体。这个时间限度即是购买方暂时

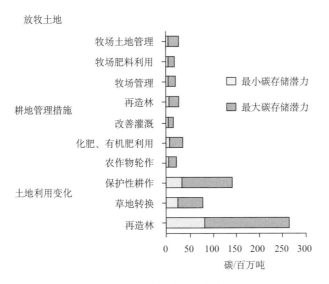

图 5.2　碳储存潜力评估

拥有碳抵消额的时间限度。在合同结束后，土地管理者/卖方通过此项目固碳的义务也相应结束。购买方需要通过续约或购买新的抵消合同来完成减排的指标。

5.2.3　碳排放项目集成开发

5.2.3.1　集成服务及其作用

土地使用项目往往需要"中间人"代表农民或土地管理者将单个项目集成打包出售。通过项目集成能够大大提高农业和林业项目的规模和市场竞争力。项目集成开发提供的服务，例如计量、监测和风险管理等是单个土地管理者难以独自承担的。正如前文所说，美国的碳市场有 25 亿 tCO_2e 的潜在需求。若平均每笔交易为 10 万 tCO_2e，则每年需要有 2.5 万笔交易；显然，在工业购买者力图寻找大单生意的市场里，由单个土地管理者完成的 100 多吨甚至 1000 多吨的小规模减排额将面临昂贵的交易成本。

图 5.3 诠释了温室气体抵消额的集合机制以及集合多个小的抵消项目所实现的市场优势。例如，600 个独立的平均 1000 英亩[①]土地的小型减排项目，平均每英亩土地的减排额为 $1tCO_2e$，项目每年的总减排额达到 60 万 tCO_2e。如果被集成开发为一个大项目，集成者将有很好的机会与一家或多家大型购买者协商。

除了将小项目捆绑以增加市场竞争力外，项目集成者还扮演其他的角色。通过改变土地使用方式和技术实现温室气体减排是一种商业活动，需要在几年的时间内投入相应的资金，因此需要规划。项目集成者需要提供既适合自身也适合其客户，即参与项目的小土地管理者的商业计划书。集成者很可能需要为客户提供投资服务，寻找相应的资金以协助客户完成真实可信的农林业减排额。

————————

① 1 英亩＝0.404686hm²。

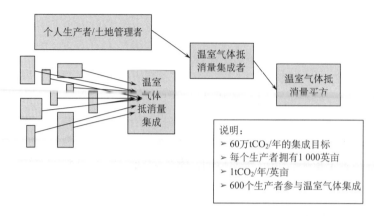

图 5.3　土地部门的温室气体集成

说明：
➢ 60万tCO$_2$/年的集成目标
➢ 每个生产者拥有1 000英亩
➢ 1tCO$_2$/年/英亩
➢ 600个生产者参与温室气体集成

　　尽管项目的开发商不一定是项目的集成者，后者可以扮演前者的角色。开发商需要确保项目的实施符合特定的减排标准，项目的集成者也可以承担这一任务。例如，集成者可以负责确定和测量项目的减排额，并在减排额上市时提供必要的监测、测量和核准计划书。第三方认证机构需要参与减排额的核证过程，集成者可以负责选择认证机构并与其签署服务协议。集合者必须与参与项目的农场、林场以及抵消额的购买者签署协议。风险管理，特别是对于没有完成合同规定的减排额的管理是集成者的主要任务之一。风险决策包括对多种选择的评估，如保险的获取、自保险缓冲、建立多供应商储备账户以及参与项目的土地管理者默认的管理等。

5.2.3.2　温室气体集成者资质

　　集成者需要在很多方面有资格提供可靠且有效的服务参与农业及森林项目。如前所述，集成开发者必须有能力从单个的土地管理者手中汇集足够多的温室气体抵消额度，以适应市场经济的规模。为扮演好这样的角色，集成者不仅需要有丰富的经验，还需要在土地管理者中具有良好的声誉及可信度。由于集成开发者需要管理与农民和林务员签订的多个合同，需要具有制度上的能力来管理资金和合同，因此不仅要有良好的经营能力，还需要具备一系列的专业能力，包括生产和管理温室气体抵消额的专业知识。集成者还需要有能力与土地管理者和购买者进行磋商，而这些人的谈判能力和专业的法律知识往往使他们难以对付。最后，集成者还需要和第三方核证及监督机构打交道，处理关于监督、定量及核准的计划。

　　在美国，土地部门中有一些组织已经或正在考虑成为温室气体抵消额的集成者。这些组织中的大多数都已经具备土地管理者的关系网，足以汇集抵消额。例如，保护区、农场局地方分会、农产品组织、食品加工机构、农场及林场协会、保险公司及农业投入品供应商都是很好的例子。其中一些组织，如保护区和农场局地方分会，可能缺乏商业管理及与客户进行财务交易的能力。另外一些，如农产品组织、食品加工机构和保险公司，则具备这些财务能力。因此，成为温室气体抵消额集合者对于来自不同背景的组织来说，提出了不同的挑战。

5.2.4　温室气体项目开发的基本要素

5.2.4.1　项目定义

图 5.4 描述了开发温室气体减排及抵消项目的必要步骤。土地管理者定义一个项目时需要明确产生温室气体抵消额所需要采取的措施及技术。例如，一个项目可能会在土壤或树木中封存碳、或使用厌氧分解技术来捕获粪肥中产生的甲烷排放。项目的空间和时间边界也需要界定出来，用以对项目的温室气体抵消额进行定量及核准。

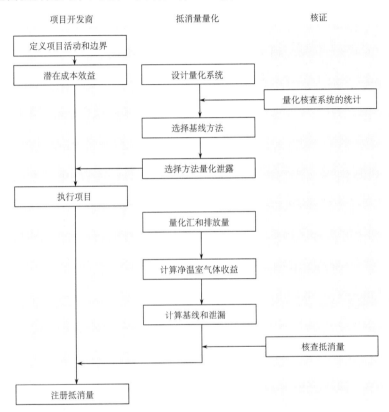

图 5.4　温室气体项目开发程序及步骤

项目的空间边界可以通过调查来确定。但是这种方式通常较为昂贵。可以选择较为廉价方法，例如依靠规划地图或全球定位系统（GPS）接收器来确定项目的范围。具有法律效力的记录或进行了适当标记的航拍相片也可以提供借鉴。对那些位于特定设施的项目来说，例如有牲口棚及相连的粪肥处理区域，一个地址也许就足以确定该项目空间界限。如果土地管理者具有多种减排方式，那么项目边界需要涵盖与项目有关的所有土地及设施。否则，只需把产生温室气体排放的行为移出项目所在地就可以获取温室气体抵消额。

温室气体抵消项目具有时间和空间的边界。时间边界的确定相对容易。项目通常自签约日起生效，或始于土地管理活动启动，或从一个设施或程序（例如从牲畜粪便中捕获甲烷）开始运作算起。项目可以无限期的运作，或到某一确定时间终止。

5.2.4.2 界定项目的成本和收益

项目界定指对预期产生的温室气体抵消额及成本进行估算，用以决定该项目是否会产生净投资回报。这是决定是否执行一个项目的基础。进行温室气体抵消额项目的界定有三步：①确定该项目可产生温室气体抵消额；②界定项目的收益及成本；③拟制温室气体抵消额的报价单。

一个项目的成本包括执行成本、与参与者签订合同以及测量、核准、登记及营销温室气体减排额过程中产生的费用。在评估净投资回报的过程中，土地管理者、项目开发者和买方须考虑在项目的生命周期中何时会产生成本及温室气体收益。估算一个项目产生抵消额的潜在能力需要经过一些步骤，它们大体上与温室气体抵消额量化的步骤相当。然而，与实际上监测项目成果相比，在这一阶段通常会采取较为宽松及省时廉价的方法，如估算与预测，对项目进行界定。

报价单----基本要素
从_____农业项目产生CO$_2$e抵消量
地点_____，美国，_____，2008
项目类型
项目地点　　　　　　　价格及支付方式
所用方法　　　　　　　总碳评估
组织/个人　　　　　　　预计产生的二氧化物排放抵消
项目总报价(美元)　　　量(吨CO$_2$或碳当量)
项目描述　　　　　　　抵消量核证
抵消量的期限和所有权　销售或租赁协议的终止

图5.5　气体项目报价单

通过项目的界定最终可以获得一份温室气体抵消额的报价单。这份报价单提供一个简短的摘要（一般不超过两页），通常包括集合者卖出各土地管理者生产的温室气体抵消额的销货要约，预计产生的温室气体抵消额的总量，产生这些温室气体抵消额所需采取的措施及技术，以及报价。图5.5为气体项目报价单样本。

5.2.4.3 建立额外性和基准线

为确保一个项目的温室气体抵消额有效且可交易，项目土地上的温室气体排放或碳储量的改变必须与不执行该项目时的情况有所差别，且这种差别必须可以量化。这些问题可以通过决定额外性和基准线来解决。

判断一个项目是否具有额外性需要寻找具有相似起始条件的场地，并且预期在项目周期内这些地方可能产生的土地管理的改变。这将决定一个项目是否真正产生了超过"常规情景"的温室气体减排。虽然确定一个项目是否具有额外性有一定难度，但这些努力是至关重要的。如果一个项目的温室气体获益并不具有额外性，那么这个项目宣称的抵消额就不是真实的，总量控制和排污权交易系统也不会认可这些抵消额。

根据不同的标准，决定额外性有不同的测试方法。最常见的测试方法包括管理盈余、资金、障碍检测和惯例检测。可以采取一种或多种测试方法对项目的额外性进行逐一的分析。另外，也可以采用绩效标准。

不执行任何项目时一块土地或设施中将会产生的温室气体排放构成了基准线。由于管理或环境条件的改变，基准线可能会随时间产生变化。项目的净温室气体效益是指基准线与项目执行期间实际温室气体排放的差值。

如果使用一个甲烷消解器对温室气体排放进行捕捉，那么在项目开始前没有消解器的情况下产生的温室气体排放的数值，就可以作为基准线。其他类型的项目必须在开始时确定基准线，说明区域内条件相当的土地上环境和土地管理行为的改变。包括《京都议定书》在内的一些体系，将额外性和基准线定为不同的步骤。该体系确定一个项目是否具有额外性，如果具有额外性，则指定一种独立的方法来确定基准线。这种程序对于额外性的测试通常是非此即彼的。但是，这种走极端的方式易于妨碍那些真正能够实现温室气体减排措施的使用，因而可能适得其反。一种替代方案是明确一个涵盖多种标准的折现因子体系，在项目的温室气体抵消额量化过程中准予计算 0～1 之间的因子。

5.2.4.4 泄漏

泄漏是指从一个项目的边界之内转移到边界之外的排放源。当商品的生产从项目所在地区转到边界之外的其他区域，就会产生泄漏。项目边界内商品生产减少的影响可以通过标准的经济分析来进行评估。市场需求和供给弹性可以用来估算因项目边界内商品生产减少而带来的边界之外的产量。

在所有项目中，在为增加现有林地的碳储量而控制砍伐的项目中可能产生的碳泄漏最为令人关注。美国的林产品市场非常活跃，因此在一个地区的供给减少往往会刺激其他地区进行更多的补偿。例如，美国太平洋西北部地区为保护斑点猫头鹰而放慢了伐木的速度，而砍伐却在东南地区兴盛了起来。与控制木材砍伐的项目不同的是，那些在边缘农业用地上造林的项目不大可能带来显著的泄漏。美国农田生产了过多的农产品，因此这些项目不大可能促使其他农民将林业用地转化为农业用地来补充粮食的供给。采用免耕法的农业项目也不大可能产生泄漏，因为用免耕法替代以前的耕作方法改善了土壤的肥力，因而增加了粮食的生产。因此，排放不会转移到其他地点。

5.2.4.5 监测和量化计划

采用公开透明的方法创造并量化一个项目的温室气体抵消额需要予以记录，以保证其可核准，并可以被管理者和买方接受。项目开发者需要在项目开始前拟订一份监测和量化计划。如果条件的改变要求对项目的土地管理或量化行为进行修改，可以通过附录来对这些修改做记录。为提高适销性，项目的温室气体抵消额需要进行独立的核准。核准人将会参照详细记录的计划，以保证土地管理者和项目开发者执行了计划，以及量化者计算的净温室气体效益真实可信。

监测及核准计划应该包括以下几方面内容：

（1）项目边界（当计划拟定时，如项目边界已知应记录在内）。

（2）该项目中潜在的温室气体排放源和碳汇的清单。

（3）用以测量项目条件的详细协议，包括测量的频率、记录、管理及存储数据的程序。

（4）抽样调查项目温室气体效应的计划，包括监测活动的地点、鉴别这些地点的机制，如在航拍照片上做标记、GPS 坐标或物理标记。

（5）在项目测量基础上分析数据和量化抵消额的程序、因子和公式。

（6）量化者形成报告的内容和时间。这些报告需要包括原始数据的摘要，而不仅仅是数据分析的结果。

  (7) 质量控制标准和方法，包括备份数据以免遗失。

  (8) 基准线或确定基准线的程序。

  (9) 泄漏比率或评估泄漏的程序。

5.2.4.6 测量计划

  监测和量化计划最重要的部分就是明确采用何种方法监测该项目的土地管理行为导致的温室气体排放或碳储量的改变。为确保减排量和碳汇量是真实的，量化者必须要使用可信赖的、恰当的、完整的、公正的及透明的技术。在这一点至关重要的一步是小心取样，以收集具有代表性且准确的数据，从而测出实际排放量或碳汇量的改变。

  不同种类的土地管理项目要求使用不同的技术来测量项目周期内的排放量和碳汇量的净变化值。当一个项目设计生态系统的不同组成部分时，量化者进行测量时需要对每一个组成部分都采取其各自适用的技术。设计完整且精确的测量系统需要对量化对象的生物和物理属性有透彻的理解。如果一个测量系统不是建立在这些知识之上，那么它就不足以评价该项目将会影响的所有温室气体变化。项目抵消额的精确性通常会反映所采用的测量和量化方法的严密程度。一个较为严密的测量计划通常会产生出更为准确的量化抵消额，但这也意味着测量成本的上升。

  1) 林业温室气体测量

  森林碳汇是一个复杂的过程，林业项目通常有数十年的持续期需要，因此设计良好的生物质取样测量系统是非常重要的。森林项目的界定可以通过使用一个已校准的林业碳模型获得改善，例如由美国林务署开发的林业碳模型（Forest Vegetation Simulatory，FVS）。林业项目的抽样调查应做到精确，并且长期内可以反复进行。可适应各种不可预见的情况，如野火、林业管理改变、项目用地的增加或减少用地。尽可能的简单，以允许行业外的人员对结果进行审计。尽量做到固碳量的量化，以减少不确定性、控制成本，从而鉴别一个项目可能实现的固碳量，可参照以下步骤：

  (1) 设计一个森林抽样系统，在不同地点测量碳的累积量。

  (2) 在一个森林中的不同场地进行初步的碳储量测量。

  (3) 选择或建立新的异速生长方程，将实地测量数据转化为碳值。

  (4) 开展后继的实地测量，决定碳储量的变化。

  这一方法的关键在于开展无偏差的取样，选择足够多的取样场地，并决定是否以及如何将取样分层化。

  每隔5～10年重复一次定量的实地测量，在此期间，依靠每年对质量和数量的观察来判断一个项目是否依计划而行，还是需要开展补救措施。10%的不确定性和90%的可靠度对于估算碳的净封存量来讲已经足够，因为更高的准确度带来的收益与其耗费的成本相比微不足道。

  2) 土地温室气体管理

  为了准确地估算项目持续期内土地中碳的变化，必须制定详细的抽样和分析测量方法。抽样和土样测量成本很高，因此抽样设计在很大程度上影响项目的成本及其收益。进行抽样选择的目的是在保证准确性的基础上，既能测量碳的固定量，而又不至于花费过高。适当的抽样设计、分析过程、翔实的实地调查以及高质量的实验室测试可以保证在可接受的成本范围内获得较高的准确度。

土地管理者和项目开发者可以通过下列方式来量化项目所在地土壤中封存的碳：

（1）使用已经校准过的土壤碳模型（如 C-STORE）。

（2）设计一个测量土壤中碳储量变化的系统。

（3）在项目启动初期开展实地碳储量测量。

（4）随监测项目进展情况决定是否需要调整估算及（或）措施。

（5）重新测量碳储量并计算该值的变化。

量化土壤碳封存是很具有挑战性的，因为在大部分项目中土地中碳储量的增加通常不超过土壤中总碳储量的 10%——如果土壤取自于地下较深的部分，这个比值会更小。这意味着量化者测量净封存值（或土壤中碳含量的变化）的准确度需要达到 10%，而测量土壤中总碳含量的准确度需要至少达到 1%。

土壤抽样规则应包括对从不同样地土壤样本的收集，并制定一套详细的抽样规则。这份抽样规则应明确：①每个样地土壤样本的数量及空间安排；②当在某一指定地点不能成功获取样本时，实地采集员应当采取的步骤；③土柱的直径以及每个土柱的采集深度；④采集员如何处理土壤表面物质，如何标记、包装及处理样本的导则。

3）直接温室气体减排测量

土地管理和农业操作直接产生的温室气体减少需要通过间接的方式和模型进行量化。这是因为直接测量减排量需要昂贵的设备，尤其是气体测量在几乎所有涉及直接减排的土地项目都不具备经济可行性。

例如减少农场机械（如免耕法）或水泵设备（如滴灌项目）使用获得的二氧化碳减排。这些减少的二氧化碳排放可以通过直接测量减少的燃料和电力使用计算出来。根据燃料种类、发动机效率等计算二氧化碳排放量。

通过"脱氮-分解"模型估算甲烷和氧化亚氮排放是一个前景非常好的方法，它也被称为 DNDC（DeNitrification-DeComposition）模型。DNDC 模型需要提供关于天气、土壤种类、作物种类/美国每个郡的土壤面积的数据，以及由用户确定的在每个植物轮作周期或每年内施肥、耕作及其他管理行为的数据。用于估算土壤碳储量的变化、甲烷和氧化亚氮的排放变化，以及这些排放的全球变暖效应[1]（Li et al, 1992, 1996, 2000；Li, 2001）。这一模型需要大量关于样地的详细信息，且模型指定的措施和投入可能与项目需求有很大出入。一个替代方案是在少数易于测量的因子（如土壤中碳含量、土地管理者施用氮的数量以及作物所需要氮量）的基础上使用简单的公式对排放进行估算（Willey，Chameides，2007）。

---

[1]　请参考 http://www.dndc.sr.unh.edu/，包括该模型使用说明及关于其应用的详细讨论。

5.2.4.7　签订合同

温室气体抵消额是财产，因此管理财产的法律条例都适用于在土地管理者、项目开发者、集合商和买方之间进行的所有权流转。购买合同[①]通常在一个温室气体项目启动前签订，这就使土地管理者和项目集合商必须采取特定的措施或递交一定数量的温室气体抵消额。涉及土地使用的温室气体抵消额的销售和转让大致有两种类型的合同，一是单个的土地管理者与集合商签订合同，同意由集合商从一定数量的农业或林业操作中汇集温室气体抵消额。二是集合商直接与买方就累积的温室气体抵消额签订合同。

个体农民及土地管理者与集合商签订的合同包含以下一些要素：

（1）明确合同期/年数及项目用地；

（2）项目活动的次序及时刻表；

- 约定抵消额的固定数量或固定的减排行动；
- 估算预期的抵消额；
- 对实现的抵消额进行量化；
- 买方与卖方的责任；

（3）集合商（买方）责任；

- 设定并执行监测和核实计划；
- 进行支付；
- 建立准备金账户/风险管理；

（4）土地管理者责任；

- 在租期内采用能够产生温室气体抵消额的生产方式；
- 将温室气体抵消额度转让给集合商；
- 允许第三方核准人员进入土地；
- 准备年度报告，保证遵守合约；
- 对于持续或禁止特定土地管理行为具有永久权益（如契约、地役权）；
- 土地租用合同；
- 仅进行与温室气体生产者合同相符的行为；
- 如行为与温室气体合同不符，出租人退出一切温室气体抵消额的申领，并放弃租期内产生的所有温室气体抵消额，将其让给土地拥有者；

（5）温室气体抵消额价格及支付额计算；

- 明确每吨 CO_2e 温室气体的价格，以及当前执行行为的支付额；
- 对于多重付款，最终付款根据实际温室气体抵消额的情况而支付；
- 采用现值估价法计算抵消额的租价；

（6）其他条款（包括担保/代理人、中止条款、调解、合作、告知、保密性、责任范围、赔偿、终止、不可抗力）。

---

① 合同样本可以在下列网址找到：（i）http://www.environmentalmarkets.org；（ii）http://www.ieta.org；（iii）http://www.climatetrust.org.完善政府管理的新工具：对排污交易及其他基于市场的管理工具的评估一书也可以提供有益的帮助，该书由政府事务中心出版，提供了关于抵消额合同的基础内容。

项目集合商与买方的购买合同中也包括类似的要素。

5.2.4.8 注册及核准抵消额

项目温室气体抵消额的可销售性，透明度及核准是非常重要的。因此，得到量化的抵消额之后，项目开发者在最终出售这些额度之前还需要完成几个步骤。项目开发者与（或）集合者需要公开一个简短的书面报告，涵盖项目地址的信息，明确项目执行者，声明由谁来完成量化和核准，以及列出该项目将要产生的温室气体排放，并明确温室气体抵消额从何时起产生，且需告知其抵消的效果会持续多长时间。

发布的报告可以对用来进行温室气体量化的方法及卖方/土地管理者的法律义务进行公开，但同时要保护私人信息。独立的核准人需要参与其中，且温室气体抵消额需要注册。核准人像审计员一样对项目的温室气体抵消额产生过程进行核准。为避免利益冲突，核准员不得以任何其他方式参与项目。为提高可交易性，项目的温室气体抵消额需要向适当的注册实体进行注册，注册后抵消额拥有者将获得一个独一无二的识别码。如果温室气体抵消额售出，注册就被修改，从而反映出拥有权已经转让。注册同时还保证温室气体抵消额不能多次出售。

5.2.4.9 土地使用行业温室气体减排及抵消标准

为保证从土地项目中产生的温室气体抵消额度真实可信且准确，标准必不可少。前面的讨论已经涉及从项目开发到获得可交易的温室气体抵消额过程中的基本要素。简单说，这些要素包括：①项目描述；②温室气体减排的量化；③基准线/额外性；④泄漏；⑤监测方法学及计划；⑥第三方核准计划。

目前在世界范围内，已经有一些温室气体抵消的标准被制定出来，还有一些正在制定过程中。图5.6列出了一些标准。美国环保协会目前正在调查这些标准的优缺点，并为其是否能保证高质量的温室气体补偿提供一个粗略的排名。这些标准中有些适用于强制性温室气体控制计划，而另外一些则适用于全球的自愿减排市场。随时间的发展，这些标准有可能逐渐融合成为综合性、统一的标准。但这可能在未来很多年后才会实现，因此在这个过渡期之内，了解现存的这些标准，了解当采用这些标准评估土地行业的温室气体抵消项目时可能发生的性质变化非常重要。

清洁发展机制造林和再造林项目方法林	CarbonFix标准
自愿性核实减排标准	指定经营实体1605 (b)
ECIS自愿减排标准	ECIS自愿减排标准
CCAR林业协议	区域温室气体减排行动
自愿碳标准	世界资源研究所温室气体协议
杜克法则	IPCC方法指南
Plan Vivo	TUV SUD自愿减排方法
友好型温室气体方法	气候中和网络
气候、社区及生物多样性标准	
Green E气候协议	
芝加哥气候交易标准	
黄金标准	

图5.6 温室气体抵消标准

5.2.5 农业温室气体减排案例分析——美国

最近几年美国已经开展了一些农业温室气体减排的示范项目。这些项目包括不同农业作物类型的土地管理、造林碳汇及牲畜粪便处理等。下面是其中五个项目的具体情况。

5.2.5.1 精确农业（西北部）

项目种类：作物生产过程中通过采用精确农业技术和措施实现二氧化碳减排。

项目地点：美国太平洋西北部地区——俄勒冈东北部，华盛顿东部，北爱达荷北部。

推行的措施：农民采用直播及精确农业技术，如 GPS 导航系统、变量控制技术、自动开关技术，避免重复的农业生产投入，提高效率。

组织/个人：太平洋西北地区种子协会，一个代表约 500 个农民的非政府组织。

项目描述：太平洋西北地区种子协会将在太平洋西北部地区汇集近 2.5 万英亩的农业用地，在这些地方采取种子直播技术及各种水平的精确农业技术。土地管理者将提供相关数据，包括所采用的精确农业技术，并记录由此获得的效率。通过这些数据，太平洋西北地区种子协会将计算出由于燃料使用及农业生产投入效率提高而获得的二氧化碳减排当量。这些结果将与美国农业部农业研究所及自然资源保护署的研究结果相比较。

温室气体减排的测量/量化：项目界定通过氮和其他含化石燃料的农业生产投入品使用量的减少来估算。换算为温室气体减排值时使用默认的转换因子。后续的量化过程使用脱氮-分解模型。使用 PA 法对下列化石燃料的减少而产生的温室气体减排量进行估算：

（1）使用种子直播系统节省的柴油燃料。

（2）使用 GPS 导航系统节省的柴油燃料。

来自于下列方式的氧化亚氮减排：

（1）使用 GPS 导航系统。

（2）使用变量控制技术。

减少使用杀虫剂获得的二氧化碳减排当量：

（1）使用 GPS 导航技术。

（2）使用自动开关控制系统。

（3）使用传感器喷洒器技术。

基准线/额外性：通过计算该地区不采用精确农业技术和措施的情况下，常规耕作中农药和含化石燃料的使用确定温室气体排放基准线。项目经过管理、常规措施法及障碍检测法确定其额外性。

泄漏：在这个项目中不存在商品生产减少的情况，因此没有产生泄漏。

监测方法学与计划：遵守杜克法则。由地方保护区的工作人员进行监测。

第三方核准计划：核准计划按照杜克法则中的格式进行。项目确认（预评估）及后续项目效果评估由第三方核准员完成（SCS 有限公司）。

合同/所有权：起始期为 3 年（2008～2010 年），可更新。如温室气体减排效果低于预期，卖方对此负责，通过支付包含利息的补偿或提供其他区域中相当的温室气体减排量进行赔偿。温室气体减排量的所有权在合同期内转计给买方。合同到期后所有权转归卖方。

5.2.5.2 免耕（中西部）

项目种类：减少玉米、大豆等作物耕种时化石燃料的使用，增加土壤碳的固定以实现二氧化碳减排。

项目地点：东北堪萨斯三个郡的农业用地。

推行的措施：在 1200 英亩土地上自 2007～2016 年持续使用免耕法。

组织/个人：AgraMarke Inc 是一家代表来自堪萨斯、密苏里、内布拉斯加、爱荷华的近 1000 名农民的非政府组织。ArgarMarke 作为其农民会员的代表拥有并掌管谷物加工设备的运行。

项目描述：项目地位于密苏里州 St.Joseph 附近，该地区的玉米和大豆产量很高。与 AgraMarke 签约的生产方出于环境和经济因素采取了免耕措施。免耕法将前一年粮食生产的作物残留物留茬，以减少水土流失及水的蒸发，并通过增加土壤中有机物的含量提高土壤肥力。与传统耕作方式相比，实施免耕法需要的实际操作力也更少。免耕农业的环境效益在于用减少实地操作、增加土壤二氧化碳的固定，减少温室气体排放。

测量/量化温室气体减排：项目界定利用区域内的碳封存因子及燃料使用的数据。每英亩的土壤预计每年可平均减少 750kg 的 CO_2e。采用免耕操作预计每年每英亩可以节约 3.02 加仑^①的柴油使用。项目合同期的第 5 年和第 10 年利用土壤碳储量测量对项目温室气体减排进行调整。

基准线/额外性：温室气体排放的基准线由测量该区域内土壤碳储量及采用耕种法时燃料使用的平均值确定。项目将经过管理、常规措施法及障碍测试确定其额外性。注意该区域内非持续性的免耕操作较为常见，而不是持续的免耕操作。

泄漏：该项目不会造成商品生产减少，因此不会引起泄漏。

监测方法学与计划：遵守杜克标准的协议。监测由 AgraMarke 员工完成。

第三方核准计划：核准计划依照杜克标准进行。项目确认（预评估）及后续项目效果评估由第三方核准员完成（SCS 有限公司）。

合同/所有权：项目起始期为 10 年（2007～2016 年），可更新。如温室气体减排效果低于预期，卖方对此负责，通过支付包含利息的补偿或提供其他区域中相当的温室气体减排量进行赔偿。AgraMarke 将通过在相当于项目总占地面积 20% 的地方采用免耕法，以为项目提供保险。温室气体减排量的所有权在合同期内转让给买方。合同到期后所有权转归卖方。

5.2.5.3 灌溉效率（加利福尼亚）

项目种类：通过采用农田滴灌技术，以减少农业用燃料及氮肥施用从而实现二氧化碳和氧化亚氮减排。

---

① 1 加仑≈0.0038m³。

项目地点：美国加利福尼亚州圣华金河谷附近的灌溉农田。

推行的措施：自 2009 年起，在近 8000 英亩中耕作物（如玉米和棉花）用地上安装并运行滴灌技术。

组织/个人：若干水资源区；JM Lord 有限公司。

项目描述：农场通过采用滴灌技术及措施种植作物实现减排，将比在同样的土地上采用垄沟灌溉法种植作物消耗更少的化石燃料。采用滴灌法种植作为还可以减少水/能源使用，提高氮肥摄入的效率。温室气体减排量将来自于总面积为 8000 英亩的 8 个农场。

温室气体测量/量化：项目界定采用默认因子。通过向 DNDC 模型输入实地数据进行模拟量化。

基准线/额外性：通过计算该区域内垄沟灌溉法生产粮食所排放的温室气体确定基准线。项目将经过管理、常规措施及障碍测试以确定其额外性。

泄漏：该项目不会造成商品生产减少，因此不会引起泄漏。

监测方法学与计划：遵守杜克法则。监测由 JM Lord 有限公司进行，这是一家提供灌溉技术服务的公司。

第三方核准计划：核准计划依照杜克法则进行。项目确认（预评估）及后续项目效果评估由第三方核准员完成（SCS 有限公司）。

合同/所有权：项目起始期为 3 年（2009～2011 年），可更新。如温室气体减排效果低于预期，卖方对此负责，通过支付包含利息的补偿、或提供其他区域中相当的温室气体减排量进行赔偿。温室气体减排量的所有权在合同期内转让给买方。合同到期后所有权转归卖方。

5.2.5.4 水稻用水和秸秆管理/加利福尼亚

项目种类：通过水稻生产过程中用水和秸秆管理减少甲烷排放。

项目地点：美国加利福尼亚州萨克拉门托河谷水稻种植区。

推行的措施：减少冬灌时间并移除水稻残余秸秆。甲烷补偿的基准线建立在不存在残余的冬灌及不进行冬灌时的残余结合的基础上。

组织/个人：加利福尼亚水稻委员会及郡水稻加工企业。

项目描述：加利福尼亚水稻委员会从布尤特郡 4～6 个农场主处汇集了近 2 万英亩的稻田。目前的水稻生产管理包括延长冬灌时间及将水稻残余秸秆与土壤混合。参与项目的稻田管理者将缩短冬灌期，并去除水稻秸秆残余的含量。这些行为将减少项目用地上甲烷的排放。

温室气体减排的测量/量化：通过用水和水稻秸秆管理有可能实现大幅度的净温室气体排放减少。初步的结果表明仅水稻秸秆管理就可在每公顷田地上实现 1000～5000kg 的 CO_2e 减排，减排平均值近 $3500kgCO_2e/hm^2$。采用 DNDC 模型计算来自缩短的冬灌期及秸秆管理的温室气体减排。通过向该模型输入水管理、秸秆及氮肥施用情况的现场数据及当地环境数据（如降水、温度及土壤）来计算温室气体排放量的变化。

基准线/额外性：基准线情景为采用延长的冬灌期及将秸秆与土壤混合的做法时的温室气体排放。项目将经过管理、常规措施法及障碍测试以确定其额外性。

泄漏：该项目不会造成商品生产减少，因此不会引起泄漏。

监测方法学与计划：遵守杜克法则。监测由地方水稻加工企业进行。

第三方核准计划：核准计划依照杜克法则进行。项目确认（预评估）及后续项目效果评估由第三方核准员完成（SCS 有限公司）。

合同/所有权：项目起始期为 3 年（2009～2011 年），可更新。如温室气体减排效果低于预期，卖方对此负责，通过支付包含利息的补偿、或提供其他区域中相当的温室气体减排量进行赔偿。温室气体减排量的所有权在合同期内转让给买方。合同到期后所有权转归卖方。

5.2.5.5　再造林项目（西北）

项目种类：在爱达荷州中部将耕种用地转为松树林，从土壤及生物质固碳中获得二氧化碳减排。

项目地点：美国爱达荷州刘易斯郡 Nez Perce 东北 5 英里①的范围内。

推行的措施：耕地上改种松树。

组织/个人：Nez Perce 部落林产，拉普瓦伊，爱达荷。

项目描述：Nez Perce 部落的土地包括在 20 世纪年代早期由森林被开垦为农场的几千英亩耕地。这个项目将目前每年耕种的农田转变为松树林。如没有退耕还林的资金支持，目前的农业租期很有可能获得延期。种植近 400 英亩培育的西黄松幼苗，通过下述方式（但不局限于）保证退耕还林的效果：植被控制、安装幼苗保护材料，苗死后立即补种等以实现成活率的目标。对幼苗存活率进行半年度的调查，直到被认定幼苗可以"自由生长"为成活。经与美国林业服务-落基山研究站合作，长期监测土地碳固定量和树木生物质固碳量。管理行为包括（但不局限于）前商业化及商业化间伐，采用有控制的火烧，目的是限制树木之间的竞争，保持活力，以减少野火燃烧所需的材料及连续性。

在部落 NP 03-190 决议中规定：从碳排放核准量交易中收获的资金盈利将被存入一个特殊账户，用以推广此类项目。附加的环境及社会效益将超过碳储存获得的经济效益。这些效益包括但不局限于水质改善及大鳞大马哈鱼和虹鳟鱼产卵栖息地的修复，水土流失减少，杀虫剂使用减少，生物多样性增加及野生动物自然栖息地的恢复。社会及文化效益包括增加的林地面积为聚会和娱乐场所提供了地点，以及给 Nez Perce 部落及其成员带来的经济收益，如植树、球果收集及间伐带来的工作机会。

温室气体减排的测量/量化：美国林业协会认证的 FVS 模型中预测的碳封存率将用来界定此项目。在项目合同期内，每 5 年将采用森林勘测法中的实地取样程序测量实际的碳封存率。将碳含量转化为二氧化碳当量的计算采用抽样生物质密度方法。

基准线/额外性：温室气体排放基准线通过该地区灌溉作物生产的平均排放确定。项目将经过管理、惯例法及障碍测试以确定其额外性。

泄漏：计算减少的粮食作物生产，并从项目的净温室气体排放中排除。计算由于木材制品增加而减少的温室气体泄漏需要被计算到净温室气体减排产出中。泄漏计算依照杜克法则规定的步骤进行。

---

①　1 英里≈1.6093km。

监测方法学与计划：遵守杜克法则。监测由 Nez Perce 部落林业部门进行。

第三方核准计划：核准计划依照杜克标准进行。项目确认（预评估）及后续项目效果评估由第三方核准员完成（SCS 有限公司）。

合同/所有权：项目起始期为 80 年，可更新。如温室气体减排效果低于预期，卖方对此负责，通过支付包含利息的补偿或提供其他区域中相当的温室气体减排量进行赔偿。Nez Perce 部落通过预留退耕还林地使项目更为保险。温室气体减排量的所有权在合同期内转让给买方。合同到期后所有权转归卖方。

5.2.5.6 牛奶厂（东北部）

项目种类：通过厌氧消解对牛奶厂产生二氧化碳、甲烷、氧化亚氮进行捕获，使用甲烷燃料替代化石燃料，通过使用消解残留物减少氮肥施用。

项目用地：美国纽约州北部的几家牛奶厂。

推行的措施：将牛奶厂产生的甲烷收集并置于厌氧消解系统中。消解后的甲烷可用作燃料，消解残留物可作为农业用肥料。

组织/个人：中部纽约资源保护和发展公司。

项目描述：牛奶厂通过安装及运行厌氧消解设备处理产生的甲烷来减少温室气体减排。收集从粪肥中产生的甲烷，使用甲烷燃料减少了化石燃料的燃烧，消解残留物可作为肥料，减少氮肥的使用。

温室气体减排的测量/量化：项目界定采用乳品业肥料生产因子、厌氧消解甲烷因子及氮肥施用的氧化亚氮因子。在项目合同期，将对粪肥数量和成分进行抽样，对消解甲烷生产进行计量，通过当地电网计算化石燃料使用的减少。通过 DNDC 模型计算因减少氮肥施用带来的氧化亚氮减排。

基准线/额外性：基准线包括从未经限制的乳品厂粪肥中排放的甲烷、地方电力公司发电产生的二氧化碳及施用氮肥造成的氧化亚氮的排放。项目将经过管理、惯例法及障碍测试以确定其额外性。

泄漏：该项目不会造成商品生产减少，因此不会引起泄漏。

监测方法学与计划：遵守杜克法则。监测由地方保护区工作人员完成。

第三方核准计划：核准计划依照杜克法则进行。项目确认（预评估）及后续项目效果评估由第三方核准员完成（SCS 有限公司）。

合同/所有权：项目起始期为 3 年，可更新。如温室气体减排效果低于预期，卖方对此负责，通过支付包含利息的补偿或提供其他区域中相当的温室气体减排量进行赔偿。温室气体减排量的所有权在合同期内转让给买方。合同到期后所有权转归卖方。

5.2.6 结 束 语

全球控制温室气体排放的努力为农业经济和土地管理者带来了很多的机会。土地行业现有的措施和技术为减少温室气体排放提供了很多选择，既可以直接减排，又可以通过提供碳汇进行间接减排。农业对所有国家的福利来讲都至关重要，且人们对于可持续的食物生产方式的需求正在变得比以往任何时期都更迫切。但农业同时又对气候变化极为敏感和脆弱，与大多数经济部门相比，其可持续性都面临着更大的调整。

农业温室气体减缓的投资产生的效益是多重的。可以减少温室气体排放，采用可持续的措施及技术可以增加农业的经济附加值，提高资源的使用效率，降低生产成本，增加农业生态系统对气候变化的适应性。获得资金效益对资源和环境来说都是一件好事。但是发展这些效率必须要有相应的激励措施。温室气体补偿投资的额外效益就是一个新的激励。在农业领域通过使用环境友好的措施及技术获得的效率对于所有国家和社会来说都是一个重要的效益。但是所有国家和社会需要达成共识，在全球范围内对土地管理者提供生态补偿的激励措施，这样的一个全球性挑战依然存在。

第6章 农村适应和减缓气候变化的政策选择

大部分农户不能够单纯依靠常规农作业收入来弥补减缓和适应气候变化的费用。到2030年，适应气候变化每年的花费将达到2500亿～3800亿美元，其中中国需要承担50%以上。

中国大部分适应气候变化的费用和一半的减缓费用的支出都会发生在农村地区。也就是说，到2030年，农村地区的贫困人口在能源和环境方面的支出将达到830亿～1270亿美元，即世界全部支出的1/3。这些支出中，550亿～650亿的支出需要用于减少农业作业、土地利用变化、森林砍伐排放的温室效应气体，例如，管理农场草原、牧场、施肥、家畜来减少甲烷和氮氧化物的排放，以及减少森林退化、管理现有森林和规划新造林。

为了满足这些需求，中央政府需要建立政策和基金制度来提高农村地区减缓和适应气候变化的能力，其中包括通过节能建筑和依靠可再生能源。这些做法已经在试点项目中显露头角，且有更宏伟的规划将被实现。为加强这些项目，中国可以引入国际基金机制向农户购买他们减排的温室气体排放指标。中国还可以考虑调整贸易政策使其支持应对气候变化。

6.1 政策支持下的农村节能建筑

6.1.1 有关政策法规

我国《民用建筑节能条例》自2008年10月1日施行。条例规定"国家鼓励和扶持在新建建筑和既有建筑节能改造中采用太阳能、地热能等可再生能源。在具备太阳能利用条件的地区，有关地方人民政府及其部门应当采取有效措施，鼓励和扶持单位、个人安装使用太阳能热水系统、照明系统、供热系统、采暖制冷系统等太阳能利用系统"，"县级以上人民政府应当安排民用建筑节能资金，用于支持民用建筑节能的科学技术研究和标准制定、既有建筑围护结构和供热系统的节能改造、可再生能源的应用，以及民用建筑节能示范工程等项目提供支持。民用建筑节能项目依法享受税收优惠"。"设计单位、施工单位、工程监理单位及其注册执业人员，应当按照民用建筑节能强制性标准进行设计、施工监理"。

住房和城乡建设部建筑节能与科技司2009年3月透露，建设部将加强与节能有关的政策、规章法规、标准制定。力争到2009年底，90%以上全国新建建筑和6000万 m² 的现有建筑在施工阶段执行节能强制性标准。

为实现这些目标，政府会加快北方地区已有建筑的节能建设并鼓励当地政府建立有效的基金。政府部门还需建立节能建筑示范项目，以加强新建建筑的节能标准，发展节能的经济刺激机制，土地节约建筑并进行相关研究。

同时，科技部门还应研究太阳能、生物质能、压缩秸秆和其他先进的农村可再生能源技术并调研这些技术的经济性。例如，扩大可再生能源建筑应用示范规模，以太阳能热水系统城市级示范、太阳能光伏屋顶及幕墙、长江流域及沿海地区应用淡水源和海水源热泵为重点，积极引导可再生能源建筑应用向更高水平发展。

6.1.2　农村地区的节能建筑案例

清华大学建筑技术科学系的农村建筑节能课题组在新农村建筑节能方面的研究是国内首次大规模尝试，在节能评价体系、系统优化、技术集成方面综合示范。美国国家科学院院士克·史密斯教授对该研究也给予高度评价，并将推进申报首个中国农村节能清洁发展国际专项。著名学术期刊 Nature 也对本成果进行了专门报道。

课题组已经在北京房山地区完成了村级生态节能型农宅集中示范工程，并联合北京市可持续发展促进会等单位，在平谷、石景山、怀柔、密云等多个郊区县完成了 500 多户农户住宅实际改造工程。

青龙满族自治县祖山镇山神庙村的节能示范项目正在实施中。青龙满族自治县是典型的山区，传统的灰瓦房抗寒能力差，冬季大多住房室温在 0℃ 以下，农民主要依靠柴和煤来取暖。

由于这个计划的实施，100 多户农民将住进使用新型建筑结构体系和太阳能采暖的住宅中。为保持热量，建筑墙体采用保温新型页岩空心砖，窗户为塑钢中空玻璃。农户家里只需要烧很少量的煤作为补充供暖，比传统住宅能够节约用煤量 2/3，预计在最寒冷的冬天，室温能保持在 10～15℃。如果中国北方地区全部采用这种方法，将会减少对 500 万 t 煤当量的需求，相当于节约资金 5000 万元。

据青龙满族自治县建设局负责人介绍，新民居的造价比传统民居要高一些，但每栋新民居能够使用 60 年左右，而且平时采暖等使用要比传统的民居采暖成本低 50％ 以上。因此这个项目能带来很大的经济收益。

为了取得锦上添花的效果，该县县委、县政府还将投资 1000 万元对水、电、路、通信、街道亮化等基础设施配套项目进行补贴。为确保工程质量，该县选择了具有相应资质的建筑公司，同时还聘请了专门的监理公司为农民建房监督施工质量。

6.2　中国农村可再生能源政策

《中华人民共和国节约能源法》第四条规定："国家鼓励开发、利用新能源和可再生能源"；第十一条规定："国务院和省、自治区、直辖市人民政府应当在基本建设、技术改造资金中安排节能资金，用于支持能源的合理开发利用以及新能源和可再生能源的开发。"

《中华人民共和国可再生能源法》第十八条规定："国家鼓励和支持农村地区的可再生能源开发利用。县级以上地方人民政府管理能源工作的部门会同有关部门，根据当地经济社会发展、生态保护和卫生综合治理需要等实际情况，制订农村地区可再生能源发展规划，因地制宜地推广应用沼气等生物质资源转化、户用太阳能、小型风能、小型水能等技术。县级以上人民政府应当对农村地区的可再生能源利用项目提供财政支持。"

例如，新建秸秆气化发电厂不论规模大小均可享受政府补贴 15 年每度电 0.25 元。秸秆发电厂所发电量由电网全额收购，且进口设备的关税和进口环节增值税全免。具体优惠政策包括：享受政府最优惠价怵批地；享受银行的贴息贷款；购买国产的设备还可退还增值税；享受大部分及多项税收的减免税 15 年；作为环保和创新技术。2008 年 4 月，国家发展和改革委员会和中华人民共和国国家电力监管委员会再次发出《可再生能源电价附加补贴和配额交易方案的通知》，对纳入补贴范围的秸秆直燃发电厂电价给予每度 0.1 元的补贴[1]。

农业部《全国农村沼气建设规划》提出：2002 年底全国沼气池总量达 5000 万户以上，到 2010 年全国 20% 的农户可使用沼气。这些沼气池通过对动物和人类产生的固体废弃物进行厌氧消化产生沼气，沼气将被用于取暖、做饭和照明。

到 2010 年为这些设备进行的投资将达到 610 亿元，中央投资 449 亿元。中央对投资者的补助标准为：西北、东北地区每户 1200 元，西南地区每户 1000 元，其他地区每户 800 元。为提高环境标准和生活质量，从 2005 年开始，中央政策层面开始加速沼气普及工程以在各省、市落实和执行。

为保证沼气项目平稳有效的执行，各省、市地方财政按照中央财政补贴的相应比例，也投入部分资金在资助扶贫、退耕还林、天然林保护资金、建设社会主义新农村等政策中拿出一部分资金直接补贴农户。当经济发展好时，各地市、县、乡在经济条件允许的情况下，也对农户建造沼气池进行了补助。

2000 多万户家庭目前使用沼气池，每年能产生 80 亿 m³ 沼气。有超过 4000 个地区在使用大规模沼气池，每年这部门沼气池能产生出超过 100 万 m³ 的沼气。有超过 100个大中型以沼气为燃料的电厂，每年能发电 2 亿度。每年沼气的产生量有 154 亿 m³，相当于 2420 万 t 标准煤、1.4 亿亩林地，每年可为农民节省开支 200 亿元。

6.3　退耕还林项目

中国的人均二氧化碳排放量远低于发达国家。但中国还是在大规模的发展植树造林。中国的土地和森林碳汇每年能超过 1 亿 t。

例如，2000 年 3 月，经国务院批准，国家林业局、国家发展计划委员会、财政部联合发出了《关于开展 2000 年长江上游、黄河上中游地区退耕还林还草试点示范工作的通知》。

退耕还林工程是我国政策性最强、投资最大、涉及面最广、群众参与程度最高的一项生态建设工程。实施 8 年来，全国已完成退耕还林造林 1.39 亿亩、荒山荒地造林 2.05 亿亩、封山育林 2000 万亩，改善了中西部地区的生态环境。

在 1999 年中国政府开展退耕还林工程以前，四川、陕西和甘肃就已经开始试点。经过 3 年的试验，该项目在 2002 年全面启动。项目范围涉及 25 个省和自治区，1897

---

[1]　委员会是按照《可再生能源电价附加补贴和配额交易方案的通知》提供经费。

个县、3200万农户和1.24亿新疆生产建设兵团农民。至今已经让这些省区完成了530万 hm² 的退耕还林，800万 hm² 的荒山造林，防止水土流失3600万 hm²，防风固沙7000万 hm²。

通过大规模还林还草，中国在中西部地区已经让森林覆盖面积提高了2%以上，其中，内蒙古提高近4%，陕西延安提高约25%。水土流失和风沙危害明显减轻。

为继续退耕还林还草工程，国家还设立了一系列的资金和补贴机制。包括：按照"谁造林还草、谁管护、谁受益"的原则，鼓励农民承包退耕地和宜林荒山荒地。为了调动农民群众的积极性，农民承包期一律延长到50年，到期后还可以根据有关法律和法规继续承包。有条件的地区，可本着协商、自愿的原则，由农村造林专业户、社会团体、企事业单位等租赁、承包退耕还林还草，其利益分配等问题由双方协商解决。鼓励在有条件的地区实行集中连片造林、种草，鼓励个人兴办家庭林场和草场，实行多种经营。

例如，农户可以因保持经济林而得到经济林补助5年；因保护生态林而得到8年的补助。签订生态林合同和还草合同的农户可得到税收优惠。这些项目通过检查之后耕户将无偿获得一定的粮食或现金收入。其中，长江上游地区每亩退耕地补助300kg 原粮，黄河上中游地区补助200kg 原粮。给退耕户适当现金补助，按每亩退耕地每年补贴20元，现金补助的期限与粮食补助期限相同。现金补助以户为单位发放到农民手中。向退耕户提供种苗补助费50元，并直接发给农民，由农民自行采购种植。

为集中力量解决影响退耕农户长远生计的突出问题，中央财政安排一定规模资金，作为巩固退耕还林成果专项资金，主要用于西部地区、京津风沙源治理区和享受西部地区政策的中部地区退耕农户的基本口粮田建设、农村能源建设、生态移民以及补植补造，并向特殊困难地区倾斜。中央财政按照退耕地还林面积核定各省（区、市）巩固退耕还林成果专项资金总量，并从2008年起按8年集中安排，逐年下达，包干到省。专项资金要实行专户管理，专款专用，并与原有国家各项扶持资金统筹使用。具体使用和管理办法由财政部会同国家发展和改革委员会、西部开发办、农业部、林业局等部门制定，报国务院批准。

退耕还林的地区将接到不同渠道的基金来减少贫困，管理村与农业土地，保持水土。例如，中央政府补助地方政府来弥补这个项目中产生的损失。

2007年9月开始，国务院决定再安排2000多亿元资金，用于今后8年延长退耕还林补助期限，巩固退耕还林成果，解决退耕农户长远生计问题。例如，实现西南地区退耕农户人均不低于0.5亩、西北地区人均不低于2亩高产稳产基本口粮田的目标。

中央安排预算内基本建设投资和巩固退耕还林成果专项资金给予补助，西南地区每亩补助600元，西北地区每亩补助400元。这项新政策将使中西部地区1.24亿农民直接受益，对加快中西部地区生态建设，促进当地经济和社会的可持续发展影响深远。

6.4 农村水利工程基金

我国农村水利已经进入全面改革时期，农田灌溉和农村供水更加有效，尤其是主要的粮食生产地区、旱区和贫困地区。目标是鼓励灌区、旱区发展的同时提高农村环境质量。其投资体制包括：

1）为小型节水项目建立农田水利建设补助专项资金

2005 年中央 1 号文件要求中央和省级财政建立农田水利建设补助专项资金。同年，国务院办公厅转发《关于建立农田水利建设新机制的意见》，明确要求以规划为依托，大幅度增加政府投入，逐步建立农田水利建设资金稳定增长机制、规范资金使用，并完善村级"一事一议"筹资筹劳政策。目前我国小型农田水利工程建设补助专项资金已经建立。

2）改革对国有大中型灌溉项目和抽水站系统的拨款

2002 年财政部、水利部编制了《水利工程管理单位维修养护标准》。同年，国务院办公厅转发《水利工程管理体制改革实施意见》。根据这些政策，国有大中型灌区及泵站管理机构被定性为公益或准公益单位，可从地方财政获得管理和维护经费。

3）改革农村水利工程管理体制和运行机制

这些改革包括：加强这类项目的计划、指导和监督。通过对所有权的分类，寻求更有效的大、中、小型农村灌溉系统的管理办法，并分配管理职责。例如，政府可以鼓励农户合作监督用水管理，且这些农民合作协会能通过政府资助拥有设备。改革水价机制。

6.5　温室气体减排信用基金

很多国内外的项目已经建立了购买农户和其他方式减排的温室气体指标的机制。这些项目能成为中国提高能效、可再生能源和可持续发展提供重要的资金源。

6.5.1　中国清洁发展机制基金

2007 年 11 月国务院批准建立中国清洁发展机制基金（China Clean Development Mechanism Fund），用于生产联合国清洁发展机制指标[①]。它是长期性的、不以营利为目的的国有独资基金，旨在国家可持续发展战略的指导下，支持和促进国家应对气候变化的行动。

基金将支持项目建设、提供技术支持、分享和管理信息，培训人员并注重机构能力建设和增强公共意识。这一基金是个重要的创新，它能协调国内企业和外国政府和机构。

6.5.2　欧洲碳基金

欧洲碳基金（European Carbon Fund，ECF）是一家由欧洲多家金融机构成立的专

---

① 国家发展和改革委员会、财政部、外交部和科技部 2005 年 10 月发布《清洁发展机制项目运行管理办法》。

门基金，投资全球范围内的温室气体减排项目及碳减排市场交易。欧洲碳基金在最近的研究资料中指出：在欧盟的排放交易方案下，将形成每年约有 22 亿 t 二氧化碳排放量的交易市场，欧洲企业的排放限额每年大约有 6000 万～1.2 亿 t 的缺口。欧洲碳基金将努力通过清洁发展机制项目置换的碳资产来弥补上述缺口。该基金还表示，将在中国投资 10～20 个项目。

6.5.3　世界银行基金

世界银行管理着 9 个与碳有关的基金，这些基金使用公共和私人基金购买来自低收入国家和团体的温室气体减排指标。中国的伞形碳基金是世界银行的 9 个碳基金之一，其从世界银行得到的基金总额已超过 19 亿美元。中国伞形碳基金产出的是双重红利，这是由于中国政府承诺将伞形基金 65％ 的收入投入到清洁发展机制基金。

2006 年，世界银行宣布完成总额达 10.2 亿美元的伞形碳基金第一笔交易的份额分配，这部分收入被用来购买中国两个工业天然气温室气体减排项目产生的指标。

6.5.4　全球环境基金

中国于 1993 年签署了《生物多样性公约》和《联合国气候变化框架公约》。为履行公约、完成自己的职责，中国与全球环境基金（Global Environment Facility，GEF）进行了密切合作。截至 2002 年 6 月底，我国已获得 GEF 的赠款承诺 3 亿多美元，在所有受援国中位居第一。

例如，GEF 第一期（1994 年 7 月 1 日～1998 年 6 月 30 日）的总承诺捐资额约为 20 亿美元，中国捐款 560 万美元；GEF 第二期（1998 年 7 月 1 日～2002 年 6 月 30 日）的总承诺捐资额约为 20 亿美元，中国捐款 820 万美元。那些基金支持已完成和正在实施或准备中的项目达到 55 个。我国所获批的 GEF 项目涉及范围广泛，包括生物多样性保护、工业节能、可再生能源、国际水域保护、土地退化防治以及相关机构能力建设等多个领域。

6.5.5　私人企业基金

2007 年 10 月，美国国际集团（American International Group，AIG）宣布，将通过购买二氧化碳排放指标的方式，投资支持新疆和四川的农业温室气体减排项目。这些项目将帮助两个省的农民产生大约 31 万 t 的二氧化碳指标。按照美国国际集团 2006 年的温室气体排放总量计算，这一数字约占其全球业务部门温室气体排放总量的 1/2。

这个项目由美国环保协会（Environmental Defense Fund，EDF）开发。这些项目最显著的益处包括降低了农作物需水量，减少了对化石燃料的消耗量，提高了氮肥的使用效率，将人和动物的固体排泄物产生的沼气用于做饭和照明。同时通过在沙漠地区植树造林，从而保持水土、防风固沙和降低土壤侵蚀。

6.5.6 其他国际环境保护基金

总部设在伦敦的气候变化资本集团（Climate Change Capital），计划在未来的2～3年内为中国投资50亿元人民币（7.32亿美元）发展诸如工业废物处置和发展清洁能源技术等环保项目。

其他非政府组织，像世界自然基金（World Wide Fund，WWF）和国际爱护动物基金会（International Fund for Animal Welfare，IFAW）也都提供了资金来支持中国的环境项目，并与政府、民间组织就相关项目进行合作。

6.6 利用贸易政策保卫气候变化情况下的食品供应安全

中国和其他主要经济体在国际贸易中对农业生产、能源使用、气候变化有很大的影响力。Fisher（2009）的研究报告揭示了这一影响[①]，其研究观点与已经出版的几项研究意见相同，一致认为在不考虑气候变化的情景下，21世纪农业能够满足世界的粮食需求。这是因为技术变化会提高农业生产力，假设提高农业生产的历史趋势仍将继续，这种改变将大于气候变化所带来的任何生产方面的负面影响。

Fisher 的主要研究结论：

在全球范围内，气候变化和贸易自由化的影响将不会发生完全一致的变化，在一些地区农业生产力将增长，而在其他的地区将下降。对于中国、欧盟、北美和巴西，气候变化将对农业产生积极影响；产生负面影响的地区包括东非、中非和南部非洲、北非和西非、中东和俄罗斯。气候变化还将轻微削减在印度和南亚和东亚的农业生产力。

贫穷地区的人们比许多其他地区的居民更加依赖农业活动来维持生计和收入。因此气候变化危害最贫穷的地区，将意味着对于全球财富的重新分配。

即使气候变化改善了某一个特定区域作物生产力，这并不一定意味着农业生产向该地区转移。如果其他地区有更大的改善，在输入丰富且价格有竞争力的情况下，农业生产将转向这些地区。

在气候变化的条件下，中国、澳大利亚和前苏联地区肉类加工和奶制品行业的生产力提高最大。而在东非、北非和西非，中东、非洲的中部和南部，南亚和东亚这些地区产品的生产率下降最多。

东非、北非、西非、中东和俄罗斯的食品加工部门应对气候变化的表现最差；而中国、巴西、澳大利亚的食品加工部门在应对气候变化时表现要稍好一点。

不同的气候情景下，对食品生产的影响通常不同。

所有地区可以通过消除边境税和补贴来改善他们的福利。因此，贸易自由化可以成为各国抵消部分气候变化的负面影响的一项较好策略。

研究显示，在中国取消边境税和补贴将会使除大米和畜牧业外的其他商品产量增

---

① 对于这个结论的主要质疑在于：用于本研究的农业生产的冲击不包括可能的气候变化、灾害的变化、海平面的升高、改变淡水（非降水）供应的初期影响。这些影响给未来的农业生产产生带来巨大的不确定性。

加。自由贸易下，中国的大米出口将大幅增长，到2030年将多达14万t。中国的玉米出口将适度增长，其他的农产品出口基本上不受影响，中国的大米进口在贸易自由化下将会增加，到2030年中国的大米进口也将上升约30万t（与基准情况相比），到2080年将更高，达到3600万t，而小麦和玉米的进口会略有下降。

在自由贸易下，中国所有农业商品的实际价格将有所上升。但是，收入增加能够抵消这些负面影响，使人民的福利整体提高。事实上，如果中国能在2050年免去边境税和补贴，当实际消费到2050年增加0.7%～0.8%时，中国在任何气候情景下都会有良好的发展。

第7章 农村应对气候变化的案例研究

确保粮食安全和消除贫困是中国农村发展目标之一。然而，鼓励农业发展和经济增长，在有些农村地区可能意味着政府忽视节约能源和控制污染等环保目标。

尽管某些农村地区污染所造成的经济和社会损失，有时甚至超过了城市地区，但许多现行政策仍主要关注城市企业的节能减排。目前，中国仍有1.3亿人生活在国际贫困线之下，中国迫切需要制定具备成本效益的政策，在消除贫困的同时，提高农村地区能源利用效率，减少生产生活造成的环境影响。

为满足上述需求，中国可以通过提供直接的政府补贴，鼓励使用高效和可再生能源，同时，允许农村地区居民通过减排获得可交易的排放许可。事实上，中国已经开展了大量相关项目，对节能、污染控制和应对气候变化进行了大量投资，显示出中国促进经济发展的巨大潜力。

7.1 畜牧业节能清污增产增收案例

改革开放30年，我国畜牧业取得了举世瞩目的成就。畜产品产量持续上升，到2007年底，我国生猪存栏43989.5万头、出栏56508.3万头；牛存栏10594.8万头、出栏4359.5万头；羊存栏28564.7万头，出栏25570.7万头；家禽出栏957867万只。生猪存栏、牛存栏和羊存栏分别是1978年的1.5倍、1.5倍和1.7倍，生猪出栏、牛出栏、羊出栏分别比1978年增长了2.5倍、17.1倍和8.8倍，家禽出栏比1986增长了5倍。

2007年全国肉产量达到6865.7万t、禽蛋产量2513.4万t，分别占世界产量的24.7%和37.7%，居世界第一位；奶类产量3633.4万t，占世界产量的5.4%，居世界第三位。1978～2007年，我国肉、蛋、奶产量年递增率分别为10.8%、15.2%和19.0%。畜产品人均占有量迅速增加，1978年全国人均肉、蛋、奶占有量分别只有8.9kg、2.4kg和1.0kg，2007年人均占有量分别是1978年的5.8倍、7.9倍和27.5倍（图7.1），我国人均肉蛋奶的消费已经达到中等发达国家的水平。同时，全国畜牧业产值也由1978年的209.3亿元，提高到2007年的16125.2亿元，并由1978年占农业总产值的15%上升到33%，成为我国农业和农村经济的支柱产业。

在我国畜产品总量增长的同时，畜牧业规模化和集约化的程度也在不断增加。改革开放之初，我国畜禽养殖主要以集体饲养和农户饲养为主，到2007年末，我国生猪、肉牛、羊、奶牛、肉鸡和蛋鸡的规模化程度分别达到了48.4%、34.6%、41.3%、58.9%、80.1%和72.0%。

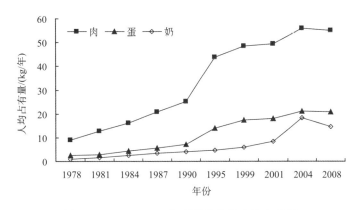

图 7.1　1978～2008 年畜产品全国人均占有量

7.1.1　畜牧业发展对能源与环境的影响

我国是畜牧业大国，畜禽的饲养量大，畜牧业发展在为改善城乡居民的生活水平和帮助农民增收方面做出巨大贡献的同时，其产生的大量废弃物对环境的威胁也与日俱增。2007 年我国畜禽粪便的总量达到 27 亿 t，养殖污水量达 110 亿 t。

在现代规模化养猪场，畜禽在封闭的高密度环境中饲养，动物生产过程中因代谢所产生的湿气和废气、分发饲料和舍内打扫所产生的粉尘以及畜禽排泄的粪尿等都必须及时排出舍外，否则将导致畜禽舍一系列的化学、物理和微生物指标超标，给动物带来应激，应激的长期作用将使动物的生产性能下降，对疾病的抵抗力降低，甚至诱发疾病；另外当遭遇不利的环境条件时，畜禽行为调节能力在有限的空间内受到极大的限制甚至完全丧失，因此现代规模化养殖必须借助工程措施给畜禽创造适宜的生活条件并帮助其克服极端的环境，例如畜禽舍日常的通风换气、夏季的通风降温以及冬季的保暖等都需要能源。随着我国畜牧业的发展以及我国畜牧业规模化程度的不断提高，畜禽养殖对能源的需求不断加大，尤其在全球气候变暖的条件下，高温季节降温的能源需求将进一步增加。

随着近年来规模化养殖场的发展，污水排放量迅速增加，由于废弃物处理投资大且没有直接的产品回报，畜禽养殖场自身效益低，没有能力投入大量资金进行废弃物处理，因此除部分养殖场建有沼气工程外，绝大多数养殖场没有粪便污水处理设施，大量粪便污水随意排放，大量养殖污水未经处理直接进入水体，对周围环境造成了严重威胁。

（1）污染水体。畜禽养殖场未经处理的污水中含有大量的污染物质，其污染负荷很高。高浓度畜禽养殖污水排入江河湖泊中，由于含氮、磷量高，造成水质不断恶化，导致水体严重富营养化；大量畜禽废弃物污水排入鱼塘及河流中，会使对有机物污染敏感的水生生物逐渐死亡，严重的将导致鱼塘及河流丧失使用功能。而且，畜禽废弃物污水中有毒、有害成分一旦进入地下水中，可使地下水溶解氧含量减少，水体中有毒成分增多，严重时使水体发黑、变臭，造成持久性的有机污染，使原有水体丧失使用功能，极难治理、恢复。

（2）污染空气。畜禽养殖过程会产生大量的恶臭气体，其中含有大量的氨、硫化物、甲烷等有毒有害成分，污染养殖场及周围空气，影响养殖场员工的身心健康。同时有的畜禽养殖场离文教区、居民生活区较近，由于恶臭污染问题，导致养殖场与周围群众关系十分紧张，有的甚至引发社会矛盾。

（3）传播病菌。畜禽废弃物中的污染物中含有大量的病原微生物、寄生虫卵以及孳生的蚊蝇，会使环境中病原种类增多，病原菌和寄生虫大量繁殖，造成人、畜传染病的蔓延，尤其是人畜共患病时，会导致疫情发生，给人畜带来灾难性危害。

（4）危害农田生态。高浓度的畜禽养殖污水长期用于灌溉，会使作物陡长、倒伏、晚熟或不熟，造成减产甚至毒害作物出现大面积腐烂。此外，高浓度污水可导致土壤孔隙堵塞，造成土壤透气、透水性下降及板结，严重影响土壤质量。

畜禽在饲养过程中由于新陈代谢要不断排出二氧化碳，另外畜禽因肠道发酵产生和排放甲烷，尤其是牛、羊等反刍动物的甲烷排放量比禽类和非禽类单胃动物要高得多，因此动物生产成为农业排放温室气体的重要组成部分。

根据《中华人民共和国气候变化初始国家信息通报》，1994 年中国温室气体的总排放量为 36.50 亿 tCO_2e，其中二氧化碳、甲烷、氧化亚氮分别占 73.05％、19.73％和 7.22％。农业源温室气体排放占全国温室气体排放总量的 17％，其中动物饲养过程中的甲烷排放为 1104.9 万 t，动物粪便和放牧管理过程排放的氧化亚氮 15.5 万 t（表 7.1）。由于近些年我国畜禽的饲养量飞速增加，畜牧业对气候变化的贡献也会有所增加。

表 7.1　1994 年畜牧业甲烷和氧化亚氮排放量

温室气体类型	排放源	排放量/万 t	占农业排放比例/％	占全国排放比例/％
甲烷	动物肠道发酵	1018.2	59.21	29.70
	动物粪便管理系统	86.7	5.04	2.53
氧化亚氮	放牧	11.0	14.03	12.94
	粪便燃烧	0.1	0.10	0.12
	动物粪便管理系统	4.4	5.56	5.18

7.1.2　动物废弃物管理的综合效果

在中国农村地区开展的两个动物废弃物管理项目，旨在提高农牧民的收入，减少能源消耗，改善当地环境，削减温室气体排放。

7.1.2.1　山东民和股份有限公司特大型沼气工程案例

山东民和牧业股份有限公司（原农业部蓬莱良种肉鸡示范场），是目前亚洲最大的父母代肉种鸡生产企业，年存栏父母代肉种鸡 130 多万套，年可孵化 1 亿多只商品鸡鸡苗，存栏商品鸡 370 万羽（年出栏 1800 万羽），生产饲料 40 万 t，屠宰加工商品鸡

3000万只,加工鸡肉产品6万t,已形成以父母代肉种鸡饲养和商品代肉鸡苗生产为核心,肉鸡养殖、屠宰加工与肉鸡苗生产相结合的较为完善的产业链。

公司主营的民和鸡苗以其抗病力强、成活率高等优点成为全国鸡苗第一品牌,畅销上海、云南等二十多个省市及中东、香港等十几个国家和地区。鸡肉产品通过了ISO9001:2000、HACCP质量体系认证,公司获得诸多荣誉和奖项。2008年5月16日,公司作为国内唯一的一家肉鸡苗生产企业,成功登陆A股市场。

山东民和股份特大型沼气发电工程应用热电肥联产的沼气发电技术对鸡粪废弃物进行资源化开发和多层次利用,其工艺流程如图7.2所示,包括原料的预处理、厌氧消化、沼气净化及输配、发酵残留物后处理以及控制等,工程总投资6000万元。沼气工程的装机容量为3500kW,持续功率2500kW,年运行成本为550万元/年。

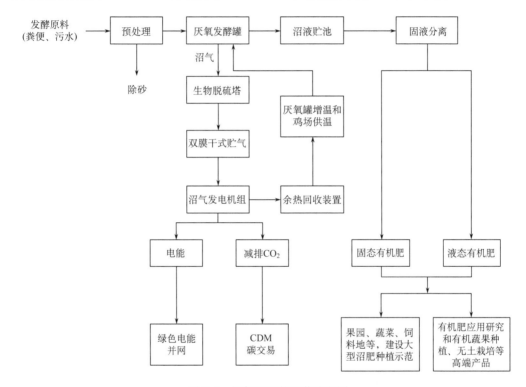

图7.2 沼气工程的工艺流程图

该沼气工程的主要产品是沼气、沼渣和沼液。所生产的沼气用做动力燃料,供发电机组生产绿色电能,发电机组产生的余热大部分用于冬季厌氧发酵罐的加温,使之保持中温发酵温度;剩余部分用于鸡场供暖,减少化石能源的消耗。

山东民和牧业股份公司建设的特大型沼气发电工程项目,选址在蓬莱市民和肉鸡产业化基地内,建设3000m³的高效厌氧反应器共8座(图7.3)。

该工程利用公司23个种鸡场和8个肉鸡养殖区的500t粪便(20%的干物质)和500t养殖场污水调配成干物质10%的粪污浓度进行中温厌氧发酵,发酵后日产沼气3万m³,年产沼气1095万m³。

图 7.3　山东民和特大型沼气工程的厌氧发酵罐

利用沼气发电，沼气发电机组装机容量 3MW，日发电量 6 万 kW·h，发电并入电网，年上网电量 2.19 万 MW·h，每度电的售价为 0.35 元。每年的售电收入 760 万元。

厌氧发酵后每天产生含水率为 70％的沼渣 46.83t，折合成含水率 20％的有机肥 17.5t；每天的沼液（固体物含量为 1.3％）产生量约 850t。畜禽粪便经过厌氧发酵后，其中的氮、磷、钾等营养成分几乎没有损失，均存在于发酵后的沼渣和沼液中，沼液和沼渣是高效的绿色肥料。

其被广泛应用于种果树、养鱼、种花等种植业上，本项目所产生的沼渣沼液应用于周边 55.6 万亩耕地（粮食作物 35.32 万亩，花生等经济作物 9.64 万亩，蔬菜瓜类 10.6 万亩，葡萄 8 万亩，其他果树 24.5 万亩），进行有机蔬菜、花卉、水果的种植和生产。

如果有机肥料的售价按 500 元/t 计算，该沼气工程每年出售固体有机肥的收益为 320 万元；另外沼液全部用于周围农田灌溉，每年可节约清水 31 万 m³，自来水的价格按照 1.0 元/m³ 计算，每年节约自来水的收益为 31 万元，即沼渣和沼液的经济效益共计为 351 万元。

因此沼气工程的沼气发电、沼渣和沼液的总经济收益为 1111 万元/年，扣除运行费用，工程的净经济收益为 561 万元/年。如果不考虑温室气体减排效益，沼气工程的静态投资回收期为 10.7 年，但可以给当地带来很好的环境和社会效益。

该公司已经与世界银行签订温室气体减排量转让协议，这是国内农业领域第一个在联合国注册的农业清洁发展机制（CDM）项目，已经通过联合国核查和审定，并获得国家发展和改革委员会批准。该沼气工程每年减排温室气体约 8.6 万 t 二氧化碳当量，可核证的排放削减量（Certificated Emission Reduction，CER）的销售价格为 10 美元/tCO₂e，CDM 每年收益约为 580 万元，CDM 计入期 10 年，该公司将获得近 5800 万元的温室气体减排经济补偿。

如果将沼气工程的温室气体减排效益与发电、有机肥的经济效益结合起来，该沼气工程的年总收益为 1691 万元，扣除运行费用后的工程总的净收益为 1141 万元/年，投资回收年限为 5.3 年。即将大型沼气工程开发为 CDM 项目获得减排补偿，能大大缩短投资回收年限。

从该案例分析可以看出，在大型养殖场中建设沼气工程，不但可以为当地带来良好的环境和社会效益，而且也可以产生较好的全球温室气体减排效益。将产生的减排量在国际市场上出售，可以使沼气工程获得减排补偿，能大大提高沼气工程的经济性，从而有效地促进大型养殖场沼气工程的发展。

7.1.2.2 湖北恩施农村小型沼气工程案例

"湖北省恩施土家族苗族自治州生态家园户用沼气池"项目于 2009 年 2 月 19 日获联合国批准，成功注册为清洁发展机制（CDM）项目。这是第一个根据我国专家提出的 CDM 方法学开发并获准注册的农村户用沼气 CDM 项目，该项目位于湖北省西南部的贫困地区。

恩施土家族苗族自治州全州国土面积 2.4 万 km^2，耕地面积 379 万亩，共有 88 个乡镇、2476 个村，农业人口 93 万户 330 万人。恩施土家族苗族自治州位于湖北省西南部，处于湘、鄂、渝、黔四省市结合部的武陵山区，是云贵高原向洞庭湖平原过渡的衔接地带，自古就是进入大西南的大通道和门户。恩施州与我国西南各省（市、区）的历史文化、地理环境和资源、经济社会发展程度十分相似，所辖六县二市均被国家列为重点扶贫开发县市。

2003 年恩施州委和州政府明确提出建设生态大州的构想，决定把农村以沼气建设为中心的生态家园文明新村建设作为解决"三农"问题和保护生态环境的重要战略。

计划用 5 年时间，全州农村适宜地区建设 70 万口沼气池，建成全国沼气第一州。全州围绕沼气建设大力实施"五改三建"，努力推进"四个结合"，促进农村能源及农村经济持续、快速、健康发展。经过几年的努力，以农村沼气为中心的生态家园文明新村建设取得显著成效。截至 2006 年年底，全州已累计建成家用沼气池 41 万口，占适宜地区农户的 44%。

通过实施以户用沼气池建设为重点的"一池三改"模式，把沼气池建设同改厨、改圈、改厕结合起来，改变农村现有开放式厌氧猪粪便及污水管理方式，减少农户猪粪便及污水的甲烷排放；收集户用沼气池处理农户猪粪便及污水产生沼气，替代包括做饭、烧热水、做猪食等在内农户生活用能，从而避免了相应的燃煤所造成的二氧化碳排放。

利川市五一村村民认真地算过账：他家 6 口人，过去每天要烧 12kg 柴。小村村朱家堡七组组长说，建成沼气池后，每户一年至少少烧 2500kg 柴，全组 51 户就要砍伐 250 多亩森林，根据初步测算，农村推广沼气后，全州每年少砍 150 多万亩薪炭林。

近三年恩施的森林覆盖率提高了 5%，村容村貌明显改观。同时也使农民从繁重的砍柴劳动中解放出来，用于农业生产或发展副业，外来收入增加。

根据农业部的研究和调查，一个 $8m^3$ 的户用沼气池，可处理 4～6 头猪的粪便，平均年产沼气 $385m^3$。按照等量有效热计算，可分别替代煤炭 847kg。沼气替代煤炭不仅节约了不可再生的燃料，也大大减少了二氧化硫对空气的污染。

恩施市茶叶种植历史悠久，质地优良，虽然限制了施用农药、化肥，但由于过去家家户户烧煤，污染了环境，导致茶叶二氧化硫超标，产品被挤出国际市场。近两年由于茶园周围农民用沼气代煤，2004年恩施茶叶又重返欧盟市场。

根据农业部的研究结果，一个 $8m^3$ 的户用沼气池，平均年产沼气 $385m^3$。沼气的价格按照 1.2 元/m^3 计算，每个沼气池所生产沼气直接经济效益为 462 元/年。农户沼气发酵后产生的沼渣和沼液，都作为有机肥料用于大田作物或经济作物生产。沼液和沼渣有机肥的综合利用，每口沼气池每年可节约化肥和农药费用 100 元。沼气池建设通过节约资源、节约成本、节约劳力和促进增收，使农民的人均收入增加 40 多元；另外优质茶叶、白术等经济作物和家庭养殖收益，农村经济总收入年均增长 10% 以上，农民人均纯收入年增长近 100 元。

农户建设沼气池及其配套设施，需要投入资金 3000~5000 元，其中国家对农民的补助为每口沼气池 1000 元，即使按照沼气池及其配套设备的最大投入 4000 元计算，农户投入资金的静态投资回收期为 7.1 年。

按照等量有效热计算，每年沼气池的产气量可替代煤炭 847kg，按照 IPCC2006 年推荐的方法学计算，一个沼气池如按处理 4 头猪粪便计算，每年最大可减排温室气体 $4.1~5.2tCO_2e$。项目所覆盖农户每年温室气体减排收入为 181 元。

如果将户用沼气所产生沼气以及利用沼渣和沼液所节约农资的经济收入与 CDM 项目的温室气体减排效益结合起来，户用沼气池的年总收益为 743 元，农民建设沼气池的投资回收年限最长为 5.4 年。将户用沼气开发为 CDM 项目所获的温室气体减排补偿，也能有效缩短沼气池投资的回收年限。

户用沼气因替代煤炭和改变猪粪管理方式可减少温室气体 $59153tCO_2e$，项目 10 年可为 3.3 亿农户带来 6000 万元的直接经济效益。

从该案例分析可以看出，户用沼气池的建设不仅能改变农民传统的生活方式，而且农业种植生产方式由原来的半自给自足的粗放式经营方式向以市场为导向的、以高投入高产出为特征的集约化经营方式转变。中共中央政治局委员、原湖北省委书记俞正声称其为"现阶段欠发达地区农村发展的新模式"。农业部将其誉为生态家园建设的"恩施模式"。

7.2 农村地区生物质能发电案例

生物质是指通过光合作用形成的各种有机体，包括所有的动植物和微生物。而生物质能（biomass energy），是太阳能以化学能形式贮存在生物质中，是以生物质为载体的能量。它直接或间接地来源于绿色植物的光合作用，可转化为常规的固态、液态和气态燃料，是一种可再生能源，同时也是唯一一种可再生的碳源。依据来源不同，可以将生物质能分为林业资源、农业资源、生活污水和工业有机废水、城市固体废物和畜禽粪便等五大类。生物质能仅次于煤炭、石油和天然气居于世界能源消费总量第四位，在整个能源系统中占有重要地位。有关专家估计，到 22 世纪中叶，采用新技术生产的各种生物质替代燃料将占全球总能耗的 40% 以上。

由于中国地广人多，常规能源不可能完全满足广大农村经济日益增长的需求，而且由于全球气候变暖的威胁，限制二氧化碳等温室气体排放成为当务之急。在这种情况下，立足于农村现有的生物质资源，研究新型转换技术，开发新型装备既是建设社会主义新农村的迫切需要，又是减少排放、保护环境、实施可持续发展战略的需要。

7.2.1 农村生物质能的概况

我国生物质能资源丰富，2003 年农村生物质能（秸秆、沼气、薪柴）的使用量达 2.62 亿 t 标准煤，占当年全国总能耗的 22.4%（国家林业局，2003），但是我国农村生物质能源的使用和处理方式基本上是以焚烧、废弃为主，生物质能利用效率十分低下，不仅造成能源的浪费，也严重污染了农村环境，影响农村经济社会环境的全面进步。

改变农村生物质能的开发利用方式，并以此为核心构建新的发展模式，是实现农村可持续发展的重要突破点。采用现代技术开发利用生物质能在我国还处于起步阶段，但已经显示出快速增长的发展趋势和发展前景。如果能够改善农村能源利用结构，把这部分生物质能资源充分利用，将能够完全满足农村生活用能的需要，极大地缓解我国的能源需求压力，改善农村地区环境状况，促进农村经济社会全面发展。2007 年 6 月 7 日国务院常务会议审议并通过了《可再生能源的中长期发展规划》，提出了我国未来将重点发展生物质发电、沼气、生物质固体成型燃料和生物液体燃料。

到 2010 年，生物质发电总装机容量达到 5.50MkW，生物质固体成型燃料年利用量达到 100 万 t，沼气年利用量达到 190 亿 m³，增加非粮原料燃料乙醇年利用量 200 万 t，生物柴油年利用量达到 20 万 t。到 2020 年，生物质发电总装机容量达到 30MkW，生物质固体成型燃料年利用量达到 5000 万 t，沼气年利用量达到 440 亿 m³，生物燃料乙醇年利用量达到 1000 万 t，生物柴油年利用量达到 200 万 t。

为实现这些目标，需要一系列广泛的政策。为减低生物燃料的成本，政府需为可再生能源的使用和温室气体的减排提供直接补贴、税收减免、可交易的排放许可等优惠措施。提高生物燃料的市场份额同样有助于减少对化石燃料的补贴。

7.2.2 生物质能发电的成本核算

使用生物质能发电可以带来巨大的经济和环境效益。以宁波农作物秸秆发电的情况为例介绍生物质能利用的成本。

宁波秸秆资源丰富，年均高达 185 万 t。如果能将秸秆资源总量的 50% 即 92.5 万 t 秸秆用来发电，则可提供折合 46.25 万 t 标煤的热量。具体的项目设计如下：

土地征用。秸秆发电项目建设占地约 10hm²，一期装机容量为 2.5 万 kW，根据宁波荒地工业用地每亩大约 15 万元，土地投资约 2250 万元。

固定资产。秸秆发电固定资产投资包括：设备、厂房、管理用房、堆场及附属设施。分项见表 7.2 所示。

表 7.2　固定资产投资分项表

项目	装机容量/(kW/m²)	单位费用/(元/m²)	总费用/万元
设备	25 000	3000	7500
厂房	8000	2500	2000
管理用房	3000	1500	450
堆场	20 000	500	1000
附属设施（道路、围墙等）			100
固定资产总投资			11 050

原料成本。向农民的原料收购价一般在 100 元/t（秸秆是干燥的），秸秆收购公司收取相应的运输费为 30 元/t。即秸秆收购公司卖到发电厂的价格为 130 元/t。2.5 万 kW 的秸秆发电项目年秸秆消耗量约 45 万 t，每吨收购费用 130 元，合计 5850 万元。

工人工资、运行费用及流动资金费用。项目定员 150 人，平均每人月薪 3500 元，一年计 630 万元；项目各项运行费用一年预计为 500 万元；流动资金按年 3000 万元计，利息 300 万元。合计为 1430 万元。

主营收入。采用 2.5 万 kW 机组，全年发电时间为 8000 小时，可发电 2.0 亿 kW·h。秸秆发电项目每度电上网电价是 0.35 元，在运行 15 年内，享受地方政府每度电 0.25 元的电价补贴，电厂自用电率为 6%，则年电力收入 1.128 亿元。

政府补助。秸秆发电具有明显的社会和环保效益，根据现有政府政策，可获得一次性补助 800 万元，同时享受 15 年税收减免。

成本核算。按折旧率为 7% 计算，则每年土地、厂房和设备等的固定成本为 875 万元；材料、工资、运行费和流动资金费用等变动成本为 7280 万元；因此税前利润 3125 万元。项目静态投资回收期 4 年。

农村地区可以从建造此类工厂获得可持续的经济收益。通过将生物质变为高附加值的商品，不仅可以增加农民收入，同时可以生产清洁能源，保护环境，创造循环经济。

7.2.3　生物质能发电面临的挑战

农村生物质能发展取得了不少成效，国家针对生物质发电的优惠政策已经在各地相继实施，生物质发电厂实现盈利应该不成问题。然而，电厂在实际运营中并非如此，从其长期发展来看，还存在诸多发展瓶颈和不利因素。具体表现如下：

原材料（秸秆）供应不稳定，成本偏高。一是收购难。我国生物质秸秆的收购和组织面对的是千万家的小农户，农民多年来都是把秸秆作为生活燃料的主要来源，出售秸秆的意识不强。加之农作物秸秆的收购往往在农村大忙季节，收集秸秆的力量不足。二是储存难。秸秆收购具有很强的季节性，无法均衡收购，要维持企业的正常运转，必须有半年的储存量。因秸秆比重轻，体积大，堆入存储场地广大，还需一系列的防雨、防潮、防火等配套设备，投资建设和维护费用大。另外，秸秆供应还受到灾害气候的影响，实际材料成本比预计往往高出很多。

生物质（秸秆）收集的机械化程度低。原料收储运所需的农业机械稀缺，国产高秆作物的收获机械尚处在中试阶段，生物质成型燃料加工设备还不尽完善。

生物质（秸秆）转化利用技术不成熟。生物质的转化主要采用热化学和生物学技术。我国用来秸秆发电的锅炉及燃料输送系统的技术和设备绝大部分依靠进口，由于与国外生产运输方式、工作习惯和文化的差异，加之我国专业技术人才匮乏，很可能在技术和设备引进以后造成消化不良，使机组无法安全、稳定、满发运行。另外，由于缺乏核心技术，投产后生物质发电企业很有可能将长期受制于国外企业。

生物质发电企业内部电耗大。企业内部的用电损耗往往比设计的比率要高很多，主要是由于技术和管理的不完善造成的。

7.2.4 促进生物质能发电的相关建议

首先，加大企业技术创新力度和技术改造。加强企业内部对生物质发电设备的技术改造、改进，实现"两降两升"的目标：使电厂的单位发电燃料消耗和发电厂用电率降下来；让发电利用小时和单位装机容量发电量升上去。

其次，通过加强对生物质发电的经营管理，实现"三个控制"，使电厂建设造价有效控制，秸秆收购单位得到有效控制，电厂各项费用开支得到合理控制。企业要把成本控制作为当前的首要任务。不能因为电价政策不到位的外部因素，而掩盖电厂自身管理方面存在的问题，努力降低企业内部的用电量，减少损耗，以提高电厂自身的生存能力。

分散建设生物质燃料加工基地。生物质燃料加工基地是生物质能发电厂燃料收集、储运和预处理中心，应当采取以电厂为轴心分布式多点布局设置，每个加工基地应设在生物质资源密集区域内，考虑到运输成本，其收集辐射半径在5km以内为宜，厂区面积应不低于10亩，可充分利用荒地或空闲地。燃料加工基地就像燃煤电厂的煤矿一样为生物质能发电厂供应燃料，生物质能发电厂可以以投资方式参与其中，以便控制生物质燃料的收集处理。

生物质燃料加工基地应从小规模的关键设备入手，逐步向大规模最大化机械生产发展。为有利于大规模收集利用燃料，加工基地应尽可能地使用机械作业，配备基本的机械设备和运输工具。有关单位应进一步研究改进生物质收集和预处理等机械设备。

寻求当地政府的配合。政府部门可以在禁烧生物质、取缔小型造纸厂、普及推广环境保护等方面加大宣传和治理力度，政策上扶植农区从事生物质收集和预处理加工的经纪人，对生物质收购价格提出保护性意见；同时，应当避免生物质利用的其他项目建设，减少争资源状况，并且改进生物质收集区域的农业种植结构和农民作业习惯，以适应生物质回收的需要，为生物质能发电厂控制生物质资源给予帮助和协调，保障生物质燃料加工基地的生物质资源供应量。

提高业务素质，壮大技术队伍。生物质能的利用主要是在农村，而用高技术开发它，就需要有一大批相应的技术人员，包括科研、管理、生产、推广等方面。号召企业与高等院校、中等专业学校相结合，举办各种类型的进修班，派出学习，请进指导，参观访问等；并要制定一些激励政策，使懂技术的人员能坚持在这个行业里工作。要有计划地培养一大批本行业的技术骨干力量，提高研究层次，实现管理与生产科学化，推广使用不走样。

7.3 农林部门温室气体减排案例

7.3.1 评估中国土地减排的潜力

二氧化碳、甲烷和一氧化二氮是人类活动直接排放最为普遍的三种温室气体。森林和农业部门既是这些温室气体的来源，也可以作为它们的碳汇。

耕地和牲畜是甲烷和一氧化二氮排放尤为巨大的来源，甲烷和一氧化二氮的温室气体效应分别是等量二氧化碳的 23 倍和 310 倍。农业占全球甲烷排放的 50%，全球 85% 的一氧化二氮来自于人类活动。

幸运的是，林业和农业活动也有助于降低和避免温室气体在大气中的积聚。每年全球人类活动造成的排放中，土地利用的改变（主要是热带的滥砍滥伐）所造成的排放就占到了 20%。不过，森林从大气中吸收的二氧化碳，超过了土地利用改变所释放的二氧化碳，全球化石燃料燃烧造成的二氧化碳排放中，有 11% 被森林抵消掉。

减少农业甲烷和一氧化二氮排放的措施：采用减耕或免耕耕作。改变农作物混种和轮作方式。改变施用化肥及其他消耗能源的肥料的时机、数量和频率。改善水浇地与旱地的搭配。提高灌溉效率。改善牲畜粪便的管理。改变牲畜种类和其饮食，减少牲畜消化道中排放的甲烷。改善大米生产中水和稻田管理的方式。

减少农业二氧化碳排放的措施：减少耕作和其他机械生产活动。改变农作物混种和轮作方式。改善水浇地与旱地的搭配。提高灌溉效率。

通过农业活动储存、吸收土壤和生物质中的二氧化碳的措施：减少耕作。改变农作物混种和轮作方式。改变施用化肥及其他消耗能源的肥料的时机、数量和频率。将耕地变为牧地。提高牧场草料的数量和质量，增加轮牧频率。

通过林业封存土壤或生物质中的二氧化碳的措施：将农业和其他用地变为林业用地（造林）。林地再植（森林再造）。延长木材砍伐的间隔期，加强林业管理。保护现有森林。

减耕或免耕、精细化施肥、高效灌溉、增强大米生产中水和稻田的管理等四种实践，每年可以减少 13 亿 tCO_2e，约占中国温室气体排放的 15%～20%（表 7.3）。这种尝试有助于遏制中国二氧化碳排放的增长。这些措施同时也有其他益处，例如保护庄稼免受风沙影响，防止水土流失，保护水资源，减少污染物和固体废物，极大地改善农村环境。

2007 年 6 月，科技部启动了一个科技特别行动计划（Science and Technology Special Action Plan）。计划中强调，农业和土地利用是中国减少温室气体排放的一种可行的途径。为评估这些途径的实际潜力，政府应该详细评估它们的经济和环境效益，考虑市场激励措施。这些措施应该包括允许在国内和国际市场出售减排额度。

四川和新疆的试点项目继续从事这些实践。下面具体介绍这些项目。

表 7.3　四种耕作方式的减排潜力

项目	减排量/(t/hm²/年)			可用耕地/亿 hm²	减排量/(亿 t/年) 采用 100%的措施			减排量/(亿 t/年) 采用 50%的措施		
耕作措施	低	中	高		低	中	高	低	中	高
减少耕地	0.74	1.73	2.72	1.942	1.44	3.359	5.279	0.72	1.68	2.639
精确施肥	0.69	1.16	1.66	1.942	1.344	2.255	3.215	0.672	1.128	1.608
高效灌溉	0.74	1.24	1.73	0.78	0.578	0.964	1.349	0.289	0.482	0.675
稻田用水管理	3.09	5.51	11.12	0.316	0.976	1.741	3.514	0.488	0.871	1.757
总减排量/(亿 t/年)					4.338	8.319	13.357	2.169	4.161	6.679

7.3.2　新疆柽柳温室气体减排项目

新疆拥有丰富的水资源、土壤资源、光资源和地热资源。日照长、昼夜温差大和无霜期时间长等特点使得该地区易于农事活动，农业总产值占全区国内生产总值（GDP）的 25%。新疆的农产品名扬国内外，新疆是中国最大的棉、麻和西红柿的产区，也是家畜、甜菜糖和葡萄的重要产地。然而，新疆地区的外国投资项目非常少，新疆以及中国整个西部地区的经济发展已经落后于其他地区。在新疆进行柽柳造林计划可产生良好的环境效益，同时还可以给当地农民带来经济效益。

柽柳是适应性很强的灌丛植物，它是新疆的本土植物，成熟的柽柳可以成活 100 多年。柽柳造林项目所能带来的温室气体减排主要来自柽柳生物量的增加对二氧化碳的吸收和土壤碳汇增加。随着柽柳的生长，柽柳本身的生物质不断积累，起到了生物固碳作用；同时，随着凋落物的增加和土壤微生物的作用，林下土壤有机质含量增加，土壤的碳含量也随之增加，具备了增加土壤碳汇的作用。该项目产生的碳减排量可以通过对柽柳的生物量监测和林下土壤含碳量测定得到。除生物固碳，柽柳造林还能起防风固沙、防止土壤侵蚀、改善当地的生态环境的作用。对固定的碳进行交易以及大芸的销售可增加当地农民的收入，帮助农民脱贫致富。新疆的柽柳造林项目可以集温室气体减排，改善生态环境和脱贫致富于一体，对当地的经济发展和生态环境建设具有重要意义。

7.3.2.1　新疆柽柳温室气体减排项目实施

新疆有国家级贫困县 30 个，人口 153 万人，现有人工林面积 284.1 万亩，新疆的柽柳造林项目主要分布在塔里木盆地南缘的和田地区，准噶尔盆地南缘的奇台县、呼图壁县、玛纳斯县。

准噶尔盆地南缘荒漠平原具有典型的荒漠气候特征，其特点是气候变化剧烈，年温差、日温差变化大；春温多变，秋温下降迅速，夏季炎热；年降水在 100~150mm，绿洲平原区年降水可达 200mm。

主要分布有梭梭、柽柳等植物，以地貌类别不同，植被盖度不一。历史上，自玛纳斯县北部的绿洲边缘地区，至呼图壁县与奇台县的绿洲边缘，长 300 多 km、宽 10～15km 的地区，曾分布有茂密的梭梭、柽柳等植物，由于过度滥伐，植被退化严重。

和田地区是一个多民族聚居、以农业为主体经济的地区，人口 180 万人，面积 25 万 km²，其中山地占 43.73%，沙漠占 42%，绿洲占 3.96%。耕地面积为 262.05 万亩，占绿洲面积的 17.95%，人均耕地 1.62 亩。当地农民主要以种植棉花、小麦、果树为主。

2008 年，和田地区已完成柽柳造林 10 万亩，接种大芸 6 万亩，栽培大芸产量已达到 20～40t，计划 10 年内扩大再造林 30 万亩，通过柽柳造林所能带来的温室气体减排潜力巨大。

该项目在玛纳斯县、呼图壁县、奇台县三个县实施的柽柳人工造林面积 36.5 万亩，初步估计生物固碳 28.8 万 tCO_2e（表 7.4）。

表 7.4 新疆柽柳人工造林生物固碳量

项目	2008 年	2009 年	2010 年	2011 年	2012 年	合计
奇台柽柳面积/万亩	5	10	15	15	15	
呼图壁柽柳面积/万亩	0.5	1	1.5	1.5	1.5	
玛纳斯柽柳面积/万亩	6	13	20	20	20	
固碳量/万 tCO_2e	4.6	9.6	14.6	14.6	14.6	28.8

7.3.2.2 新疆柽柳温室气体减排项目效益

新疆柽柳人工造林温室气体减排项目的一个关键性动机就是通过项目的实施发展可销售的温室气体减排量。这种想法认为项目产生的所有的温室气体减排量都是额外的。作为可以交替使用的测量额外性的方法，杜克法则描述的额外性供应比例可以应用到新疆柽柳种植项目中。柽柳人工造林生物固碳量由第三方来认证、具体核实项目产生的温室气体减排量。认证过程将在可接受的精度水平下，验证该项目中温室气体排放减排量的真实性、盈余性以及温室气体排放减排量的数量。

按照准噶尔盆地项目在玛纳斯县、呼图壁县、奇台县三个县实施的柽柳人工造林面积 36.5 万亩计算，至 2010 年，生物固碳量达 28.8 万 tCO_2e。按排放抵偿额度 5 美元/tCO_2e 交易价格（项目合同价格），上述 28.8 万 tCO_2e 排放抵偿额度可以获得 144 万美元收益，平均每亩获益 28 元。

按照和田项目实施的柽柳人工造林面积 30 万亩计算，预计生物固碳量为 40 万 tCO_2e。按排放抵偿额度 5 美元/tCO_2e 交易价格，上述 40 万 tCO_2e 排放抵偿额度可以获得 200 万美元的碳汇收益。

大芸的销售也可以增加当地农民的收入，帮助农民脱贫。2008 年和田地区种植柽柳 10 万亩，接种大芸 6 万亩，实际收获大芸产量已达到 20～40t。按照当年大芸市场价格 80～100 元/kg 计算，可以获得 160 万～400 万元收益，平均每亩 27～67 元。按照准噶尔地人工种植柽柳 36.5 万亩，实际接种大芸面积 20 万亩计算，预计栽培大芸收益可达 540 万～1340 万元。

准噶尔盆地项目区位于沙漠边缘，生态环境恶劣。人工营造柽柳、梭梭防风固沙林36.5万亩，使原本裸露的沙漠披上绿装，自玛纳斯县北部的绿洲边缘地区，至呼图壁县与奇台县绿洲的边缘，形成长300多km、宽10～15km的防风固沙林带，植被盖度增加到54%，植物种类也由原来的4种增加到现在的46种，形成了乔灌草三层立体结构群落，增加了生物多样性，提高了荒漠的生产潜力，阻断了沙漠向绿洲的侵袭，使人们赖以生存的绿洲生态环境逐步得到改善。

7.3.3 新疆和四川户用沼气项目

为缓解农村地区的能源短缺问题，我国尝试了沼气、节能灶、小水电、太阳能、风能、地热能等各种方法。其中，沼气项目是推广较早，且辐射范围较广的项目。2003年国家农业部、国家发展和改革委员会启动了2003年农村沼气建设国债项目，在全国22个省（自治区、直辖市）共投资8.4亿元用于户用沼气建设，并从2005年开始将以前的每年10亿元左右增加到25亿元，其中20亿元用于户用沼气池建设。

标准沼气池建设成本在2000～3000元。政府补贴以水泥、河沙、砖、沼气灶等实物形式提供给农户，价值1000元左右。其余资金由农户自筹。

四川省南充市的西充县和仪陇县分别在2004～2006年期间推广了沼气国债项目。但在此次项目之前，已有少部分农户在政府补贴的支持下建造了沼气池。根据入户调查获得的信息，仪陇县早在20世纪80年代就已有小部分沼气池投入使用。因此，该地区农户对沼气项目的接受程度普遍较高。样本村平均沼气推广率为42.75%，其中最高的村达到70%。该项目以沼气池建设为主，结合改厕和改圈，但比例不是很高。牲畜圈的改造比例为29.17%，进行改厕的农户仅为13.89%。

大多是农户选择将沼气池建在院内空地上，占样本项目户的74.29%。有21.43%的农户选择将沼气池建在暖圈周围，另有4.29%的农户建在厨房附近。在材料选择上，以砖混结构为主，比例高达90.28%。另有9.72%的沼气池采用混凝土建成。玻璃钢材料尚未被采纳。所用样本项目户中，34.72%的农户选择建造8～10m³的标准沼气池。另外，31.94%的沼气池容积小于8m³，大于10m³的比例为33.33%。样本农户中，经常使用沼气做饭的农户达88.89%，不经常使用的比例为6.94%，另有4.17%的农户由于畜禽养殖规模小、沼气设备问题、劳动力缺乏或已采用液化气替代等原因，沼气池闲置。33.99%的户用沼气可用来洗澡。其中经常使用的农户比例为14.08%。

位于准噶尔盆地呼图壁县的样本村2003～2005年期间陆续推广了沼气项目。项目地区沼气主要用于做饭烧水，但由于气候、建造质量和后期维护等原因，有产气慢且不足的问题。根据调查，每年沼气可用来做饭的时间大致为2～3个月。

在沼气技术推广中，沼气池的建造布局和质量是影响产气量的关键因素。①位置：北疆地区冬季气温很低，将沼气池建在大棚或暖圈周围可以提高沼气池的温度，进而提高产气量。调查结果显示：目前，选择在暖圈或大棚建造沼气池的农户仅为1/3；另外2/3的项目户将沼气建造在自家院内空地上。②材料：沼气是厌氧条件下产生的，需要沼气池良好的气密性做保障。因此选择气密性好、保温性高的沼气池建造材料有助于提高产气量。调查发现，60%的沼气池为造价相对较低的砖混结构。其次是混凝土结构。玻璃钢是很好的沼气池建造材料，但由于建造成本大，且有些玻璃钢本身质量不过关，导致推广工作并未收到显著成效，目前项目地区采用玻璃钢结构的沼气池仅占沼气池总数的 11.43%；③容积：由于户用沼气池发酵原料有限，为提高有效利用率，户用沼气池容积不宜过大。经调查，为提高能源利用效率，同时适应不同家庭人数的需要，大部分项目户选择建造容积在 0~10m³ 的沼气池。

由于沼气项目造价高投入大，且北疆地区气候寒冷致使沼气产气率较低，农户参与项目的热情不高。截至调查期间，沼气项目的推广率为 13.1%。

在沼气项目推广的前后，新疆和四川的沼气项目样本农户能源消费结构如图 7.4，可以看出沼气项目对案例地区农户的煤消耗量有显著影响，降低了农户煤的消耗量。

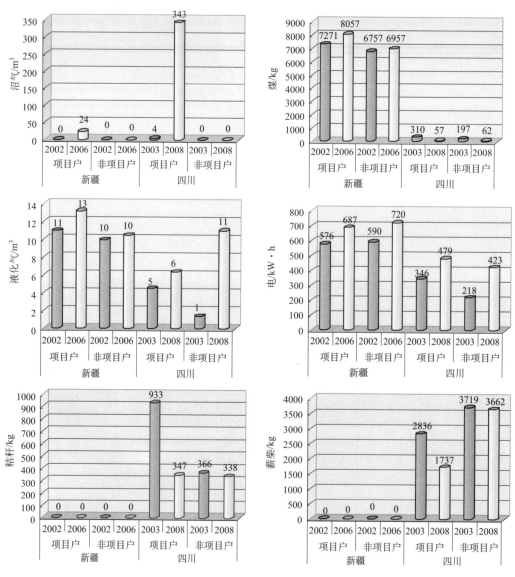

图 7.4　新疆、四川能源消费变化比较

数据来源：北京大学环境学院 2007 年和 2009 年入户调查结果

对四川地区沼气使用户在项目前和项目后的能源结构进行比较可以发现，按照项目户沼气使用量和家庭生活用能的平均水平计算，沼气供能占家庭生活用能的 16% 左右，主要替代了燃烧秸秆和煤的使用。以前用做燃料的大部分秸秆目前被还田，还田的秸秆可以增加土壤有机质含量，改善土壤质量。项目户能源结构见图 7.5。

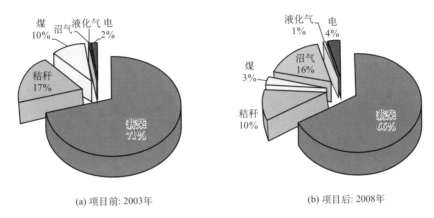

(a) 项目前: 2003年　　　　　　　　　(b) 项目后: 2008年

图 7.5　四川沼气项目户项目前后年生活用能结构比较

数据来源：北京大学环境学院 2007 年和 2009 年入户调查结果

在沼气发酵过程中，由于多菌群共生作用，使沼气发酵液中不仅含有丰富的氮、磷、钾等元素，还含有许多生物活性物质——丰富的氨基酸、微量元素、多种植物生长激素、B 族维生素、有机酸、较高浓度的氨基以及某些抗生素等。这些物质的存在使沼气发酵残留物对农作物病虫害具有良好的防治效用（卢旭珍等，2003）。沼渣、沼液不仅可以替代传统的化肥农药，还可以进一步并有效减少氧化亚氮的排放，为缓解气候变化做出贡献。

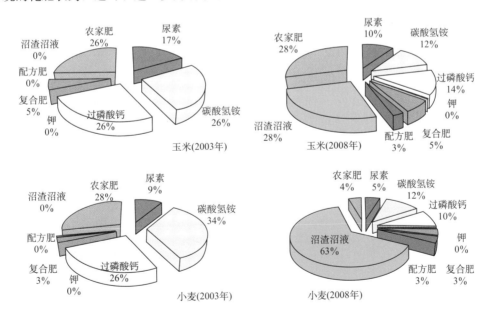

图 7.6　沼气项目前后主要作物的肥料投入比较

数据来源：北京大学环境学院 2007 年和 2009 年入户调查结果

化肥主要包括氮、磷、钾、复合肥和配方肥，有机肥包括沼渣沼液以及牲畜粪便、草木灰、油枯菜枯等农家肥。通过比较发现，样本地区的水稻、玉米和小麦种植以氮肥、磷肥为主，钾肥使用量较低，沼气项目户的沼渣沼液投入对玉米和小麦的化肥、农家肥投入有明显的替代作用（图7.6）。

7.3.4　四川测土配方肥项目

在样本地区，传统的农业耕作需要施一次底肥，并在作物生长过程中进行若干次追肥。测土配方项目后，大部分参与农户把测土配方肥用作底肥，替代了尿素、碳酸氢铵和过磷酸钙等传统化肥，并显著地减少了追肥的次数。很多农户表示用测土配方肥后可以完全不用追肥，大大节省了劳动力。而且作物的产量有所提高。

广元市剑阁县是全国200多个测土配方肥项目试点县之一，项目于2005年前后开展。测土配方项目通过测土、配方、配肥、供肥几个环节，根据土壤质量和作物需求，向农户提供氮、磷、钾和各项微量元素配比精准的肥料。目前在剑阁县已建成土壤监测点5000个，拥有实验室和两个配方肥生产厂。作物覆盖小麦、水稻、玉米、油菜等。农户反映采用配方肥后，虽然化肥方面的开销变化不大，但吸收效率提高，总使用量有所减少，另外可以起到节约劳动力和增产的作用，因此农户对该项目的接受度较高。

采用测土配方肥的农户没有直接补贴。剑阁县共获得该项目拨款3000万元，主要用于土壤监测点建设和试验田管理。

测土施肥项目根据土壤质量和作物需求，向农户提供氮、磷、钾和各项微量元素配比精准的肥料，提高肥料利用效率，从总量上节约化肥投入。从2003～2008年，项目户和非项目户的尿素、碳酸氢铵、过磷酸钙和钾肥等单元素肥料投入量都大幅下降，且在不同程度上被复合肥和配方肥所取代。以水稻为例，2008年与2003年相比，项目户尿素、碳酸氢铵、过磷酸钙的使用分别下降了44.4%，92.1%和98.39%。同期，非项目户以上化肥的使用量也分别下降了20.0%，51.8%和62.3%。配方肥的使用极大的替代了传统单元素化肥。没有参与项目的农户通过施用复合肥替代部分单元素化肥（图7.7）。

项目对农民种植业收入和总收入均有显著的正向影响，对畜牧业收入和非农就业收入的影响不显著。

农民使用新的方法没有获得政府补贴，为鼓励更多农民测试土地和使用配方肥，应对该实践提供直接补贴，允许减排获得可交易的排放额度。随着农民看到这种实践的益处，政府可以逐步取消补贴。

7.3.5　新疆滴灌项目案例

位于玛纳斯县的样本村于2003～2005年期间陆续推广了农田滴灌技术。该项技术主要针对棉花和番茄等矮秆作物栽培。滴灌地块须有专人负责统一供水供肥。截至2007年5月，项目村滴灌技术平均推广率为9.125%，即参加项目的农户占全村总户数的比例不到1/10。

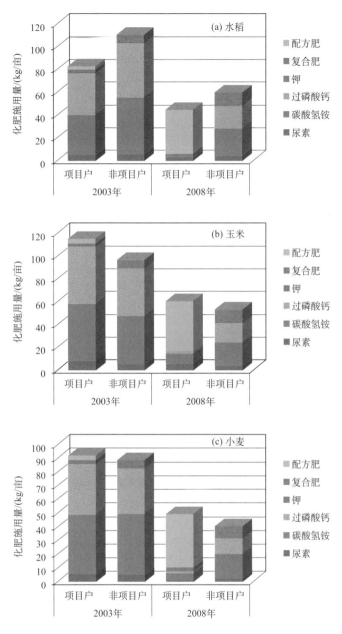

图 7.7 沼气项目前后主要作物的肥料投入比较

在项目初期的 2003 年，主要推广的技术是膜下常压滴灌，当地俗称小白龙。该技术成本较低，但滴灌主管和支管的更新周期较短，每 1~2 年需要换新，后期维护费用较高。另外滴灌管道回收体系尚不完善，被替换而废弃的管道会造成新的环境污染。项目后期主要推广主管深埋式高压滴灌。主管深度为地下 80~150cm 左右，更换周期一般在 10 年左右。针对所有滴灌项目户，采用主管深埋式的农户比例为 73%。膜下常压滴灌的比例为 27%。

由于滴灌设备不同，各村滴灌的建设投资也不同。高压深埋式滴灌设施建设成本为

900～1300 元/亩。项目建设费用主要以上级政府补贴为主，村委会投资和农户贷款为辅。农户需承担设施的后期维护费用，支管的更新费用为 50～65 元/亩。

以项目地区最重要的农作物之一棉花为分析对象，从 2002～2006 年，滴灌样地和非滴灌样地上的化肥施加总量分别都略有提高（图 7.8）。其中尿素、碳酸氢铵等含氮肥料的使用量都有不同程度的增加。调查数据并没有显示项目有明显的节肥效果。以施用量最高的尿素为例，滴灌项目地块上 2002 年尿素的亩均投入为 26.55kg，到 2006 年增长到 29.54kg，提高了 11.26％。同期，非项目地块的尿素投入略有下降。滴灌项目地块的施用量高于非项目地块。但是考虑到滴灌地块的单位产量有明显提高，从 2002 年的 210.98kg 上升到 260.62kg，增产了 25.53％，如果把增产考虑进来，那么单位产量的化肥投入均有所下降，说明肥料的利用率有所提高。

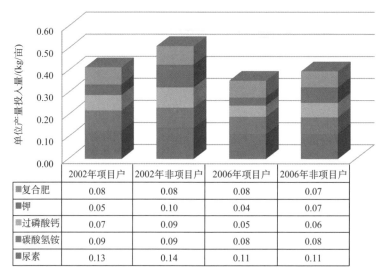

	2002年项目户	2002年非项目户	2006年项目户	2006年非项目户
■复合肥	0.08	0.08	0.08	0.07
■钾	0.05	0.10	0.04	0.07
■过磷酸钙	0.07	0.09	0.05	0.06
■碳酸氢铵	0.09	0.09	0.08	0.08
■尿素	0.13	0.14	0.11	0.11

图 7.8　滴灌项目前后农户化肥使用量亩均变化

数据来源：北京大学环境学院 2007 年入户调查结果

地膜投入维持在 3kg 左右，基本保持不变。用水量的变化比较显著。项目户从 2002 年的 639.24m³ 下降到 564.18m³，下降 11.74％，同期非项目户灌溉量下降 3.05％，降幅低于项目户。由于滴灌采用全村统一供水供肥的模式，灌水季节农户需要按时到自己的地块开关管道阀门，因此劳动力投入提高。项目对农业机械的柴油消耗量影响不大。

7.4　灾后重建案例分析

2008 年 5 月 12 日，四川汶川 8.0 级特大地震造成了巨大人员伤亡和财产损失的同时，也引发了大面积的滑坡、崩塌和泥石流等次生灾害，引起一系列生态环境问题，造成大范围植被破坏、水土流失加剧、野生动物生境破坏与隔离、河道堵塞、耕地毁坏，生态系统和生物多样性受到严重破坏。此次地震是新中国成立以来破坏性最强、波及范围最广、救灾难度最大的一次地震。

据初步测算，地震造成 122136hm² 生态系统丧失，占生态破坏重灾区的自然生态系统的 3.4%（欧阳志云等，2008）。

地震主要影响区位于四川盆地西缘，是四川盆地向青藏高原的过渡地带。该区地质构造复杂，山高谷深坡陡，是我国生态环境十分脆弱的地区，同时也是重要的生态服务功能区[①]。

此次受汶川大地震后危害较大的地区均为高山峡谷区，地震对生态系统的巨大破坏使得当地本已十分紧张的人地矛盾更加尖锐，因此植被恢复和生产发展必须统筹兼顾。

此次地震将本已不适合耕种的土地破坏殆尽。在灾后重建过程中，应避免对坡地再次进行大面积开荒，否则将极易引起水土流失。应合理利用在地震中保存下来的林地资源，发展林下经济。同时对可以进行人工恢复的坡地采取必要的措施进行人工恢复，种植兼具生态效益和经济效益的牧草和灌木，加快植被恢复速度的同时兼顾农民的需求。

地震之后的农房重建对当地的森林资源具有相当大的需求，这种需求是刚性的，当农房重建完成后农户对森林资源的压力主要来自于能源方面的需求，如果仍以薪柴作为农户的主要能源供给形式，这势必会对本已在地震中遭受破坏的森林资源造成极大的压力，不利于植被恢复和生物多样性保护。

由于灾后基础设施和房屋重建工作的全面展开，灾区建筑材料价格人工费用大幅度上涨（表 7.5）。调查中发现灾区大多数农户无法负担，因此国家有必要出台相关政策，加大扶持力度，加快农户由消耗薪柴向利用可持续能源的过渡，这不仅有利于灾后重建工作，而且有利于保护森林资源，加快震区生态环境的恢复速度。

表 7.5　可持续能源设施建造成本（单位：元）

项目	地震前	地震后
沼气池	2200	3500
节柴灶	400	600
太阳能热水器	1900	2500
多功能取暖炉	1300	2000
厕所与牲畜圈舍	2600	4000
总计	8400	12 600

针对山区的地形、气候、植被特点，建议发展山地复合农林系统，构建果树、蜜蜂、牧草、牲畜、沼气、有机肥等多种因素有效连接的生态农业模式（图 7.9）。在物质和能量的良性循环中，降低了外来化学物质（农药、化肥、油料）的使用量，使废弃物排放最小化，实现了"减量化—再利用—资源化"的循环经济目标。这在实践中证明是行之有效的，生态效益和经济效益十分明显。

该复合农林循环系统的生态效益包括：减少了传统果园生产过程中产生的水土流失；提高了土壤肥力，改善了土壤理化性状；增加了天敌数量，降低了病虫害；实现了

① 据初步统计，四川省在本次地震中森林碳汇储备能力每年损失 78.1 万 t，价值 2.5 亿元，森林释放氧气能力降低 67.38 万 t，价值 2.7 亿元。全省森林生态系统生态服务价值损失 1055.88 亿元，综合生态损失 2527.31 亿元，属于生态系统严重经济损失等级。

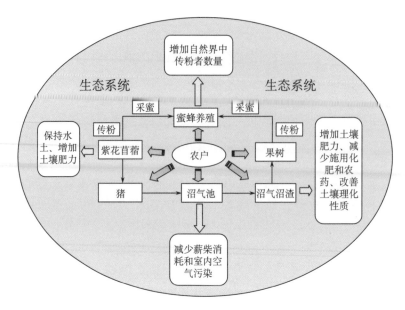

图 7.9　复合农林循环系统

空间的立体利用，提高了土地使用效率。复合农林循环系统的经济效益包括：改善了果实品质，提高了单产效益；蜂产品、牲畜、牧草增加了收益渠道；化肥、农药等外来物质输入的减少降低了生产成本。产品的深加工提高了产品附加值，同时带动产业的快速发展形成当地的特色产业。

近些年来在重灾区安排了大量退耕还林、天然林保护、长江防护林、小流域治理等生态保护工程项目，这些大多建在河谷坡耕地上的项目在地震中损失严重。

生态恢复不但是自然的、技术的过程，更重要的是经济的过程，因为农民是生态建设的主体，他们的生存和发展是第一位的。很多研究表明，在贫困的状态下，保护生态的社会公德和政策法规在农民生存压力面前往往没有效果，此时的农民只重视短期直接经济利益，使生态经济系统陷入生态破坏与贫困的恶性循环之中。

7.4.1　平武县"生态保护与发展综合项目"案例

平武县位于四川盆地西北部，青藏高原向四川盆地过渡的东缘地带，长江的二级支流涪江的上游地区，地处东经 $103°50'\sim104°58'$、北纬 $31°59'\sim33°02'$。全县辖区面积为 5974km²，人口 18 万余人。平武县地处山区，具有典型的山地地貌景观，多年平均气温 14.7℃，多年平均降水量 866.5mm，森林覆盖率为 72%，栖息着大熊猫、金丝猴、扭角羚等珍稀野生动物。

平武县作为地震灾区的 12 个极重灾区县之一，作为灾后植被恢复的研究对象具有很好的典型性和代表性，加之研究团队在该地区已经开展了十余年的研究，积累了大量社会、经济和环境方面的本底资料和数据，因此选择该县作为本项研究的对象。自 2005 年至今，本研究对参加该项目的 120 个农户进行了为期 3 年多的跟踪研究（图 7.10）。

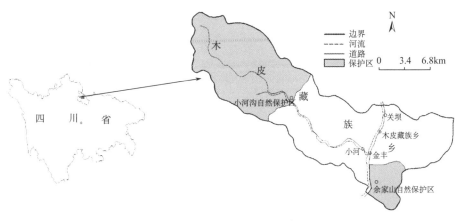

图 7.10　研究区域的地理位置

平武县"生态保护与发展综合项目"为农户提供沼气池、太阳能热水器、多功能取暖炉等设备，以达到降低农户薪柴消耗量的目的。该项目帮助农户将肉牛放养改为圈养，减小森林生态系统的压力，开展蜜蜂饲养等替代性生计，提高农户家庭收入（图 7.11）。

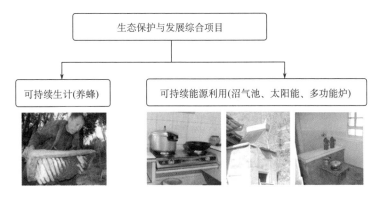

图 7.11　生态保护与发展综合项目框架

农户生态足迹变化。项目实施以来，120 户被调查农户家庭的人均生态足迹由 2005 年的 2.7hm² 下降为 2007 年的 1.6hm²。林地和草地的人均生态足迹大幅度下降，化石能源用地、耕地、建筑用地和水域的人均生态足迹略有上升（图 7.12）。

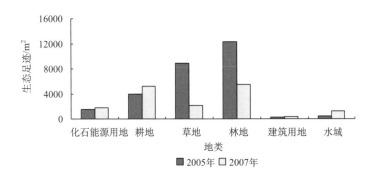

图 7.12　不同土地利用方式农户生态足迹的变化

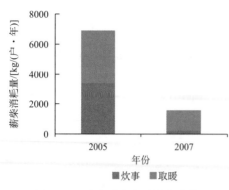

图 7.13 农户的薪柴消耗量变化

农户的薪柴消耗量大幅度下降，2005 年农户的薪柴消耗量为 6920hm²/(户·年)，2007 年为 1570kg/(户·年)，仅为 2005 年的 22.69%（图 7.13）。

沼气池、节柴灶、多功能取暖炉的使用极大地减少了薪柴消耗量，保护了存量森林资源的同时，减少了薪柴燃烧时产生的大量有害气体和烟雾，改善了农户的人居环境，对于保护农户身体健康和减少火灾隐患具有重大意义。

农户收入变化。自 2006～2009 年农户的家庭收入和结构都发生了很大变化（图 7.14）。2006 年农户的家庭平均收入为 1.39 万元，到 2007 年变为 2.16 万元，增长了 7700 元，增长幅度为 55%，主要来源于打工和养蜂业。2008 年农户家庭收入减少到了 1.62 万元，比 2007 年减少了 25%，这主要是由于金融危机和地震的双重影响，在外打工的农民大批返乡，打工收入锐减，来自于养蜂业和畜牧业也由于地震的影响而减少。2009 年由于金融危机的持续，外出打工人数比 2008 年又有所降低，打工收入继续减少。

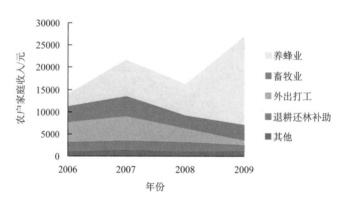

图 7.14 农户的收入结构变化

农户人居环境。项目实施之前，农户的炊事与取暖方式非常原始，薪柴燃烧效率很低，造成严重的空气污染。牲畜圈舍和厕所条件很差，滋生大量苍蝇、细菌等有害生物，这些都对农村居民的健康构成很大威胁（图 7.15）。

项目实施之后，农户家庭卫生状况发生了很大变化（图 7.16）。薪柴燃烧时产生的烟雾以及有害气体大幅度降低，人居环境和动物福利状况都得到了极大改善。

以平武县为例，从 1999 年 10 月实施退耕还林工程以来，截至 2006 年，共完成 12.3 万亩退耕还林，其中生态林 8 万亩，经济林 5.3 万亩。工程涉及 24 个乡镇，165 个村，22829 户。在灾后重建过程中，应利用好前一阶段所取得的成果，巩固生态林，利用经济林，对经济林产品进行深加工，平武县退耕还林地中栽种核桃 2.5 万亩，占经济林种植面积的 48%，现在已经进入盛果期，成为农户的重要经济来源之一。

图 7.15 项目实施前农户家庭卫生状况

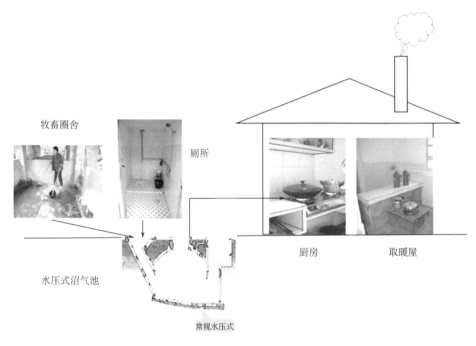

图 7.16 项目实施后农户家庭卫生状况

当前正在发生的全球金融危机造成我国许多企业开工不足，吸纳农村剩余劳动力的能力锐减。加之灾后重建工作的全面展开，许多在外地打工的农民纷纷返回家乡。这些返乡农民工具有一定的知识和技能，回到家乡后将对当地的自然资源进行开发，应该对他们进行积极引导，利用当地的资源发展可持续产业，这对于灾后重建、增加就业机会、实现科学发展具有重大意义。

7.4.2 发展水电实现农村电气化

作为促进能源利用和灾后重建的一部分，政府应该帮助农户对当地的水电资源进行有效利用。地震灾区也是我国西南水电资源富集地区，但是当地百姓却没有享受到廉价的电力资源。

以平武县为例，当地拥有大型水电站1座，中型水电站3座，但是生活在电站周边的农民生活用电价格为0.55元/kW·h，比北京市的居民生活用电0.49元/kW·h高出12%。

2008年12月课题组对平武县木皮乡200户农户进行调查后发现，使用电力进行炊事和取暖的农户比例非常低。电价过高成为农村电气化的主要障碍（表7.6）。

表7.6　农村电力使用情况调查

使用电力进行炊事、取暖的农户	电磁炉4户（2%），电暖器2户（1%）
期望使用电力进行炊事的农户	88户（44%）
期望使用电力进行取暖的农户	180户（90%）
不使用电器进行炊事、取暖的原因	电器价格过高90户（45%），电力价格过高180户（95%）
期望电器价格	电磁炉160元/台，电暖气200元/台
期望电力价格	0.13元/kW·h

44%的农户希望使用电力进行炊事，而90%的农户希望使用电力取暖。这主要是因为当地农户的薪柴消耗中用于冬季取暖的占绝大部分，因此农户希望能够以电代柴，减轻他们的负担。调查中农户表示家用电器虽然初期投入较大，但是使用时间长，平均下来后单位时间内的投入并不高，只有45%的农户认为电器价格较高，55%的农户认为当前电器价格合理，这也和当前国家实施的"家电下乡工程"有关。95%的农户认为当前电力价格过高是导致他们不使用电器的主要障碍。农户的平均期望电力价格仅为0.13元/kW·h，为当前电力价格的22%，即当前电价需要降低78%才能达到农户的期望值。

值得注意的是调查中一部分农民表示，由于该地区建有大型水电站，利用的是当地的水能资源，且对他们的生存环境造成了一定影响，如渔业收入的降低，因此认为用电应该全部免费。

在灾后重建过程中，政府应出台政策对农户生活用电进行补贴，在农户购买电磁炉、电暖气等设备时进行补贴。实施以电代柴，让农户享受到清洁、方便、高效的电力，这不仅有利于保护森林资源，也可以拉动农村地区消费，加快灾后重建和建设社会主义新农村步伐。

第8章 政策建议

为了满足农民对高质量能源的需求，中国需要充分利用广大农村地区的可再生能源资源。政府应当启动市场机制，调动政府各部门、企业和农民积极性，统筹解决农村能源和环境问题。为此我们提出以下建议。

改变生物质能的传统利用方式。现代化的气化或炭化技术可将秸秆和薪柴等生物质资源转化成高品质能源，从而大大提高能源的利用效率，降低废弃物的处理成本。相关政府部门需要建立战略目标和具体的政策措施加速生物质能利用的现代化，加大对农村气化设施的投资，并着手实施新的激励政策。相关的政策应当要求农民把部分秸秆留在田里以保持土壤的质量。

因地制宜地进行生物质能源建设。根据不同地区农村经济发展水平和农村居民生活习惯，开发不同类型的现代化生物质能技术。西南地区人多地少、气候湿热、养殖业发达，适合以人畜粪便为主，结合作物秸秆、其他种植业有机废弃物，发展小型沼气池，满足农村居民的能源需求。

北方平原地区作物秸秆资源丰富，易于收集并开展规模化处理，适合对秸秆进行深加工，既可以直接作为压块燃料，也可以生产饲料；此外，结合新型的太阳能增温沼气池技术，还可以推广沼气生产，改变北方地区冬季温度过低，不适合发展沼气的局面。其他农村和农业地区可以依靠中型生物质气化设施将农业废弃物转化为能源。

政府部门要为不同区域的生物质能开发提供有针对性的技术指导。首先，政府应当在充分考虑其对土壤和环境影响的基础上，为不同的生物质能项目制定技术指南，然后派出技术人员深入田间协助农民和企业根据技术指南实施项目。达到技术指南要求的项目应当能够拿到相应的贷款、赠款和温室气体减排额。

加强农村地区小水电、小风电、太阳能和地热能的开发和使用，加快清洁煤技术的研发。农村可再生能源利用具有明显的区域特点，微水电主要集中于水能资源丰富的西南山区，风能则集中于西北、内蒙古以及沿海地区，太阳能的利用相对普遍，除四川盆地等少数辐射资源条件差的地区外，大部分地区均可利用太阳能，其中华北、西北干旱区太阳能资源丰富，利用普遍。

可再生能源的利用是我国经济发展的迫切需要。但由于经济效益和环境效益并不明显，社会资本和金融资本都不愿意参与产品研发和生产。目前可再生能源发展的主要障碍有技术不成熟、成本过高、无法持续供能等。因此，需要政府出台扶持政策，一方面降低终端用户的能源利用成本，另一方面，利用增加基建投资、补贴、税收优惠等手段引导更多社会资本进入农村可再生能源技术研发和生产，培育可再生能源走产业化道路。

除了直接补贴、低息贷款、优惠税收政策等经济手段以外，可再生能源开发所带来的温室气体减排额可以在市场上出售，从而增加可再生能源的市场竞争力。政府还需要通过加大对能源基础设施的投资力度来鼓励私营部门积极参与可再生能源的研发和使用。我们也建议政府在适当的地区开展高效气化项目的示范，如煤气和天然气的示范。

提高能源供应效率，保障农村能源需求的可持续增长，加强能源保护，提高终端能源的利用效率。中国应当大力推广气化炉和秸秆炉等高效炉具，提高农业机械，特别是灌溉和排水机械的能效；通过调整生产结构、淘汰高耗能设备等方式提高乡镇企业的能效。

新技术的应用需要经济投入，政府需要使用经济激励措施鼓励家庭和乡镇企业采用新技术。相关部门还需要为新建筑和设备提供能效标准。

强化农村能源消费统计。国家有关主管部门需要加强对农村生活和生产终端能源消费的统计工作，为政策研究和制定提供更坚强的基础。首先需要结合农村能源和乡镇企业的发展形势统一农村能源和农村经济的定义、内涵、外延以及相关指标的统计口径，使农村能源统计能够反映农村生活用能以及乡镇企业生产用能的真实状况。

其次，需要加强县级地方政府的能源统计管理和组织能力。调查结果表明，县级统计过程是我国能源统计的一个薄弱环节，受人员编制的影响很多县统计部门表示拿不出系统准确的能源统计数据，因此加强农村能源统计工作必须从完善县级的统计部门抓起。建议在地方统计局的组织和指导下，由农业局、林业局以及各工业部门的具体分管机构分别统计和上报各自领域的能源消费数据，由统计局汇总、校核并统一发布，以确保农村能源统计数据的权威性和真实性。

推广低碳高效农业技术。发展低碳农业经济是改善农村环境、提高农民生活质量的重要手段和紧迫需要。农牧民可以通过植树、减少耕作、扩大植被作物的种植面积、改善草地管理、减少化肥、农药、农用薄膜的使用，用农家肥替代化肥，用生物农药、生物治虫替代化学农药，用可降解农膜替代不可降解农膜等方式减少二氧化碳的排放。

减少温室气体排放、增加碳汇（将碳储存在土壤和生物质当中的过程）的技术不仅有助于减少大气中的二氧化碳，还可以使耕地更迅速地恢复肥力，增加作物的产量。低碳农业技术减少了能源的使用，降低了空气污染和农业废弃物的产生，有助于达到改善农村环境和增加农民收入的双重效果。

节能技术的推广减少了农耕机械和养殖部门的能源消费量。在很多地方，农民已经开始采用测土配方施肥。立体种植、养殖充分利用土地、阳光、空气、水，拓展了生物生长空间，增加农产品产量，提高了产出效益。节水的灌溉和排水方式减少了水资源的使用。

然而，在最近颁布的建设社会主义新农村和减少城乡差别等政策的基础上，政府需要更加重视节能、低碳、高效技术的推广。通过培训、技术指导和提供经济刺激鼓励农民采用新技术应当是工作的重点。"绿色"新技术的推广也必将促进农村地区经济的发展，有利于消除经济危机的影响和减少贫困。

因地制宜和综合规划是发展低碳农业的重要环节。政府和农民需要合作建立长期的政策和补贴措施、改革农业结构、提高生产技术和土地管理技术。具体措施包括：①为农民提供低碳技术经济援助；②建立多级的咨询服务网络推广低碳农业和清洁生产技术；③为高效农业机械的研发提供资金；④规范农作物市场，发展低碳作物；⑤建立农业温室气体减排额的出售程序；⑥依靠低碳低能耗农业进行灾区重建；⑦改善低能效的农产品；⑧加强宏观指导，保证在市场被大机构占领的情况下小项目仍能正常运转。

确定粮食和农业生物多样性并评估其对气候变化影响的脆弱性，制定将生物多样性分布图与不同气候情景分布图匹配，以支持制定相关的国家战略。政府需要在国家和国际基因库中保存生物多样性信息，制定应对气候变化战略，帮助农民利用生物多样性应对气候变化，并指导农民、牧民和渔民采用正确的适应方法。

加快推进农村建筑中可再生能源的利用比例。农村建筑耗能占能源总消费量的比例很大。在中国北方，农村建筑冬季取暖能耗相当可观。随着农村地区的城市化和农民生活水平的提高，农村建筑的能耗总量将迅速增加。

在北方地区，传统的以生物质能为主的取暖模式正迅速向化石能源为主的模式转变。研究表明，农村建筑业和农业经济的进一步发展将导致环境恶化。然而，正如前文所指出的，在广大的农村地区蕴藏有丰富的太阳能和浅层地热能等可再生能源资源和良好的利用条件，可以为建筑供电和供热。

中央对示范区的农村可再生能源建筑已经有了明确的补贴和支持措施。2009年农村可再生能源建筑应用补助标准为：地源热泵技术应用 60 元/m²，一体化太阳能热利用 15 元/m²，以分户为单位的太阳能浴室、太阳能房等按新增投入的 60％ 予以补助。以后年度补助标准将根据农村可再生能源建筑应用成本等因素予以适当调整。每个示范县补助资金总额将根据上述补助标准、可再生能源推广应用面积等审核确定。每个示范县补助资金总额最高不超过 1800 万元。

使用新技术加快农村可再生能源建筑与建筑节能的发展必须坚持多管齐下。可采纳的政策包括：①强化建设标准控制，结合区域实际，推行标准化应用模式；②制定系列应用技术方案，并配套制定相关标准规范、工法、图集，指导工程建设；③确保建筑节能项目建设与使用安全，设计、施工、监理人员应经过培训；④委托专门机构对应用效果进行评估，及时进行项目跟踪；⑤相关设施建成后要采取有效措施，确保系统安全、高效和长久的运行；⑥整合设备生产企业、科研单位、勘察设计单位、施工企业等各方面专业力量，推动与示范推广工作相关的生产、勘察、设计、施工等环节有效结合，提高应用水平；⑦为进一步推广建筑节能制定政策基础，包括补贴、贷款和能效标准等；⑧打破地方垄断，发展环保产业；⑨为能效项目提供可出售的温室气体减排额。

以上政策有助于提高农村居民的生活水平，推动清洁能源及相关产业的发展，提高家庭清洁能源需求，减少传统化石燃料的消费，优化能源供应结构。

收集和分析人类抗击自然灾害的经验并系统地加以利用，提高预测水平帮助农业部门适应气候变化。政府应当对气候变化引起灾害的规模、速度和范围进行评估，强化社区防灾和备灾培训。例如，加强农民田间学校等农村组织，开发预警和监测区域气候变化和灾害发生的技术和系统，以帮助当地农民和主管部门了解气候变化对区域和社区的影响。

政府必须在人口密集区和生态脆弱地区加大对农民，特别是种粮农民的灾害补贴和信贷；制定和研究针对不同地区特点的农业补贴、信贷和农业保险政策和措施，以增加农业生产特别是粮食生产抗击气候风险的能力。但不同地区可根据自身需要选择有弹性的经济刺激方式。

推动经济、社会和环境的统筹发展，实现绿色扶贫。在生态资源严重退化、生活水平低、自然条件恶劣的"天然困难区"，政府需要为农民的财产损失提供补偿，并在符合农民意愿的前提下制订移民和发展计划，以减轻人口压力对当地环境的影响。

可持续发展要求创造"绿色就业机会"。政府应当鼓励可再生能源、能效和低碳农业项目的开发。经济刺激措施和具备"绿色"技能的劳动力是这些项目成功的前提。因此政府有必要规范"绿色工作和技能"的定义，并提供补贴、贷款和培训推动劳动力技能的提高。

确保国家的粮食安全。事实经验和模型模拟结果都表明气候变化将对中国的食品安全产生深远影响。国际社会正试图通过减缓和适应两类措施应对这一挑战，最终目标是使公共和私营部门、社区、基础设施和经济在调整自身行为、减少温室气体排放的同时做好适应变化的准备。

以下步骤对中国至关重要：

（1）确保相关部门制定政策鼓励农业减排、可再生能源和能效项目的推广；

（2）为开发和检测农业节能减排项目及相关新政策框架和组织形式提供更多资金；

（3）整合农村信用社、供销社及技术合作社资源，建立综合的农村合作服务体系；

（4）加强乡镇企业、农产品加工企业、农村合作组织和社会团体之间的合作；鼓励其参与项目的研发和执行；

（5）完善农村金融信用政策，加大贷款抵押创新力度，积极推进农村基层金融改革；

（6）将农村信用体系与现有银行体系结合，促进社会资本参与农村清洁能源的开发；

（7）支持各地区参与为气候变化减缓和适应筹集资金的各种机制，包括联合国气候变化框架公约的机制、各种由公共和私人伙伴建立的自愿和强制性碳市场；

（8）加强低碳农业和能源国际合作，敦促国际组织和发达国家分享先进技术和成功经验；

（9）取消补贴和边界税，减少农产品交易的政策障碍。

建立促进温室气体减排的市场机制。科学界已经达成共识，由人类活动引起的温室气体排放所导致的气候变化威胁着世界的可持续发展。由所有主要排放国参与的减排行动是应对气候变化的关键。

提高能效和发展可再生能源是应对这一挑战的基础。碳埋存——即将碳储存在土壤和生物质里，也有助于减少大气中的二氧化碳含量。

适应和减缓活动也可以增加农牧民和其他土地管理者的收入。他们可以通过改变耕作方式和农作物品种将大气中的二氧化碳埋藏在泥土中，也可以通过改变牲畜和稻田的管理方式减少温室气体（如甲烷）的排放。造林—在非林地植树—可以将碳储存在生物质、泥土和农产品中。所有这些改变都会在减排的同时为农牧民带来经济补偿。

为了确保农林业温室气体减排额的可信性，中国需要建立完善的测量和统计体系，体系的设计需要从实际出发，以适用中国各式各样的土地活动。

该体系必须明确：

（1）达到高质量项目标准的活动类型；

（2）量化减排额的方法；

（3）评估"额外性"和"碳泄漏"的方法；

（4）测量和认证的方法；

（5）管理减排额度不确定性的方法，以及针对不同项目制定保险等风险控制手段。

参考文献

卞有生. 2005. 生态农业中废弃物的处理与再生利用. 北京：化学工业出版社

蔡承智，梁颖，李啸浪. 2008. 基于 AEZ 模型预测的我国未来粮食安全分析. 农业科技通讯，2：15～17

蔡祖聪，谢德体，徐华等. 2003. 冬灌田影响水稻生长期甲烷排放量的因素分析. 应用生态学报，14（5）：705～709

曹国良，张小曳，王丹. 2005. 中国大陆生物质燃烧排放的污染物清单. 中国环境科学，25（4）：389～393

邓根云，于沪宁. 1992. 温室气体增加对气候和农业的影响问题. 见：邓根云主编. 气候变化对中国农业的影响. 北京：科学技术出版社，3～18

邓可蕴，贺亮. 2000. 我国农村地区中长期能源需求预测. 中国工程科学，2（6）：16～21

董保成，鞠笑非，甘静等. 2006. 东北地区沼气分户供暖的可行性初探. 农业工程学报，22（1）：101～103

董红敏. 2008. 湖北恩施启用沼气 CDM 项目实例. 农业工程技术（新能源产业），05：23～26

段茂盛，王革华. 2003. 畜禽养殖场沼气工程的温室气体减排效益及利用清洁发展机制（CDM）的影响分析. 太阳能学报，24（3）：386～389

高春雨，毕于运，赵世明等. 2008. "五配套"生态家园模式经济效益评价——以陕西省洛川县"果-畜-沼-窖-草"模式为例. 中国生态农业学报，16（5）：1287～1292

韩广轩，朱波，江长胜. 2005. 川中丘陵区稻田甲烷排放及其影响因素. 农村生态环境，21（1）：1～6

黄柏权，田敏. 2008. 少数民族山区建设社会主义新农村的有益尝试——恩施州生态家园文明新村调查. 青海民族研究，19（2）：125～132

黄耀，张稳，郑循华等. 2006. 基于模型和 GIS 技术的中国稻田甲烷排放估计. 生态学报，6（4）：980～988

黄耀. 2006. 中国的温室气体排放、减排措施与对策. 第四纪研究，26（5）：722～732

居辉，熊伟，马世铭等. 2008. 气候变化与中国粮食安全. 北京：学苑出版社

孔祥智，庞晓鹏，张云华. 2004. 北方地区小麦生产的投入要素及影响因素实证分析. 中国农村观察，4：2～7

李晓锋，陈明新. 2008. 全球气候变暖对我国畜牧业的影响与分析. 新视点，44（4）：50～53

李永华，王五一，杨林生等. 2002. 燃煤污染型氟中毒流行特点及氟安全阈值研究. 中国地方病学杂志，20（1）：41～43

李智文，任爱国，关联欣等. 2006. 山西省农村地区室内燃煤空气污染状况调查. 中国公共卫生，22（6）：728～729

林而达. 1997. 气候变化与农业——最新的研究成果与政策考虑. 地学前缘，4（1～2）：221～226

刘宇，匡耀求，黄宁生. 2008. 农村沼气开发与温室气体减排. 中国人口·资源与环境，18（3）：84～89

刘源，张元勋，魏永杰等. 2007. 民用燃煤含碳颗粒物的排放因子测量. 环境科学学报，27（9）：1409～1416

卢旭珍，邱凌，王兰英. 2003. 发展沼气对环保和生态的贡献. 可再生能源，6：50-52

陆慧，卢黎. 2006. 农民收入水平对农村家庭能源消费结构影响的实证分析. 财贸研究，3：28～34

罗国亮，张媛敏. 2008. 中国农村能源消费分析. 中国农学通报，24（12）：535～540

农业部科技教育司，农业部能源环保技术开发中心. 2008. 全国农村可再生能源统计. 北京：农业科技教育司

农业部科技教育司编. 2008. 中国农村能源年鉴 2000～2008. 北京：中国农业出版社

欧阳志云，徐卫华，王学志等. 2008. 汶川大地震对生态系统的影响. 生态学报，28：5801～5809

秦晓波，李玉娥，刘克樱. 2006a. 长期施肥对湖南稻田甲烷排放的影响. 中国农业气象，27（1）：19～22

秦晓波，李玉娥，刘克樱. 2006b. 不同施肥处理稻田甲烷和氧化亚氮排放特征. 农业工程学报，22（7）：143～148

孙芳，杨修，林而达等. 2005. 中国小麦对气候变化的敏感性和脆弱性研究. 中国农业科学，38（4）：692～696

孙永明，李国学，张夫道等. 2005. 中国农业废弃物资源化现状与发展战略. 农业工程学报，21（8）：169～173

孙振钧. 2004. 中国生物质产业及发展取向. 农业工程学报，20（5）：1～5

孙振钧，袁振宏，张夫道等. 2004. 农业废弃物资源化与农村生物质资源战略研究报告. 国家中长期科学和技术发展战略研究

谭贤楚，刘伦文. 2008. 少数民族地区生态建设模式研究——以恩施市新农村建设的"生态家园"模式为例. 安徽

农业科学，36（8）：3337~3338

田宜水. 2009. 中国生物质固体成型燃料产业发展分析. 农业工程技术：新能源产业，2：13~17

王飞，王革华. 2006. "四位一体"户用沼气工程建设对农民种植行为影响的计量经济学分析. 农业工程学报，22
（3）：116~120

王效华，冯祯民. 2001. 中国农村家庭能源消费研究——消费水平与影响因素. 农业工程学报，5（17）：88~92

王效华，冯祯民. 2004. 中国农村生物质能源消费及其对环境的影响. 南京农业大学学报，27（1）：108~110

王效华，高树铭. 2003. 中国农村能源可持续发展：现状、挑战与对策. 中国沼气，21（4）：41~43

王效华，吴争鸣. 1999. 中国农村家庭生活用能需求预测方法的探讨. 农村能源，5：1~3

王铮，郑一萍，冯皓洁. 2001. 气候变化下中国粮食和水资源的风险分析. 安全与环境学报，1（4）：19~23

谢立勇，侯立白，高西宁等. 2002. 冬小麦 M808 在辽宁省的种植区划研究. 沈阳农业大学学报，33（1）：6~10

熊伟，许吟隆，林而达等. 2005a. IPCC SRES A2 和 B2 情景下我国玉米产量变化模拟. 中国农业气象，2（1）：11~15

熊伟，许吟隆，林而达. 2005b. 两种温室气体排放方案下我国水稻产量变化模拟. 应用生态学报，16（1）：65~69

熊伟，许吟隆，林而达等. 2005c. 气候变化导致的冬小麦产量波动及应对措施模拟. 中国农学通报，21（5）：380~385

徐浪，贾静. 2003. 化肥使用量对粮食产量的贡献率分析. 四川粮油科技，1：58~62

徐新惠. 2006. 棉秆压缩成型特性的试验研究. 石河子大学硕士学位论文

杨修，孙芳，林而达等. 2004. 我国水稻对气候变化的敏感性和脆弱性. 自然灾害学报，13（5）：85~89

杨修，孙芳，林而达等. 2005. 我国玉米对气候变化的敏感性和脆弱性研究. 地域研究与开发，24（4）：54~57

于康震. 2009. 2008 年畜牧饲料经济运行形势及 2009 年预测分析. http://www. feedtrade. com. cn/news [2009-1-
19]

于文金. 2008. 地震灾害对四川省区域生态系统危害及损失评价. 生态学报，28：5785~5794

虞江萍，崔萍，王五一等. 2008. 我国农村生活能源中 SO_2、NO_x 及 TSP 的排放量估算. 地理研究，27（3）：547~555

张国威，何文勤. 1998. 我国干旱区洪水灾害基本特征：以新疆为例. 干旱区地理，21（1）：40~48

张培栋，王刚. 2005. 中国农村户用沼气工程建设对减排 CO_2、SO_2 的贡献——分析与预测. 农业工程学报，21
（12）：147~151

张文学，孙刚. 2008. 我国农业及畜牧业发展 CDM 项目的潜力分析. 江西能源，1：21-23

赵行姝. 2003. 中国农村能源消费的趋势和面临的挑战. http://www. ccchina. gov. cn/cn/NewsInfo. asp? NewsId=3957
[2003-3-21]

赵宗慈. 2006. 全球气候变化预估最新研究进展. 气候变化研究进展，2（2）：68~70

中国农村能源年鉴编辑委员会. 1999. 中国农村能源年鉴 1998~1999. 北京：中国农业出版社

中国农业年鉴编辑委员会. 2007. 中国农业年鉴 1996~2007. 北京：中国农业出版社

中华人民共和国国家发展和改革委员会. 2004. 中华人民共和国气候变化初始国家信息通报. 北京：中国计划出
版社

中华人民共和国国家发展和改革委员会. 2007. 中国应对气候变化国家方案

朱四海. 2007. 中国农村能源政策：回顾与展望. 农业经济问题，9：20~25

朱兆良，孙波. 2008. 中国农业面源污染控制对策研究. 环境保护，8：4~6

85-913-04-05 攻关课题组. 1994. 我国农用氮肥氧化亚氮排放量变化趋势预测（1990~2020）. 农业环境保护，13
（6）：259~261

Alexandrov V，Eitzinger J，Cajic V et al. 2002. Potential impact of climate change on selected agricultural crops in
north-eastern Austria. Global Change Biology，8：372~389

Barnes D，Foley G. 2004. Rural Electrification in the Developing World：A Summary of Lessons from Successful
Programs. Energy Sector Management Assistance Program. Washington D. C.

Barnes D. 2007. The Challenge of Rural Electrification，Strategies for Developing Countries. Resources for the Fu-
ture，（1）：1~18

Chen F J，Wu G，Ge F et al. 2004. Impacts of elevated CO_2 on the population abundance and reproductive activity of
aphid Sitobionavenae Fabricius feeding on spring wheat. J. Env. Nutr，128（9-10）：723~730

Ferraro P，Kiss A. 2002. Direct payments to conserve biodiversity. Science，298（29）：1718~1719

Fischer G, Van Velthuizen H T. 1996. Climate change and global agricultural potential project LA case study of Kenya. International Institute of Applied System Analysis, Lazenburg, Austria

Fuhrer J. 2003. Agroecosystem responses to combination of elevated CO_2, ozone, climate change. Agriculture, Ecosystems and Environment, 97: 1~20

Gunasekera D, et al. 2007. Climate change: impacts on Australian Agriculture. Australian Commodities: Forecasts and Issues, 14 (4): 657~676

Hector A, Schmid B, Beierkuhnlein C et al. 1999. Plant diversity and productivity experiments in European grasslands. Science, 286: 1123~1127

Hitz S, Smith J. 2004. Estimating global impacts from climate change. Global Environmental Change, 14: 201~218

Hulme M. 1996. Climate Change and Southern Africa. Norwich, United Kingdom: Climatic Research Unit. University of East Anglia. 104~115

IPCC. 2007. Summary for Policymakers. In: Metz B, Davidson O R, Bosch P R et al. Climate Change 2007: Mitigation. Contribution of Working Group III to the Fourth Assessment Report of the Intergovernmental Panel on Climate Change. Cambridge: Cambridge University Press

Javier Blas, Geoff Dyer. 2009. China sows seeds of food self-sufficiency, Financial Times

Ju H, et al. 2008. Adaptation Framework and Strategy Part 1: A Framework for Adaptation. AEA Group, UK

Kevan P G, Clark E A, Thomas V G. 1990. Insect pollinators and sustainable agriculture. American Journal of Alternative Agriculture, 5: 13~22

Li C S. 2001. Biogeochemical concepts and methodologies: Development of the DNDC model. Quaternary Sciences, 21: 89~99

Li C S, Aber J, Stange F et al. 2000. A process-oriented model of N_2O and NO emissions from forest soils: 1. Model development. Journal of Geophysical Research, 105 (4): 4369~4384

Li C S, Frolking S, Frolking T A. 1992a. A model of nitrous oxide evolution from soil driven by rainfall events: 1. Model structure and sensitivity. Journal of Geophysical Research, 97: 9759~9776

Li C S, Frolking S, Frolking T A. 1992b. A model of nitrous oxide evolution from soil driven by rainfall events: 2. Applications. Journal of Geophysical Research, 97: 9777~9783

Li C S, Narayanan V, Harriss C R. 1996. Model estimates of nitrous oxide emissions from agricultural lands in the United States. Global Biogeochemical Cycles, 10: 297~306

Lin E D, Xiong W, Ju H et al. 2005. Climate change impacts on crop yield and quality with CO_2 fertilization in China. Philos. T. Roy. Soc. B, 360: 2149~2154

Ma S et al. 2006. "Efficient System Design and Sustainable Finance for China's Village Electrification Program". Midwest Research Institute, Batelle. Available on: http://www. osti. gov/bridge [2006-12-4]

Markandya A. 2008. Rural Electrification and Rural Energy in China. Paper prepared for the 2nd Meeting of the Task Force on Rural Development and its Energy, Environment and Climate Change Adaptation Policy, CCICED, Beijing, China

McCarthy J J, Canziani O F, Leary N A et al. 2001. Climate Change 2001: Impacts, Adaptation, and Vulnerability. Cambridge: Cambridge University Press, 235~342

Mirza M Q. 2003. Climate change and extreme weather events: can developing countries adapt. Integrated assessment, 1: 37~48

NakiCenovic N, Alcamo J, Davis G et al. 2000. Special Report on Emissions Scenarios. A Special Report of Working Group III of the Intergovernmental Panel on Climate Change. Cambridge: Cambridge University Press

Nearing M A, Pruski F F, O'Neal M R. 2004. Expected climate change impacts on soil erosion rates: A review. Journal of Soil and Water Conservation, 59: 43~50

Niesten E, Rice R. 2004. Sustainable forest management and conservation incentive agreements. International Forestry Review, 6: 56~60

Parry L M, Carter R T, Knoijin T N. 1988. The Impact of Climatic Variations on Agriculture. Dordrecht: Kluwer

Academic Publisher

Peng S B, Huang J L, Sheehy E J et al. 2004. Rice yields decline with higher night temperature from global warming. Proceedings of the National Academy of Sciences of the United States of America, 101 (27): 9971~9975

Reiche K, Covarrubias A, Martinot E. 2000. Expanding Electricity Access to Remote Areas: Off Grid Rural Electrification in Developing Countries. World Power, 52~60

Ringius L, et al. 1996. Climate change in Africa: Issues and challenges in agriculture and water for sustainable development. Report 1996: 8, Oslo: University of Oslo, Center for International Climate and Environmental Research, 128~136

Rosenweig G E, Parry M I. 1994. Potential impact of climate change on food supply. Nature, 367: 133~138

Scherr S, et al. 2004. Tropical forest provides the planet with many valuable services. Are beneficiaries prepared to pay for them? ITTO Tropical Forest Update, 14 (2): 11~14

Shiel M J. 2007. Electricity for Social Development in Ireland. In: Barnes D eds. The Challenge of Rural Electrification: Strategies for Developing Countries. Resources for the Future, Washington D. C. and Energy Sector Management Assistance Program, Washington D. C.

Stern N. 2006. The Economics of Climate Change: The Stern Review. Cambridge: Cambridge University Press

Strzepek K, Simth J B. 1995. As climate changes: International Impacts and Implications. Amsterdam: Springer

Van Ittersum M K, Howden M S, Assent S. 2003. Sensitivity of productivity and deep drainage of wheat cropping systems in a Mediterranean environment to changes in CO_2, temperature and precipitation. Agriculture Ecosystems and Environment, 97: 255~273

Wang J, et al. 2008. Can China Continue Feeding Itself? —— The Impact of Climate Change on Agriculture. Policy research working paper 4470, The World Bank

Wang X H, Feng Z M. 1996. Survey of rural household energy consumption in China. Energy, 21 (7-8): 703~705

Wang X H, Feng Z M. 1997. A survey of rural energy consumption in the developed regions of China. Energy, 22 (5): 511~514

Wang X H. 1994. Situations and trends of China's rural household energy consumption. Journal of Nanjing Agricultural University, 17 (3): 134~141

Willey Z, Chameides B. 2007. Harnessing Farms and Forests in the Low-Carbon Economy: How to Create, Measure, and Verify Greenhouse Gas Offsets. Durham: Duke University Press

Xiong W, Lin E D, Ju H et al. 2007. Climate change and critical thresholds in China's food security. Climatic Change, 81: 205~221

Yu H N. 1993. The Impact of Climate Change to Food Production in China. Beijing: The Science and Technology Publish of Beijing, 118~127

致　谢

在此，我们谨对课题发起方——中国环境与发展国际合作委员会表示特别感谢。同时，对国家发展和改革委员会应对气候变化司以及中国-联合国气候变化伙伴框架项目对课题组的支持、组织和帮助表示衷心的感谢；感谢中国环境与发展国际合作委员会、联合国开发计划署、美国环保协会为该项目提供的资金支持；感谢商务部中国国际经济技术交流中心对项目资金管理和协调所做的工作，并对给予本项目支持和帮助的所有专家和工作人员表示衷心的感谢，尤其对国合会的祝光耀秘书长、沈国舫院士、汉森博士、李永红处长、卢雪云、张鸥；联合国环境规划署的张卫东、张玉；国家发展和改革委员会的李丽艳处长、吴建民、李彦；商务部中国国际经济技术交流中心的祝端倪处长、李斌、田缘诗、高京等表示衷心的感谢。

1 Introduction

China's large, scattered rural population—and varying natural conditions and level of economic development—make energy issues even more complicated in the countryside than in urban areas. Since the reform and opening-up, China's rural economy has been developing rapidly, and that development has brought significant challenges in energy use and climate change. First, total rural energy use has rapidly increased from 560 million tons of coal equivalent in 1995 to 730 million tons of coal equivalent in 2007 with an annual increase of 2.3%. In 2007, commercially produced energy only accounted for 23.2%; total rural household energy consumption was 350 million tons of coal equivalent. Straw and firewood accounted for the majority of non-commercially produced energy at 60% and 35%. In 2007, rural per capital energy consumption was 1.7 times that of urban levels but household energy consumption was only 40% of the urban levels. Second, environmental problems are getting more serious than before: from 1980~2004, total SO_2 emissions and CO_2 emissions from coal consumption increased about 4 times, and biomass and wood became a major source of indoor pollution. Finally, rural communities and resource users are very vulnerable to climate change impacts. In the meantime, from land use and forest perspectives, rural areas also hold the largest potential of carbon sequestration. Thus, CCICED recommends:

The Chinese government should integrate rural energy and environmental issues into the strategic task of Building the New Countryside, strengthen management and adopt comprehensive strategies, develop clean and renewable energy sources in the rural areas and establish a comprehensive rural renewable energy service system and develop low-carbon and highly efficient agriculture; and pay attention to the policy measures on climate change adaptation for rural areas.

(1) **Increase the role of rural energy development in the national energy strategy and national climate strategy.** China should speed up the upgrading of rural electrical grids and increase efficiency of rural energy use; strengthen the development of energy-saving technology and new energy technology/products suitable for various rural regions; determine how to establish national rural energy financing mechanisms to promote sustainable energy construction in rural areas; improve rural renewable energy development plans and relevant regulations; develop rural biomass energy subject to local conditions; incorporate rural biomass facility, especially large or medium-scale methane facility, into national rural infrastructure plans; and meanwhile, strengthen rural environmental improvement to reduce health risks such as those associated with

burning of coal for cooking and heating in homes.

(2) Adopt integrated measures to stimulate the development of clean and renewable energy sources. Growing rural use of commercial energy sources such as coal, petroleum products, and electricity results in significant pollution and GHG emissions. Developing clean and renewable energy sources such as biogas (marsh gas) and biomass for electricity generation could help relieve gaps between energy supply and demand, curb pollution, increase farmers' income, and control GHG emissions.

First, a rural renewable energy strategy and related laws and regulations are necessary both to improve the rural environment and to tackle climate change.

Second, the government should promote renewable energy technologies to bring them into widespread rural use. The government could do so by expanding its own investment in modern biomass facilities, and by providing subsidies and tax incentives to encourage private capital to invest in R&D for rural renewable energy technology. Only with government guidance can China fulfill the goal of fully commercializing its extensive renewable energy resources. A Rural Energy Construction Fund could promote sustainable energy development, while "transfer payments" could subsidize electricity use among farmers.

Third, China should spur the rural use of biogas by integrating the construction of biogas facilities into efforts to rebuild rural infrastructure, and to set up market mechanisms in support of biogas development.

Fourth, China should expand the use of renewable energy sources to provide heat and electricity for rural buildings. Rural buildings already account for a large proportion of energy use in China, and the amount of energy they consume is rising fast. Thus, it is important to strengthen the monitoring and evaluation of energy conservation technologies, subsidies, and the promotion of energy saving materials under the rural building energy saving policies. Greater reliance on renewable technologies to heat rural buildings can help to conserve energy. To promote that goal, it is now appropriate to scale up activities such as the use of solar and shallow geothermal technologies in rural buildings as part of the modernization of the Chinese countryside.

(3) Optimize land use, increase carbon sequestration potential and support the development of high quality low carbon, low pollution agriculture; introduce a new rural carbon sequestration compensation mechanism, with provision for fiscal transfers and possibly for international financial transfer mechanisms. China should maintain and increase forest, farmland and grassland carbon sequestration, and promote these GHG-reducing practices to a wider audience. The practices include afforestation, improved protection of natural ecosystems, low-till or no-till farming, improved grassland management, alternative varieties of animals and fodder, and more efficient use of fertilizer. The government should establish consulting services at all levels to ensure that farmers have access to energy-saving technologies and information on low carbon farming. The government should provide subsidies, insurance, and credits to advance these goals, especially in areas with fragile ecosystems and large numbers of farmers. A program that enables farmers to obtain credits for reducing GHG emissions through changes in production practices, and that markets and trades those credits, could achieve the dual goals of removing CO_2 from the atmosphere and providing new income sources to farmers and land managers. A low-emission, high-efficiency, recycling agricultural industry will help China reduce both pollutants and rural GHG emissions. Many good practices are available in China now. China should rely on a comprehensive, long-term strategy based on local circumstances to develop low pollution, low carbon high quality agriculture and to protect natural ecosystems, with subsidies to encourage investment in new technology and management approaches. National voluntary carbon trading mechanisms, and payments to impoverished farmers for reducing pollutants and GHG emissions are a cost-effective way to promote low pollution and low carbon practices while also contributing to the goal of alleviating poverty.

(4) Improve the capacity of farmers and rural regions to adapt to climate change. Enhancing farmers' ability to adapt to climate change is essential in order to sustain the rural economy, improve rural living standards, protect ecological services and biodiversity, and ensure food security. Towards these ends: ①China should evaluate the speed and scale of potential disasters, with systems for monitoring regional climate change, and early warning systems; ② authorities at all levels need to consider adaptation to climate change when creating development strategies, and bolster community-based disaster prevention and training; ③ China will need to adjust the structure of the nation's agricultural production and consumption; ④ China should import agricultural products with high resource input values in order to ensure self-sufficient supply of other foods and to relieve pressure on domestic resources and the environment; ⑤ as part of its climate change strategy, China should pay greater attention to the protection of biodiversity, including preservation of genetic material in national and international gene banks.

(5) Enhance the statistical analysis of rural energy use. To ensure that rural energy becomes an integral part of China's energy system, authorities need to strengthen their statistical analysis of rural energy end-use by both households and producers. First, authorities need to unify the definition of rural production, to ensure that statistics reflect actual energy use of township enterprises. Second, national officials need to bolster the ability of county governments to organize and manage energy statistics. Agricultural Bureaus, Forestry Bureaus, and other industry bureaus should then calculate and report statistics on local energy consumption under the guidance and organization of local statistics bureaus. The National Statistics Bureau can collect, check, and issue the overall results, to ensure the authority and authenticity of the nation's rural energy statistics.

2 An Overview of Rural Energy, Environment, and Climate Change in China

In rural regions, energy is not only critical for agricultural production and everyday life—its development and use are also closely linked to preserving the rural environment and tackling climate change. A sound rural energy supply is therefore an essential foundation for building a well-off society in an all-around way and achieving sustainable development in China's countryside.

2.1 The Evolution of Rural Energy Use in China

2.1.1 The Concept of Rural Energy

We can define rural energy in two ways: narrow and broad. In its narrow sense, it refers to commercial energy transported from other places and used in rural areas, as well as local forms of energy, usually renewable. In its broad sense, it refers to the notion that rural areas of Third World countries must rely on local sources of renewable energy because their economies are underdeveloped and commercial supplies are limited. In its essence, rural energy refers to the overall challenge of providing energy to rural areas (Wang, Gao, 2003).

China has long differentiated between cities and countryside in tackling its energy problems, heavily weighting construction toward ensuring enough energy to meet industrial and urban demand. That means vast rural areas have long lacked basic commercial energy services. They have responded by becoming self-sufficient in local renewable resources. These have largely included traditional forms of biomass, such as crop straw, firewood, methane gas, and cow muck, as well as some hydropower, small-scale wind power, and small coalmines.

Ensuring China's rural energy supply is often seen simply as managing these noncommercial resources. However, energy sources and methods have quietly begun to change during 30 years of rural economic development and construction. As Chinese farmers become more urbanized and their standard of living rises, new forms of commercial energy and of renewable energy are appearing on the horizon. Energy management is advancing with these changes, with accelerated application of market incentives and prices.

2. 1. 2　The Environmental Impact of Rural Energy Use

Because China's rural population is massive and its rural areas vast, agricultural production, farmers' life, and rural development will inevitably consume a huge amount of energy. And that means energy and environmental issues in the nation's rural areas will always be closely linked.

On the one hand, energy use puts great pressure on the rural environment and ecology. Because rural residents and industries depend mainly on the direct use of biomass for energy, poor efficiency and rising energy demand have led to a series of rural environmental problems. As a national 1979 survey revealed, the use of firewood and crop straw to provide energy for everyday life and agricultural products had reached more than 600 million tons annually. For example, energy users relied on gathering and cutting to plunder some $30\%\sim40\%$ of the $240\sim260$ million tons of firewood used that year, which led to severe soil erosion, a loss of soil fertility, and desertification (Wang, Gao, 2003).

Since the reform and opening-up in 1978, commercial energy consumption, including the use of fossil fuel, in China's rural areas has been rising along with farmers' income. And growing fossil fuel use has substantially increased all kinds of pollutant discharges in countryside, including sulfur dioxide (SO_2), nitrogen oxide (NO_x), dust, smoke, and solid wastes. Because energy use is scattered throughout rural areas and reuse of energy byproducts is lagging, producers and households release wastes and pollutants directly into the environment, without any treatment. For example, pollutants from indoor burning of coal and crop straw for cooking and heating are exhausted directly into the air, and residues such as coal-fired waste pile up in more populous areas.

On the other hand, the construction of new and renewable energy sources in rural regions could promote more effective use of agricultural wastes, such as livestock manure and crop straw, playing a pivotal role in improving the rural environment and accelerating rural sustainable development. To encourage that outcome, the nation must create economic incentives and regulatory structures that reward developers and consumers of new renewable energy supplies and curb rural pollution and damage to human health and the environment.

2. 1. 3　Rural Energy Use and Climate Change

With the rapid growth of the rural economy and rising rural living standards, rural energy consumption is becoming linked with the need to address global climate change by reducing greenhouse gas (GHG) emissions.

Chinese farmers have long relied on traditional cookers with a thermal efficiency of less than 10% for household use, which have wasted a great deal of straw, wood, and coal. These forms of energy have also brought energy shortages and greenhouse gas emissions in rural areas. Because of China's dual development structure, which differentiates between urban and rural areas, living standards are much higher in urban areas than in rural areas, as are per capita energy consumption and carbon emissions. However, that means that the transformation of rural society will spur much higher rural energy consumption, and thus GHG emissions (Zhao, 2003)

Fortunately, new and renewable energy resources that replace conventional sources can improve the efficiency of rural energy use and reduce GHG emissions. From 1990 to 2000, China promoted the development and use of more than 10 kinds of renewable energy technologies in rural areas, including biogas and wind. The use of these technologies prevented the release of 158. 72 million tons of carbon dioxide (CO_2) and 231 000tons of methane (CH_4) emissions (Wang et al, 2002).

If China vigorously accelerates the use of methane and other forms of efficient biomass-based energy, as well as wind, solar, geothermal and ocean energy, and also encourages afforestation, it can prevent the release of 100 million tons of CO_2 and sequester 50 million tons of carbon by 2010 (Zhu, 2007). (Forestation is one of the best ways to increase carbon sequestration—or the storing of carbon in biomass and soil.) Given the diversity and size of China's rural population, the nation can pursue these goals most effectively by providing economic incentives to suppliers and consumers of these energy sources.

2. 2 The Evolution of Policies on Rural Energy, Environment, and Climatic Change

China is now in an important historical period, as it aims to build a well-off society in an all-round way. The need to tackle the global financial crisis, build a new socialist countryside, create an ecological civilization, and fight climate change provide an unprecedented opportunity to accelerate rural energy construction while improving the rural environment and ecology. However, this opportunity also presents new challenges. China has developed several policies to address these challenges.

2. 2. 1 Tackling the Global Financial Crisis

The financial crisis triggered by America's subprime mortgage meltdown reverberated around the world in 2008. As an organic part of the global economy, China's economy has been hit hard by this financial crisis, and domestic uncertainties have grown.

For example, the economic crisis directly affects China's countryside and farmers. Because of a sharp drop in exports, some domestic industries have too much capacity, and some enterprises have had trouble remaining in operation. As a result, millions of migrant workers have flocked home, which affects farmers' income and rural stability. Many farmers, too, have lost jobs.

The financial crisis may also slow the growth of government revenues at all levels and curb agriculture-related expenditures, rural infrastructure construction, and supplies of rural public goods. Thus the large gap between urban and rural development could widen, and rural pollution could worsen.

However, China's core response to the financial crisis has been to expand domestic demand, and rural areas have much potential in that regard. Therefore, in the current national and international economic climate, rural China also has great development opportunities. In 2008, for example, under dual pressure from the global financial crisis and serious natural disasters at home, the Chinese government adopted positive coping strategies such as expanding investment in "agriculture, countryside and farmers" and the construction of an ecological civilization. This approach has proven effective in stimulating domestic demand and sustaining economic development.

In 2008, for example, government spending rose by 1000 billion Yuan RMB, with the funds invested mainly in livelihood projects, infrastructure, the construction of an ecological environment, and post-disaster reconstruction. This spending, in turn, stimulated a total investment of 4000 billion Yuan RMB. Of that amount, 370 billion Yuan has been used for rural infrastructure construction and livelihood projects, such as the provision of water supplies, electricity, roads, gas, and homes; 210 billion Yuan for energy-saving and emission-reduction projects as well as ecological engineering; and 1000 billion Yuan for post-disaster reconstruction. At the same time, to raise consumption in rural areas, the Ministry of Finance and the Ministry of Commerce issued the Action Program for Promoting Home Appliances to the Countryside, which entailed providing direct subsidies to help farmers buy household electrical appliances.

These important policies will exert far-reaching influence on rural energy use and emissions, helping to improve the environment and enabling rural areas to adapt to climate change. However, the government needs to supplement these efforts with new energy and environmental pricing policies that encourage the development of clean renewable energy supplies and reduce GHG and other emissions.

2.2.2 Building a New Socialist Countryside

To prevent growing polarization between rich and poor and the widening gap between urban and rural areas in China—as well as the wider gap between East and West—and also to ensure long-term economic stability, the Chinese Communist Party released requirements for building the new socialist countryside at the Fifth Plenary Session of the Sixteenth Central Committee in 2005. These requirements included "developed production, better-off life, civilized village culture, clean and tidy countryside, democratic management." These measures will prove important in strengthening agriculture, rural areas, and farmers, and in vigorously promoting construction of a well-off society in an all-around way through modernization and construction.

The development of new sources of rural energy is an important component of the effort to build a new socialist countryside. Using economic incentives and market pricing, such development can ensure a thriving rural economy, raise farmers' income and help transform their lifestyle, promote the reuse of resources, improve the rural environment, and integrate urban and rural economic and social development.

2. 2. 3   Building an Ecological Civilization

The 17th Congress of the Chinese Communist Party regards the construction of an ecological civilization as its primary development strategy. In the Report of the 17th National Party Congress, President Hu Jintao pointed out that one way to realize the goal of constructing a well-off society in an all-round way by 2020 is by establishing an energy-efficient and environmentally friendly industrial structure, and growth and consumption pattern. China's recycling economy has since seen a large-scale increase, and renewable energy now accounts for a considerable proportion of total energy consumption. This initiative aims to bring the discharge of major pollutants under effective control, thus improving the nation's environment and firmly establishing the notion of ecological civilization throughout Chinese society.

With the continuous development of the rural economy, ecological and environmental problems are becoming more obvious. Because of the lack of effective regulatory structures and energy and environmental pricing systems, agricultural wastes are not being effectively used, farms and households are discharging large amounts of chemical fertilizers, pesticides, and other pollutants, household garbage and industrial wastes from township enterprises are accumulating, and air and water quality is deteriorating. The construction of a rural ecological civilization is an important measure for sustainably developing agriculture and ensuring that farmers have a rich, healthy, and happy material and spiritual life. It is also a way to solve the "three rural issues."

Indeed, the goal of building an ecological civilization is spawning new development ideas. These emphasize the application of market pricing and regulatory structures to comprehensively address energy construction, environmental protection, and building the capacity of the Chinese countryside to mitigate and adapt to climate change.

2.2.4 Controlling Greenhouse Gas Emissions and Adapting to Climate Change

Climate change presents human society with a huge challenge. Although some uncertainties in the science of global warming still exist, nearly every country has resolved to take active steps to reduce greenhouse gas emissions while strengthening the ability of social and economic systems to adapt to climate change.

China has long been an active participant in formulating and executing international policies related to global climate change. In 2007 the Chinese government issued a national action plan to respond to global warming. This plan proposed that, by 2010:

- Energy consumption per unit of GDP will fall by 20% from 2005 levels.
- The discharge of major pollutant will decline by 10%.
- Renewable energy, including large hydropower, will account for more than 10% of the nation's primary energy supply.
- Forests will cover 20% of the nation's area, storing some 50 million additional tons of carbon dioxide.

To achieve those goals, the nation must pursue large-scale changes in its economic structure, energy system, and consumption patterns. Those shifts, in turn, will create opportunities for rural economic development and revolutionize agricultural production, the development and use of rural energy, waste disposal, and rural environmental protection. To achieve those goals, the nation will need to vigorously develop renewable energy, strengthen the comprehensive processing and use of agricultural and other rural waste, and continue to pursue carbon sequestration, such as by planting forests.

Of course, global climate change means that extreme weather events such as floods and droughts are becoming more frequent and ferocious, undermining the stability of agricultural production and threatening rural sustainable development. China must therefore strengthen the ability of its agriculture and countryside to adapt to climate change, to ensure steady development of agricultural production and a sound rural ecology. Toward that end, the nation must provide economic rewards to encourage farmers to adopt agricultural practices and technologies that can both mitigate and withstand climate change.

3 Trends and Challenges in Rural Energy Use

Since the reform and opening-up, under the nation's diversified development policy and in light of local conditions, China has developed rural renewable energy resources to produce heat and power, such as marsh gas systems, straw briquettes, small hydropower stations, wind energy, and solar energy. The nation has also reformed rural power grids, improved the energy efficiency of rural production and everyday life, and brought power to 30 million people in far-flung areas (Luo, Zhang, 2008). At the same time, with the vigorous support and coordination of the UN Development Programme (UNDP) and other international organizations, the nation has successfully completed several projects designed to address energy shortages in remote mountainous regions and areas with ethnic minorities and impoverished populations[①], thereby helping to relieve rural poverty.

However, China is a huge agricultural country with a rural population of nearly 800 million, and investment and overall planning in the rural energy system continue to lag behind those in urbanized regions. These longstanding problems also mean that energy demand will grow more strongly in rural areas than in urban regions for quite some time, and that relying on conventional sources to supply enough energy for rural economic and social development will be difficult. If new energy and environmental pricing and regulatory structures do not solve these problems, they will seriously undermine the nation's ability to improve farmers' quality of life, sustainably develop the rural economy, and ensure social stability.

3.1 The Current Situation

3.1.1 Total Rural Energy Consumption

China's rural economy has developed rapidly since the reform and opening-up. And that development has brought huge changes in the quantity, structure, and sources of rural energy use.

Total rural energy consumption—including that used for both production and everyday life—tripled over the past decades, from 328 million tons of coal equivalent in 1980 to 956. 5

---

① These efforts include the Brightness Program, Upgrading of Rural Power Grids, Rural Hydropower, and Electrification and Power Transmission to the Countryside.

million tons of coal equivalent in 2006. The proportion of rural energy used for agricultural production also increased steeply, from 20. 4% in 1980 to 47. 6% in 2006.

Driven by national agricultural policy, the per capita income and living standards of rural residents have dramatically increased, and household energy consumption has also increased commensurately (Table 3. 1).

Table 3. 1   Rural energy consumption for household needs and production, 2000~2005

Year	Energy used for rural production, in mtce	Percent of total	Energy used by rural households, in mtce	Percent of total
2000	3. 0048	44. 8	3. 6999	55. 2
2001	3. 1175	42. 9	4. 1428	57. 1
2002	3. 2933	42. 1	4. 5347	57. 9
2003	3. 5037	43. 2	4. 6127	56. 8
2004	3. 5965	42. 9	4. 7932	57. 1
2005	3. 8286	44. 0	4. 8397	56. 0

Source: Ministry of Agriculture.

Note: mtce=million tons of coal equivalent.

China's rural energy supply includes both noncommercial sources such as straw, wood, animal waste, and domestic biogas, and commercial sources such as electricity, coal, oil, natural gas, and coal gas. The proportion of total rural consumption accounted for by commercial supplies rose dramatically, from 30% in 1980 to 67. 3% in 2006 (Table 3. 2 and Figure 3. 1). As in the rest of the country, coal accounts for two-thirds of this supply. Consumption of noncommercial energy sources remained largely stable, fluctuating only slightly from year to year.

Table 3. 2   Rural energy consumption, 1991 and 2004

Item	Consumption of 1991 in mtce	Consumption of 2004 in mtce
Total energy consumption	568. 22	838. 79
Energy used for household needs	360. 04	479. 32
Straw	162. 13	145. 80
Firewood	103. 03	120. 43
Coal	77. 52	162. 83
Electricity	11. 63	29. 34
Petroleum products	1. 33	11. 36
Methane	—	3. 99
Other	0. 0404	5. 67
Energy used for production	208. 18	359. 47
Coal	119. 96	191. 28
Petroleum products	38. 34	64. 15
Electricity	29. 26	56. 23
Firewood	20. 62	32. 76

Source: Department of Science and Technology Education of the Ministry of Agriculture.

Note: "Other" includes liquid petroleum gas, coal gas, and other sources such as solar water heaters.

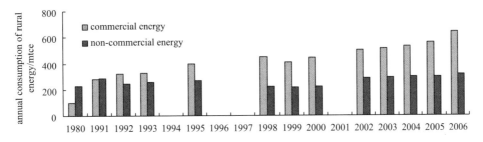

Figure 3.1　Annual consumption of rural energy, 1980~2006

In 1978, at the beginning of the reform and opening-up, rural consumption of electricity stood at just 25.31 billion kW·h. By 2004, annual electricity use had reached 393.3 billion kW·h—15.5 times the former (Figure 3.2). The annual growth rate of 11.2% exceeded GDP growth over that period.

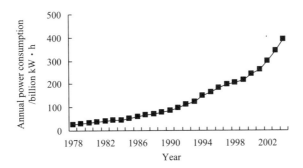

Figure 3.2　Rural electricity consumption, 1978~2004

As our comprehensive analysis of growth in power consumption revealed, the continuous development of the rural economy since 1978 is the main driver behind growing use of electricity. This growth stems from both larger-scale production among rural township enterprises and rising quality of life in rural areas, including growing use of household appliances. Residents of developed rural regions use more electricity than rural residents of more backward areas. In 2006, rural per capita income was positively correlated with domestic use of electricity in every province (Figure 3.3).

Indeed, as the economic structure in rural areas continues to change, energy consumption will move from a focus on irrigation, drainage, and lighting to the use of electrical appliances in industry and everyday life. In rural areas, the proportion of total energy use devoted to irrigation and drainage, sideline occupations, other production, township enterprises, and everyday life changed from 44.3%, 22.1%, 16.1%, and 17.5% in 1978 to 13.3%, 12%, 45.1%, and 24.2% in 2000. Thus the proportion of energy used for township enterprises and everyday life already exceeds that used for irrigation and drainage and sideline occupations.

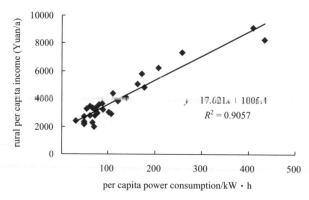

Figure 3. 3   Annual rural per capita income and household electricity use

Coal and electricity account the largest percentages of energy used for production. But use of petroleum products has grown at the highest rate, increasing eightfold from 1991 to 2004. Urban forms of energy such as liquefied petroleum gas (LPG) have become part of rural energy consumption (Figure 3. 4).

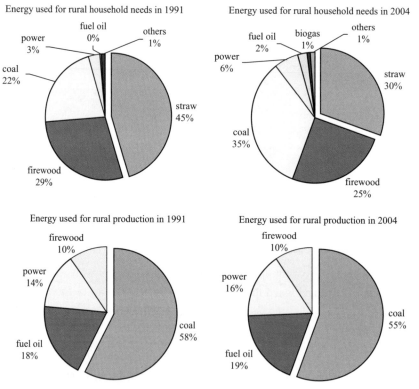

Figure 3. 4   Structural changes in energy used for rural production and household needs, 1991 and 2004
Source: Department of Science and Techology Education of the Ministry of Agriculture

In rural areas, straw and firewood account for 60% and 35% of noncommercial energy supplies respectively. Commercial energy supplies are based mainly on coal, which accounts for 62.6% of that sector. Electrical power provides 22.4% of commercially produced energy (Table 3.3).

Table 3.3 Energy end-use by rural households

Type	Amount	Reference quantity/tce	Per capita consumption	Percent
Commercial energy sources		80 151 000	110kgce	23.2
Coal	71 737 200tons	50 138 600	69kg	14.5
Electricity	145942000000kW·h	17 926 800	201kW·h	5.2
Petroleum products	3631200tons	5 327 900	5.0kg	1.5
LPG	3 787 100tons	6 492 200	5.2kg	1.9
Natural gas	161 000 000m³	215 700	0.2m³	0.1
Coal gas	173 000 000m³	49 800	0.2m³	0.0
Noncommercial energy sources		265 606 400	365kgce	76.8
Straw	339 975 200tons	159 788 300	467kg	46.2
Firewood	182 168 900tons	92 906 200	250kg	26.9
Methane	10 239 626 000m³	7 311 100	14.1m³	2.1
Solar energy	58 100 900m³	5 600 800	0.08m³	1.6
Total		345 757 400	475kgce	100

Note: tce=tons of coal equivalent. ce=coal equivalent.

Rural areas have seen rapid development in the use of renewable energy sources— including the use of biogas and other advanced forms of biomass—to satisfy growing energy demand. Waste from agricultural production and household garbage have also served as rural energy resources, easing environmental pressures, expanding the energy supply, reducing the use of commercial energy, and cutting household costs.

Traditional reliance on biomass energy is good for the energy cycle, but direct burning is inefficient and hostile to the environment, and does not help improve living standards. Thus the old ways of producing energy become insufficient as rural incomes rise (Table 3.4). Coal, meanwhile, is relatively cheap and easily accessible, and coal ovens are easy to use. The result is rising reliance on commercial energy such as coal. However, this leads to even higher levels of ambient pollution and more burdens on the rural environment.

Table 3.4 Comparison of coal and traditional rural energy sources

Item	Coal	Crop straw and firewood
Consumption costs	Must be purchased with cash at higher cost than traditional energy sources, but cheaper than other high-quality commercial sources.	Noncommercial sources composed mainly of agricultural waste from scattered locations—can be obtained without cash. Costs stem from the need to collect, transport, and store the biomass.
Attributes	Relatively convenient and efficient.	Traditional burning is low efficiency, resulting in poor sanitation of inhabited areas.
Greenhouse gas emissions	High CO_2 emissions.	Low CO_2 emissions; minimum methane emissions.

Item	Coal	Crop straw and firewood
Pollutants	High emission.	Direct burning has produced serious indoor air pollution.
Solid waste	Large volumes with no other uses and high disposal costs, so most have been directly abandoned, creating environmental problems in rural residential areas.	Plant ash that can be used as fertilizer.
Recycling of materials		Circulates materials through the agricultural production process.

Consumption of fossil fuels such as coal spells a great threat to the rural environment. That is especially true in northern China, where residents have begun to depend largely on coal rather than crop straw and firewood to provide heat in winter. The solid wastes from burning coal are unfit for any use, and rural areas cannot process these solid wastes centrally. The efficiency of coal burning is also far lower in rural areas than in urban areas, while CO_2 emissions per unit of caloric value are much higher.

3. 1. 2   Rural Energy Consumption for Household Needs

China's countryside and small-scale peasant economy have long been largely self-sufficient. Noncommercial sources—especially biomass resources such as straw and firewood—have therefore dominated rural energy consumption, especially household consumption. Rural household energy use depends heavily on inferior, low-efficiency sources, such as straw, wood, and coal. These noncommercial energy resources are usually burned directly, and used mainly for cooking and for heat in winter.

At the beginning of the reform and opening-up, noncommercial energy supplies accounted for more than 85% of rural household consumption. However, with economic development and the transformation of rural lifestyles, the proportion of household energy use stemming from noncommercial sources has been in protracted decline (although it has remained steady since 2000) (Figure 3. 5).

From 1995 to 2007, rural household energy use fluctuated, as did the sources of this energy (Figure 3. 6). For example, the consumption of wood and coal for household use fell 10. 7% and 7. 2%, respectively. However, the consumption of straw rose 5. 9%, electric power 241%, petroleum products 343%, methane 575%, solar energy 865%, and liquefied petroleum gas 1246% (Figure 3. 6). The use of natural gas for household needs—concentrated in villages near big cities such as Beijing and Shanghai—also grew rapidly from near zero. Still, the contribution of high-quality resources to rural energy household use remains low.

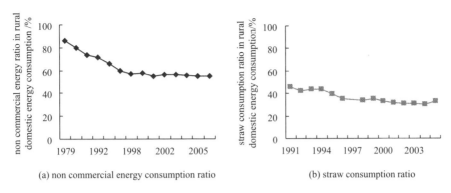

(a) non commercial energy consumption ratio   (b) straw consumption ratio

Figure 3.5　Rural household energy use from noncommercial supplies, and from straw

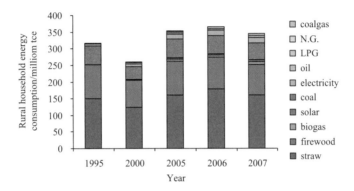

Figure 3.6　Total volume of rural household energy consumption, 1995~2007

During this period, the per capita use of commercial energy for household needs grew 3.4% (Figure 3.7), while the use of noncommercial energy supplies rose 1.8%.

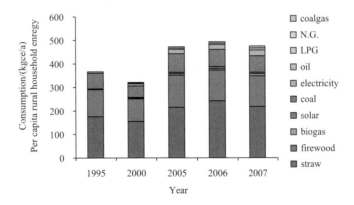

Figure 3.7　Per capita rural household energy consumption, 1995~2007

The level and structure of household energy use vary regionally, reflecting each area's level of economic development, resources, climate, and living habits. Both total household consumption and per capita household consumption are higher in western areas of China, for example, than in central and eastern areas (Table 3.5). The proportion of household energy from noncommercial sources is also far higher in the West than in the East. Low efficiency is the main factor that makes the per capita domestic energy consumption in the west above the national average.

Table 3.5 Rural household energy use in different regions, 2007

Region	Total energy consump-tion for household needs/tce	Per capita /kgce	Noncommercial energy Amount /tce	Noncommercial energy Per capita /kgce	Noncommercial energy Percent /%	Commercial energy Amount /tce	Commercial energy Per capita /kgce	Commercial energy Percent /%
China	34 575 700	475	265 606 000	365	76.8	80 151 000	110	23.2
Eastern China	107 095 000	463	75 976 000	329	71.1	31 119 000	135	29.5
Central China	113 542 000	465	89 222 000	365	78.5	24 320 000	100	21.5
Western China	125 120 000	547	100 408 000	439	80.3	24 712 000	108	19.7

Note: tce=tons of coal equivalent. ce=coal equivalent.

1. Commercial sources include coal, electricity, petroleum products, LPG, natural gas, and coal gas. Noncommercial sources include straw, firewood, methane, and solar energy.

2. Eastern China includes Beijing, Tianjin, Hebei, Liaoning, Shanghai, Jiangsu, Zhejiang, Fujian, Shandong, Guangdong and Hainan. Central China includes Shanxi, Anhui, Jiangxi, Henan, Hubei, Hunan, Jilin, and Heilongjiang. Western China includes Chongqing, Sichuan, Guizhou, Tibet, Gansu, Qinghai, Ningxia, Xinjiang, Shaanxi, Yunnan, Inner Mongolia, and Guangxi.

China's rural regions have seen uneven development in per capita power consumption for everyday life, with levels in the East high and those in the West low. For example, in 2006, per capita consumption in rural areas around Beijing reached 434.38 kW • h, while consumption around Shanghai reached 408.59 kW • h, and topped 100 kW • h in Tianjin, Fujian and Zhejiang, Jiangsu, Guangdong and Liaoning, Hebei, Shandong, Chongqing, and Sichuan—all in the East. However, in the western areas of Xinjiang, Gansu, Qinghai, Yunnan, and Tibet, per capita annual consumption remained below 50 kW • h (Figure 3.8).

Household energy use has become more diversified and commercialized in more developed rural areas. For example, in the developed areas of East China, higher-quality energy sources such electricity and LPG account for a larger proportion of household energy use, dramatically improving the efficiency of energy use.

The use of straw and firewood is higher—and the use of electricity, petroleum products, and liquefied petroleum gas far lower—in the West than in central and eastern areas. Domestic biogas is relatively well-developed in the West, having reached 16% of rural households (Figure 3.9). Eastern area, in contrast, use higher percentages of solar energy: some 16% of households in that region have solar water heaters.

As noted, local resources are a major determinant of rural household energy use. Agricultural areas tend to use straw, mountain and forest districts use firewood,

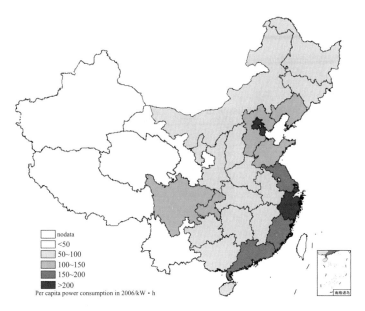

Figure 3. 8　Per capita rural power consumption for everyday life, 2006

Source: Survey of China's rural residents, 2007.

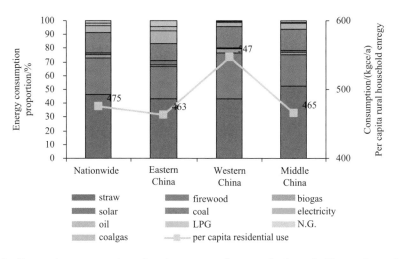

Figure 3. 9　Per capita consumption of various types of energy for household use, by region, 2007

pastoral areas rely mainly on animal excrement, and coal production areas prefer coal. Thus, central regions have a bias toward straw, while western regions rely on firewood. In central and western regions, where coal resources are cheap and abundant, coal also accounts for a significant share of rural household energy use.

　　Because of both climate and living habits, western regions need heat for long periods in winter. Thus the per capita consumption of biomass for rural household needs is also significantly higher in this region than in central and eastern areas (Figures 3. 10~ 3. 12).

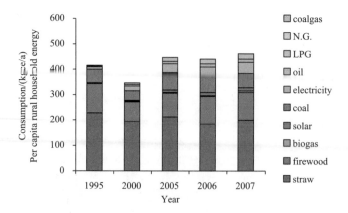

Figure 3. 10　Rural per capita energy use for household needs in eastern China，1995～2007

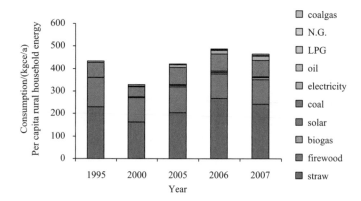

Figure 3. 11　Rural per capita energy use for household needs in central China，1995～2007

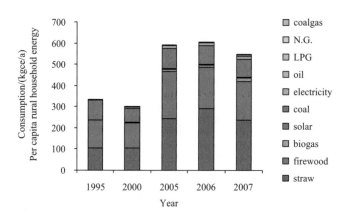

Figure 3. 12　Rural per capita energy use for household needs in western China，1995～ 2007

Energy use also varies by province. Straw consumption was highest in North China, Sichuan, Chongqing, and Heilongjiang because these regions are major grain-producing areas (Figure 3.13). The Tibetan Autonomous Region had the lowest straw consumption, at just 103 400tce, while the area with the highest straw consumption is Sichuan Province, where consumption was 21 232 100tce.

The Tibetan Autonomous Region also posted the lowest levels of firewood consumption, at 112 200tce. In Guizhou province, in contrast, firewood consumption reached 10 568 100tce. Firewood consumption is higher in southwest China, including Sichuan, Guizhou, Yunnan, Guangxi, and Guangdong, because those areas benefit from extensive land resources.

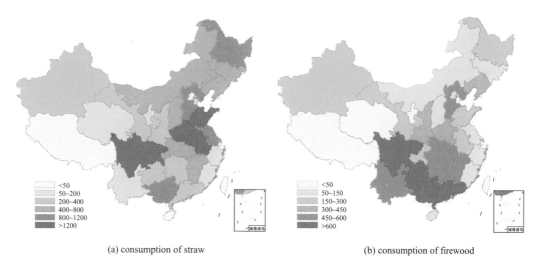

(a) consumption of straw   (b) consumption of firewood

Figure 3.13   Straw and firewood consumption, by province, 2006
Source: *China Energy Statistics Yearbook* 2007.

3.1.3   Rural Energy Consumption for Production

The rural economy consists of two key components. One is agricultural production, which includes agriculture, forestry, animal husbandry, and fisheries. The other is township enterprises—businesses run by rural residents.

Total output of agriculture, forestry, animal husbandry, and fisheries rose from 1251.3 billion Yuan in 1995 to 1902.8 billion Yuan in 2006 (in 2000 prices), with an annual increase of 3.8%.

The value added by township enterprises rose from 1440.5 billion Yuan in 1995 to 5118.4 billion Yuan in 2006 (in 2000 prices), with yearly growth of 11.5%. By the end of 2006, this added value accounted for 29.2% of the country's GDP. ①

End-use energy consumption for rural production reached 380.98 mtce in 2007. ②Commercial sources provided most of this energy, including coal (62.4%), petroleum products (17.3%), coke (5.9%), and electricity (5.4%) (Table 3.6).

Township enterprises are major energy users, accounting for 84.5% of all energy consumed for rural production in 2007. Coal provides 68.8% of the energy used by these enterprises, while petroleum products supply 11.0%.

Table 3.6   Energy used for rural production, 2007

Item	Total energy used for production/tce	Percent of total/%	agriculture, forestry, animal husbandry, and fisheries/tce	Percent /%	township enterprises/tce	Percent of total/%
			Amount used by			
Coal	237 882 000	62.4	16 880 000	27.8	221 454 000	68.8
Coke	22 299 000	5.9	794 000	1.3	21 526 000	6.7
Petroleum products	65 812 000	17.3	31 092 000	51.1	35 550 000	11.0
Electricity	20 473 000	5.4	12 031 000	19.8	8 763 000	2.7
Straw	34 516 000	9.0		0	34 516 000	10.7
Total	380 982 000	100	60 797 000	100	321 809 000	100

Source: Calculated by the authors from *National Rural Renewable Energy Statistics*, 2008, and *China Energy Statistics Yearbook*, 2008.

Annual growth in energy demand from 1995 to 2006 averaged 4.1%—higher than the growth in output during those years. Meanwhile demand for petroleum products and electricity rose 5% annually. These changes are mostly due to spreading mechanization, which has driven huge demand for oil and electricity. By the end of 2007, total rural electricity consumption had reached 766 million kW.

From 1995 to 2007, end-use energy consumption in agriculture, forestry, animal husbandry, and fisheries rose steadily, at an annual rate of 4.1%. That growth stemmed mainly from rising use of petroleum products and electricity, whose growth rates topped 5% (Figure 3.14).

---

① Though many township enterprises have become highly urbanized and industrialized, the nation still includes the value they create in the rural economy, and these enterprises must account for a large part of the total rural energy consumption. However, in the next 20 years, they will continue to industrialize and urbanize, so their energy use will disappear from the scope of rural energy consumption. We will therefore not address their energy demand while examining rural energy needs.

② At present, information on rural energy use is scattered throughout the *China Energy Statistics Yearbook*, published by the National State Bureau, and the *China Rural Energy Statistics Yearbook* and the *National Rural Renewable Energy Statistics*, published by the Department of Science and Technology Education of the Ministry of Agriculture. These bureaus use different criteria for defining and calculating primary energy sources. And some of the data are incongruous. In particular, information on the end-use energy consumption of rural enterprises cannot reflect their actual energy use, structure, or efficiency.

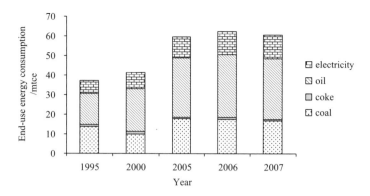

Figure 3.14　End-use energy consumption in agriculture, forestry, animal husbandry,
and fisheries, 1995~2007

The intensity of end-use energy consumption in agricultural production rose, given growing mechanization, from 29.8tce in 1995 to 32.8tce in 2006 (Figure 3.15), posting an annual growth rate of 0.9%.

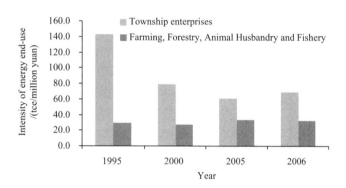

Figure 3.15　Intensity of energy end-use by township enterprises and agriculture, forestry,
animal husbandry, and fisheries, 1995~2007

From 1995 to 2007, end-use energy consumption by China's township enterprises rose sharply, posting an annual growth rate of 5.0%, although energy use fell by 9.2% from 2006 to 2007 (Figure 3.16). Coal occupied first place in supplying these incremental needs, followed by firewood, petroleum products, and coke.

In contrast to the agricultural sector, the energy intensity of China's township enterprises declined steadily, to 69.3tce—below that for the nation's industrial enterprises as a whole (148.3tce). However, official figures underestimate the energy intensity of township enterprises, as those figures include the output from these enterprises but not their energy use as part of the rural economy.

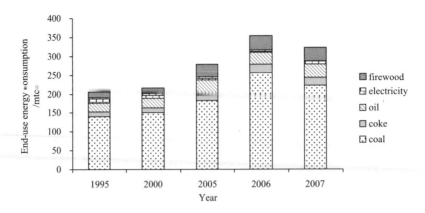

Figure 3.16   End-use energy consumption by township enterprises, 1995~2007

3.2   Problems with Rural Energy Consumption

As rural energy consumption has risen and its structure has changed, problems have become more evident. The heating efficiency of traditional straw and firewood is only 10%~15%, and the efficiency of family stoves is about 20%. In 2006, more than 50% of peasant households in North China used adobe kang and indigenous heaters with a heating efficiency of about 40%. Thus a great deal of rural energy ends up as waste. And most areas simply store energy residues and household garbage in open inner yards or nearby areas, without any treatment.

As noted, the consumption of commercial energy, especially coal, has caused severe environmental problems. Burning coal produces huge quantities of waste. The average ash content of China's coal is as high as 23%, and rural residents use poor-quality coal whose ash content may be even higher than the national average. Honeycomb briquettes—which usually consist of 40% clay added to straw, and thus also have low combustion efficiency—have also been widely used in the countryside. Burning these generates the same amount of solid waste as burning coal, per ton of coal equivalent.

Because rural residents usually burn coal indoors, they face serious indoor air problems from total suspended particles (TSP), sulfur dioxide (SO_2), carbon monoxide (CO), and other pollutants (Li et al, 2006). In some areas where fluorine content exceeds government standards, coal-burning fluorosis remains serious (Li et al, 2002). Directly burning conventional fuels such as straw and firewood can also result in environmental problems, mainly from TSP, SO_2, methane (CH_4), and nitrogen oxide (NO_x) (Wang, Feng, 2004).

The development of cleaner sources of rural energy has suffered from a dearth of long-term financial support. Development of rural renewable energy for the countryside, in particular, relies heavily on government funding. And the gap between government funding and the need for new sources of rural energy is widening day by day.

For example, the central government spends 1 billion Yuan annually to build biogas (methane) digesters in the countryside. However, these funds can supply only 1 million families yearly with such units—just a fraction of demand.

The lack of start-up capital has greatly restricted the development and use of such renewable energy supplies. A small, standard biogas unit built according to specifications costs about 1600 Yuan, including materials and professional wages. Of that amount, the government has agreed to provide 1200 Yuan, with peasants themselves paying 400 Yuan. However, the central government pays just 360 Yuan initially—awarding the rest only after a completed project passes inspection. A peasant household must therefore initially invest 1240 Yuan to build one methane pool. Many poor households must therefore abandon construction despite public subsidies.

Farmers' difficulty in obtaining loans is another important brake on the construction of rural renewable energy supplies. Under collective land ownership, peasants cannot get credit, because they cannot put land or homes into market circulation. Because peasants cannot find a guarantor or have no proper mortgage, most cannot get financial support for expanding their energy supplies.

3.3　Supplying Future Rural Energy Demand

China's economic goal is to reach the level of moderately developed countries by 2050. Because the rural population accounts for 70% of the total population, the country cannot modernize unless the countryside also modernizes. The history of developed nations suggests that rural energy consumption rises with social productivity. Thus, as China's rural economy continues to grow by leaps and bounds over the next 10 years, a rapid increase in rural energy consumption seems inevitable (Zhao, 2003).

Rural energy demand reflects the size of the rural population, the level of a region's economic development, income levels and living standards, the price of energy, and levels of energy efficiency. China's current economic development strategies and rural energy policies suggest that these factors affecting rural energy consumption will undergo significant changes.

3.3.1　Rural Population

The major contributors to the size of the rural population are its natural growth rate and the rate of urbanization. In China, urbanization occurs at a higher rate than natural population growth. That means the rural population is shrinking. In 2010, China expects to have a rural population of 700 million, accounting for 51% of the total population. By 2020, those numbers will fall to 610 million and 42%, respectively. By 2030, the rural population will decline by another 530 million, while still accounting for 36% of the total.

Still, although the rural population is shrinking, the nation must meet its growing demand for energy.

3.3.2   Income Levels, Living Standards, and Energy Pricing

The higher rural residents' incomes, the higher their requirements for energy that provides "comfort, convenience, and cleanliness" (Lu et al., 2006). Thus energy consumption interacts closely with income levels.

The net income of rural households soared from 2253 Yuan in 2000 to 4140 Yuan in 2007, to be more exact, income in eastern, areas rose from 3137 to 5626 Yuan, in middle areas from 2017 to 3878 Yuan, and in western areas from 1685 to 3033 Yuan. Rising income levels give rural families an incentive to buy more electric appliances, vehicles, and farm equipment, to help them move away from manual farming. That, in turn, raises energy demand.

Under the national goal of building a well-off society in an all-around way, per capita net income of China's peasants will keeping growing at an annual rate of 5%~6% over the next two decades. A moderately prosperous society in all respects means not only higher living standards but also a cleaner environment, because these changes will spur demand for commercialized, high-quality energy, and people will gradually abandon their traditional approach to using biomass. The structure and trend of energy prices will help determine overall energy demand, as will the types and quality of energy production and consumption.

3.3.3   National Policies on Rural Energy Use

Since 2000, given continuous economic growth and the accumulation of national wealth, China has underwritten the construction and management of the energy industry. The national government has also emphasized the exploration of renewable resources to supply rural energy, especially biomass, small hydropower plants, and small coalmines. Since 2000, efforts such as renovating the electricity system in rural areas, constructing new electricity facilities, and exploring new forms of energy such as marsh gas systems have boosted the rural energy industry.

Under the goal of balancing urban and rural development and constructing a new socialist countryside, the rural energy system will finally become a part of the nation's energy system. Rural areas will have equal opportunities to enjoy commercial energy services. Making good use of their natural renewable energy resources, in turn, will enable them to help ensure energy security, protect the environment, and mitigate global climate change. New energy and environmental pricing policies that encourage the development of clean renewable energy and reward cuts in emissions, including greenhouse gases, are essential to achieving these results.

3.3.4   Renewable Energy Resources in Rural Areas

Renewable energy resources—such as biomass, hydropower, wind power, solar power, and geothermal—are widely available in China's countryside. Biomass primarily consists of crop straw, twigs, animal waste, and energy crops.

The annual gains in grain yields and ratio of grain to straw suggests that crop straw resources can total 600 million tons. Some of this is used for soil fertilizer, livestock feed, and raw materials for making paper. However, some 300 million tons can be used to produce 150 million tons of energy.

Twigs and other waste from the lumber industry can total 900 million tons. Transforming just 300 million tons of that waste into energy would yield about 200 million tons.

The theoretic yield of marsh gas from animal waste is 70 billion m^3. Farmers could plant energy-supplying crops—including sugarcane, sorgum, cassava, sweet potato, Jatropha, Chinese pistache, and tung tree—on about 20 million hm^2. That could provide 50 million tons of organic liquid fuel equivalent to 70 mtce.

Together these biomass resources total about 600 mtce.

The economically exploitable installed capacity of small hydropower resources— with single stations ranging from 100 kW to 50 000 kW—is about 128 million kW. Some 90% of these exploitable resources occur in Hubei, Hunan, Guangdong, Guangxi, Henan, Zhejiang, Fujian, Jiangxi, Yunnan, Sichuang, Xinjiang, and Tibet.

China also has considerable wind energy resources, as it is favored by prevailing monsoons. In particular, southeastern coast and islands, Inner Mongolia, the Northwest, and some areas in the Northeast have abundant wind resources, with wind speeds above 3 meter per second for as many as 5000 hours each year.

Finally, most of China lies below north latitude 45°, so the nation enjoys abundant solar resources. Sunshine tops 2200 hours annually in Xinjiang, Tibet, Qinghai, Gansu, Inner Mongolia, Shanxi, and Hebei. In fact, solar energy is already well-developed in those areas, especially in the Northwest and Qinghai-Tibet.

3.3.5   A Plan for Meeting Growing Rural Energy Demand

To meet rural energy demand over the medium and long term, Deng Keyun and other researchers have designed a program to strengthen the development and use of renewable energy, based on the following assumptions:

- Rural energy demand has been growing faster than demand in urbanized areas, and will account for a growing proportion of national energy consumption.
- Modernizing China's agricultural production will require greater reliance on high-quality commercial energy sources.
- Rural industries can focus on improving energy efficiency, conserving energy, and reducing emissions while increasing their energy expenditures.

This work shows that—under a conventional scenario—rural energy demand will reach 1262. 48 mtce in 2010, 1574. 17 mtce in 2020, and 1993. 20 mtce in 2050. In an energy-intensive scenario, demand will be 6. 55 mtce higher in 2010, 3. 54 mtce higher in 2020, and 104. 82 mtce higher in 2050 (Table 3. 7).

Table 3. 7   Forecast of China's rural energy demand/mtce

Year	1995	2010	2020	2050
Conventional situation	689. 89	1262. 48	1574. 17	1993. 20
Energy-intensive situation	689. 89	1269. 03	1577. 71	2098. 02

We, too, analyzed rural energy demand and carbon emissions in 2010, 2020 and 2030, taking 2005 as the base year. We used qualitative and quantitative analysis of historical trends in population, income levels, grain yields, and the added value of agriculture, forestry, animal husbandry, and fisheries (Table 3. 8).

In this analysis, we considered industry restructuring and energy technology that may emerge in the next two or three decades, based on China's Long-Term Energy Alternative Plan (LEAP), as well as the impact of various social, economic, and environmental uncertainties on rural energy demand and greenhouse gas emissions. Our model then used this information to calculate future end-use energy demand of rural households and agricultural production under two scenarios: conventional, and intensive renewable energy (Tables 3. 9, Table 3. 10).

Table 3. 8   Rural population and income levels in 2005, 2010, 2020 and 2030

Item	Unit	2005	2010	2020	2030
Rural population	10 000people	74 544	70 695	62 997	55 298
Eastern China	10 000people	24 256	22 855	20 052	17 249
Western China	10 000people	24 179	23 162	21 127	19 092
Central China	10 000people	26 109	24 679	21 818	18 957
Annual per capita net income (in 2005 prices)					
China	Yuan	3255	4333	7375	12 032
Eastern China	Yuan	4523	5911	10 097	16 448
Western China	Yuan	2389	3197	5725	9780

Item	Unit	2005	2010	2020	2030
Middle China	Yuan	2977	3984	7135	12 187
Added value of agriculture, forestry, animal husbandry, and fisheries	100 million Yuan	23 070	28 069	41 548	61 502
Growth rate of agriculture, forestry, animal husbandry, and fisheries	Percent	4	4	4	4
Grain yield	10 000tons	48 402	50 871	56 193	62 073
Average annual growth rate in grain yield	Percent	1	1	1	1

Under the conventional scenario, with the mechanization and modernization of production, our model found that end-use energy consumption in China's agriculture, forestry, animal husbandry, and fisheries sectors will rise to 120 mtce—a lower level than that forecast (Deng et al, 2000). The proportion of coal in the energy mix will drop to 10%.

Given new rural construction and rising living standards—including larger homes—peasants will gradually increase their demand for energy for heating, cooling, boiling water, electrical appliances, and transportation, even as the average number of people per rural household declines.

Under our conventional scenario, traditional use of biomass for household energy needs will continue to drop, in both absolute quantity and proportion of total energy use. Some straw and firewood resources will be converted into more efficient forms of renewable energy, and the ratio of modern to traditional use of straw will reach 1 : 1 by 2030.

The contribution of small hydropower stations, small wind-powered electricity plants, methane, solar energy, and other modern forms of renewable energy has been rising to meet rural demand for high-quality energy for household use. With growing household use of modern sources of renewable and other high-quality energy, household coal consumption will continue to decline. Under the conventional scenario, some developed regions of the countryside will begin to use more natural gas and coal gas, but the contribution of those sources to rural energy consumption will remain negligible.

Table 3. 9   Rural energy demand for production and household use: Conventional scenario/mtce

Year	2005	2010	2020	2030
Energy used for agriculture, forestry, animal husbandry, and fisheries				
Coal	18.094	17.51	17.56	22.23
Coke	0.592	1.09	1.74	2.47
Petroleum products	30.249	35.43	53.06	67.92
Electricity	10.77	14.36	24.12	30.87
Subtotal of energy used for production	59.705	68.39	96.48	123.49
Energy used for household needs				

Year	2005	2010	2020	2030
Commercial energy	76. 013	88. 712	105. 657	117. 333
Coal	58. 141	57. 17	53. 90	47. 88
Electricity	9. 125	16. 29	28. 67	39. 94
Petroleum products	3. 776	6. 73	10. 48	13. 19
LPG	4. 905	8. 20	12. 05	15. 54
Natural gas	0. 032	0. 27	0. 47	0. 66
Coal gas	0. 034	0. 052	0. 087	0. 123
Traditional domestic biomass	262. 691	242. 99	194. 16	122. 61
Straw	159. 596	154. 07	119. 23	68. 75
Firewood	10 3. 095	88. 92	74. 93	53. 86
Modern renewable energy	13. 647	38. 92	83. 89	128. 75
Straw	0	10. 20	34. 22	60. 09
Firewood	0	6. 95	15. 77	21. 48
Small hydropower stations	4. 28	5. 65	8. 40	11. 14
Small wind-powered electricity	0. 28	0. 45	1. 17	3. 03
Methane	4. 927	8. 81	13. 30	17. 81
Solar energy	4. 16	6. 86	11. 03	15. 20
Subtotal of household energy consumption	352. 351	370. 622	383. 707	368. 693
Total rural energy use	412. 056	439. 012	480. 187	492. 183

Note: We assume that energy from rural small hydropower stations and small wind-powered electricity plants will be used only for local household consumption.

In the intensive renewable energy scenario, China can meet rural demand for high-quality energy through full and modernized use of renewable energy resources, which, as noted, are widely distributed throughout China's countryside. The development of small hydropower stations, small wind-powered electricity plants, methane, and solar energy will occur more quickly than in the conventional scenario. Biomass energy will see "skip-type" development, as modern use of straw and firewood replaces traditional biomass burning, with the ratio of modern to traditional biomass use reaching 2 : 1 by 2030 (Table 3. 10). Demand for coal will shrink even more than under the conventional scenario.

**Table 3. 10　Rural energy demand for production and household use:
Intensive renewable energy scenario/mtce**

Year	2005	2010	2020	2030
Energy used for agriculture, forestry, animal husbandry, and fisheries				
Coal	18. 094	17. 51	17. 56	22. 23
Coke	0. 592	1. 09	1. 74	2. 47
Petroleum product	30. 249	35. 43	53. 06	67. 92
Electricity	10. 77	14. 36	24. 12	30. 87
Subtotal of production energy consumption	59. 705	68. 39	96. 48	123. 49

Year	2005	2010	2020	2030
Energy used for household needs				
Commercial energy	76.013	85.522	97.187	97.113
Coal	58.141	54.50	47.57	31.77
Electricity	9.125	15.77	26.53	35.83
Petroleum products	3.776	6.73	10.48	13.19
LPG	4.905	8.20	12.05	15.54
Natural gas	0.032	0.27	0.47	0.66
Coal gas	0.034	0.052	0.087	0.123
Traditional domestic biomass	262.691	241.02	175.17	85.48
Straw	159.596	153.41	107.63	48.13
Firewood	103.095	87.61	67.65	37.35
Modern renewable energy	13.647	44.84	113.55	189.10
Straw	0	13.61	51.47	96.45
Firewood	0	7.72	20.20	31.14
Small hydropower stations	4.28	6.06	10.25	14.49
Small wind-powered electricity	0.28	0.56	1.46	3.79
Methane	4.927	9.80	18.12	26.43
Solar energy	4.16	7.09	12.05	16.80
Subtotal of domestic energy consumption	352.351	371.382	385.9107	371.693
Total rural energy use	412.056	439.772	482.387	495.183

Note: We assume that energy from rural small hydropower stations and small wind-powered electricity plants will be used only for local household consumption.

Our model shows that China's rural per capita use of energy for household needs will reach 700 kg of coal equivalent by 2030. However, as the rural population continues to decline, the amount of energy used for household needs will first rise slowly and then gradually drop. Incremental rural demand for energy for household needs will mainly be met through commercial sources from other areas. However, noncommercial energy sources—including traditional and modern forms of biomass as well as hydroelectric power, wind power, and solar energy—will remain the primary energy sources for household use.

4 The Environmental Effects of Rural Energy Use

Unlike traditional use of biomass energy sources, waste from the large-scale use of commercial energy—mainly fossil fuels, including coal and petroleum products—cannot be recycled. And unlike in urban areas, central treatment of these wastes is difficult because of the dispersed nature of rural energy use and backward rural infrastructure. Rural households also burn coal indoors, so the emissions of various pollutants cause serious indoor air pollution. If they are not addressed, these environment problems will constrain the development of the rural economy and society.

4. 1 The Environmental Impact of the Use of Commercial Energy

Since the reform and opening-up, the proportion of total rural energy use supplied by commercial sources, including coal, electricity, and petroleum products, is increasing. Coal is the primary commercial energy source. The pollutants emitted from coal combustion include sulfur dioxide (SO_2), nitrous oxide (NO_x), and solid wastes. The volume of these wastes is large because rural areas lack the needed control technology, especially compared with urban areas. Most coal combustion pollutants are therefore emitted directly into the rural environment, creating significant effects.

4. 1. 1 SO_2 Emissions from Rural Coal Combustion

SO_2 causes respiratory disease, and is the main cause of acid rain. Because China has large reserves of high-sulfur coal, operators of urban power plants that produce electricity from coal must use equipment to reduce SO_2 emissions. However, rural coal combustion rarely includes such equipment.

In Chinese inventories, the discharge of SO_2 is calculated as

$$SO_2 \text{ discharge} = \text{amount of coal consumption} \times f \qquad (4\text{-}1)$$

$$f = T \times S \times R \qquad (4\text{-}2)$$

f is the emission factor; T is the SO_2 conversion factor (2. 0); S is the average amount of sulfur in coal (1. 1%), and R is the non-desulfurization rate, which is equal to 1-desulfurization rate, The desulfurization rate is 0 in rural areas, so R is 1 in formula.

In 2004, China rural coal consumption produced 10. 91 million tons of SO_2, with agricultural production accounting for 5. 89 million tons of that amount, and household use accounting for 5. 02 million tons (Table 4. 1) (Yu et al, 2008). Rural coal consumption has produced growing amounts of SO_2. In 1980, SO_2 totaled just 2.01 million tons. By 2004 that amount had increased 4 times.

Table 4.1 SO_2 Emissions from Rural Coal Combustion, 1980~2004/million tons

Year	Emissions from Production	Emissions from Household Use	Total
1980	0.86	1.14	2.01
1991	3.47	2.39	5.86
1995	4.66	2.65	7.31
2000	4.94	3.64	8.58
2002	5.57	4.85	10.41
2004	5.89	5.02	10.91

Table 4.2 shows SO_2 emissions from household coal use in every province, based on SO_2 conversion factors confirmed the province.

Table 4.2 SO_2 from Coal Combustion by Rural Households, 2004*

Province	Household coal consumption/ million tons	SO_2 emission factor	SO_2 emissions/ million tons	Province	Household coal consumption/ million tons	SO_2 emission factor	SO_2 emissions/ million tons
Beijing	1.8953	0.0352	0.0667	Hubei	2.5482	0.0352	0.0897
Tianjin	0.3988	0.0318	0.0127	Hunan	2.10	0.0352	0.0739
Hebei	9.4709	0.0318	0.3012	Guangdong	0.4957	0.0352	0.0174
Shanxi	6.0042	0.0318	0.1909	Guangxi	0.0489	0.0352	0.0017
Inner Mongolia	3.9352	0.0188	0.0740	Hainan	0.00	0.0222	0.00
Liaoning	1.2067	0.0188	0.0227	Chongqing	1.7002	0.0352	0.0598
Jilin	0.6422	0.0222	0.0143	Sichuan	6.5761	0.0352	0.2315
Heilong Jiang	0.1838	0.0222	0.0041	Guizhou	9.4710	0.0352	0.3334
Shanghai	0.3913	0.0318	0.0124	Yunnan	3.3340	0.0222	0.0740
Jiangsu	0.4802	0.0318	0.0153	Shaanxi	1.2073	0.0188	0.0227
Zhejiang	0.1368	0.0318	0.0044	Gansu	3.1122	0.0188	0.0585
Anhui	2.51	0.0318	0.0798	Qinghai	0.6140	0.0318	0.0195
Fujian	0.4668	0.0352	0.0164	Ningxia	0.65	0.0188	0.0122
Jiangxi	1.6256	0.0352	0.0572	Xinjiang	3.35	0.0188	0.0630
Shandong	2.20	0.0318	0.07	Tibet	—	—	—
Henan	5.1050	0.0352	0.1797				

* Missing Hong Kong, Macao and Taiwan data.

Differences in SO_2 emissions reflect differences in the level of coal consumption (Figure 4.1). Because rural residents of coal-producing areas can get coal more easily and cheaply, those areas—which include Hebei, Shanxi, Henan, Sichuan, and Guizhou Provinces—have high coal consumption and high SO_2 emissions.

The highest per capita SO_2 emissions occur in Beijing, where they reached 26.47 kg in 2004, while the second-highest per capita emissions occur in Guizhou (12.24 kg).

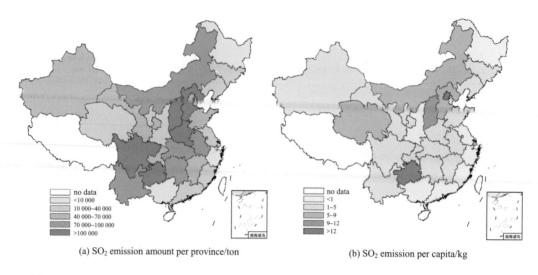

<table>
<tr><td></td><td>no data</td></tr>
<tr><td></td><td><10 000</td></tr>
<tr><td></td><td>10 000~40 000</td></tr>
<tr><td></td><td>40 000~70 000</td></tr>
<tr><td></td><td>70 000~100 000</td></tr>
<tr><td></td><td>>100 000</td></tr>
</table>

	no data
	<1
	1~5
	5~9
	9~12
	>12

(a) SO_2 emission amount per province/ton   (b) SO_2 emission per capita/kg

Figure 4.1   Per Capita Coal Consumption and SO_2 Emissions for rural household needs, in 2004

4.1.2 NO_x and TSP Emissions from Rural Coal Burning

NO_x and total suspended particles (TSP) are primary pollutants from rural coal combustion. According to an analysis of different documents by Yu et al (2008), the NO_x emission factor is 1.88g/kg, while the TSP emission factor is 1.3g/kg.

According to this analysis, rural coal combustion released 932 000tons of NO_x and 644 400tons TSP in 2004, with agricultural production accounting for 503 400tons of NO_x and 348 100tons of TSP, and household use accounting for 428 600tons of NO_x and 296 300tons of TSP (Table 4.3).

Table 4.3 NO_x and TSP Emissions from Rural Coal Consumption, 1980~2004/ton

Year	NO_x emissions from production	NO_x emissions from household use	Total	TSP emissions From production	TSP emissions from household use	Total
1980	73 700	97 400	171 100	51 000	67 300	118 300
1991	296 500	204 200	500 700	205 000	141 200	346 200
1995	397 800	226 500	624 300	275 100	156 700	431 800
2000	422 200	310 800	733 000	292 000	214 900	506 900
2002	475 600	414 400	890 000	328 900	286 500	615 400
2004	503 400	428 600	932 000	348 100	296 300	644 400

Like SO_2 emissions, NO_x and TSP emissions from rural coal consumption are rising, with emissions from agricultural production growing more quickly than those from household use of coal. In 1980, NO_x and TSP emissions from rural coal consumption were just 171100tons and 118300tons, respectively, but those figures had quadrupled by 2004.

4.1.3 Solid Waste from Rural Coal Combustion

The large amount of solid waste from coal combustion includes non-flammable ash (Chinese coal averages an ash content of 23%) and carbon (the Chinese rural oxidation rate is about 80%, which means that 20% of the carbon in coal is not burned). Most of this waste from household use is discarded with other garbage, without any treatment. Piles of waste in rural settlements pollute the environment greatly (Figure 4.2).

Figure 4.2   In rural settlements, waste from household coal use piles up with other garbage

Total waste can be calculated as

solid castoff amount = coal consumption × average ash content + average carbon × non-oxidation rate   (4-3)

The results show that in 2004, solid wastes from rural consumption totaled 184.85 million tons, with agricultural production accounting for 99.85 million tons and household use accounting for 85 million tons (Table 4.4). Those wastes quintupled from 1980 to 2004.

Table 4.4   Solid Waste from Rural Coal Consumption, 1980~2004/million tons

Year	Waste from production	Waste from households	Total
1980	14.62	19.31	33.98
1991	58.80	40.49	99.29
1995	78.90	44.93	123.83
2000	83.74	61.63	145.37
2002	94.33	82.18	176.51
2004	99.85	85.00	184.85

These calculations do not include the coal in honeycomb briquettes and coal balls, which include clay. The amount of waste from the use of honeycomb briquettes is several times that from by the direct use of coal.

4.1.4 Other Pollutants from Rural Coal Combustion

Coal combustion also emits pollutants such as carbon monoxide (CO) and benzopyrene (BaP). People exposed to these substances for long periods may suffer from respiratory diseases and cancer, and their children often have birth defects.

Air pollution in areas with high coal consumption has a strong impact on public health, especially if people burn coal for cooking or winter heat. Air samples from households in Pingding and Taigu counties of Shanxi Province showed higher amounts of CO, SO_2, BaP in kitchens than in bedrooms and outdoors, and higher levels in winter than in summer. The most serious problem was BaP in kitchens and bedrooms in winter, with the maximum amount recorded 558 times higher than the regulatory limit (Li et al, 2006).

Coal combustion also causes fluorosis in many areas, especially in Southwest China. When the coal is burned, 50% of the fluorine content can become fluoride gas, contaminating indoor air. The fluoride remains in the room for a long time, entering people's bodies through their respiratory tracts, or through dust that attaches to food. The result is a growing rate of fluorosis of the bone.

Epidemiological investigations show that fluorosis from the burning of high-fluorine coal stems mainly from consumption of food cooked over coal and smoke inhalation. In Southwest China, local residents use crude coal to bake food and heat their homes. In that region, the prevalence of fluorosis of the bone correlates with the duration and amount of coal combustion (Li et al, 2002).

4.2 The Environmental Effects of Traditional Energy Sources

Traditional noncommercial energy sources consist mainly of straw and firewood, which can be burned directly. The pollutants from such energy sources include TSP, SO_2, methane (CH_4), and NO_x (Yu et al, 2008; Wang et al, 2004; Cao et al, 2005). Unlike energy sources such as coal, biomass energy sources such as straw and firewood contain carbon absorbed from the air during photosynthesis. CO_2 emissions from the burning of biomass will therefore not raise atmospheric levels of CO_2.

According to the Initial National Information Notification on Climatic Change, methane emissions from biomass burning accounted for 6.26% (2.147 million tons) of China's total methane emissions in 1994. A large proportion of these emissions result from the rural use of straw and firewood for energy.

Cao et al (2005) analyzed pollutants from the burning of straw and firewood for cooking and heating, the open combustion of discarded straw during harvest, and forest and grassland fires, based on information from each province and emission factors (Table 4.5). Provinces vary widely in the amount of pollutants this burning emits, reflecting differences in geography, climate, level of economic development, the size of the population, the consumption of biomass fuels.

Eastern, southern, and central China have trouble acquiring enough commercial supplies of coal, given their high rural population density. As a result, consumption of biomass fuels is quite high in those regions, with correspondingly large amounts of all pollutants. Shandong Province occupies first place, while Jiangsu and Heilong jiang Provinces come in second.

Table 4.5 Pollutants from the Combustion of Biomass in Different Provinces, 2000 * /ton

Province	SO_2	NO_x	NH_3	CH_4	EC	OC	VOC	CO
Beijing	550	2860	2420	7280	880	3550	13 110	112 430
Tianjin	770	3160	2800	9360	1090	4720	6170	129 190
Hebei	10 560	66 390	46 690	114 260	18 660	77 880	420 140	2 321 030
Shanxi	2430	14 200	9320	22 160	4090	18 140	81 190	478 360
Inner Mongolia	3600	18 600	14 680	43 720	6190	26 920	87 850	703 520
Liaoning	6810	41 600	30 560	78 530	11 870	48 850	253 480	1 493 160
Jilin	11 290	67 670	42 520	95 460	19 220	86 160	401 070	2 223 560
Heilong Jiang	17 130	93 170	62 300	156 610	28 200	126 880	483 780	3 176 730
Shanghai	0	0	0	0	0	0	0	0
Jiangsu	17 400	88 650	63 720	174 500	27 170	120 740	391 250	3 164 900
Zhejiang	4000	35 120	24 120	50 250	8880	33 440	306 580	1 196 920
Anhui	10 650	61 830	46 430	123 930	18 020	74 660	349 600	2 252 720
Fujian	1800	10 960	5980	11 080	3560	16 590	80 520	326 690
Jiangxi	3160	26 680	18 890	41 390	6 900	25 820	227 930	926 020
Shandong	24 890	138 040	91 680	226 400	40 600	181 940	722 570	4 693 340
Henan	11 800	67 760	46 730	117 210	19 710	85 750	375 950	2 350 220
Hubei	8510	57 710	42 740	106 140	15 880	62 550	400 690	2 073 490
Hunan	4960	53 180	38 070	78 060	12 650	43 040	517 500	1 849 920
Guangdong	5280	41 330	28 390	61 900	10 800	42 300	330 000	1 414 120
Guangxi	4660	42 380	30 950	68 390	10 610	37 780	376 890	1 497 220
Hainan	3590	20 510	16 610	46 970	6070	24 210	113 090	782 400
Chongqing	2850	20 690	15 800	39 300	5570	20 930	154 120	755 550
Sichuan	7050	51 700	38 940	95 580	13 850	52 480	386 720	1 873 330
Guizhou	1640	21 900	15 860	31 100	4970	15 530	234 400	763 510
Yunnan	1810	26 400	18 890	35 630	5830	17 800	290 230	912 900
Tibet	0	10	0	0	0	10	50	120
Shaanxi	3440	25 260	17 650	40 200	6720	26 650	190 110	874 690
Gansu	2590	15 440	11 980	32 410	4470	17 980	90 560	573 020
Qinghai	440	2320	1960	5880	710	2870	10 870	91 320
Ningxia	430	2080	1520	4310	660	2960	7890	75 100
Xinjiang	1350	7230	5000	13 180	2210	9960	35 490	252 670
Total	175 420	1 124 820	793 190	1 931 190	316 030	1 309 080	7 339 770	39 338 120

* Missing HongKong, Macao and Taiwan data.

Source: Cao et al, 2005.

Straw and firewood account for about 98% of these pollutants (Table 4.6).

Table 4.6　The Contribution of Different Materials to Pollutants from Biomass/%

Pollutants	Straw	Firewood	Forest fires	Grassland fires
SO2	97.98	0.78	1.08	0.16
NOx	75.29	23.65	0.86	0.19
NH3	75.20	24.08	0.61	0.11
CH4	84.78	14.62	0.47	0.12
EC	83.21	15.00	1.53	0.25
OC	91.18	6.67	1.76	0.39
VOC	46.93	51.66	1.31	0.11
CO	76.08	23.10	0.65	0.17

Source: Cao et al, 2005.

Yu et al (2008) used this information to calculate the emission factors for the combustion of straw and firewood in rural areas (Table 4.7).

Table 4.7　Emission Factors for the Combustion of Straw and Firewood/(g/kg)

Item	SO_2	CH_4	NO_x
Straw	0.53	3.28	1.29
Firewood	0.63	2.07	0.7

Those factors can be used to calculate total emissions of SO_2, CH_4, and NO_x from straw combustion in China (Table 4.8).

Table 4.8　Pollutants from Rural Combustion of Straw and Firewood, 2004/ton

Item	Consumption for production	SO_2 emissions	CH_4 emissions	NO_x emissions
Straw	291 600 000	154 500	956 400	376 200
Firewood	268 300 000	183 700	603 600	204 100

Emissions in different areas are positively correlated with the level of straw consumption. Sichuan, Jiangsu, Shandong, and Anhui have the highest emissions, while emissions in Beijing, Qinghai, Fujian, and Hainan are lower (Table 4.9).

Table 4.9　Pollutants from Rural Straw Combustion* /ton

Areas	Straw	SO_2 emissions	CH_4 emissions	NO_x emissions
Beijing	1 380 000	730	4520	1780
Tianjin	1 830 000	970	6010	2360
Hebei	17 420 000	9230	57 140	22 470
Shanxi	4 470 000	2370	14 670	5770
Inner Mongolia	15 190 000	8050	49 810	19 590
Liaoning	13 140 000	6960	43 100	16 950
Jilin	12 790 000	6780	41 950	16 500

Areas	Straw	SO$_2$ emissions	CH$_4$ emissions	NO$_x$ emissions
Heilong Jiang	23 670 000	12 550	77 640	30 540
Jiangsu	32 790 000	17 380	107 540	42 300
Zhejiang	3 020 000	1600	9900	3890
Anhui	26 070 000	13 820	85 520	33 630
Fujian	2 020 000	1070	6620	2600
Jiangxi	5 620 000	2980	18 420	7250
Shandong	28 820 000	15 270	94 520	37 170
Henan	23 660 000	12 540	77 600	30 520
Hubei	14 740 000	7810	48 340	19 010
Hunan	7 290 000	3860	23 910	9400
Guangdong	14 910 000	7900	48 900	19 230
Guangxi	8 350 000	4430	27 390	10 770
Hainan	2 160 000	1150	7090	2790
Chongqing	8 240 000	4370	27 030	10 630
Sichuan	35 430 000	18 780	116 200	45 700
Guizhou	8 440 000	4470	27 670	10 880
Yunnan	5 180 000	2740	16 980	6680
Shaanxi	7 370 000	3910	24 180	9510
Gansu	6 480 000	3440	21 260	8360
Qinghai	1 280 000	680	4180	1640
Ningxia	3 010 000	1590	9860	3880
Xinjiang	5 110 000	2710	16 750	6590

* Missing HongKong, Macao and Taiwan data.

4.3   Environmental Effects of the Rural Use of Renewable Energy

Renewable energy includes wind, solar, hydropower, biomass, geothermal, and ocean energy. In China's rural regions, the most promising sources of renewable energy are the more efficient, modern use of biomass, as well as solar energy and micro hydropower.

Most renewable energy sources produce little pollution during use. In 2005, China used 166 million tons of coal equivalent in renewable energy (excluding traditional use of biomass), accounting for about 7.5% of the nation's total consumption of primary energy. Use of those energy sources avoided the release of 3 million tons of SO$_2$ and 400 million tons of CO$_2$.

Greater reliance on renewable energy can relieve conflicts between energy supply and demand, curb pollution, and raise farmers' income. The government therefore needs to provide economic incentives to ensure the full and timely development and use of such resources. Those incentives could include providing marketable credits to farmers who reduce their greenhouse gas (GHG) emissions through the use of renewable energy, providing direct subsidies to users of renewable energy sources, and ensuring that producers of electricity from renewable sources such as biogas or wind have low-cost access to transmission lines.

4. 3. 1　The Development and Environmental Impact of Biogas

China first began to produce biogas in the 1970s, to address a shortage of rural energy supplies. In the mid-and late-1980s, to satisfy farmers' need for clean, convenient. and low-cost energy, the nation focused on improving the materials used to produce biogas, and on qualifying the sources of those materials. Biogas is therefore gradually becoming the preferred new source of rural energy, especially because it can protect the environment.

Raw materials for biogas include straw; waste from livestock, poultry, and people; and other organic waste. Farmers can use the byproducts of biogas production—which include liquid and dregs, or solid waste—as fertilizer, creating a closed production cycle.

The direct burning of straw and firewood in traditional rural stoves has low thermal efficiency—less than 10%, 15%, respectively. When straw and human and animal waste are made into biogas, thermal efficiencies can rise to 60%.

Economic incentives to encourage biogas production can include loans and subsidies for building biogas production facilities such as anaerobic digesters, payments for cuts in GHG emissions resulting from the use of biogas to produce electricity, and guaranteed low-cost access to transmission lines for excess power from biogas. Even more vigorous efforts to encourage rural households to use high-efficiency stoves that burn biogas are also important.

Because biogas developed earlier than other renewable energy sources, the technology is more mature and less costly, so it has seen rapid development. Production of biogas for household use grew from 1. 11 billion m^3 in 1991 to 9. 88 billion m^3 in 2007—a eightfold increase in 17 years (Figure 4. 3). Estimates show that biogas production in China will reach 15. 6 billion m^3 in 2010, and 38. 5 billion m^3 in 2020.

Biogas is cheaper than fossil fuels, and more efficient than the traditional method of burning biomass directly. Biogas production also makes large-scale use of waste from agriculture and rural households, and reduces GHG emissions (Figure 4. 4).

The use of biogas curbs the pollution that would have resulted from the use of coal, straw, and firewood. According to Zhang et al (2005), if biogas had replaced household direct use of 4. 24 million tons of straw, 3. 18 million tons of firewood, and 2. 55 million tons of coal from 1996 to 2003 (1. 43%, 1. 93%, and 1. 43% of total annual household energy use, respectively), annual SO_2 emissions would have dropped by 21 300 ~ 62 000tons.

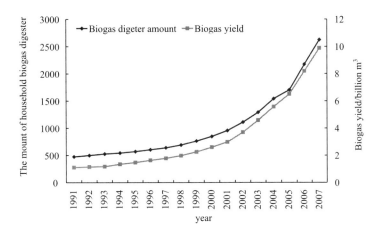

Figure 4. 3　Biogas Use in Rural Households, 1991~2007

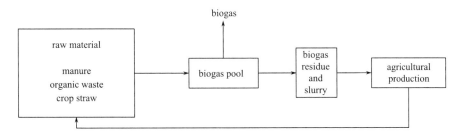

Figure 4. 4　Recycling of Materials in Biogas Production

4. 3. 2　The Uses and Environmental Impact of Straw

Straw is the main byproduct of agricultural production, as well as a key traditional energy resource. Some 0. 6 billion to 0. 7 billion tons of straw various kinds is available annually, so it is a huge energy resource.

However, the developed proportion of that annual output is rather low. In 2005, for example, only 28% of straw output was used as fuel, mainly in the form of direct combustion for rural cooking and heating. Up to 17% of straw output that year was directly burned in the field (Figure 4. 5). That is a great waste of a valuable resource, as well as a cause of air pollution.

Straw is a clean renewable energy source. The thermal value of 2 tons of straw is equal to that of a ton of standard coal, while the average sulfur content is 3. 8‰, compared with 1% in coal.

As noted, traditional combustion of straw is rather inefficient. More-efficient techniques for using straw include not only biogas but also cured straw, straw pyrolysis and gasification, and the direct firing of straw to produce electricity.

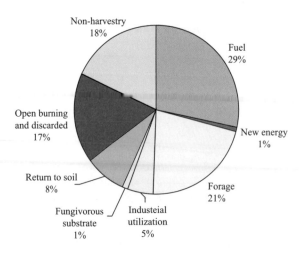

Figure 4. 5   Uses of Chinese Straw, 2005

For cured straw, heat is used to compress straw into rod-shaped lumps, making it easier to transport and store, improving its combustion efficiency, and expanding its uses. When the straw is cured, its volume decreases by six to eight times, and density rises from 1. 1 tons/m^3 to 1. 4 tons/m^3. The energy density of the cured straw is equivalent to that of mid-quality of coal. The cured straw can replace firewood and coal in rural cooking and heating (and also replace natural gas and boiler fuel used in urban areas). The thermal efficiency of family stoves that burn cured straw can exceed 80% (Tian, 2009).

Straw pyrolysis and gasification make full use of straw, rice hulls, wood chips and branches, and other rural organic castoffs, which are burned in a gasifier without oxygen. This technique, mainly used in villages, controls the combustion process to produce burned gas CO, hydrogen, firedamp for rural energy for household needs. Straw pyrolysis and gasification can reach thermal efficiencies of 80%.

In direct-fired power generation, straw is burned in a gasifier, which releases heat that is used to produce high-pressure steam. As the steam expands, it pushes a turbine, transforming the energy into mechanical energy for generating electricity. This technique is basically mature, with commercialized use in agricultural areas west of China's plain areas.

These new techniques can reduce straw use 50%, and also reduce the volume of rural waste. The household stoves designed to use modern straw-based fuel also reduce indoor air pollution, improving rural life.

To encourage wider reliance on these new techniques, the government must create additional economic incentives. The government could pay farmers and other producers for supplying the raw resources, as well as for reducing regional air pollutants. Because these techniques reduce GHG emissions compared with burning fossil fuels, the government could also pay farmers for those reductions, and sell the resulting credits on domestic and international markets.

4.3.3 The Use and Environmental Effects of Other Renewable Energy Sources

The practicality of micro hydropower, wind energy, solar energy, and other rural renewable energy sources obviously varies from region to region. Micro hydropower is available mainly in the southwestern mountainous region, which has rich water resources. Wind resources are largest in the Northwest, Inner Mongolia, and coastal areas. Except in some areas with little sunshine such as Sichuan Basin, most rural areas can rely on solar energy, especially North China and the arid region of Northwest China.

These energy sources are the cleanest, as they produce little waste and few GHG emissions. The principal challenges are the immaturity of the technologies, their high cost, and the instability of the energy supply. To reduce the cost to developers and users of these energy sources, the government could offer tax credits, subsidies, low-interest loans, and other incentives. Because these energy sources produce few GHG emissions, developers and consumers could receive credits and payments for reducing those emissions.

4.3.4 The Bottom Line on Renewable Energy Sources

China is developing renewable energy sources as an important approach to meeting rural energy needs, reducing pollution, and promoting the economic development. According to the 2007 Long-term Development of Renewable Energy Plan from the State Development and Reform Commission, China's renewable energy capacity could reach 300 mtce in 2010, and 600 mtce in 2020. This extensive capacity can replace coal use and compensate for insufficient supplies of natural gas and oil.

Annual biogas amount is 24 billion m^3 of natural gas, and annual combustion of ethanol and biodiesel equals 10 million tons. The use of solar and geothermal energy takes an important role in improving the energy structure and saving the energy resources. While meeting the need of energy, the renewable energy development will bring a remarkable economic benefit.

If the nation reaches the 2010 goal, the use of renewable energy could reduce annual SO_2 emissions by 4 million tons, NO_x emissions by 1.5 million tons, dust emissions by 2 mill-ion tons, and CO_2 emissions by 600 million tons, while also saving 1500 million tons of water and protecting 150 million mu[①] of woodland. If the nation reaches the

---

① 1mu≈0.067 hm².

2020 goal, the use of renewable energy could reduce annual SO_2 emissions by 8 million tons, NO_x emissions 3 million tons, dust emissions by 4 million tons, CO_2 emissions by 1200 million tons, while saving 2000 million m^3 of water and protecting 300 million mu of woodland.

The nation cannot achieve these important goals without additional economic incentives for both suppliers and consumers of renewable energy. Again, such incentives fall into two categories. First, payments, low-interest loans, and tax credits can reduce the costs of renewable energy. Second, because the use of these energy sources reduces pollution versus the use of fossil fuels, suppliers and consumers could receive payments for these reductions. The environmental benefits include fewer regional air pollutants as well as GHG emissions, less water pollution and greater efficiency of water use, and protection of terrestrial resources from fossil fuel extraction.

4. 4　Rural Energy Use and Climate Change

The rapid development of the rural economy and swift rise in the quality of rural life are bringing continuous changes to rural energy use. These changes are clarifying the relationship between the development and use of rural energy, reductions in GHG emissions, and global climate change.

4. 4. 1　Rural Energy Use and Greenhouse Gas Emissions

Although the direct burning of straw and firewood is inefficient and creates unhealthy living conditions, the resulting CO_2 emissions come from carbon that the biomass stored during photosynthesis, and thus are not counted in national GHG inventories. When commercial energy sources—which mainly include fossil fuels such as coal and petroleum—replace these traditional fuels, in contrast, China's GHG emissions—as measured under the standards of the Intergovernmental Panel on Climate Change (IPCC) —will greatly increase. Greater reliance on fossil fuels also means that huge amounts of straw will become waste rather than fuel, and recycling or treating those wastes will require an extra investment.

New and renewable energy sources may also produce some GHG emissions. For example, the principal constituent of biogas is methane (CH_4), whose greenhouse effect is 21 times that of CO_2. The research results from Energy Research Institue Showed that GHG emissions from the combustion of biomass in rural areas reached 450 million tons of CO_2 equivalent in 2004.

4. 4. 2　CO_2 Emissions from Rural Coal Combustion

Rural coal combustion is the main source of CO_2 from energy use in the Chinese countryside. According to the 2006 IPCC Guidelines for National Greenhouse Gas Inventories, the CO_2 produced from rural coal consumption can be computed using the following formula:

CO_2 emissions $=$ raw coal consumption $\times$ mean carbon content $\times$ average oxidation coefficient $\times 44/12$ (4-4)

In this formula, mean carbon content is 71.43%, and can be converted from China's coefficient of 0.7143 kilogram coal equivalent per kilogram from raw coal to standard coal. The coal combustion oxidation coefficient mainly reflects the type of stove, combustion process, and household habits.

Rural use of coal in China occurs mainly through direct combustion. Combustion is usually inadequate, and the oxidation coefficient is low. (The oxidation coefficient of cooking stoves is less than 80%, while the oxidation coefficient of coal-fired heating stoves used in northern China is generally above 90%). Coal combustion for rural production is usually more efficient than coal burning by rural households. However, in our analysis, we chose to use an average oxidation coefficient of 80% for rural coal consumption.

Our results show that rural coal consumption emitted 1.03872 billion tons of CO_2 in 2004, of which 561.09 million tons came from rural production and 477.63 million tons stemmed from household use (Table 4.10). China's CO_2 emissions from rural coal consumption have been rising. In 1980, those emissions totaled 190.96 million tons, but by 2004 that figure had quintupled, with an average annual increase of 7.3%.

Table 4.10 CO_2 Emissions from Rural Coal Consumption, 1980~2004/million tons

Year	Emissions from production	Emissions from household use	Total
1980	82.13	108.53	190.96
1991	330.43	227.55	557.98
1995	443.36	252.48	695.84
2000	470.60	346.35	816.95
2002	530.11	461.80	991.91
2004	561.09	477.63	1038.72

4.4.3   The Impact of Biogas on GHG Emissions

Rural reliance on biogas significantly reduces GHG emissions and other pollutants (Liu et al, 2008), and also saves large amounts of energy. More widespread use of biogas can therefore greatly improve the rural environment and advance the construction of a new countryside. Research has shown that biogas can reduce average annual net GHG emissions by 1.88 kg/m^3 (with a range of 1.76~2.11kg/m^3).

From 1991 to 2005, biogas provided 28.4 mtce, and reduced GHG emissions by

73. 16 million tons of CO_2 equivalent, with an average annual reduction of 4. 88 million tons, or 0. 07% ~ 0. 16% of total national GHG emissions. The use of biogas avoided the release of 84. 24 million tons CO_2, 3. 56 million tons CO_2 of equivalent of methane, and 0. 26 million tons of CO_2 equivalent of N_2O.

Before 1990, reductions in GHG emissions from the use of biogas were relatively low. However, from 1998 to 2001, those reductions began to grow, and then rose rapidly to 11. 54 million tons in 2005 (Figure 4. 6).

ERES: Reduced emission amount by energy substitution effect

ERMM: Reduced amount of Manure management

EBC: Emission amount of biogas utilization

NER: Net reduced emission amount

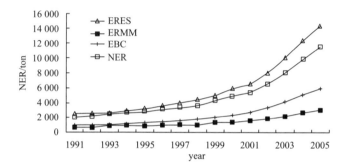

Figure4. 6　Reductions in GHG Emissions from the Use of biogas, 1991~2005

Note: Net reduced emissions stem from energy substitution, better management of manure, and the use of biogas.

According to China's long-term plan for biogas development, output can reach 15. 6 billion m^3 in 2010 and 38. 5 billion m^3 in 2020, which can reduce GHG emissions by 29. 33 million tons and 79. 38 million tons of CO_2 equivalent, respectively. This plan can not only satisfy growing rural energy demand but also improve the rural environment and help the nation cope with climate change.

Over the long term, two main sources contribute to rising GHG emissions from rural regions. The first is the shift from the use of biomass to commercial energy use. Today biomass supplies one-third of the total energy used in rural areas, mainly for household cooking and warming. However, with rising rural living standards, households are using more and more commercial energy rather than burning straw and wood.

The second factor in rising rural GHG emissions is growing energy demand caused by urbanization. Per capita energy use and GHG emissions are much lower in rural areas than in urban areas. In 2000, per capita annual rural energy use was 0. 77 tons of coal equivalent, compared with 2. 58 tons of coal equivalent in urban areas. Urbanization therefore increases energy consumption. External commercial energy sources will supply most of this extra demand, increasing rural GHG emissions and harming the rural environment.

According to the LEAP model, direct rural CO_2 emissions from both production and household energy use will rise in the coming 20 years—whether or not the nation expands its reliance on renewable energy sources (Table 4.11). Under normal circumstances, China's carbon emission will be total 78.7 million tons, 91.56 million tons, and 103.31 million tons in 2010, 2020, and 2030, respectively, representing an increase of 8.1%, 25.7%, and 41.9% over 2005 levels.

Table 4.11　Direct Carbon Emissions from Rural Production and Household Energy Use under Different Circumstances/million tons

Year	2005	2010	2020	2030
Normal circumstances	72.83	78.70	91.56	103.31
Household energy use	42.89	45.72	47.77	47.22
Strengthened reliance on renewable energy	72.83	76.95	87.39	92.72
Household energy use	42.89	43.96	43.61	36.63

If the nation strengthens it reliance on renewable energy sources, carbon emissions will be total 76.95 million tons, 87.39 million tons, and 92.72 million tons in 2010, 2020, and 2030, respectively, with an increase of 5.7%, 20.0%, and 27.3% over 2005 levels.

Future increases in carbon emissions from rural energy use will mainly come from production. Under normal circumstances, household GHG emissions will fall after peaking in 2020, to 47.22 million tons in 2030, representing a 10% increase over 2005 levels. If China emphasizes renewable energy, household carbon emissions will fall after peaking in 2010 to only 36.63 million tons in 2030, representing an increase of 14.6% over 2005 levels.

Thus the development of rural renewable energy supplies can greatly slow GHG emissions. Additional economic incentives for renewable energy developers and users are needed to realize this potential. Per capita carbon emissions from both rural production and household energy use will keep rising under both scenarios, given the narrowing gap in energy use between rural and urban regions. However, rural commercial energy use and the rural per capita emissions will not surpass those in urban areas.

4.4.4　Relying on Renewable Energy to Cope with Climate Change

All renewable energy sources can reduce GHG emissions, which can help China cope with climate change in three key ways. The first is by improving energy efficiency and controlling excessive increases in energy use. The second is by replacing conventional energy sources and satisfying rising energy demand. And the third is by relying on energy use to achieve multiple goals, including strengthening the rural economy and reducing rural GHG emissions and other pollution.

Investigating and promoting renewable and more efficient sources of energy—including a shift from traditional use of biomass to biogas and the use of solar heating (hot water), micro hydropower, wind, and energy-saving stoves—are important. However, the accurate evaluation of the environmental effects of these new forms of energy is not yet systematic.

Persuasive research on the total amount of renewable energy available under different circumstances, and the resulting impact on the rural energy structure, is not yet available. Some scholars have clearly ignored rapid increases in total energy use. Still, to safeguard the energy supply and improve energy efficiency, active development of energy-saving technologies to improve the rural environment and reduce GHG emissions within "the strategies of coping with climate change" have important practical significance.

4.5 Strengthening the Capacity of Rural Areas to Adapt to Climate Change

China is feeding 20% of the world's population with only about 10% of the world's farmland and 6% of the world's water resources. Chinese agriculture faces severe challenges because of its reliance on a large population of small farmers, the shrinking amount of land devoted to agriculture, and the deteriorating quality of that land.

Increases in greenhouse gases, especially CO_2, and the resulting climate change, have already undermined rural development and the stability of rural production. Strengthening the capacity of rural areas to adapt a changing climate is therefore critical to ensuring food security, maintaining the stability of the rural economy, and raising farmers' revenue and living standards.

In the past 100 years, China's average annual temperature has risen 1.1℃, with higher temperatures especially obvious in the most recent 50 years. The location and timing of precipitation and extreme weather events has also changed.

(1) Rising temperatures mean both advantages and disadvantages for rural production. Temperature increases within a certain range allow agriculture at mid and high latitudes and on plateaus to restructure, increasing opportunities for multiple cropping and greater output, and expanding the area for growing rice and winter wheat northward. However, rising temperatures have also undercut approaches to farming developed over many years, especially in low-latitude areas, increased agricultural demand for water, and aggravated damage from pests and diseases.

(2) Increases in atmospheric concentrations of CO_2 within a certain range can promote crop output by improving the efficiency of photosynthesis. However, the limitations and long-term impact of these changes remain unclear, and deserve further

research.

(3) Extreme climate is an important factor in a significant drop in agricultural output and variations in crop yield. According to the Civil Administration and Social Welfare Department, droughts in the past 20 years have reduced GDP by 1.2%, while floods have reduced GDP 0.8%.

In 2008, 100 million people suffered from a severe snowstorm and freezing rain, with direct losses surpassing 150 billion Yuan. In the future, high temperatures will be an important factor limiting agricultural production, causing severe droughts in water-deficient areas and making the agricultural ecology more fragile. Drought as well as heavy rainfall can reduce and even wipe out harvest and production of some crops.

Droughts, floods, pests, and diseases now common in northern China will also occur in other regions. That is already happening in northeastern China, where drought and black-stem disease have caused huge losses to rapeseed crops. However, China lacks good quantitative information on the extent of agricultural losses the nation can expect in the future.

According to Xiong et al (2007), the per-unit yield of the three main food crops could remain steady in the face of a 2.5~3℃ rise in average temperatures, if farmers adjust their planting structures (leaving out CO_2's fertilizer effect and adaptive measures). However, if average temperatures rise further, per-unit yields will fall (Figure 4.7).

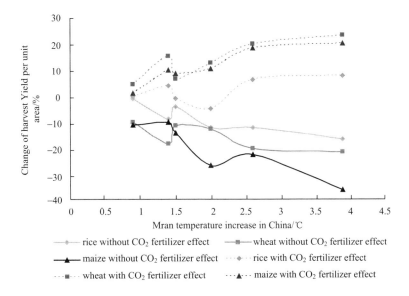

Figure 4.7　Temperature Threshold of per-Unit Grain Yields in China

Under a high-emissions scenario, China will see a food gap around 2030, assuming a per capita grain intake of 300 kg—the minimum food supply for social development. Under medium- and low emissions scenarios, China will not see a problem unless it aims for a per capita intake of 400 kg—the amount needed for sustainable development. Still, if we consider CO_2's fertilizer effect, the anticipated temperature increase will not cause a negative effect on the nation's future food production (Figure 4.8) (Xiong et al, 2007).

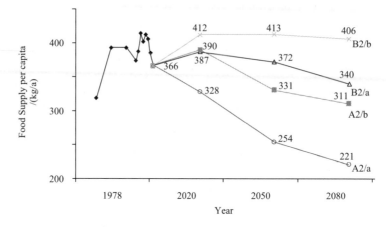

a. The fertilizer effect of not taken into account.

b. The fertilizer effect of CO_2 taken into account.

Figure 4.8　Future Variations in China's per Capita Food Supply

If we combine the latest research on water resources, variations in land use, social and economic development, and adaptive measures, the results show that rising temperatures, declining amounts of water available for agriculture, and shrinking amounts of arable land will mean a $14\% \sim 23\%$ drop in food production in 2050 from 2000 levels. However, if we consider the maximum CO_2 fertilizer effect, these three factors will influence China's grain production by $-7\% \pm 2\%$. Thus climate change over the next 30 to 50 years will not substantially affect the nation's food supply (Xiong et al, 2007, 2009; Cai et al, 2008). However, according to Lin et al (2005), wheat, rice, and corn output will fall $24\% \sim 37\%$ in the latter half of the twenty-first century.

As temperatures in China continue to rise over the next century, so will the frequency and intensity of extreme climate events. A correlation between agricultural disaster areas and rising temperatures has already become obvious. Thus, although high atmospheric concentrations of CO_2 could raise the output of some crops, dwindling water resources and land suitable for agriculture will require stringent efforts to ensure food security when the population peak arrives in 2030. These efforts include raising the national investment in agriculture and agricultural technology, controlling the loss of agriculture land, and safeguarding agricultural water supplies.

Research on the impact of climate change on food security remains very challenging: there is no accepted approach, so results vary greatly. Research on adaptive measures and their effects is especially thin, with studies having evaluated only spontaneous adaptations by farmers, such as changes in planting dates and crop cultivars. Research on large-scale strategies for ensuring the nation's food security, such as diverting water supplies from south to north and protecting farmland, as well as the interaction between adaptive measures and climate change, is also scarce, and needs to be strengthened.

Given this uncertainty, China's food security will largely depend on the effectiveness of adaptive measures, such as eco-agriculture and progress in agricultural technology. The willingness of farmers to use such measures will be critical, and that, in turn, will depend largely on the impact of such measures on their incomes. If farmers can be reasonably assured that their incomes will rise, they will adopt them. Government policies that provide financial support to farmers for shifting to these measures will therefore be pivotal.

To reduce GHG emissions, China needs to control rural reliance on commercial energy supplies to some extent. Today such supplies are used mainly for agricultural activities, such as irrigation, the application of chemical fertilizers, and the use of farm machinery. Irrigation is especially important: according to recent research, the association between irrigated areas and grain yields is as high as 0.92, while the association between the use of chemical fertilizers and grain yields is 0.59, and the association between the use of farm machinery and grain yields is 0.55.

Under climate change, grain yields in northern areas will depend more on irrigation. And rising temperatures and accelerating decomposition of soil organic matter will shorten the release cycle of chemical fertilizers, so that means farmers will need to apply more of those fertilizers.

Thus, an effort to safeguard the food supply, China may increase its energy consumption and the use of chemical fertilizers. However, that will pose more obstacles to rural energy efficiency and reductions in GHG and other emissions. Farming practices and technologies that increase the efficiency of fertilizer and water use and other inputs can counter this trend, lower production costs, reduce emissions, save energy, and raise farmers' income. However, farmers will not widely adopt these practices and technologies without government support.

4.5.1 Biomass Energy and Food Security

Food security affects not only people's livelihood but also world peace and stability. Many nations foresee a new food crisis, and the food security problem has become a global challenge:

(1) This new crisis is closely related to climate change, as global food production has declined because climate change has led to more extreme and frequent natural disasters. The decisions of some countries to limit or forbid food exports to guarantee domestic food supplies have further inflamed tensions in global markets.

(2) Rising energy prices have also pushed up food prices. Global oil prices quintupled from 2002 to 2007, and the global price of chemical fertilizers nearly tripled. Rising oil prices also increased the costs of transporting agricultural production.

(3) Higher energy prices increase the demand for crops used to produce biofuels such as ethanol, further increasing the price of agricultural products. The rapid development of ethanol and biodiesel has consumed large amounts of food and seed oil resources.

For example, today 12% of global corn output, 20% of U. S. corn output, and 50% of Brazil's sugar cane is used to produce ethanol. Some 20% of global supplies of rapeseed oil, 65% of the European Union's rapesed oil output, 20% of global bean oil output, and 30% of Southeast Asia's palm oil is already used to produce biodiesel.

According to the UN Economic and Social Commission for Asia and the Food and Agriculture Organization, prices of the world's main food staples have increased 80% since 2005. In 2007, soybeans price hit their highest point in 34 years, corn prices reached their highest level in 11 years, rice prices were the highest in 19 years, and the prices of wheat and rapeseed reached historic highs.

Thus, within only a few years, large amounts of grain, sugar, and oil crops have poured into the energy industry, pushing up food prices. Demand for biofuels will only intensify in the future, greatly affecting food prices.

Rising prices for key commodities have caused social unrest in many lower-income countries, especially in Africa and South America. To stabilize domestic food prices, traditional food-exporting nations such as Vietnam, Thailand, and Ukraine have begun to limit or forbid food exports.

(4) Rapidly rising and shifting food consumption in developing countries has also raised food demand and prices. These changes include growing demand for edible oil, meat, eggs, milk, and other fine food, and a steep rise in demand for oil crops and feed grain. According to the Food and Agriculture Organization, global grain consumption grew to 2. 043 billion tons in 2006, greatly intensifying stress on global food markets.

These are practical reasons for taking steps to restore world food prices to normal levels.

Many studies suggest that higher atmospheric concentrations of CO_2 can improve the efficiency of photosynthesis and raise the amount of water stored in grain, which in turn will increase agricultural yields. Estimates suggest that if CO_2 concentrations double, global grain yields will increase 10%~30%.

However, by accelerating the growth and development of grains, rising temperatures will also shorten their reproductive cycles. If the average temperature surpasses 40° C, some physiological processes of grain will collapse (Alexandrov et al, 2002; Hulme, 1996).

Temperature increases will also bring new diseases, pests, and weeds to grain, affecting its growth (Chen et al, 2004; Fuhrer, 2003). But many studies predict that changes in the timing and location of precipitation will exert the largest effect on agriculture (Hulme, 1996; Fischer, 1996; Strzepek, Smith, 1995). The impact of these climate-related factors on grain yield will vary among regions. Generally speaking, they will increase grain yields at high latitudes and decrease them at low latitudes (Table 4.12) (Lin, 1997).

Table 4.12　Impact of Climate Change on Grain Output

Region	Percentage Change in Grain Output				
	Corn	Wheat	Soybean	Rice	Others
Latin America	-61~Incr.	-50~-5	-10~40		
Soviet Union (former)		-19~41			-10~13 (G)
Europe	-30~incr.	decr. / incr.			Incr. (V)
North America	-55~62	-100~234	-96~58		
Asia	-65~6				-79~-63 (M)
South Asia	-62~10	-61~67		-22~28	
China	-19~5	-21~54	-44~83	-21~28	15~49 (C)
Other regions in Asia and Oceania		-41~5		-45~30	-1~35 (P)

Source: Lin E D, 1997, based on the Double Equilibrium General Circulation Model.

Note: G=grain, V= vegetable, M=millet, C=cotton, P=pasturage, incr. =increase, decr. =decrease.

4.5.2　Rural Development Policies and Climate Change

China is a large agricultural country with a huge population. Ensuring food security is the primary task of agricultural production. However, if the single goal of agricultural policies and activities is to increase grain yield, the country will face growing risks from climate change.

For example, according to the 2008 National Mid- and Long-Term Food Security Plan, China needs to increase grain yields by 50 billion kg by 2020, with one-third of that increase occurring in northeastern China. However, efforts to raise grain yield put ecological stress on the region, increasing its fragility in the face of climate change.

The old agricultural development policies focus mainly on technology. However, under climate change, traditional technologies and cultivars will not work anymore. The agricultural production model that relies on intensive use of chemical fertilizers and other farm chemicals cannot cope with diminishing resources and deteriorating environmental conditions.

To safeguard grain yields, Heilong Jiang Province has been expanding the area devoted to growing rice, which reached 2.45 million hm² in 2008. However, the province is now facing a series of climate disasters that are greatly increasing the uncertainty of rice yields. For example, the 2000~2001 drought prevented large areas from growing rice. Many paddies were converted to dry farmland, and even then farmers had to increase the frequency of irrigation, stressing local efforts to reduce energy use and agricultural emissions. Then, in late July 2006, severe low temperatures occurred in Heilong Jiang, reducing rice yields by 10%.

As this example shows, adjusting regional agricultural development policies and strengthening regional adaptability to climate change are essential to ensuring the stability of food production. The government has recently expanded its investment in rural infrastructure, mainly to improve irrigation and water conservancy facilities, improve the rural environment, and expand the use of biogas. The economic stimulus plan created to respond to the global financial crisis has also provided some new investment in agricultural infrastructure. China can use those investments to reduce GHG emissions, improve grain yields, boost living standards, and mitigate the adverse effects of climate change.

For example, improving irrigation facilities and developing new water-saving technology will help farmers withstand droughts and floods. And expanding farmers' ability to store rainfall, reduce soil runoff, and increase the infiltration of precipitation can help farmland retain water, soil, and fertilizer. Because global warming will worsen pest and disease disasters—more pests will survive, they will appear earlier, and they will stay longer—pest monitoring, prevention, and control will also be essential.

5　International Experience in Rural Energy, Environment and Adaption to Climatic Change

5.1　International Experience in Rural Energy

As an economy develops, it uses more of the modern forms of energy, such as electricity, petroleum products and gas, and less of the traditional forms, such as fuel wood, animal wastes etc. The two clearly go together but it is less obvious whether it is an increase in the supply of modern energy that promotes development, or whether it is demand for development that is responsible for an increased supply of such energy.

Certainly, most countries (those now developing and those that developed in the first half of the 20th Century) have sought to promote modern energy in rural areas by various means. The reasons for this have been partly social and partly economic. With electricity, for example, the ability to read and work when there is no natural light and the ability of families to be able to provide their children with facilities to study all depend are all greatly enhanced. Women also benefit as they have to spend less time cooking and gathering fuel wood and other traditional sources of energy. Finally there is now clear evidence that traditional energy, when used inside the house for cooking and heating, causes serious health problems (Markandya, 2008).

Apart from these social benefits the programs of rural energy modernization have also been driven by a strong belief that access to modern energy will increase productivity. The efficiency of electricity-based operations relative to manual or animal powered ones, for example, is significant and helps reduce costs. Furthermore the availability of electricity allows agro-industries to be established in rural areas. By both these means it can improve rural living standards and boost economic development.

The main difficulty with promoting modern energy in rural areas is the divergence between what customers demand and can pay for and the cost of supply. It is generally recognized that promoting rural electrification requires some subsidies to the providers or the consumers. The amount depends on what system is used (e.g. grid connections can be more expensive than mini-grids or solar home systems but are less liable to maintenance problems) and the income level of the communities being connected[①]. Subsidy programs are often not sustainable: e. g. if utilities are expected to provide at below cost and are not reimbursed for this provision they allow supplies to deteriorate and tend to disconnect rural consumers when the system is under pressure. In other cases the subsidies are provided by donor grants but when these grants stop the program also comes to a halt.

A review of experience in rural electrification shows a range of approaches has been adopted to deal with this problem. Sometimes the subsidies are given directly to "deserving consumers", and at other the subsidy is given to the supplier to cover losses on rural consumers. There is also the issue of whether to subsidize capital costs or operating costs. Additionally there are institutional questions of which entities should provide the services and how they should be organized. (Barnes, Foley, 2004; Barnes, 2007).

The relationship between modern energy demand and rural development were described through below two cases, and the existent obstacle were identified, which would provide some experience and lessons for China.

5. 1. 1 The Experience of the Developed World

5. 1. 1. 1 The Case of the United States

Before the Second World War the United States relied mainly on traditional energy in its rural areas. As late as the mid-1930s nine out of ten homes were without electricity. The farmer milked his cows by hand in the dim light of a kerosene lantern. His wife was a slave to the wood range and washboard. The unavailability of electricity in rural areas kept their economies entirely and exclusively to agriculture. Factories and businesses, of course, preferred to locate in cities where electric power was easily acquired.

Although electricity was available in the urban areas, private companies did not consider it profitable to expand supply to rural communities, which had low densities of users and were relatively far from the main centres of production. The extension of electric power to these communities came about as a result of two factors.

First, to entice electric companies to electrify rural America, President Franklin D. Roosevelt decided to offer low interest loans to those companies that would extend lines

---

① The choice of grid connection or mini-grid or stand alone systems depends on the density of the communities being electrified and distance of the communities from the grid lines (Reiche et al, 2000). In China typical off-grid systems, electricity costs are relatively high. For the conditions considered here, levelized cost of electricity varies between \$0. 57 and \$1. 04/(kW · h) for individual home systems. For a village mini-grid with 100 homes, levelized cost is between \$0. 87 and \$1. 09 (Ma et al, 2006).

into the countryside. On May 11, 1935, President Roosevelt established the Rural Electrification Administration (REA) as an emergency agency through Executive Order 7037. A year later, Congress passed the Rural Electrification Act of 1936 and moved the agency to a more permanent status. The Act gave the agency the authority to make $410 million in favourable loans to achieve rural electrification[1].

But by itself this would not have worked. Indeed the first administrator of the REA could not convince the power companies that there were farms that were willing to be connected under this program. These companies claimed that the number of such farms was too small to justify the investment in transmission and distribution even with the loans. This problem was solved by the farm people themselves taking the initiatives. Encouraged by the REA, they set up cooperatives, which would purchase electricity in bulk and undertake local distribution. In 1938 the REA approved $88 million in loans to rural cooperatives and by 1939 this had gone up to $227 million. Rural electrification was on its way.

The cooperatives were critical to the success of the US rural electrification program. REA officers, meeting day and night, outlined procedures and principles to the rural leaders. It took a tremendous effort, a lot of patience and hard work, as these committed men and women went up and down the country roads, working from farm to farm, to get the needed signatures of new members, obtaining the hard-to-come-by $5 "sign-up" fees. This amount was required to ensure that the community would have enough revenue to cover the costs of purchase and distribution of power from the suppliers.

As more and more communities got connected, demand per household began to grow. Farmers and ranchers began to realize the potential for electricity in their daily work. Electricity could grind feed, shell corn, pump water and saw wood. It powered milking machines and lifted hay into the barn. Electricity furnished the bright lights in the barnyard, giving precious extra hours to bring in the harvest. At the heart of all these lightened labors and the increased productivity was the electric motor—the new "hired hand." Of course the consequence was a huge increase in use. Initially in 1939 cooperatives had thought they would do well if per household demand reached 40 kW • h a month. By 1948 demand had tripled to 120 kW • h and continued to rise for decades thereafter[2].

The growing activity within the farm spread outside and into the community more widely. Schools, churches and meeting places now had lights and other electric conveniences for the first time. All the electric improvements created new economic activity along Main Street. New business and new kinds of businesses began to appear-electric wiring, plumbing and new electric appliances could be found in the stores. In

---

① For more details see www. NRECA, accessed July 1st 2009.
② http://www. powersouth. com/news. aspx? id=119, accessed July 3rd 2009.

addition, electricity brought new industry. With electric power available from the co-op, factories could locate in rural areas, consequently generating more jobs. These new employment opportunities gave hope, promise and a future to the younger generation in rural America-rural opportunities.

The cooperative movement for energy has now become a feature of energy supply in the USA, involved in all aspects of generation, transmission and distribution. In 1997 there were 3190 utilities in the country. Of these 935, or 29%, were cooperatively owned, serving 32 million people in 46 states and accounting for 45% of the electric distribution lines. Yet rural supply networks remain ones with relatively low concentration. At present cooperatives serve an average of 3.6 customers per kilometre of line (Griffiths, 2008).

The current role of the cooperative movement is to provide electricity at a competitive price to its rural customer base, in a competitive environment, which it does well. At the same time rural energy users are being targeted by a number of subsidies designed to increase their energy efficiency and reduce their use of fossil fuels. The 2008 Farm Bill has a number of renewable energy provisions, providing funds for a range of renewable energy projects, the establishment of bio-refineries, the development of advanced biofuels, efficiency improvements in hydro generation and the empowerment of rural communities to increase their energy self-sufficiency. Grants for renewable energy projects range from $2500 to $500 000 but must not be more than 25% of the total project costs. In addition loan guarantees are available for up to 50% of eligible costs and ranging from $5000 to $10 million.

5.1.1.2 The Case of Ireland

Even more than the United States, rural Ireland was dependent on traditional energy late into the 1940s. In 1946, when its rural electrification program started, virtually no rural households had electricity. Thirty years later virtually the entire rural population was electrified. The motivations on the part of the Irish government were social and economic (Shiel, 2007).

The programs, started in 1946, had been prepared carefully over the previous five years, studying in particular the cases of the USA, Canada and Scandinavia. The biggest problem it faced was financial: how to ensure that enough customers would wish to be connected to make the program viable and able to meet its target with the subsidy that was available. A tariff high enough to meet the full capital cost of rural electrification was beyond the means of most rural householders.

The government decided at the outset on a number of measures. First, it would exclude initially the 30% of rural households who were located in the most remote areas, thus saving costs overall. Second it would not provide a cross subsidy from urban to rural consumers, simply because the urban base was too small to allow that to be a feasible option. Third it was decided to provide the electricity board a capital subsidy, the amount of which would depend on finances available. The company then had to set tariffs to recover the rest of its costs. Accounts produced for a few years show that the company made small surplus at the beginning on its rural operations but eventually this turned into a deficit.

A number of institutional features of the program are important. Areas were selected for coverage if there were enough customers who had signed up for a connection to warrant the service. Local communities were responsible for ensuring this was the case, so the system had a feature of local involvement similar to that of the US, although not as structured. In any event, a lot of emphasis was put on local support and communication with the residents of the areas being electrified.

The charge consisted of a two part tariff, with a fixed and a variable component. The variable charge was quite high: around 18 US cents in today's prices per kW • h for consumption of up to 80kW • h a month. As consumption increased the marginal rate fell, until for units over 360 kW • h the rate was only 5.4 cents/(kW • h) (Shiel, 2007).

We have noted the importance of local support and this consisted not only of recruiting customers but educating the communities about the benefits of electricity.

The biggest problem faced by the authorities was over the fixed charge, which was seen as akin to a detested ground rent under the British landowners. Changes in this charge to reflect increased costs were particularly difficult.

At the end of the day, however, the program was a success and electrification was achieved. Agricultural productivity rose significantly, as new industries started to locate in the countryside. It took about 15~20 years, however, before the major increases in demand and use of electricity took place.

5.1.1.3 Lessons for China

There are important lessons from these two case studies of rural energy and development as far as China is concerned. We should note here that China's program in this area is already well advanced. Since 1949 more than 900 million rural residents have been connected and the rate of connection across the population is nearly 99%. There now remain about around 4.6 million households spread over 9300 villages and 608 townships who are without electricity. They are mostly located in remote areas and will be increasingly more difficult to connect to the grid. Hence the China Village Electrification Program is a scheme to provide renewable electricity to 3.5 million households by 2010, to be followed by full rural electrification using renewable energy by 2015.

The other feature of China's rural energy use is that modern energy is only a small part of total energy consumption. In 2000 about one-third of rural energy use was from "non-modern" sources (i.e. wood, straw etc.). Moreover electricity accounted for only 11% of the total and coal, which is a polluting source when used at the household level, accounted for around 45%. So an effort is needed to increase electricity use.

Based on the US and Irish experience there could be a role for cooperatives to assist in achieving this. The main purpose would be to help lower costs of distribution so that electricity becomes cheaper to rural households. Eventually they could even take responsibility for some generation and transmission. At present rural consumers pay around twice what urban consumers' pay, so it not surprising their consumption is so low. With cooperatives setting up local distribution networks these costs could fall. Cooperatives could also help in providing access to the remaining 4.6 million households.

The other lesson is that local community involvement in showing the benefits of electricity can help spread its uses outside the limited applications of lighting. This played an important part in both the USA and Ireland, where demand grew rapidly once people could see how electric power could help reduce costs and increase business opportunities[1].

Of course it is important to remember that the cooperative movement did need some government support in the early years of electrification and the Irish program likewise would not have succeeded without funds from the central government. Although these funds were necessary, they were not sufficient, and local involvement was a key condition for success.

Finally, as peri-urban areas expand in China, and capacity for local innovation increases, there is a potential for renewable energy programs similar to those in the US to promote renewable energy sources and energy efficiency. It is critically important, however, to ensure that these subsidies are allocated to projects that have been well designed and carefully vetted. As in the US, only co-funding should be provided and the programs monitored to see what lessons can be learnt.

5.1.2 Experience and lessons from Other Developing Countries

5.1.2.1 Experience from developing countries

The outstanding fact from the experience of developing countries is the slow rate of electrification. In many African and Asian countries it is slower than the rate of population growth.

National programs frequently run into financial difficulties. The highly subsidized Indian program, for example, has drained the resources of many of the state power companies, with highly damaging effects on their overall performance and quality of service.

---

[1] Although electricity use in rural areas for non-domestic purposes has gone up considerably (it is now between 44% and 67% depending on which figures you take) there is scope for increase the amount further as per capita levels are still low.

The reasons for the financial difficulties lie in three factors. First, the programs are over ambitious in terms of what can be sustained with the resources available for subsidy. Once those resources disappear, the programs run into difficulty.

Second the selection of the areas to be electrified areas not the most appropriate, given the resources and the ability and willingness of the residents to pay for the electricity. Politicians interfere with the orderly planning and running of programs, insisting on favoured constituents being connected first and preventing the disconnection of people not paying their bills.

Third, in some cases not enough care is taken to ensure that those being provided the electricity are able to afford it and are willing to pay for it. The consequence is that revenues do meet expectations and problems arise in recovering payments from defaulters.

Yet in spite of these problems, a number of countries have been quietly and successfully providing electricity to their rural areas. In Thailand, over 80% of rural people have a supply. In Costa Rica, cooperatives and the government electricity utility provide electricity to almost 95% of the rural population. In Tunisia, 75% of rural households already have a supply and the national electricity company confidently expects the proportion to rise to well over 80% by the year 2001.

The lessons learnt from the experience of developing countries has been summarised by Barnes and Foley (2004); Barnes (2007). The following are identified as necessary conditions that have to be met:

1) Setting up effective institutional structures

Large scale grid-based rural electrification is a relatively complex business and an effective implementing agency is one of its most basic requirements. The exact institutional structure, however, does not appear to be critical, as a variety of approaches have been successful. They include a separate rural electrification authority (Bangladesh); setting up rural electric cooperatives (Costa Rica, following in part the US experience); allocating rural electrification to a department of the national distribution company (Thailand); or delegating it to the regional offices of the utility (Tunisia).

Although no one institutional model appears unquestionably superior, there are common factors between those which have worked well. A high degree of operating autonomy—in which the implementing agency can pursue rural electrification as its primary objective—seems to be essential. But with autonomy must come responsibility as well. A typical example was Ireland, where the rural electrification agency had its own budget and control over access to materials and labor, and worked to its own realistically drawn up and costed plans, but it also was strictly accountable for meeting its targets.

Less tangible but even more important, experience shows that implementing agencies need dynamic leadership with a capacity to motivate staff and bring a sense of dedication to the task of rural electrification. In Thailand and other countries with successful programs, the extent to which the staff of the implementing agencies felt they were laying the foundation for the development and advancement of their country is notable.

2) Dealing with the political dimension

The use of public funds for rural electrification often leads to political interference at national and local levels. The politicians regard public funding as giving them rights to interfere, but experience shows that nothing is more damaging.

Once technical and financial decision-making in the implementing agency becomes based on political string pulling, professional discipline is destroyed and the organizational structure is undermined. Waste of resources, low staff morale and operational ineffectiveness are the characteristics of rural electrification programs suffering from a high degree of political interference.

Sometimes this can be turned into a positive force as in Thailand where local politicians were encourage to raise and contribute funds, so that their constituents could receive electricity before the planned time. It is even more important to ensure that rural electrification planning is open and objective. Successful programs use clearly defined criteria to rank areas in order of priority for electrification, so that the decision-making is clearly seen by all to be fair.

3) Criteria for rural electrification

Countless failed initiatives show the futility of premature rural electrification. Providing an electricity supply will only make a significant contribution to sustainable rural development when the other necessary conditions are present.

Security of land tenure, availability of agricultural inputs, access to health and education services, reliable water supplies, and adequate dwellings are among the more obvious of these conditions. If farmers are to invest in increased agricultural production they must have access to markets where they can obtain fair prices for their higher outputs. Families must have a level of disposable income that allows them to place improved lighting, and ownership of TVs and other electricity-using appliances among their expenditure priorities before they will pay for a supply.

Successful rural electrification programs have all developed their own system for ranking or prioritizing areas for obtaining a supply. Capital investment costs, level of local contributions, numbers and density of consumers, and the likely demand for electricity are among the factors normally taken into account. In Costa Rica, the ranking of communities was based on their population density, level of commercial development, and potential electricity load. Thailand developed a numerical ranking system taking account of a variety of factors such as level of income, the number of existing commercial enterprises, and the government's plans for other infrastructural investments in the area.

4) Importance of cost recovery

Cost recovery is probably the single most important factor determining the long-term effectiveness of rural electrification programs. When cost recovery is pursued, most of the other program elements fall easily into place. All the successful programs reviewed in the case studies placed a strong emphasis on covering their costs, though there is a wide variation in how it was approached.

In contrast, electricity supply organizations depending on operational subsidies are critically vulnerable to any downturn in their availability. When the subsidy is reduced, as inevitably happens, the virtue of increased sales turns into the vice of greater losses, creating a significant disincentive to extend electricity to new customers, especially poor people. The contradictory signals to management make proper running of the organization impossible.

In Kenya, for example, where the rural electrification program depends on the availability of grant funds from donors, progress has been slow and intermittent. In Malawi, the state electricity company states flatly that it has no interest in rural electrification, because electricity prices, by government order, are too low to cover even operating costs.

Capital investment subsidies raise different questions. In most successful programs, a substantial proportion of the capital has been obtained at concessionary rates or in the form of grants; at commercial rates of return a substantial proportion of the rural areas in would never be electrified. The program in Costa Rica started with low interest loans from USAID. In Ireland, a proportion of the investment costs, which varied depending on the state of the national exchequer, were covered by government grants.

Provided it is used wisely, and operating costs are covered, having access to such concessionary capital need have no ill-effects on the implementing agency or the rural electrification program. But concessionary capital should never be provided to organizations which are not covering their operating and maintenance costs; it will simply worsen their financial position.

5) Charging the right price for electricity

There is a widespread belief that electricity tariffs need to be extremely low, often well below their true supply costs, if rural electrification is to benefit rural people. The facts do not support this. Rural electrification only makes sense in areas where there is already a demand for electricity-using services such as lighting, television, refrigeration and motive power. In the absence of a grid supply, these services are obtained by spending money on kerosene, LPG, dry-cell batteries, car battery recharging and small power units, all of which are highly expensive per unit of electricity supplied. Recent surveys in regions without electricity in Uganda and Laos indicate that people spend approximately 5 dollars per month on these energy sources. Private suppliers often find a ready market for electricity at more than one US dollar per kilowatt hour.

Rural electrification tariffs set at realistic levels do not prevent people making significant savings in their energy costs, as well as obtaining a vastly improved service. Charging the right price allows the provider to supply electricity in an effective, reliable, and sustainable manner to an increasing number of satisfied consumers. In Costa Rica, the price of electricity is set through a regulatory process, but it is high enough for the cooperatives to make a modest profit. In 1996, the price for residential electricity started with a fixed charge of $2.59 for the first 30 kW • h, and the variable tariff increased steadily to over 25 cents a kilowatt hour for people consuming over 150 kW • h of electricity per month.

6) Lowering the barriers to obtaining a supply

The initial connection charges demanded by the utility are often a far greater barrier to rural families than the monthly electricity bill. Reducing these charges, or spreading them over a several years, even if it means charging more per unit of electricity, allows larger numbers of low income rural families to obtain a supply.

In Bolivia, for example, a small local grid, in spite charging 25 to 30 cents per kilowatt hour, immediately doubled its number of consumers when it offered them the option of paying for the connection cost over 5 years. By contrast, in Malawi where the electricity company charges the full 30 year cost of line extension to new customers, the rural electrification rate is just 2%.

7) Benefits of community involvement

Traditional thinking in many utilities is often oblivious to the importance of local community involvement. Rural electrification is seen simply as a technical matter of stringing lines to grateful consumers. The case studies show clearly that rural electrification programs can benefit greatly from the involvement of local communities-or suffer because of its absence.

Setting up a rural electrification committee to represent the local community can do, much to smooth the implementation of the program. The committee can play a crucial role in helping assess the level of demand, educating consumers in advance, encouraging them to sign up for a supply, and promoting the wider use of electricity.

In Bangladesh consumer meetings were held before the arrival of the electricity supply, helping to avoid costly and time-consuming disputes over rights of way and construction damage. Community contributions, in cash or kind, were often the decisive factor in bringing areas within the scope of the rural electrification program in Thailand. The efforts to recruit customers made by parish rural electrification committees in

Ireland ensured that the utility received an adequate return on its investment and contributed to the rapid implementation of the country's rural electrification program.

8) Reducing construction and operating costs

There are major opportunities for the reduction of construction and operating costs of rural electrification in most countries. In many cases, careful attention to system design enables construction costs to be reduced by up to 30%, contributing significantly to the pace and scope of the rural electrification program.

Where the main use of electricity is expected to be for lights and small appliances, typical of many rural areas, there is no reason to apply the design standards used for much more heavily loaded urban systems. The rural distribution system can be designed for the actual loads, often no more than 15 kW • h per month, imposed on it by rural households. Although consumption normally grows, this is usually at a slow pace and provided the necessary design provisions are made, systems can be relatively cheaply upgraded later.

Each country will have its own cost-saving opportunities for rural electrification planners. In Thailand, materials were standardized and manufactured locally, reducing procurement, materials handling, and purchasing expenses. In Costa Rica, the Philippines and Bangladesh, adoption of the well proven single-phase distribution systems, used in the US rural electrification program of the 1930s, brought major savings over the three-phase system still widely used in Africa and elsewhere. The case studies show that careful and critical analysis of design assumptions and implementation practices invariably reveals potential for significant cost savings.

9) Alternatives to the grid

Grid-based rural electrification is often portrayed as being in competition with alternatives, especially photovoltaic systems. This is a mistake as there is little conflict between the two.

The grid allows people to use standard electrical equipment and appliances without any practical constraint on the quantities of electricity they consume. It provides a level of service which cannot be approached by the alternatives and where technically and financially feasible will always be the first choice among consumers.

In remote or hard to reach areas where grid supplies are impractical on cost, technical or institutional grounds, people generally meet their need for lighting and electricity-using services by using kerosene, LPG, dry-cell and car batteries, and occasionally, small diesel or gasoline generators. Photovoltaic systems are increasingly demonstrating that they can be competitive on cost and service grounds with these conventional energy sources.

5. 1. 2. 2　Lessons for China

By and large China has avoided many of the pitfalls that have bedeviled rural electrification in other developing countries. The key messages it can take away from their experience are the following.

(1) As the country moves to ever remote and difficult areas for electrification the programs need to take account of the criteria that have to be met for such services to succeed. Primary among them is affordability at the sustainable tariff.

(2) As these areas will be relatively poor a scheme for recovering the initial connection charge through installment payments would make more households willing to connect.

(3) The benefits of active community involvement cannot be overstated; from the basic level of mobilizing local groups, to perhaps even forming local associations for distribution and beyond.

(4) Measures that reduce costs and take advantage of the fact that demand levels are low can help maintain lower tariffs and make programs more sustainable.

(5) Alternatives to the grid, already being used in China will have a greater role in remote locations.

5. 2　The Experience and Implications of the Adaptation to the Climate Changes in Rural Areas in Foreign Countries

Changing land use and management practices help to both adapt to and mitigate climate change. Reductions of greenhouse gas (GHG) emissions associated with these changes can also add economic value and alleviate poverty in rural areas. This section discusses agricultural and forestry GHG emission reduction projects and experiences in the United States. It enumerates the key elements in a system for defining and evaluating GHG emission reductions produced by projects that change land uses and management practices. Demonstration projects are described in detail to illustrate how GHG reductions can be defined, measured, and made real, credible, and cost-effective. The lessons learned in the US are useful for rural energy and environmental sustainability in China's countryside.

5. 2. 1　Economic Incentives for Agricultural GHG Emission Mitigation Investments are Already in Place in China Through Eco-Compensation

Greenhouse gas reduction projects in the land sector require changes in practices and technologies. These changes can be shown to measurably reduce GHG emissions either by storing carbon in soils or biomass or by reducing direct emissions. To make these changes, economic costs are involved. To provide the land manager with a way to cover those costs, mechanisms facilitating compensation to the land manager are needed. The concept of eco-compensation provides a means of achieving reductions in GHG emissions by providing payment to land managers making changes in practices and technologies.

China already has the framework providing economic incentives for GHG emission reductions in its rural areas. The Chinese Council for International Cooperation on Environment and Development (CCICED) defines[①] eco-compensation as "a type of institutional arrangement to protect and sustainably use ecosystem services, and to adjust the distribution of costs and benefits between different actors and stakeholders, mainly through economic measures." The key economic concepts for ecosystem management underlie eco-compensation: ecological conservation has costs; ecosystem productivity has opportunity costs when it is degraded; and ecosystem services have economic values. To account for these costs and benefits, governments and markets must provide economic rewards for protections and impose costs for damages to ecological and natural resources. CCICED includes the following underlying tenets of eco-compensation:

- Polluter Pays—the source of ecological damage pays for that damage.
- User Fees—users pay for the scarcity of ecological resources, compensating the government where use is external to an existing market or the government owns the resources.
- Beneficiary Compensation—the beneficiary of an ecological service pays the provider.
- Investor Returns—those investors or underwriters of ecological projects receive payment in return.

Several eco-compensation payment policies have been implemented by a number of nations, including the US:

- Private entities pay land resource managers for ecosystem services.
- Governments pay land managers and other providers of ecosystem services.
- Product labeling and "green" certification provide a price premium to suppliers of ecosystem goods and services.
- Governments provide tax incentives for land managers to produce ecosystem services.
- Governments implement cap-and-trade programs wherein a limit or target is set for ecosystem degradation and users or polluters must comply with this limit. These programs are important for control of GHG emissions, and policy experiments in Europe, Japan, and other nations are underway pursuant to the Kyoto Protocol.

---

① CCICED Task Force on Eco-Compensation Mechanism, Summary Report, 2008.

5.2.2　GHG Mitigation in Agriculture

Improving land management practices and technologies can reduce the level of GHGs in the atmosphere. Biomass and soils in forests and crop lands store carbon, called sinks. As forests grow, they absorb CO_2 from the atmosphere, storing (or sequestering) carbon in wood, leaves, roots, and soils. Agricultural practices such as no-till or low-till farming, grassland restoration, and the use of cover crops also sequester carbon in soils. By protecting and restoring forests, replanting grasslands, and improving cropland-management practices, land managers can reduce GHGs in the atmosphere. Better land-use practices can also reduce emissions of potent GHG such as methane and nitrous oxide. For example, using fertilizer more precisely can reduce emissions of nitrous oxide from soil. Reducing the saturation of soil with water (particularly during rice cropping) can curb methane emissions, as can the capture and burning of methane emitted from manure.

5.2.2.1　The Potential of GHG Reductions and Offsets from Improved Land Management Practices and Technologies

Land-management practices have the potential to significantly reduce GHG emissions. China's land sector has significant potentials which could be estimated through a research project. Such research has been done in the US, and the results are significant. Total GHG emissions in the US exceed 6000 million tons of CO_2 each year, as well as the equivalent of another 1000 million tons of CO_2 in the form of other GHG, including methane, nitrous oxide, and chlorofluorocarbons. Overall, annual GHG emissions total the equivalent of some 7000 million tons of CO_2. In 1990, US GHG emissions were equivalent to about 6100 million tons of CO_2 per year; in 2004, they totaled nearly 7100 million tons, for an annual rate of increase of about 1%. Without a limit on such emissions, this 1% rate will result in an additional 1600 million tons per year by 2025, to the equivalent of about 8700 million tons of CO_2 annually.

For the period through 2025, an often suggested target for the US is to lower GHG emissions by roughly 15% of current rates, which would require cutting about 1000 million tons of CO_2e per year[①]. Adding the estimated annual increase in GHG emissions during this period of 1600 million tons, the USA would need to cut GHG emissions approximately 2600 million tons of CO_2e per year.

Land management practices and technologies in the USA could contribute

---

① 　CO_2e is a measure of equivalents for all GHG accounting to global warming potential (GWP), where 1 metric ton of CO_2 is one unit of GWP, or one unit of CO_2e. Other GHG have different GWP, for example one metric ton of methane is equivalent to about 23 metric tons of CO_2 in terms of GWP.

significantly to reaching this target of 2600 million tons of CO_2e per year. A key factor in determining what amount of GHG reductions and offsets farmers and land managers will supply is the price of such reductions and offsets. The higher the price, the more farmers and land managers will participate in the market (Figure 5. 1), producing an increasing amount of GHG offsets. [1]At a price of $15 per ton of CO_2, land management projects could produce nearly 1500 million tons of CO_2 per year by 2025, or around 60% of the reduction needed for the USA to meet its target of 15% below current GHG emission rates. At $50 per ton, almost 2000 million tons of CO_2 per year could be produced by the land sector —nearly the total required cut in emissions.

Current conditions offer some insight into the potential of GHG markets to deliver prices sufficient to stimulate the land sector to produce significant amounts of GHG reductions and offsets. The GHG market in the USA is currently based on voluntary transactions so that demand is relatively weak, resulting in prices in the $1 ~ $10 range per ton of CO_2. In the European Union, which has adopted a mandatory cap under the Kyoto Protocol, CO_2 prices have risen well over $35 per ton of CO_2 in recent years. If the USA enacts a mandatory GHG cap as currently contained in several national legislative proposals, the price for GHG offsets will be high enough for the land sector to become a major producer of offsets.

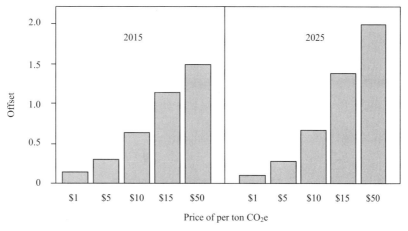

Figure 5. 1　Carbon offsets that U. S. land sector could produce, as a function of year and price (in millions of metric tons of CO_2e) With the rising price of offsets the total amount of offsets available should increase, as more farmers and land managers perceive an opportunity to profit and participate in the market. Note: From US EPA 2005

---

① For carbon sequestration in soils and forests, eventually additional carbon saturation will limit further increases in the future.

5.2.2.2　Types of Agricultural Practices to Reduce GHG Emissions

Land managers, farmers, and GHG offset project developers have many options to reduce GHG emissions. Types of projects include:

- Projects designed to sequester carbon in biomass, such as the cultivation of new forests and grasslands or through delays in the harvesting of forests, and decreasing the loss of carbon stored in trees.
- Projects designed to sequester carbon in soils through changes in farming practices, such as through the adoption of no-till farming and switching to perennial species such as grasses and improving grassland conditions.
- Projects designed to reduce greenhouse emissions of methane and nitrous oxide through changes in farming practices, such as reduction in nitrogen fertilizer applications, changes in the chemical composition of fertilizers applied, and changes in flooding and residue management in rice production.
- Projects designed to reduce greenhouse emissions of methane through changes in the practices used to process and dispose of manure, such as the collection of manure and processing through anaerobic digestion facilities.

While there is considerable variation in the costs per unit of CO_2e produced by land sector projects, in general these types of GHG offset projects can produce relatively large amounts of low-cost offsets per unit of land (Figure 5.2). There are often overlaps between types of projects—for example, a project that shifts from cultivating annual crops through plowing and applying nitrogen fertilizer to growing and permanently conserving forest could produce several types of GHG benefits. These include sequestering carbon in trees and soil and reducing fossil fuel emissions from the

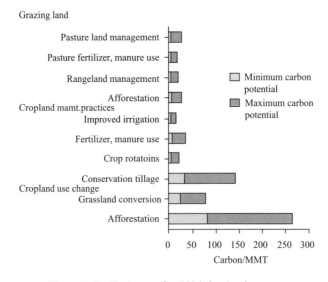

Figure 5.2　Estimates for USA land sub-sectors

machines and nitrous oxide emissions from the fertilizer. All these benefits count in assessing the amount of GHG offsets produced by such a project.

5. 2. 2. 3　GHG Reduction and Offset Transaction Types

Land sector GHG offsets can be marketed in two contractual forms—outright and permanent sales, and term leases or rentals. Permanent sales are possible for GHG offsets from projects that directly reduce GHG emissions. These include, for example, methane reductions from livestock manure management, nitrous oxides reductions from fertilizer reduction, and carbon dioxide reductions from reduced fuel use associated with adoption of no-till soil management. In addition, outright and permanent sales of GHG offsets are possible for soil and biomass carbon sequestration with in perpetuity commitments to maintain stored carbon. While carbon sequestration can be permanently contractually committed, contractual assignment of liabilities for reversal/release of stored carbon is necessary for these types of projects.

Carbon sequestration in soils and biomass not involving a permanent contractual commitment to maintain stored carbon requires term lease forms of purchase contracts. For these types of projects, the land manager/GHG offset lessor agrees to sequester carbon producing GHG offsets for a specified length of time. This time period is the term of the lease governing the buyer's temporary ownership of the GHG offsets. At the end of the lease term, the land manager/seller no longer has contractual responsibility to maintain the carbon stored by the project. The buyer then has the responsibility to either renew the lease or to replace the GHG offsets from the leased project with other GHG offsets.

5. 2. 3　GHG Aggregators

5. 2. 3. 1　Aggregation Services and Functions

Land-sector GHG offset projects usually require an "aggregator" entity to represent individual farms and land managers in the marketing of offsets. Aggregators improve marketability of the GHG offsets producer by individual farming or forest operations. Economies of scale in GHG offset development and marketing are provided by the aggregator. The aggregator can provide services such as quantification, monitoring, and risk management that would be typically difficult for individual land managers to access on their own. It is helpful to understand the size of the emerging GHG market in the USA-as noted above, a market demand of 2. 5 billion tons of CO_2 e is quite possible. An average transaction size of 100 000 tons CO_2 would entail 25 000 transactions each year. Clearly, small blocks of offsets, such as those in the 100 or even low 1000 of tons that would be produced by individual land managers, would face high transactions costs in attempting to market to industrial buyers looking for large blocks of GHG offsets.

Figure 5. 3 illustrates the mechanics of GHG offset aggregation and the marketing leverage that results from combining the offsets of a number of individual producers. In this example, 000 individual producers with an average land holding of 1000 acres[①] and an average GHG offset production rate of 1. 0 tons of CO_2e per acre per year would be required to aggregate into a 600 000 tons of CO_2e block of offsets. An aggregator with 600 000 tons of CO_2e of offsets would be well-prepared to deal with one or a few large industrial GHG offset purchasers.

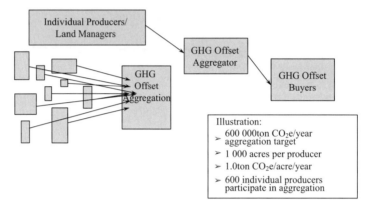

Figure 5. 3 The mechanics of GHG offset aggregation and the marketing leverage

In addition to the physical accumulation of GHG offsets from individual producers into a substantial block of GHG offsets for marketing leverage, aggregators have a number of other functions. Producing GHG offsets by changing practices and technologies in land management is a business activity that requires investments over a period of years. This requires planning, and aggregator entities require business plans. Those plans pertain not only to the operation of the entity doing the aggregation but also to the plans of individual producers who are the clients of the aggregator. It is conceivable that the aggregator will play an investment finance role for its clients, facilitating and even brokering funds required for participating farms and forest operations to implement the changes needed to produce real and credible GHG offsets.

Aggregators can also be project developers, although other entities can play that role as well. The tasks involved in project development are discussed below, but the point here is that project development requires a variety of expertise which can be delivered by the aggregator. Included in the mix of project development activities is the need to be aware of and to apply GHG offset standards in the process. Quantification and measurement of GHG offsets to be produced by a project are technical functions that the

① 1 acre＝0. 404686 hm².

aggregator can perform. Preparation of monitoring, quantification, and verification plans arc necessary tasks to deliver GHG offsets to market. Engaging independent third-party verification entities is required as well, including contracting for their services once such entities are selected. Aggregators must also engage in contracting with both individual participating farms and forest operations as well as with GHG offset purchasers. Managing risk particularly that related to the liability for underperformance in the provision of contracted-for GHG offsets is a key function for aggregators. Risk decision-making includes evaluation of several options such as acquisition of insurance, self-insuring through buffers, creation of multi-producer reserve account, and management of defaults by participating land management operations.

5. 2. 3. 2　GHG Aggregator Qualifications

Aggregators must be qualified in several ways to deliver a credible and effective service to participating farms and forest operations. As noted, aggregators must be capable of assembling GHG offsets from individual land managers in large enough blocks for marketing economies. To play this role, aggregators need to have experience, reputation, and credibility among land managers. The aggregator has to manage multiple contracts with participating farmers and foresters. It must have the institutional capacity to manage money and contracts, so it must have sound business capacities along with the array of specialized functions specifically involved with the production and management of GHG offsets from its clients. The aggregator must be able to negotiate contracts with both land managers and with purchasing entities, which often have formidable capacities in negotiation and legal matters. Finally, the aggregator must deal with third party verifiers and monitors in the context of monitoring, quantification, and verification plans.

In the USA there are a number of organizations that have become or are considering becoming GHG offset aggregators in the land sector. Most of these organizations already have networks of individual land managers necessary to assemble aggregations. Conservation districts, farm bureau chapters, agricultural commodity groups, food processing entities, farm and forest associations, insurance companies, and agricultural input suppliers are examples. Some, like conservation districts and farm bureau chapters, may lack capacities in traditional business management and financial transactions with clients and customers. Others, like commodity groups, food processing organizations, and insurance companies, have these financial capacities. So the challenge of adding a business function in the form of GHG offset aggregation will vary according to the background of these organizations.

5. 2. 4 Elements of GHG Project Development

5. 2. 4. 1 Defining a Project

The schematic in Figure 5. 4 illustrates the steps required to develop a GHG reduction or offset project. Land managers define a project by specifying the practices and technologies that will produce the project's GHG offsets. For example, a project might entail sequestering carbon in soil or trees or using anaerobic digesters to capture methane emissions from manure. The project's spatial and temporal boundaries must also be defined enabling quantification and verification of the project's GHG offsets.

Surveys can define the spatial boundaries of a project. However, this can often prove costly, and less-expensive options are available, such as relying on planning maps or a GPS receiver to record project boundaries. Legal records of land parcels or a suitably labeled and marked aerial photograph can be used as well. For projects located at a specific facility, such as a farm with animal barns and associated manure-handling areas, an address may be adequate to specify the project's spatial boundaries. If land managers have diverse operations, project boundaries should encompass all the lands and facilities

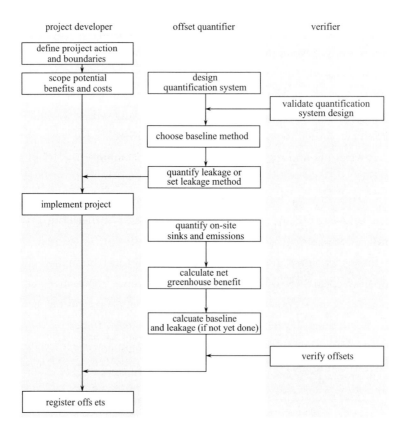

Figure 5. 4 Process and Steps of GHG Project Development

related to the project. Otherwise GHG offsets could be created simply by shifting activities that produce GHG emissions to lands or facilities outside the project.

GHG offset projects are bounded in time as well as space. Time boundaries are usually relatively easy to specify. Projects typically start on the date a contract takes effect, a land management activity begins, or a facility or process (such as capture of methane from animal waste) starts operating. Projects may run indefinitely, or a purchase contract may specify an ending time.

5.2.4.2　Scoping a Project's Costs and Benefits

Project scoping is the estimation of expected GHG offsets and costs, to determine if the project will yield a net financial return. This provides a basis to decide whether to implement a project. There are 3 steps to scoping a GHG offset project: ① confirm project GHG offset yield; ②scope project benefits and costs; ③project GHG offset sell offer sheet (s).

A project's costs include those of implementing it; creating contracts among participants; and measuring, verifying, registering, and marketing the resulting GHG offsets. In assessing the net financial return, land managers, project developers, and buyers need to consider at what point during the project's lifetime the costs and GHG benefits will occur. Estimating a project's potential for producing offsets entails a number of steps that are similar to those used to actually quantify the GHG offsets. However, at this stage, less rigorous and therefore less time-consuming and costly methods, such as estimates and projections, are used for scoping instead of actually monitoring project outcomes.

The end-product of a project scoping is the drafting of a GHG offset sell offer sheet. This sheet provides a brief (less than 2 pages) summary of the key elements of the aggregator's offer to sell GHG offsets produced by the project's individual participating land managers. Projected offset quantities to be produced; practices and technologies to be adopted to produce the GHG offsets; and asking prices are major items. A sample offer sheet template is provided in Figure 5.5.

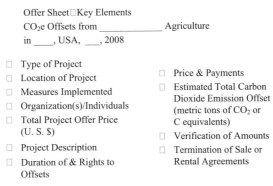

Offer Sheet□Key Elements
CO₂e Offsets from ＿＿＿＿＿ Agriculture
in ＿＿, USA, ＿＿, 2008

□ Type of Project
□ Location of Project
□ Measures Implemented
□ Organization(s)/Individuals
□ Total Project Offer Price (U.S. $)
□ Project Description
□ Duration of & Rights to Offsets

□ Price & Payments
□ Estimated Total Carbon Dioxide Emission Offset (metric tons of CO₂ or C equivalents)
□ Verification of Amounts
□ Termination of Sale or Rental Agreements

Figure 5.5　GHG Project Offer Sheet

5.2.4.3 Establishing Additionality and Baselines

In order for a project's GHG offsets to be valid and marketable, the changes in GHG emissions or carbon stocks on project lands must be different than those that would have occurred in the absence of the project, and the difference must be quantifiable. These issues can be addressed by determining additionality and baselines.

Determining whether a project is additional entails finding sites with similar starting conditions and anticipating changes in land management likely to occur on those lands during the lifetime of the project. This will determine whether the project will indeed produce GHG reductions over and above "business as usual." Although determining whether a project is additional is challenging, that effort is critical. If a project's GHG benefits are not additional, then the offsets the project claims are not real, and a cap and-trade system will not credit them.

There are a number of tests that are applied to determine additionality according to different criteria. Most common among these tests are so-called regulatory surplus, financial, barriers and common practice. One or more of these tests can be used to evaluate projects on a case by case basis. Also, performance standards can be used.

The GHG emissions from a project's lands and facilities that would have occurred in the absence of the project constitute its baseline. The baseline often changes over time due to changing management or environmental conditions. The project's net GHG benefit is the difference between the baseline and the actual GHG emissions from lands and facilities during the project's term.

If a facility such as a methane digester captures GHG emissions, measurements of emissions in the absence of the digester—that is, before the project began—can serve as the baseline. Other types of projects must establish the baseline as they unfold, to account for changing conditions and land management practices on lands with similar conditions in the region. Some systems, including the Kyoto Protocol, treat additionality and baselines as separate steps. The system establishes whether a project is additional, and if it is, the system specifies an independent method for determining the baseline. This process usually sets an all-or-nothing test for additionality. However, this all-or-nothing approach tends to discourage the increased use of practices that actually reduce GHG emissions, and thus it can be counterproductive. The alternative is to specify a system of discount factors established by various criteria, allowing factors between 0 and 1 to be applied to a project's GHG offset quantification.

5.2.4.4 Leakage

Leakage is the emissions displaced from inside the project's boundaries to sources outside it. This occurs when the production of commodities within the project area is shifted to areas outside the project boundaries. The impact of reduction in commodity production within the project boundaries can be assessed using standard economic analysis. Market demand and supply elasticities are used to estimate the amount of production that will occur outside the project boundaries in response to the reduction in commodity production within the project boundaries.

Leakage is of most concern with projects that aim to boost carbon stocks in existing forestlands by curbing logging. US markets for forest products are robust, and changes in supply in one region often spur compensation in other regions. For example, when logging in the US Pacific Northwest was slowed to protect the spotted owl, harvesting shifted to the Southeast. Unlike projects that curb timber harvesting, those that reforest marginal agricultural land are unlikely to result in significant leakage. US farmlands overproduce agricultural commodities, so such projects will probably not spur other farmers to convert forests to croplands to replenish the supply of crops. Such projects will therefore not displace emissions to other lands. Projects that entail a shift from plowing to no-till farming are also unlikely to produce leakage because the latter practice often improves soil fertility and thus boosts crop yields. Therefore, emissions will not move to other locations.

5.2.4.5 Monitoring and Quantification Plan

Transparent methods to create and quantify a project's GHG offsets must be documented to make them verifiable and thus acceptable to regulators and buyers. Project developers must write a monitoring and quantification plan before beginning a project. If changing conditions require revisions in the project's land management or quantification practices, addendums to the plan can document these revisions. To enhance marketability, the project's GHG offsets must be independently verified. Verifiers will refer to the documented plan to ensure that land managers and project developers have implemented the planned activities and that quantifiers have calculated net GHG benefits reliably.

The monitoring and verification plan should include the following:

(1) Project boundaries if they are known when the plan is written.

(2) A list of the project's potential sources and sinks of GHG emissions.

(3) Detailed protocols for measuring project conditions, including the frequency of measurements and procedures for recording, managing, and storing data.

(4) A design for sampling the project's GHG impacts, including the locations of monitoring activities and mechanisms for identifying those locations, such as markings on aerial photos, GPS coordinates, or physical markers.

(5) Procedures, factors, and equations for analyzing data (based on measurements from the project) and quantifying offsets.

(6) Contents and timing of reports that quantifiers will generate. These reports should include summaries of original data, not just the results of data analysis.

(7) Quality-control standards and methods, including redundancy in recording data in case records are lost.

(8) A baseline or a process for setting the baseline.

(9) Leakage rates or a process for assessing leakage.

5.2.4.6 Measurement Plans

The most important part of the monitoring and quantification plan specifies the methods used to monitor changes in GHG emissions or carbon stocks that result from the project's land management practices. To establish that emission cuts or greenhouse sinks are real, quantifiers must use techniques that are reliable, appropriate, complete, unbiased, and transparent. Critical in this regard is a careful sampling design for gathering representative and accurate data that can detect actual changes in emissions or sinks.

Different types of land management projects require different techniques for measuring net changes in emissions and sinks during the project. Individual projects address various components of ecosystems, and quantifiers must measure each component using techniques appropriate to it. Designing complete and accurate measurement systems requires a thorough understanding of the biological and physical attributes of what is being quantified. If not based on knowledge of such dynamics, a measurement system may not address all the GHG flows that a project is likely to affect. The accuracy of claims for a project's offsets will generally reflect the rigor of the methods used to measure and quantify them. A more rigorous measurement plan will produce more accurately quantified offsets, but it will also drive up the cost of producing them.

1) Forest GHG Measurement

Forests undergo complex changes in carbon accumulation requiring a well-designed system of biomass sampling. This is especially important because forest projects usually last for decades. Scoping forest projects can be greatly improved by using a calibrated forest carbon model (e.g. FVS, a forest carbon model developed by the U.S. Forest Service). Sampling designs for forest projects should be Accurate and repeatable over long periods of time. Adaptable to unforeseen circumstances, such as wildfires, forest management changes, and the addition or removal of lands from a project. As simple as possible to allow outsiders to audit results. Approach quantifying sequestration to reduce variability, control costs, and detect much of the sequestration a project achieves, following these steps:

(1) Designing a forest sampling system that is robust with respect to the different locations of carbon accumulation.

(2) Conducting initial field measurements of the different sites of carbon stocks in a

forest.

(3) Selecting allometric equations for converting field measurements into carbon mass, or developing new ones.

(4) Taking subsequent field measurements to determine changes in carbon stocks over time.

Crucial aspects of this approach include performing unbiased sampling, choosing an adequate number of sampling sites, and deciding whether and how to stratify sampling across a site.

Repeat quantitative field measurements every $5 \sim 10$ years, relying on annual qualitative or quantitative observations in intervening years to determine whether a project is proceeding according to plan and to take remedial action, if needed. Aim to detect net carbon sequestration with an uncertainty of 10% at a 90% confidence level, as the potential benefits of greater accuracy are generally not worth the added cost.

2) Soils GHG Measurement

A sampling design and protocol for analytic measurements must be designed at the outset to accurately quantify the changes in soil carbon over the project period. Sampling and analyzing soil samples can be costly, so the design of the sampling program can strongly affect the cost of the project and its profitability. The goal is to select a sampling program that achieves a level of precision high enough to detect tons of sequestered carbon without incurring untenable costs. An appropriate sampling design and analytical framework, careful fieldwork, and high-quality laboratory testing can provide a high level of precision for acceptable cost.

Land managers and project developers can quantify the carbon sequestered in soils on project lands by

(1) For scoping purposes, utilize a calibrated soil carbon model (e. g. C-STORE).

(2) Designing a system for measuring changes in the amount of carbon in the soil.

(3) Taking field measurements of carbon stocks at the start of the project.

(4) Monitoring project conditions over time to determine if adjustments in estimates and/or practices are needed.

(5) Remeasuring carbon stocks in soil and calculating changes in those stocks.

Quantifying carbon sequestration is challenging since the increase in soil carbon stocks in most projects will be less than 10% of the total soil carbon content—and much less if deeper soil is sampled. This means that if quantifiers need to measure the net sequestration (or change in the soil carbon content) to an accuracy of 10%, they will have to measure the total soil carbon content to an accuracy of at least 1%.

A soil sampling strategy should include a detailed protocol for collecting samples of a specified volume from numerous sites. The sampling protocol should specify: ①The number and spatial arrangement of soil samples to be taken at each site; ②The steps field crews should take if they cannot extract a sample at the specified location; ③The diameter of the soil cores and the depth to which field crews will collect each core; ④The guidelines for how crews should deal with materials on the surface of the soil and for how they should label, package, and handle samples.

3) Direct GHG Emission Reductions Measurement

Reductions in direct emissions of GHG from land management and agricultural practices must be quantified with indirect measures and modeling. This is because direct measurement of emissions reductions would require expensive facilities and gas measurement that would make nearly all land-sector projects involving direct emissions reductions economically infeasible.

One illustration involves reductions in CO_2 emissions from reduced use of farm machinery (such as in no-till) or pumping equipment (such as in drip irrigation). These reductions in CO_2 emitted can be estimated from direct measurements in reduced fuel or electricity use. Depending on site-specific factors including fuel type and engine efficiency, conversions can be made to CO_2 emissions.

A very promising approach to estimating methane and nitrous oxide emissions relies on the denitrification-decompositionprocess model, or DNDC (Li et al, 1992, 1996, 2000; Li, 2001). The GHG Wizard version of DNDC uses data provided with the model on the weather, soil types, and crop types/acreage of each county in the USA, as well as user-specified data on fertilization, tillage, and other management practices for each crop rotation and year. The model uses this information to estimate changes in soil carbon, changes in methane and nitrous oxide emissions, and the global warming equivalents of these emissions. [1] This model requires a great deal of site-specific information and the practices and inputs specified by the model may differ from those ofthe project. An alternative approach is to use simple equations to estimate emissions based on a few factors that are relatively easy to measure, such as the amount of carbon in soil, the amount of nitrogen land managers apply, and the demand for nitrogen by crops (Willey, Chameides, 2007).

5.2.4.7 Contracting

GHG offsets are property, so laws governing property can be employed to govern transfer of ownership among land managers, project developers, aggregators, and

---

[1] See http: //www. dndc. sr. unh. edu/ for the model, instructions on its use, and detailed discussions of its applications.

buyers. Purchase contracts[①] typically completed prior to the initiation of a GHG project may commit the land managers and aggregators to perform specified activities or deliver an amount of GHG offsets. There are two types of contracts involved in a land-sector GHG offset sale and transfer. First, individual land managers contract with aggregators to allow aggregators to pool GHG offsets from a number of individual farms or forest operations. Second, aggregators contract directly with buyers of the cumulative GHG offsets from all participating individual land operations.

Individual farmer or land manager contracts with aggregators contain the following elements:

(1) Specification of Contract Term/Years and Project Lands.

(2) Sequence and Schedule of Actions.

- Contracts for a fixed number of offsets versus specified actions
- Estimating Expected Offsets
- Quantifying Achieved Offsets
- Buyer Versus Seller Liability

(3) Aggregator (buyer) responsibilities.

- Create & execute a monitoring and verification plan for project properties
- Make payments
- Reserve account provisions/ risk management

(4) Land manager responsibilities.

- use GHG offset production methods for lease term
- transfer rights for GHG Offset Credits to Aggregator
- allow access to land by 3rd party verifiers
- prepare annual reports certifying compliance with contract
- permanent right to the continuation or prohibition of specified land management activities (covenant, easement)
- land lease contract
- provisions for activities on the land only if consistent with the producer GHG contract
- if activities not consistent with GHG contract, lessor quits any claim to GHG offsets during rental period & relinquishes all claims to landowner

(5) Price of GHG Offsets & Calculation of Payment Amounts.

- Specify price per ton $CO_2 e$, or payments for executing actions
- For multiple payments, final payment can vary according to actual GHG

---

① There are a number of sources of sample contracts. Websites for several are (i) http://www. environmentalmarkets. org; (ii) http://www. ieta. org; (iii) http://www. climatetrust. org. A helpful publication is *New Tools for Improving Government Regulation: An Assessment of Emissions Trading and Other Market-Based Regulatory Tools* by Gary Bryner, published by the Center for the Business of Government, provides a basic primer on offset contracts.

offset performance

- Calculate offset lease price using present valuation methods

（6） Miscellaneous provisions （including warranties/representations, severability, mediation, cooperation, notification, confidentiality, limitation of liability, indemnification, termination, force majeure).

Similar elements are contained in the purchase contract between the project aggregator and the buyer.

5. 2. 4. 8　Registering and Verifying Offsets

After quantifying offsets, project developers must complete a few more steps before they can easily sell them. In order to assure marketability of a project's GHG offsets, transparency and verification are important. Project developers and/or aggregators should make public a brief written report includes location of the project; identifies project implementers; states how and by whom quantification and verification will be accomplished; lists the quantity of GHG to be produced by the project; discloses when GHG offsets have or will occur, and how long they will last if less than permanent.

Published reports can be used to disclose GHG quantification methods and the seller/land manager's legal obligations without disclosing proprietary information. Independent verifiers should be engaged, and GHG offsets should be registered. Verifiers act as auditors of the project's GHG offsets. process. To avoid conflicts of interest, verifiers should not be involved in the project in any other capacity. To enhance marketability, the project's GHG offsets should be registered with the appropriate registry entity, which assigns the owner a unique identifying number. If the GHG offsets are sold, the registration is amended to reflect the transfer to clarify ownership and assure that the GHG offsets cannot be sold more than once.

5. 2. 4. 9　Land-Sector GHG Reduction and Offset Standards

To assure credibility and accuracy of GHG offsets from land sector projects, standards are necessary. The above discussion has touched on the key elements in project development leading to marketable GHG offsets. To summarize, these elements include: ①Project description; ②Quantification of GHG reductions; ③Baseline/Additionality; ④Leakage; ⑤Monitoring methodology and plan; ⑥Third party verification plan.

There are a number of existing and emerging GHG offset standards around the world intended in various ways to ensure offset quality. Figure 5. 6 lists some of these standards. EDF is currently investigating the relative strengths and weaknesses of these standards to provide a rough ranking of their assurances of GHG offset quality. Some of these standards govern mandatory GHG control programs while others are being applied to GHG offset projects in the global voluntary market. Over time there will likely be a convergence of most of these standards towards a comprehensive, unified standard. But that may be years into the future, so in the interim it is important to be cognizant of the existence of these many standards with their substantial qualitative variations when evaluating GHG offset projects in the land sector.

CDM A/R Methodologies		CarbonFix Standard
VER+		
ECIS Voluntary Offset Standard		DOE 1605(b)
CCAR Forestry Protocol		ECIS Voluntary Offset Standard
VCS		
Duke Standard		RGGI
Plan Vivo		WRI GHG protocol
Greenhouse Friendly		IPPC Good Practice Guide
CCBA		TUV SUD VER+
Green E		
CCX		Climate Neutral Network
Gold Standard		

Figure 5.6   GHG Offset Standards

5.2.5   Agricultural GHG Reduction Case Studies—USA

A number of agricultural GHG reduction demonstration projects have been underway for several years in the USA. These projects include several types of agricultural crop lands, forests, and livestock operations. Below are profiles of five of these projects.

5.2.5.1   Precision Agriculture/Northwest

Type of Project: CO_2 reductions from adoption of precision agriculture technologies and practices in production of grain crops.

Location of Project (s): Pacific Northwest USA-NE Oregon, Eastern Washington, North Idaho.

Measures Implemented: Farmer adoption of direct seeding and precision agriculture technologies such as GPS guidance systems, variable rate application and auto boom shutoff to increase efficiency by reducing overlap and double application of crop inputs.

Organization (s) /Individuals: Pacific Northwest Direct Seed Association, a non-governmental organization representing approximately 500 farmers.

Project Description: PNDSA will aggregate approximately 25 000 acres of cropland in the PNW where management has currently adopted direct seeding and various levels of precision agriculture technologies. The land managers will provide data on precision agriculture technologies adopted along with documentation of efficiency they have gained. Using this data PNDSA will calculate CO_2e emission reductions resulting from fuel use and crop input use efficiencies. These results will be compared to efficiency being measured by USDA-ARS research sites and USDA-NRCS extension agencies.

Measurement/Quantification of GHG reductions: project scoping using estimates of reduced use of nitrogen and other fossil fuel-based inputs. Conversion to reduced GHG emissions using default conversion factors. Follow-up quantification using DNDC model. GHG reductions estimated from the following reductions in fossil-fuel based inputs enable by adoption of PA methods:

(1) Diesel fuel reductions from the adoption of direct seed cropping systems.

(2) Diesel fuel reduction from the adoption of GPS guidance systems.

N_2O emission reductions from:

(1) Adoption of GPS guidance systems.

(2) Adoption of variable rate application technology.

CO_2 equivalent reductions from pesticide application reductions from:

(1) Adoption of GPS guidance systems.

(2) Adoption of auto boom shutoff controls.

(3) Green seeker sprayer technology.

Baseline/Additionality: Baseline GHG emissions calculated from use of agrochemical and other fossil-fuel based inputs under average farming practices in this region that do not utilize PA technologies and practices. Project passes regulatory, common practices, and barriers tests for additionality.

Leakage: no reduction in commodity production results from this project, so no leakage caused.

Monitoring methodology and plan: complies with protocols in Duke standard. Local conservation district staff performs monitoring.

Third party verification plan: Verification plan format from Duke standard. Project validation (upfront evaluation) and subsequent project performance evaluation by qualified 3rd party verifier (SCS, Inc).

Contracting/ownership: 3 years initial term (2008 ~ 2010), subject to possible renewal. Seller liable for underperformance in GHG reductions, compensation through either payment reimbursement with interest, or in equivalent GHG reductions from another source. Ownership of GHG reductions transferred to buyer during the years of the contract. Ownership of GHG reductions in subsequent years after contract expires reverts to seller.

5.2.5.2　No-Till/Midwest

Type of Project: CO_2 reductions from soil carbon sequestration with associated fossil fuel reductions in corn/soybean crop production rotation.

Location of Project (s): Selected agricultural parcels in 3 counties in Northeastern Kansas.

Measures Implemented: Continuous no-till farming implemented in 2007 through 2016 on 1200 acres.

Organization (s) /Individuals: AgraMarke, Inc. is a non-governmental organization representing approximately 1000 farmers in Kansas, Missouri, Nebraska, and Iowa. AgraMarke owns and operates grain milling facilities on behalf of its farmer members.

Project Description: The project land near St. Joseph, Missouri, is rolling cropland that is highly productive for corn and soybean production. The contracting producers of AgraMarke, Inc. who farm this land have adapted no-till farming practices for both environmental and economic reasons. No-till farming, which leaves surface crop residue from prior years' crop production, reduces soil erosion, water runoff, and water evaporation, and helps soil fertility by increasing soil organic matter. Less field operations are required in no-till farming than in conventional tillage practices. These reductions in field operations result in savings of fossil fuel. The environmental effect of no-till farming is to reduce carbon dioxide emissions by sequestering soil carbon and reducing farm fuel usage.

Measurement/Quantification of GHG reductions: Project scoping utilizes regional carbon sequestration factors and fuel use data. Soil carbon sequestration estimated to produce an average net emission reduction of 750kg CO_2e per acre per year. The average diesel use reduction resulting from utilizing no-till practices estimated 3. 02 gallons[①] per acre per year. Soil carbon measurement to adjust project GHG reductions to be implemented in years 5 and 10 of project contract.

Baseline/Additionality: Baseline GHG emissions calculated from soil carbon content and fuel use under average cultivation-based farming practices in this region. Project passes regulatory, common practices, and barriers tests for additionality. Note non-continuous no-till practices are common in this region, but not continuous no-till practices.

Leakage: no reduction in commodity production results from this project, so no leakage caused.

Monitoring methodology and plan: complies with protocols in Duke standard. Monitoring performed by AgraMarke staff.

Third party verification plan: Verification plan format from Duke standard. Project validation (upfront evaluation) and subsequent project performance evaluation by qualified 3rd party verifier (SCS, Inc).

  Contracting/ownership: 10 years initial term (2007～2016), subject to possible renewal. Seller liable for underperformance in GHG reductions, compensation through either payment reimbursement with interest, or in equivalent GHG reductions from another source. AgraMarke to implement insurance through backup reserve no-till

---

① 1 gallon≈0. 0038m³

acreage equivalent to approximately 20% of project acreage. Ownership of GHG reductions transferred to buyer during the years of the contract. Ownership of GHG reductions in subsequent years after contract expires reverts to sellers.

5.2.5.3 Irrigation Efficiency/California

Type of Project: CO_2 reductions from CO_2 and N_2O reductions and from agricultural fuel use reduction and changes in nitrogen application and use from adoption of drip irrigation in farming.

Location of Project: selected irrigated agricultural parcels in the San Joaquin Valley of California, USA.

Measures Implemented: Installation and operation of drip irrigation systems, beginning in 2009, on approximately 8000 acres of row crops, including corn and cotton.

Organization (s) /Individuals: Several water districts; JM Lord, Inc.

Project Description Emission reductions from farm operations are achieved by adopting drip irrigation technologies and practices to grow crops with less consumption of fossil fuels than crops grown on the same land using conventional furrow irrigation. Growing crops using drip irrigation reduces water/energy use and increases efficiency of uptake of nitrogen fertilizer. The resulting GHG reductions amounts are achieved on 8 participated farms with project lands encompassing approximately 8000 acres.

Measurement/Quantification of GHG reductions: Project scoping utilizes default factors. Quantification from DNDC model using site input data.

Baseline/Additionality: Baseline GHG emissions calculated from average furrow-based irrigation crop production in this region. Project passes regulatory, common practices, and barriers tests for additionality.

Leakage: no reduction in commodity production results from this project, so no leakage caused.

Monitoring methodology and plan: complies with protocols in Duke standard. Monitoring performed by JM Lord Inc, an irrigation technical services company.

Third party verification plan: Verification plan format from Duke standard. Project validation (upfront evaluation) and subsequent project performance evaluation by qualified 3rd party verifier (SCS, Inc).

Contracting/ownership: 3 years initial term (2009 ~ 2011), subject to possible renewal. Seller liable for underperformance in GHG reductions, compensation through either payment reimbursement with interest, or in equivalent GHG reductions from another source. Ownership of GHG reductions transferred to buyer during the years of the contract. Ownership of GHG reductions in subsequent years after contract expires reverts to sellers.

5. 2. 5. 4　Water, Residue Management/Rice/California

Type of Project: Methane reduction from water and straw residue management in rice production.

Location of Project (s): selected rice production parcels in Sacramento Valley, California, USA.

Measures Implemented: reduced duration of winter flooding and rice straw residue removal; methane offsets over baseline, based on (i) no residue with winter flooding; and (ii) residue incorporation without winter flooding.

Organization (s) /Individuals: California Rice Commission and county rice milling operations.

Project Description: CRC will aggregate approximately 20 000 acres of rice lands operated by 4-6 farmers in the Butte County area of California's Sacramento Valley. Current management of rice production includes prolonged winter flooding and incorporation of straw residue into the soil. Participating rice land managers will reduce the duration of winter flooding and remove portions of rice straw residue. These actions will reduce emissions of methane from project lands.

Measurement/Quantification of GHG reductions: There is potential for significant net GHG reductions through alternative water and rice straw management. Preliminary results indicate reductions from rice straw management alone in the general range of 1000kg to over 5000kg of CO_2e per hectare. Mean reduction is approximately 3500kg CO_2e/hm^2. GHG reductions for both reduced winter flooding and rice straw management estimated using DNDC model. Site data on management of water, rice straw, and nitrogen application, along with local environmental data such as precipitation, temperature, and soils will be input into the DNDC model to calculate changes in GHG emissions.

Baseline/Additionality: The baseline scenario is GHG emissions from prolonged winter flooding with rice straw residue incorporation into the soil. Project passes regulatory, common practices, and barriers tests for additionality.

Leakage: no reduction in commodity production results from this project, so no leakage caused.

Monitoring methodology and plan: complies with protocols in Duke standard. Monitoring performed by staff of local rice milling operations.

Third party verification plan: Verification plan format from Duke standard. Project validation (upfront evaluation) and subsequent project performance evaluation by qualified 3rd party verifier.

Contracting/ownership: Initial trial contract for one-year in 2009, subject to possible renewal. Seller liable for underperformance in GHG reductions, compensation through either payment reimbursement with interest, or in equivalent GHG reductions from another source. Ownership of GHG reductions transferred to buyer during the years of the contract. Ownership of GHG reductions in subsequent years after contract expires reverts to sellers.

5, 2, 5, 5　Reforestation/Pine/Northwest

Type of Project: CO_2 reductions from soil and biomass carbon sequestration from converting cultivated crop lands to pine forests in central Idaho.

Location of Project: 5 miles[①] Northeast of Nez Perce, Lewis County, Idaho, USA.

Measures Implemented: New plantings of pine trees on previously cultivated crop lands.

Organization (s) /Individuals: Nez Perce Tribal Forestry, Lapwai, Idaho.

Project Description: Nez Perce Tribal lands include several thousand acres of cultivated farm lands that were deforested and converted to agriculture in the early 1900's. This project converts land currently being cultivated on an annual basis to pine forests. The current agricultural lease will likely be renewed in the absence of funding for reforestation of these lands. Nursery raised ponderosa pine seedlings will be planted on approximately 400 acres and actions will be taken to ensure the success of the reforestation effort by implementing the following, but not limited to, vegetation control, installation of seedling protection materials, and the replanting of dead or damaged seedlings, if necessary, to meet stocking goals. Semi-annual stocking surveys will be performed to monitor survival until the stands are certified as "free to grow". Permanent monitoring plots may be established in cooperation with the US Forest Service-Rocky Mt. Research Station, to measure the amount of Carbon sequestered over time. Tree growth will also be measured as a part of ongoing forest inventory work. Management activities will include, but are not limited to, pre-commercial and commercial thinning, and the use of prescribed fire, as necessary to limit the competition between trees, maintain vigor, and reduce the amount and continuity of fuels available to wildfire.

As established by Tribal Resolution NP 03-190, financial net gains from carbon credits will be deposited into a special account which will be used to duplicate this project. The ancillary environmental and social benefits extend well beyond carbon storage. These benefits include, but are not limited to, improved water quality and restoration of spawning habitat for Chinook salmon and Steelhead trout through watershed protection, reduced soil erosion, reduced use of pesticides, an increase in biodiversity, and the restoration of wildlife habitat. Social and cultural benefits include increasing the amount of forested land for gathering and recreational opportunities as well as economic benefits to the Nez Perce Tribe and its members via tree planting, cone

---

① 1 mile≈1. 6093km.

collection, and thinning employment opportunities.

Measurement/Quantification of GHG reductions: Carbon sequestration rates are projected using the U. S. Forest Service-approved model FVS for purposes of project scoping. Site-sampling procedures developed from timber cruise methods to measure actual carbon sequestration rates every five years during the project contract term. Conversions of carbon content to CO_2 equivalents will be calculated using sample biomass densities measures.

Baseline/Additionality: Baseline GHG emissions calculated from average irrigated field crop production in this region. Project passes regulatory, common practices, and barriers tests for additionality.

Leakage: Off-project GHG leakage from reduced production of field crops calculated and subtracted from project net GHG reduction yields. Off-project reductions in GHG leakage from increased wood products on project lands calculated and added to project net GHG reduction yields. Leakage calculations follow procedures in the Duke standard.

Monitoring methodology and plan: complies with protocols in Duke standard. Monitoring performed by Nez Perce Tribal Forestry department.

Third party verification plan: Verification plan format from Duke standard. Project validation (upfront evaluation) and subsequent project performance evaluation by qualified 3rd party verifier (SCS, Inc).

Contracting/ownership: 80 year term, subject to possible renewal. Seller liable for underperformance in GHG reductions, compensation through either payment reimbursement with interest, or in equivalent GHG reductions from another source. Nez Perce Tribe to implement insurance through backup reserve of reforested acreage converted from irrigated crop production. Ownership of GHG reductions transferred to buyer during the years of the contract. Ownership of GHG reductions in subsequent years after contract expires reverts to sellers.

5. 2. 5. 6　Dairy Methane/Northeast

Type of Project: CO_2, CH_4, and N_2O reductions from capture of methane from dairy manure by anaerobic digestion, displacement of fossil fuel use from use of methane fuel, and reduction in nitrogen fertilizer use from use of digestion residues.

Location of Project (s): Selected dairy operations in upstate New York, USA.

Measures Implemented: Manure produced in dairy operations is collected and contained in anaerobic digestion systems. Methane from digester used as fuel; digester residue applied as fertilizer to farm lands.

Organization (s) /Individuals: Central New York Resource Conservation and Development, Inc.

Project Description: GHG reductions from dairy operations are achieved by installing and operating anaerobic digesters utilizing dairy manure. Prior methane emissions from uncontained manure are captured; use of methane fuel produced by digesters reduces fossil fuel combustion; and digester residues are applied as fertilizers reducing nitrogen fertilizer use.

Measurement/Quantification of GHG reductions: Project scoping utilizes dairy industry manure production factors; anaerobic digester methane production factors; and N_2O emission factor from nitrogen fertilizer applications. During project term manure volumes and composition sampled; digester methane production metered; fossil-fuel displacement from local electric utility grid calculated from utility generation source data. N_2O reductions from reduced nitrogen fertilizer applications calculated with DNDC model.

Baseline/Additionality: Baseline includes methane emissions from unconfined dairy manure; CO_2 emissions from electricity generation by local utility; and N_2O emissions from application of nitrogen fertilizers. Project passes regulatory, common practices, and barriers tests for additionality.

Leakage: no reduction in commodity production results from this project, so no leakage caused.

Monitoring methodology and plan: complies with protocols in Duke standard. Monitoring performed by local conservation district staff.

Third party verification plan: Verification plan format from Duke standard. Project validation (upfront evaluation) and subsequent project performance evaluation by qualified 3rd party verifier.

Contracting/ownership: 3 years initial term, subject to possible renewal. Seller liable for underperformance in GHG reductions, compensation through either payment reimbursement with interest, or in equivalent GHG reductions from another source. Ownership of GHG reductions transferred to buyer during the years of the contract. Ownership of GHG reductions in subsequent years after contract expires reverts to sellers.

5.2.6 Concluding Remarks

Major opportunities for rural economies and land managers are emerging with the global effort to control atmospheric pollution from GHGs. Existing practices and technologies in the land sector offer many ways to reduce GHG emissions both directly as a source and indirectly as a carbon sink. Agriculture is critical to the well-being of all nations, and the need to create sustainable food production is now more urgent than ever. But agriculture is highly sensitive and vulnerable to climate change, making sustainability an even greater challenge than most economic sectors. GHG mitigation investments in agriculture yield multiple benefits-reduction of GHG emissions, adoption of sustainable practices and technologies, economic value-added for rural economies, increased resource use efficiency, reduced production costs, increased profitability, and adaptation to the effects of climate change on agro-ecosystems. Efficiency where affordable is always a good thing for resources and the environment. But incentives to develop these efficiencies must be in place. The added benefit of payments from GHG offset production provides a major new incentive. The efficiencies gained from adoption of climate-friendly practices and technologies in agriculture are a major benefit for all nations and societies. But all nations and societies need to agree on and implement global incentives for eco-compensation for land managers to make this happen. That major global challenge remains.

6 Policy and Funding Options for Mitigating and Adapting to Climate Change in Rural Areas

Most farmers cannot rely on income from routine agricultural activities to cover the cost of mitigating and adapting to climate change. By 2030, the annual global cost of such adaptations is expected to reach $250 billion~380 billion—of which China's needs will account for more than 50%.

About almost all of China's adaptation costs, and about half of its mitigation costs are expected to occur in poor rural regions. That is, by 2030, the cost of fulfilling the energy and environmental needs of the rural population living in poverty is expected to reach $83 billion~127 billion, or one third the world's cost. Of that amount, $55 billion~65 billion will be needed to reduce greenhouse gas (GHG) emissions from agriculture, land-use change, and forestry, such as by managing farms, grasslands, rangelands, fertilizers, and livestock to reduce methane and nitrous oxide emissions, and by avoiding deforestation, managing existing forests better, and planting new forests.

To address these needs, the central government has established policies and funding mechanisms to enhance the ability of rural areas to mitigate and adapt to climate change, including through energy-efficient construction and reliance on renewable energy sources. These provisions have already paid off in pilot projects and more ambitious programs that are producing results. To reinforce those programs, China can tap international funding mechanisms created to purchase credits from farmers who reduce their GHG emissions. China can also consider modifying its trade policies to bolster its ability to cope with climate change.

6.1 Policies Promoting Energy-Efficient Rural Buildings

6.1.1 Policies and Regulations

The Energy Saving Regulation for Civil Constructions, implemented in October 2008, stipulates that the state will encourage and support the use of solar, geothermal, and other forms of renewable energy in both new and existing buildings.

The regulation directs local governments in areas with abundant solar resources to support the use of those resources to provide heat, hot water, lighting, and refrigeration. The regulation also requires governments above the county level to invest funds in research, development, and standard setting to support energy efficiency in existing buildings, the use of renewable energy, and energy-saving demonstration projects. The law provides tax incentives for energy-saving construction projects, and establishes energy-efficiency standards for designers, builders, supervisors, and other registered practitioners working on civil construction.

In March 2009, the Building Energy Conservation and the Science and Technology Division of the Department of Residential Housing and Urban and Rural Construction announced that the Ministry of Construction will strengthen policies, regulations, and standards related to energy efficiency. The goal is to ensure that more than 90% of all new construction, and 60 million m^2 of existing buildings, fulfill energy-efficiency standards by the end of 2009.

To help achieve those goals, the government will accelerate energy-saving reconstruction of existing residential buildings in northern regions, and encourage local governments to devote funds to that effort. The ministry will also establish the Special Program of Building Energy Conservation To strengthen oversight of energy-efficiency standards for new construction, develop economic incentives for energy-efficient, land-conserving buildings, and pursue research.

Meanwhile the Science and Technology Division will study the use of solar energy, biogas, compacted straw, and other modern forms of renewable energy in rural areas, and investigate the economics of these technologies. For example, the division will expand demonstration projects for buildings that rely on renewable energy, with a focus on the use of solar water-heating systems; the use of rooftop photovoltaic systems and curtain walls for producing electricity; and the use of freshwater and seawater to run heat pumps in the Yangtze River Basin and coastal areas.

6. 1. 2　Case Study on Energy-Conserving Rural Homes

A team from the Department of Building Science and Technology in the School of Architecture at Tsinghua University is pursuing the first large-scale domestic attempt to optimize and evaluate an integrated energy-saving system for rural buildings. Professor Smith Ke of the US National Academy of Sciences had put a premium on this study, and he will also promote the first international energy-efficiency project in China's rural areas. The well-known journal *Nature* reported this achievement.

The study team has now completed a pilot project in a village in the Fangshan district of Beijing. The team has also cooperated with the Council for Promoting Sustainable Development in Beijing, and completed more than 500 rural residences in Pinggu, Shijingshan, Huairou, Miyun, and other suburban counties in that province.

The pilot project occurred in Moundety Mountain Temple village in Qinglong Manchu Autonomous County. In this county, as in many mountainous areas, traditional gray tile-roofed houses have little resistance to cold, and inside temperatures are often below freezing in winter. Farmers mainly depend on firewood and coal for heat.

Because of the pilot project, more than 100 families in the village now have new residences that rely on gathering solar heat. To retain that heat, walls are built of shale and hollow brick, and windows are constructed of hollow plastic-steel glass. Families need only a small amount of coal—typically one-third of the amount they formerly used—for supplementary heat while enjoying indoor temperatures of $10 \sim 15°C$ even during the coldest winter months. If China's entire northern region adopted this approach, it could eliminate the need to burn about 5 million tons of coal equivalent for heat each year—worth about 50 million Yuan.

According to the head of the Construction Bureau in Qinglong Manchu Autonomous County, the new residences cost slightly more than traditional houses, but each will last for about 60 years, and heating costs are less than half those of traditional houses. The project therefore provides significant economic benefits.

To reinforce those benefits, the County Party Committee and the government are investing 10 million Yuan in water, electricity, roads, communications, and street lighting for the village. To ensure the quality of the project, the county chose qualified construction companies and hired specialists to help farmers supervise construction.

6. 2   Policies Promoting Rural Renewable Energy

Article IV of China's Energy Conservation Law stipulates that the government will encourage the development and use of new and renewable energy sources. Article XI of that law stipulates that the State Department and the governments of provinces, autonomous regions, and municipalities will devote funds to energy efficiency.

Article XVIII of China's Renewable Energy Law stipulates that the government will encourage and support the development and use of renewable energy in rural areas. Departments at or above the county level will formulate plans for developing renewable energy in rural areas by promoting the use of methane and other biomass resources, household solar energy, wind energy, and hydropower, among other technologies. The law also directs governments above the county level to provide financial support for renewable energy projects in rural areas.

For example, regardless of their size, new power plants that rely on gasified straw can enjoy government subsidies of 0. 25 Yuan per kW · h for 15 years. Managers of the electricity grid guarantee that they will buy all the power that such plants produce, and plant operators do not need to pay tariffs or value-added taxes on imported equipment. Other preferential policies include lower prices for land, access to bank loans, and tax breaks for 15 years. Because these plants are based on innovative technology that protects the environment, the National Development and Reform Committee and the

Electricity Supervision Committee announced in April 2008 that the government would provide a subsidy of 0. 1 Yuan per kW • h. [①]

In the National Rural Biogas Construction Plan, the Ministry of Agriculture stipulated that the total number of methane digesters would exceed 50 million by 2002, and that 20% of households would have access to methane by 2010. These digesters process animal and human solid waste under anaerobic conditions into methane, also known as marsh gas, which households then use for heating, cooking, and lighting.

The investment in these units will total 61 billion Yuan by 2010, of which the central government will have invested 44. 9 billion Yuan, including 1200 Yuan per household in the Northwest and Northeast, 1000 Yuan per household in the Southwest, and 800 Yuan per household in other regions. To improve both living standards and the environment, in 2005 the central government accelerated the popularization of biogas at the provincial and municipal levels.

To ensure smooth progress on methane projects, each province has invested some of its own funds, most by tapping financing designated for alleviating poverty, returning farmland to forests, protecting natural forests, improving rural hygiene, and constructing a new socialist countryside. When the economy is strong, each city, county, and town also provides subsidies to farmers for constructing methane digesters.

More than 20 million households now rely on methane digesters, which produce 8 billion cubic meters of marsh gas every year. More than 4000 regions also operate larger-scale biogas projects that produce more than 1 million cubic meters of methane every year. And more than 100 medium- and large-sized methane-fueled power plants produce 200 million degrees of electricity annually. The result is that methane production has reached a total of 15. 4 billion m^3 annually—equivalent to 24. 2 mtce, and wood from 140 million mu of forests, saving farmers 20 billion Yuan each year.

6. 3　Programs to Return Farmland to Forests

Per capita carbon dioxide emissions are far lower in China than in developed countries. Still, China has been playing an important role in large-scale afforestation (the planting of new forests) for many years. The result is that its lands and forests now store more than 100 million tons of carbon.

For example, in March 2000, with approval from the State Council, the State Forestry Administration, State Development Planning Commission, and the Ministry of Finance jointly issued a "notice on developing demonstration projects of returning farmland to forest and grassland in the upper reaches of the Yangtze River, the upper

---

① The committees are providing this funding under the Subsidies for the Electricity Generated Renewable Energy and Rationing Transaction Program.

and middle reaches of the Yellow River, 2000. "

This program, known as the Project on Returning Farmlands to Forests, has the strictest policies, the largest investment, the widest coverage, and the highest level of participation of any environmental effort in China. After eight years of implementation, the nation has returned 139 million mu of farmlands to forests, converted 205 million mu of barren hills and wastelands to forests, and conserved 20 million mu of forests, improving the environment in central and western regions.

In 1999, even before the central government formally launched this program, Sichuan, Shaanxi, and Gansu Provinces initiated a project to return farmlands to forests. After three years of experiments, the project became fully operational in 2002. It encompasses 25 autonomous regions and municipalities, 1897 counties, 32 million households, and 124 million farmers of the Xinjiang Production and Construction Corps. Now part of the 10-year national plan, these provinces will return 5. 3 million hm^2 of farmlands to forests, create forests on another 8 million hm^2 of barren hills, prevent 36 million hm^2 from water loss, and complete windbreaks and sand stabilization on 70 million hm^2.

Through such large-scale forestry and grassland management, China has increased its forest coverage in central and western regions by more than 2 percentage points, including nearly 4 percentage points in Inner Mongolia and about 25 percentage points in Yan'an city in Shaanxi Province. Soil erosion and threats to sand dunes have also declined in these regions.

To continue returning farmland to forests and grasslands, the central government has established several policies and funding mechanisms and subsidies: Under the principle "those who plant forests and grasslands should manage and protect them, and they will be the ones who benefit," the government is encouraging farmers to sign contracts to return farmlands to forests and plant forests on suitable barren hills and wastelands. The government is extending the contract period to 50 years, and is allowing contracts to be inherited and transferred. In appropriate regions, not only households but also social organizations, enterprises, and institutions can contract to return farmlands to forests and grasslands on a voluntary basis, resolving problems with distribution of benefits and other issues by mutual agreement. This approach will spur regions with sound conditions to create concentrated, continuous forests and grasslands, and motivate individuals to create family forests and pastures that allow a wide range of related businesses.

For example, farmers can receive income subsidies for maintaining economic forests—those with productive potential—for five years. And they can receive income subsidies for maintaining ecological forests—those set aside solely to protect the environment—for eight years. Farmers who construct ecological forests and grasslands also enjoy preferential tax policies. After their projects pass inspection, farmers can receive food subsidies and cash. For example, the government will give farmers grain allowances based on their former crop production. Farmers in the upper reaches of the Yangtze River who have returned farmlands to forests can receive 300 kg of grain per mu, while those residing near the upper and middle reaches of the Yellow River can receive 200 kg of grain per mu. And every household that returns farmland to forests receives cash subsidies of 20 Yuan per mu, as well as 50 Yuan to buy seedlings.

The central government funds a percentage of the capital investment needed for pilot projects that return farmland to forests and grasslands, to be used for scientific and technological support, through the State Development Planning Commission. For example, the Department of Central Finance ratified special funds for each province based on the area of returned land, beginning in 2008. The Ministry of Finance, Development and Reform Commission, Western Development Office, the Ministry of Agriculture, the Forestry Bureau, and other departments approve the specific uses and management practices under this program.

Regions that return farmlands to forests and grasslands can receive funds from different channels for efforts to alleviate poverty, manage remaining agricultural lands, and conserve soil and water. For example, the central government compensates local governments for revenue losses from the program.

In September 2007, the State Council decided to provide more than 200 billion Yuan to continue returning farmland to forests and consolidate the results of the program. To ensure a livelihood for the farmers whose land has been reclaimed, the central government has arranged special funds to provide land to farmers for personal use. For example, the government tries to ensure that each farmer has 0.5 mu of land for personal use in southwestern regions, and 2 mu in northwestern regions.

The central government also provides subsidies of 600 Yuan per mu in the Southwest and 400 Yuan per mu in the Northwest to farmers for investing in infrastructure, and also provides funds for rural energy, ecological resettlement, and complementary planting. This new policy will directly benefit 124 million farmers and speed up ecological construction in central and western regions, promoting local sustainable development.

6.4 Funding for Rural Water Conservancy Projects

China has embarked on a comprehensive effort to make farmland irrigation and water supplies more efficient, especially in major grain-producing areas, regions with severe water shortages, and poverty-stricken areas. The goal is to encourage the development of both irrigated and arid regions while improving the rural environment. Concrete investments include:

1) Establishing special grant funds for small-scale water-saving projects

In 2005, the Central No. 1 Document asked central and provincial governments to establish special grant funds for water conservancy projects. That same year the General Office of State Council forwarded the View on the Establishment of New Mechanisms for Water Conservancy Construction of Farmlands. This policy also asked governments to increase funds for water conservancy projects, regulate the management of such projects, and obtain funds and labor through One Project One Discussion at the village level. Special grant funds for small-scale water conservancy projects have now been established

2) Reforming the system for funding state-owned medium- and large-scale irrigation projects and pumping stations.

In 2002, the Ministry of Finance and the Ministry of Water Resources created the Standard of Water Conservancy Construction Management and Maintenance. That same year the General Office of State Council created the View on the Reform of Water Conservancy Construction Management System. Under these policies, institutions managing medium- and large-scale state-owned irrigation areas and pumping stations are now classified as public-welfare and quasi-public-welfare units, making them eligible for funds from local governments.

3) Reforming the operating mechanisms and management of water conservancy projects in rural areas

These reforms include: Strengthening the planning, guidance, and supervision of such projects. Exploring more effective approaches to managing small-, medium-, and large-scale rural irrigation districts and systems by clarifying their ownership and assigning management responsibilities. For example, the government can encourage small-scale farmers to form cooperatives to oversee water use, and those cooperatives can own assets created through national aid. Reforming the mechanism for pricing water.

6.5　Funding for Credits for Reducing Greenhouse Gas Emissions

Several programs inside and outside China have created mechanisms for purchasing credits created by farmers and others who reduce their GHG emissions. These programs could provide an important source of funding for China's efforts to promote energy efficiency, renewable energy, and sustainable development.

6.5.1 China's Clean Development Mechanism Fund

In November 2007, the State Council approved creation of the Clean Development Mechanism Fund, to be used to produce marketable credits under the United Nations Clean Development Mechanism (CDM). [1] This long-term, nonprofit state-owned fund will support action to mitigate climate change under the national strategy of sustainable development.

The fund will encourage project construction, provide technical support, share and manage information, train personnel, and build institutional capacity and public awareness. This fund is an important innovation, because it will coordinate the efforts of domestic enterprises and governments and institutions abroad.

6.5.2 The European Carbon Fund

A number of financial institutions in Europe created the European Carbon Fund (ECF) to invest in projects worldwide that reduce GHG emissions, and to market credits based on those reductions. According to a recent ECF study, the European Union's program for trading GHG emissions will create a market for reductions of some 2.2 billion tons of CO_2 emissions annually. The fund will try to find buyers for another 60 to 120 million tons of GHG reductions created through the Clean Development Mechanism. ECF officials say they intend to invest in 10 to 20 projects in China.

6.5.3 World Bank Funds

The World Bank manages nine carbon-related funds that use public and private financing to buy credits for cuts in GHG emissions from lower-income countries and communities. China's Umbrella Carbon Facility is one of the nine funds, which together handle more than $1.9 billion. The Umbrella Carbon Facility can produce double dividends, because the Chinese government has promised to invest 65% of the profits from the Umbrella Carbon Facility in its Clean Development Mechanism Fund.

In 2006 the World Bank announced completion of the first transaction under the Umbrella Carbon Facility, valued at $1.02 billion, to be used to purchase credits for reducing GHG emissions from two industrial gas projects in China.

---

① The National Development and Reform Commission, the Ministry of Finance, the Ministry of Foreign Affairs, and the Ministry of Science and Technology released the Operating and Managing Approaches for the Clean Development Mechanism Project in October 2005.

6.5.4 Global Environment Facility

China signed the Convention on Biological Diversity and the UN Framework Convention on Climate Change in 1993. To fulfill the terms of those conventions, China cooperates closely with the Global Environment Facility (GEF). By the end of June 2002, China had received more than $300 million in GEF grants—more than any other country.

For example, GEF Phase I (from July 1994 to June 1998) promised $2 billion, and China contributed $5.6 million. GEF Phase II (July 1998 to June 2002) again promised about $2 billion, and China contributed $8.2 million. Those funds supported 55 projects targeting conservation of biodiversity, energy efficiency in industry, renewable energy, protection of international waters, control of land degradation, and related institutional capacity building.

6.5.5 Funding from Individual Companies

In October 2007, American International Group announced that it would purchase GHG credits from projects in Xinjiang and Sichuan Provinces that aim to conserve energy and provide more renewable energy. These payments will help farmers produce credits for about 310 000 tons of CO_2 reductions—offsetting half the GHG emissions from the company's global business segments in 2006.

The projects are being developed by the Environmental Defense Fund, based in the United States. The projects will reduce the use of water, fossil fuel, and nitrogen fertilizer in agriculture, and produce methane from anaerobic digestion of solid waste from human and animals for use for cooking and lighting. The projects will also plant trees in desert areas to conserve soil, block winds, fix sand, and reduce soil erosion.

6.5.6 Other International Funding for Environmental Protection

Climate Change Capital, a fund based in London, plans to invest 5 billion Yuan ($732 million) in environmental protection projects in China over the next two to three years, such as for disposing of industrial waste and developing clean energy technologies.

Other nongovernmental organizations, such as the World Wide Fund for Nature and the International Fund for Animal Welfare, have also provided financial support for environmental projects in China, and cooperated with government agencies and civil society organizations on those projects.

6.6 Using Trade Policy to Safeguard the Food Supply Under Climate Change

The policies of China and other major economies on international trade have a significant impact on agricultural production, energy use, and climate change. A research report submitted to this task force explored that impact.

The report concurs with the majority of published research that agricultural production can meet the world's food needs during the remainder of this century—regardless of the climate change scenario. That is because higher agricultural productivity from technological change is highly likely to outweigh any negative effect on productivity from climate change, assuming that historic improvements in productivity continue. [1]

Other key conclusions from this research include:

- The impacts of climate change and trade liberalization will not be uniform across the globe, because agricultural productivity will rise in some regions and decline in others. The regions that will see the strongest positive impact on agriculture under climate change include China, the European Union, North America, and Brazil. The regions affected negatively include East Africa, Central and Southern Africa, North and West Africa, the Middle East, and Russia. Climate change will also undermine agriculture in India and South and East Asia, but only marginally.

  These findings have important implications for the distribution of global wealth, considering that climate change will harm the poorest regions. People in these regions are also more dependent on agricultural activities for subsistence and income than residents of many other regions.

- Even if climate change improves the productivity of a crop in a given region, that does not necessarily mean production will shift to that region. If other regions see even greater improvements, production will shift to those regions—if needed inputs are abundant and competitively priced.

- The productivity of processed meat and dairy sectors improves the most in China, Australia, and the former Soviet republics under climate change. Productivity in those sectors declines the most in East Africa, North and West Africa, the Middle East, Central and Southern Africa, Russia, and South and

---

[1] A major caveat to this conclusion is that the shocks to agricultural yields used in this research do not include possible threshold effects associated with climate change, changes in pestilence, changes in sea levels, or changes in freshwater supplies (other than precipitation). These impacts could have enormous and uncertain consequences for agricultural production around the globe.

East Asia.

- Processed food sectors in East Africa, North and West Africa, the Middle East and Russia perform worst under climate change, while those sectors in China, the former Soviet republics, Brazil, and Australia perform marginally better in the face of climate change.
- Differences in the impact of various climate scenarios on food production are typically modest.
- All regions can improve their welfare under all climate scenarios by removing border taxes and subsidies. Trade liberalization may therefore be a good strategy for countries hoping to partially offset any negative effects of climate change.

In China, the research shows that removing border taxes and subsidies will result in higher production of all commodities except rice and livestock. Under liberalized trade, the nation's rice exports increase significantly—by as much as 0. 14 million tons in 2030. China's maize exports increase modestly, and all other agricultural exports are largely unaffected. China's rice imports also rise under liberalized trade—by around 0. 3 million tons (compared with the baseline case) by 2030, and as much as 36 million tons by 2080, while wheat and maize imports fall slightly.

Under liberalized trade, real prices of all agricultural commodities rise modestly in China. However, rising incomes offset those increases, so people's welfare improves overall. In fact, China sees a positive outcome under all climate scenarios if it removes border taxes and subsidies, as real private consumption rises by 0. 7%~0. 8% by 2050.

7　Case Studies: How Rural China is Tackling Climate Change

China's rural development goals include safeguarding food security and eliminating poverty. Unfortunately, the desire to encourage agricultural development and economic growth in rural regions has sometimes meant that the government overlooks environmental goals such as energy conservation and pollution control.

Many existing policies also focus on reducing energy use and pollution from urban enterprises—despite the fact that economic and social losses from pollution in rural regions have sometimes exceeded those in urban areas. The nation urgently needs to design cost-effective policies that improve the efficiency of rural energy use and reduce the environmental impact of production and everyday life while also addressing rural poverty, given that some 130 million Chinese still live below the international poverty line.

China can fulfill all these needs by creating direct government subsidies for a shift to more efficient and renewable energy supplies, and also by granting marketable credits for reductions in GHG emissions to rural residents. In fact, a number of projects already under way reveal the nation's huge potential for promoting economic development while investing in energy efficiency and pollution control and addressing climate change.

7.1　Cases on Using Energy Efficiency to Clean Up Pollution and Raise Income from Animal Husbandry

Since the reform and opening-up, animal husbandry in China has attracted global attention for its achievements. Livestock production has seen continuous growth: by the end of 2007, farmers were raising 565 million pigs, 106 million cattle, 286 million sheep, and 9579 million chickens—at least 1.5 times the amounts in 1978. National output from animal husbandry also jumped from 21 billion Yuan in 1978 to 1613 billion Yuan in 2007, as agricultural production and the rural economy expanded from 15% to 33% of agricultural GDP.

In 2007, national output of meat and poultry ranked first in the world, with an output of 69 million tons and 25 million tons, accounting for 24.7% and 37.7% of world output, respectively. China also ranked third worldwide in milk output in 2007, producing 36 million tons, or 5.4% of global output.

From 1978 to 2007, meat, egg, and milk production grew at an annual rate of 10.8%, 15.2%, and 19.0%, respectively. Per capita output of meat, eggs, and milk also rose rapidly, reaching the level of moderately developed countries (Figure 7.1).

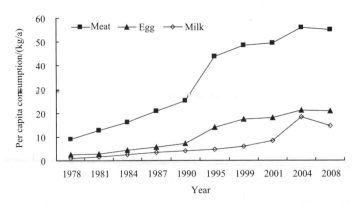

Figure 7. 1　Per Capita Output of Livestock Products, including Meat, Eggs, and Milk, 1978～2008

The scale and intensity of animal husbandry expanded commensurately. At the beginning of the reform and opening-up, rural residents cultivated beasts and birds mainly for household use. However, by the end of 2007, 48. 4% of China's pigs, 34. 6% of its beef cattle, 41. 3% of its sheep, 58. 9% of its milk cows, 80. 1% of its chickens, and 72% its laying hens were raised for commercial use.

7. 1. 1　The Impact of Animal Husbandry on Energy Use and the Environment

China's expanding animal husbandry industry is raising peasants' income and improving living standards of both urban and rural residents. However, the huge volume of wastes from these activities is posing a growing threat to the rural environment. In 2007, excrement from beasts and birds reached 2. 7 billion tons, while cultivation sewage reached 11 billion tons.

Raising livestock and poultry in modern, high-density environments also creates moisture and waste gas from metabolism, bug dust from feed distribution and indoor cleaning, and manure and urine. Farmers must remove this waste from buildings promptly to avoid stressing the animals, slowing their growth, and lowering their disease resistance. Modern cultivation also requires providing daily ventilation, cooling indoor areas in summer, and heating them in winter. The development of animal husbandry in China and a continuous increase in its scale has therefore meant growing energy demand.

Facilities for treating waste from animal husbandry require a large up-front investment, and produce no direct return. Therefore, except for farms with marsh gas tanks, most have no facilities for treating animal waste. Farmers simply discard large quantities of untreated animal waste, which enters rivers and lakes and poses serious threats to the environment.

(1) Water pollution. Pollutants in untreated sewage gradually degrade water quality, with high levels of nitrogen and phosphorus, choking off the oxygen supply of

aquatic life in a process known as eutrophication. Discharging large amounts of waste from beasts and birds into rivers and lakes also kills aquatic organisms directly.

Poisonous compounds may raise pollutant levels and decrease the amount of dissolved oxygen in groundwater. The water often becomes black and smelly—a condition that is very difficult to reverse.

(2) Air pollution. Cultivation of beasts and birds often creates malodorous gases, as well as large quantities of poisonous ingredients such as amide, sulphide, and methane, polluting the air and affecting the physical and psychological health of workers. The proximity of animal farms to institutions such as universities also creates tension between peasants and other rural residents.

(3) Transmission of pathogens. Animal waste contains numerous pathogenic microorganisms, parasitic ovums, and mosquito and fly larvae, which can harm both people and animals.

(4) Disruption of farmland ecology. If farmers apply highly concentrated sewage from beasts and birds to fields for long periods of time, those materials can reduce productivity and cause large-scale rot. High concentrations of sewage may also seriously undermine soil quality by compacting soil—preventing ventilation and reducing permeability.

Animal husbandry also account for a significant portion of agricultural GHG emissions. Livestock and poultry continuously discharge carbon dioxide created during metabolism, as well as methane produced by fermentation in their intestinal tracts. Ruminants such as cattle and sheep release methane at much higher rates than poultry and other animals. Animal waste also releases large amounts of methane and nitrous oxide during storage and treatment, so it is an important source of greenhouse gases.

In 1994, agriculture accounted for 17% of China's 3.650 billion tons of GHG emissions (in carbon dioxide equivalent). Of that amount, animal husbandry produced 11.049 million tons of methane emissions and 155 000 tons of nitrous oxide emissions (Table 7.1). Given the exploding number of cultivated beasts and birds in China since that time, animal husbandry is contributing growing amounts of greenhouse gases.

Table 7.1 Methane and Nitrous Oxide Emissions from Animal Husbandry in China, 1994

GHG type	Source	Discharge/ton	Percentage of total agricultural discharge/%	Percentage of national discharge/%
Methane	Intestinal tracts	10 182 000	59.21	29.70
	Excrement	867 000	5.04	2.53
	Grazing	110 000	14.03	12.94
Nitrous oxide	Excrement burning	1000	0.10	0.12
	Other excrement management	44 000	5.56	5.18

7.1.2　Managing Animal Waste More Effectively

Two projects in rural China are aiming to raise the income of rural residents engaged in animal husbandry while reducing energy use, improving the local environment, and cutting greenhouse gas emissions.

7.1.2.1　Case Study: Oversize Marsh Gas Project of Shandong Minhe Animal Husbandry Co

Shandong Minhe Animal Husbandry Co. Ltd. , is Asia's biggest manufacturer of breeding chickens. [①] Each year the company manages more than 1. 30 million breeding hens and hatches more than 100 million baby chicks. The company also butchers and processes 30 million chickens and 60 000 tons of chicken products annually. The combination of chicken breeding, cultivation, butchering, and processing has created a nearly perfect industrial chain.

The company's Minhe baby chicks—the leading national brand because of their disease resistance and high survival rate—are sold in more than 20 cities and provinces in China and 10 countries. All the company's chicken products have received ISO 9001 : 2000, HACCP certification, and the company has received many top prizes for its production. [②] On May 16, 2008, the company, China's only domestic manufacturer of breeding chickens, sold its first public shares.

The company uses an oversize marsh gas project to produce combined heat and power. This system—which uses chicken manure as a resource—pretreats the raw material, produces methane (or marsh gas) through anaerobic digestion, purifies and distributes the methane, and treats the residues from the fermentation process (Figure 7. 2). Major products of the system include not only marsh gas but also dregs and slurries.

The biogas is used directly as fuel, and also to generate "green" electricity. Most waste heat from the process of producing electricity is used to maintain the fermentation process and heat the anaerobic digesters in winter. The rest of the waste heat is used to warm the chicken houses in winter, to reduce the consumption of fossil fuel.

The project includes eight efficient, 3000 m^3 anaerobic digesters (Figure 7. 3). These digesters use 500 tons of excrement (20% dry matter) from 23 chicken breeding houses and 8 chicken farms, as well as 500 tons of farm sewage, to produce 30 000 m^3 of marsh gas daily, and 10. 95 million m^3 annually.

The installed capacity of the biogas power plant is 3 MW • h. The power plant,

---

① This company was formerly known as the Penglai Improved-Type Chicken Demonstration under the Ministry of Agriculture.

② Prizes include the National-Level Leading Enterprises of Agricultural Industralization, Top 50 Asian Poultry Enterprise, National Best Poultry Enterprise, National Agricultural Standardization Demo, National Chicken Export Standard Demo, and Recycling Economy Demo Enterprise of Shandong Province, among others.

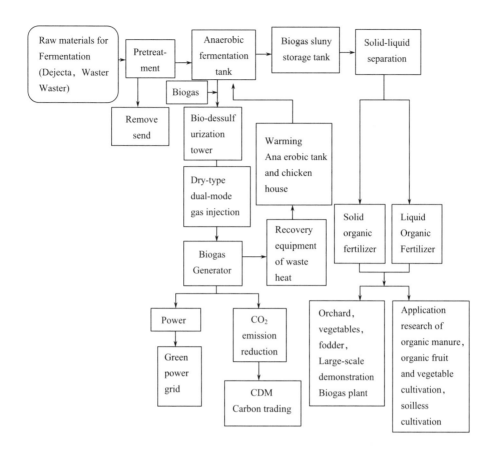

Figure 7.2　Process Flow for Shandong Minhe Animal Husbandry Co.'s Biogas Project

Figure 7.3　Anaerobic Digesters of Shandong Minhe Oversize Marsh Gas Project

connected to a grid, produces 60 000 kW · h of electricity daily, and 21 900 MW · h annually. At a per unit price of 0.35 Yuan, the plant's annual income from the sale of electricity is about 7. 60 million Yuan.

After anaerobic fermentation, the digesters produce 46. 83 tons of dregs each year (with a water ratio of 70%), which converts to 17. 5 tons of organic fertilizer (with a water ratio of 20%), as well as about 850 tons of slurry (with a solid content of 1. 3%). These substances retain most of the nutrient content of the chicken manure, including nitrogen, phosphate, and calcium, making them efficient green fertilizers.

The dregs are therefore applied to crops and fruit trees and used in aquaculture and floriculture, while the slurries are used to irrigate neighboring farmland, replacing 310 000 m^3 of fresh water every year. At a price of 500 Yuan per ton, the sale of solid fertilizer brings in 3. 20 million Yuan each year, and annual income from the sale of both dregs and slurries totals 3. 51 million Yuan.

Total annual income from the project is therefore 11. 11 million Yuan, and net income is 5. 61 million Yuan, after operating costs. Given that the project required an investment of 60 million Yuan, its static payback time is 10. 7 years. However, because the project reduces GHG emissions by 86 000 tons of CO_2 equivalent, the company has agreed to transfer credits for those reductions to the World Bank —the first agricultural project approved under the United Nations Clean Development Mechanism (CDM). At $ 10 per ton of CO_2 equivalent, the company will receive nearly 58 million Yuan for its GHG credits over a 10-years period.

That income, combined with revenue from the sale of fertilizer, brings the company's annual gross income from the mash gas project to 16. 91 million Yuan. After deducting operating costs, the company will see total net earnings of 11. 41 million Yuan per year, enabling it to recover its investment in 5. 3 years.

This case study shows that a large-scale marsh gas project can create local economic and environmental benefits while also earning income from the sale of credits for reducing GHG emissions on international markets. To provide yet another source of revenue for such projects, China can create a domestic market for GHG reductions.

7. 1. 2. 2　Case Study: Small Marsh Gas Project in Enshi Prefecture, Hubei Province

A project known as the Ecological Family-Use Marsh Gas Tank also recently won United Nations approval under the CDM program—the first rural marsh gas project for family use in China to do so. The project is in Enshi prefecture, an impoverished area of southwest Hubei Province.

Enshi prefecture encompasses 24 000 km^2 of land, including 3. 79 million mu of farmland, and an agricultural population of 3. 30 million, including 930 000 peasant households living in more than 2000 villages. A portal to Southwest China since ancient times, the prefecture has historical, cultural, and geological resources like those of other southwestern provinces, and a similar level of socioeconomic development. That is, the six counties and two cities under its administration are all key national targets for economic development and poverty relief.

In 2003, Party Committee and government of Enshi proposed creating a model ecological prefecture and villages, with construction of marsh gas tanks as the core strategy. The government saw this approach as the key to resolving the "issues of agriculture" while also protecting the environment.

To promote rapid yet sustainable development and become the nation's first prefecture that uses marsh gas as its main energy source, local leaders planned to construct 700 000 marsh gas tanks in appropriate rural areas over five years. As of 2006, Enshi had built 410 000 marsh gas tanks for home use, accounting for 44% of farm households in the chosen areas.

The project entails building a closed manure pit for human and animal excreta for each family while also updating its kitchen stove, toilet, and livestock sheds. The biogas from the pit can replace the use of traditional biomass fuels such as straw and wood for lighting, cooking, and heating, as well as the use of fossil fuels such as coal and petroleum.

One villager from Wuyi Village in Lichuan city estimated that six people in his family formerly used 12 kg of firewood daily for household needs. And a supervisor from Zhujiapu in Xiaocun village estimated that each household could save 2500 kg of firewood each year by installing a marsh gas tank. Some 51 households with marsh gas tanks could therefore avoid cutting forest covering more than 250 mu. After popularizing marsh gas tanks, an entire prefecture could save more than 1.5 million mu of forest.

Indeed, Enshi prefecture has seen its forest cover expand by 5% in the last three years, and the appearance of villages has improved remarkably. Meanwhile peasants no longer need to perform the heavy work entailed in cutting and hauling firewood, allowing them to expand their agricultural production or develop subsidiary businesses to increase their income.

According to the Ministry of Agriculture, an $8m^3$ family-use marsh gas tank can process excrement from four to six pigs, with the resulting biogas replacing 847 kg of coal. In so doing, the marsh gas tanks have greatly reduced air pollution from sulfur dioxide, benefiting farmers. Enshi has a long history of planting high-quality tea. Although the government restricts the amount of chemicals and fertilizers farmers can apply to that crop, coal burning by every family formerly contaminated the tea with sulfur dioxide, preventing the sale of tea products on international markets. However, after growers replaced coal use with marsh gas, Enshi tea reappeared on European Union markets in 2004, increasing farmers' income.

According to the Ministry of Agriculture, if marsh gas is valued at 1.2 Yuan per cubic meter, each household with a tank could save 462 Yuan per year in energy costs. Applying the dregs and slurries to food and other crops could allow farmers to save another 100 Yuan in the cost of fertilizers and farm chemicals. Reductions in costs and labor mean that peasants' net per capita annual income could nearly double if they plant economic crops such as high-quality tea.

Constructing a marsh gas tank and its supporting facilities in rural areas requires 3000~5000 Yuan, with the government providing a subsidy of 1000 Yuan. Each peasant household could therefore see a static payback time on a capital investment of 4000 Yuan of 7.1 years.

However, if each tank processes excrement from four pigs and replaces 847 kg coal each year while also reducing methane emissions from the excreta, it could cut GHG emissions by 4.1~5.2 tons of CO_2 equivalent each year. Peasants could earn 181 Yuan from the sale of GHG credits for such reductions. Annual savings from a family-use marsh gas tank could therefore total 743 Yuan, reducing the payback period to 5.4 years. By replacing coal use and the traditional approach to managing swine excrement in the entire prefecture, such a shift could reduce GHG emissions by 59 153 tons of CO_2 equivalent while providing income of 60 million Yuan to 330 million local residents over 10 years.

This case study shows that building marsh gas tanks for family use can transform everyday rural life as well as agricultural production—enabling peasants to move away from subsistence toward a market-oriented approach characterized by high investment but also higher income. Indeed, Yu Zhengsheng, a member of the Political Bureau of the Central Committee of the Chinese Communist Party and secretary of the Hubei Provincial Party Committee, has called the project the "current new mode of rural development," while the Ministry of Agriculture has pointed to the "Enshi mode" of ecological home construction as a model.

7.2　Cases on the Rural Use of Biomass to Generate Electricity

Biomass refers to plants as well as microorganisms formed through photosynthesis. Biomass stores solar energy in the form of chemical energy, which may be converted into solid, liquid, or gaseous fuels. A renewable energy resource, biomass may be classified into five groups: forest resources, agricultural resources, domestic sewage, industrial organic wastewater and solid waste, and excrement from beasts and birds.

Biomass ranks fourth in the world as source of energy, after coal, petroleum, and natural gas, and therefore plays a significant role in the global energy system. According to various experts, biomass fuels produced through the use of new technology will account for more than 40% of global energy use by the middle of this century.

In China, traditional forms of biomass energy cannot satisfy the growing energy needs of vast rural areas. Moreover, the need to reduce GHG emissions to address global warming has become urgent. The goal of building a new socialist countryside while protecting the environment and ensuring sustainable development is therefore spurring research on new technologies that allow more efficient use of biomass resources.

7.2.1 The Use of Biomass Energy in China Today

In 2003, rural areas in China used 262 mtce of biomass energy, including straw, marsh gas, and fuel wood—accounting for 22.4% of total national energy use (State Administration of Forestry, 2003). However, direct burning of biomass—as well as the practice of simply discarding unburned resources—mean that the use of biomass energy is inefficient, resulting in serious pollution of the rural environment, and undercutting rural economic and social development.

Rural sustainable development requires breakthroughs in the development and use of biomass energy. Fortunately, although this transformation is still in its early stages, the use of modern forms of biomass energy in rural China is growing rapidly. The efficient and maximum use of biomass energy will enable rural areas to meet household energy demand, relieve rising national energy demand, promote rural economic and social development, and improve the rural environment.

On June 7, 2007, the Standing Committee Session of the State Council examined and approved the Medium- and Long-Term Development Plan for Renewable Energy Sources. That plan calls for prioritizing the use of marsh gas, solid biomass fuel created by molding resources such as straw, and liquid biofuel, as well as the use of biomass to produce electricity.

Under this plan, by 2010 the installed capacity of electricity produced from biomass will reach 5.50 million kW, the nation will produce 1 million tons of solid biomass fuel each year, annual production of marsh gas will reach 19 billion m^3, annual production of ethanol from nonfood crops will rise by 2 million tons, and yearly use of biodiesel will reach 200 000 tons. By 2020, the installed capacity of biomass power will reach 30 million kW, the nation will produce 50 million tons of solid biomass fuel each year, annual production of marsh gas will reach 44 billion m^3, ethanol production will rise by 10 million tons, and yearly use of biodiesel will reach 2 million tons.

Reaching these goals will require a broad spectrum of government policies. To reduce the costs of biofuels, agencies must offer direct subsidies, tax credits, and marketable credits for the use of renewable energy and cuts in GHG emissions. Increasing the market share of biofuels will also require reducing subsidies for fossil fuels.

7.2.2 A Cost-Accounting for Electricity from Biomass

The use of straw rather than coal to produce electricity could provide significant economic as well as environmental benefits. An analysis of the use of agricultural straw to produce electricity in Ningbo, in Zhejiang Province, can shed light on the cost of biomass energy, and the income it could provide to rural communities.

Ningbo has abundant straw resources, with annual output averaging 1.85 million tons. The use of 50% of those resources to produce electricity could provide energy amounting to 462 500 tons of coal equivalent. The details follow:

Land. A 25 000 kW plant that can produce electricity from straw would require about 10 hm² of land to grow the straw. Buying enough wasteland for industrial purposes in Ningbo would cost 22.50 million Yuan.

Fixed assets. Generating electricity from straw requires a dump for biomass resources, factories, offices, and subsidiary facilities, as well as equipment (Table 7.2).

Table 7.2   Fixed Assets for a 25 000 kW Plant That Produces Electricity from Biomass

	Installed capacity/(kW/m²)	Unit cost/(Yuan/m²)	Total cost/Yuan
Equipment	25 000	3000	75 000 000
Factories	8000	2500	20 000 000
Offices	3000	1500	4 500 000
Stock dump	20 000	500	10 000 000
Subsidiary facilities such as roads and enclosures			1 000 000
Total investment in fixed assets			110 500 000

Raw materials. Dry straw purchased from peasants costs 100 Yuan per ton, and companies that buy and transport the raw material to the power plant charge 130 per ton. The 25 000 kW plant would need about 450 000 tons of straw each year. Thus the annual cost of raw materials would be 58.50 million Yuan.

Salaries and other operating costs. Such a plant would require 150 employees. At an average salary of 3500 Yuan, annual employee costs would therefore total 6.30 million Yuan. Other operating costs would total about 5 million Yuan, and interest would cost 3 million Yuan. Thus the plant would require 14.30 million Yuan for operating costs each year.

Income. If the 25 000 kW plant ran 8 000 hours a year, it would generate 200 million kW · h. The plant would receive 0.35 Yuan for each kW · h, it fed into the power grid for the first 15 years. The power plant itself would use 6% of the electricity it produced. Annual income from the sale of electricity would therefore total 112.80 million Yuan.

Subsidies: Because electricity produced from straw provides social and environmental benefits, a plant can receive a one-time government subsidy of 8 million Yuan, as well as tax relief for 15 years.

Bottom line. If the annual depreciation rate is 7%, yearly fixed costs of land, buildings, and equipment would total 8.75 million Yuan, while variable costs such as materials, salaries, and operating costs would total 72.80 million Yuan.

Pre-tax income would therefore total 31.25 million Yuan, with a four-year payback on the initial investment. Thus rural communities could see substantial economic benefits from building such plants. Turning biomass into a high-value commodity, in turn, will raise peasants' incomes while producing clean energy, protecting the environment, and creating a recycling economy.

7.2.3 Challenges to Producing More Electricity from Biomass

Given the striking environmental advantages of producing electricity from biomass, national and local governments should create policies to encourage its development. Such policies are especially important because bottlenecks and unfavorable operating conditions are inhibiting its long-term development:

An unstable supply of raw materials means higher costs. Purchasing straw from tens of thousands of small peasant farmers is difficult. Biomass brokers also find it difficult to buy enough straw because peasants traditionally use agricultural straw as a household energy source, and because the prices power plants can pay for raw materials are often lower than farmers' costs, given the need to produce electricity at a price competitive with other fuels.

Because straw resources tend to be available seasonally, buyers need to store them for half the year. And because the straw is lightweight but high volume, storing it requires large facilities that are moisture- and fireproof, so these facilities are costly to build and maintain. Major storms and other natural disasters can also affect the supply and cost of raw materials.

Collecting, storing, and processing biomass into solid fuel requires specialized agricultural machinery. Most machinery for harvesting long-stalked crops efficiently and processing them into solid fuel must be imported.

The technology is immature, as producing electricity from straw is still in the R&D stage. China also lacks core knowledge of how to run biomass-based power plants, so foreign enterprises may have to operate them in the short run. Given differences in Chinese and foreign production and transportation systems, and workplace customs and culture, as well as a shortage of qualified professionals, plant output can be unstable. That means incorporating electricity based on straw into the power network is difficult.

Costs are higher than those of producing power from coal and other fossil fuels, partly because biomass power plants themselves use a lot of energy. Technological and managerial shortcomings mean that power plants that burn biomass usually use much more energy for their own operation than their design would suggest.

7.2.4　Recommendations on Expanding Rural Biomass-Based Electricity

Rural power plants need more technological and managerial innovation. To decrease fuel consumption and increase the amount of electricity they generate per unit of installed capacity, power plant operators must reform both their equipment and management.

Some managers claim that their difficulties stem from external barriers such as tariffs on imported equipment. However, operators must reduce wear and tear on their equipment and the amount of energy they use for internal operations. Government can help by promoting the transition from foreign to domestically based, appropriate technologies and equipment.

Given the high cost of transporting biomass fuel, brokers need to create an efficient system for gathering and processing it. Brokers could build biomass processing stations on wasteland or other unused land every five kilometers, with a power plant as the axis, much the way coal mines supply coal-fired power plants. Power plant operators could help by investing in such facilities. To meet growing demand, brokers could gradually move toward larger-scale facilities based on new research and better equipment for collecting and pretreating biomass.

To help guarantee a stable supply of biomass resources, government can help coordinate their production and use for power plants. Local governments could encourage rural residents to stop burning biomass directly, educate them on how to transport and store straw, and help them improve agricultural systems to provide a consistent supply of straw. Governments also need to discourage the construction of other projects that rely on biomass such as small-scale paper mills, to decrease competition for the resource.

To stimulate the market for straw as an energy resource, government policies need to bring prices and costs in line with those of other fuels. Local governments can do that by setting the purchase price of biomass.

Power plant operators, institutes of higher learning, and vocational schools need to cooperate on training, research, and technical support for the industry. Widespread, high-tech production of biomass-based electricity will require more researchers, managers, technicians, and educators who understand the production process. Plant operators and educational institutions need to encourage technical personnel to work in the profession, and to pursue research on scientific management and production.

7.3 Cases on Reducing Greenhouse Gas Emissions from Agriculture and Forestry

7.3.1 Assessing the Potential for GHG Reductions in China's Land Sector

The forest and agriculture sectors can act as either sources or sinks of the three most prevalent greenhouse gases directly emitted from human activities: carbon dioxide, methane, and nitrous oxide. Croplands and livestock are particularly large sources of methane and nitrous oxide emissions, which are potent greenhouse gases, with a global warming potential of 23 and 310 times an equivalent mass of CO_2 emissions, respectively. Agriculture accounts for some 50% of global methane emissions and 85% of global nitrous oxide emissions from human activities.

Fortunately, forestry and agricultural activities can also help reduce and avoid the atmospheric buildup of greenhouse gases. Changes in land use—primarily tropical deforestation—account for some 20% of global CO_2 emissions from human activities each year. However, forests remove even more CO_2 from the atmosphere than changes in land use release—offsetting about 11% of the world's CO_2 emissions from burning fossil fuels.

A wide variety of changes in land management practices in China's countryside can produce cuts in GHG emission while also providing economic benefits. These changes include the following.

To reduce agricultural CH_4 and N_2O emissions:
- Use reduced or no-tillage farming.
- Alter crop mixes and rotations.
- Change the timing, amounts, and frequency of the use of fertilizers and other inputs that use energy.
- Change the mix of irrigated versus dry land.
- Increase irrigation efficiency.
- Change the management of livestock manure.
- Change the types of livestock and their diets to reduce the release of methane from their digestive tracts.
- Change approaches to managing water and straw in rice production.

To reduce agricultural CO_2 emissions:
- Reduce tillage and other machinery-based production activities.
- Change crop mixes and rotations.
- Change the mix of irrigated versus dry land.
- Increase irrigation efficiency.

To store, or sequester, CO_2 in soil or biomass through agricultural activities:

- Reduce tillage.
- Change crop mixes and rotations.
- Change the timing, amounts, and frequency of the use of fertilizers and other inputs that use energy.
- Convert cropland to grassland.
- Improve the quantity and quality of forage on grazing land, and move herds more often.

To sequester CO_2 in soil or biomass through forestry:

- Convert agricultural and other lands to forests (afforestation).
- Replant forest lands (reforestation).
- Lengthen the amount of time between timber harvests, and increase the intensity of forest management.
- Preserve existing forests.

The use of just four practices—reduced-till and no-till farming, more precise application of fertilizer, more efficient irrigation, and better management of water and straw in rice production—could reduce GHG emissions by as much 1.3 billion tons of CO_2 equivalent per year, accounting for $15\% \sim 20\%$ of China's GHG emissions (Table 7.3). Those efforts could therefore help curb the nation's significant growth in GHG emissions. All these measures also provide other benefits, such as protecting crops from wind and blowing sand, preventing soil erosion, protecting water resources, and reducing pollutants and solid waste, greatly improving the rural environment.

Table 7.3   Potential Reductions in China's GHG Emissions through Four Farming Practices

	emission reduction /(ton/hm²/a)			Available land /million hm²	emission reduction (100% adoption) /(million tons/a)			emission reduction (50% adoption) /(million tons/a)		
Cropland practices	Low	Mid	High		Low	Mid	High	Low	Mid	High
Reduced tillage	0.74	1.73	2.72	194.2	144.0	335.9	527.9	72.0	168.0	263.9
Precision use of fertilizer	0.69	1.16	1.66	194.2	134.4	225.5	321.5	67.2	112.8	160.8
More efficient irrigation	0.74	1.24	1.73	78.0	57.8	96.4	134.9	28.9	48.2	67.5
Better management of water and straw in rice production	3.09	5.51	11.12	31.6	97.6	174.1	351.4	48.8	87.1	175.7
Total reductions in GHG emissions/(million tons/a)					433.8	831.9	1335.7	216.9	416.0	667.9

In June 2007, the Ministry of Science and Technology announced a Science and Technology Special Action Plan to reduce GHG emissions through agricultural and land-use practices. To evaluate the practical potential of these practices, officials should analyze their economic and environmental benefits in detail, taking into account market incentives. Those incentives include granting credits for the sale of reductions in GHG emissions on emerging domestic and world markets.

Pilot projects in Sichuan, Xinjiang, and Shaanxi Provinces are now pursuing several of these practices. The next few sections describe those projects.

7.3.2　Case Study: Xinjiang Chinese Tamarisk Greenhouse Gas Reduction Project

The western district of Xinjiang has abundant water, soil, light, and geothermal resources. Because of those resources, and the region's large temperature differences between day and night and long frostless periods, agriculture output accounts for 25% of the region's GDP. In fact, Xinjiang is China's largest producer of cotton, hemp, and tomatoes, and also a key area for livestock, beet sugar, and grape production, and those farm products are famous at home and abroad. However, Xinjiang has seen little foreign investment, so economic development in that district—and indeed in all China's western districts—has lagged that of other regions.

The Chinese Tamarisk Forestation Project aims to reduce GHG emissions by growing more Chinese tamarisk trees, which store carbon as biomass while they grow, and also increase the amount of carbon stored in soil. Chinese tamarisk, a native tree, is found mainly in river flats, valley bottomlands, salinized plains, and dry riverbeds in central and west Asian. It is drought-resistant and saline- and alkali-tolerant, so it can adapt to arid environments, sometimes living more than 100 years. Chinese tamarisk trees protect their surroundings from wind and blowing sand, prevent soil erosion, and clean the air.

The project also includes inoculating tree roots with herba cistanches, which can be harvested without damaging the host tree. Cistanches have high herbal and medicinal values in China, and their sale can provide extra income for local peasants. Residents can also earn income from selling GHG credits for storing carbon in the Chinese tamarisk trees. The project therefore integrates reductions in GHG emissions and improvements in the local environment with economic development.

7.3.2.1　Implementing the Project

Xinjiang is home to 1.53 million people living throughout 30 counties at the south rim of the Tarim and the Junggar basins. The desert steppe at the south rim of Junggar Basin has fixed, semifixed, and wandering dunes, as well as a severe climate, including dramatic temperature changes in spring and autumn, high summer heat, and annual precipitation of 100~150 mm, with oasis plains receiving as much as 200 mm.

Chinese tamarisk seedlings thrive in the sandier soil at the margins of the oasis and the summer's plentiful floods. Dense plants such as saxoul and Chinese tamarisk have therefore traditionally grown over a large area. However, the oasis margin from North Manas to Hutubi and Qitai counties has been seriously degraded because of excessive deforestation.

The Chinese Tamarisk Forestation Project is occurring mainly in Hotan prefecture, a multiethnic region with 250 000 km² of land and a population of 1.8 million. Hotan prefecture includes seven counties and one city —all of which are high-poverty areas, and thus receive key state support. Mountains cover 44% of the prefecture, deserts 42%, and oases 4%. Agriculture is the mainstay of the economy, so farmland accounts for 18% of the oasis area, where local peasants plant mainly cotton, wheat, and fruit trees.

The prefecture planted 100 000 mu with Chinese tamarisk and inoculated 60 000 mu with herba cistanches in 2008, and plans to expand reforestation by another 265 000 mu within 10 years. Manas, Hutubi, and Qitai counties would then have artificial forestation of 365 000 mu of Chinese tamarisk, with a biologic carbon fixation of 288 000 tons of CO_2 equivalent (Table 7.4). Carbon fixation includes the amount of carbon stored in biomass and soil, minus carbon dioxide and nitrous oxide emissions from the use of fossil fuel and chemical fertilizers.

Table 7.4　Carbon Fixation of Chinese Tamarisk Forestation Project in Xinjiang

Project	2008	2009	2010	2011	2012	Total
Tamarisk areas in Qitai/mu	50 000	100 000	150 000	150 000	150 000	
Tamarisk areas in Hutubi/mu	5000	10 000	15 000	15 000	15 000	
Tamarisk areas in Manas/mu	60 000	130 000	200 000	200 000	200 000	
Carbon fixation/tons of CO_2e	46 000	96 000	146 000	146 000	146 000	288 000

7.3.2.2　Benefits of the Project

A key motivation for the project is to produce marketable credits for reducing GHG emissions. To provide a baseline for those reductions, officials measured the amount of carbon above and below ground at the start. A third party will measure the amount of additional carbon stored as a result of the project.

If artificial forestation of Chinese tamarisk carbon fixation reaches 365 000 mu and stores 288 000 tons of carbon dioxide equivalent, and credits for reducing GHG emissions earn $5 per ton of carbon dioxide emissions avoided, the project could earn a total of $1.44 million. If forestation in Hotan reaches 300 000 mu and biological carbon fixation reaches 400 000 tons of carbon dioxide equivalent, the project could earn $2 million.

Farmers could also earn $1.60 million~4 million annually from the sale of 20~40 tons of herba cistanches. If the area planted in Chinese tamarisk expands to 365 000 mu and the area inoculated with herba cistanches reaches 200 000 mu, total income from the project could reach $5.4 million~13.4 million.

The project is already providing more than economic benefits. The trees have clothed the bare desert in green, and form a windbreak and sand-fixing forest belt more than 300 km long and $10\sim15$ km wide from the oasis margin in North Manas to the oasis margin of Hutubi County and Qitai County. Vegetation now covers 54% of this land, and the number of species of vegetation has increased from 4 to 46, because the forest allows a three-layer structure of trees, shrubs, and grass. These rising levels of biological diversity are expanding the area's productive potential, preventing the desert from encroaching on the oasis, and gradually improving the environment on which human survival depends.

7.3.3 Case Studies: Marsh Gas Projects in Xinjiang and Sichuan

China has tried various methods of relieving energy shortages in rural areas, such as producing marsh gas, installing energy-saving stoves, and building small hydropower, solar energy, wind energy, and geothermal plants. Marsh gas has achieved the most widespread use.

In 2003, the Ministry of Agriculture and the National Development and Reform Commission started Rural Biogas Construction Projects Supported by Government Debt. That program invested an initial 840 million Yuan in building marsh gas tanks for family use in 22 provinces, and raised that amount to 2 billion Yuan in 2005.

The cost of a standard marsh gas tank is $2000\sim3000$ Yuan. The government often provides its 1000 Yuan subsidy in the form of cement, brick, or equipment such as a marsh gas stove, with households themselves raising the rest of the funds.

For example, from 2004 to 2006 the government supported a marsh gas project in Xichong and Yilong counties in Sichuan Province. According to information gathered during a door-to-door survey by researchers from Peking University, a minority of farm households had used government subsidies to build marsh gas tanks before the project began, with a few having installed the tanks as early as 1980.

Today nearly half of all peasant households in the project villages have now installed the tanks. Nearly a third of households have also updated their livestock facilities, and 14% have updated their toilets.

Three-quarters of farm households installed their marsh gas tank in an open courtyard, 21% installed it near a warm livestock bed, and 4.29% placed it near the kitchen. More than 90% of households used brick and concrete as their main materials, while the rest used concrete alone, and none used glass-reinforced plastics.

Some 35% of participating households built a standard marsh gas tank of $8\sim10$ m^3, while 32% built smaller tanks and another third built larger tanks. Some 89% of households reported that they often use marsh gas to cook, while just 7% rarely use marsh gas to cook. About 34% of households use marsh gas to heat water for bathing, and 14% regularly rely on the gas for that use. Some 4.17% of households do not use their marsh gas tank because they do not have enough livestock waste, they lack equipment or labor, or they use liquid petroleum gas instead.

The government also promoted a family-use marsh gas project in a village in Manas County in Xinjiang prefecture from 2003 to 2005. The project was designed to integrate construction of the tanks with updated livestock beds, toilets, and kitchen stoves. Marsh gas generated through the project is mainly used for cooking and for heating water.

Several factors have affected the output of the tanks. The first is location: winter temperatures in North Xinjiang slow the production of the gas. Building the tank in a big-arch shelter or around warm livestock beds could raise gas production. Survey results show that only one-third of farm households chose to build their tank near warm pigsties or big-arch shelters, while the other two-thirds build the tanks in open courtyards.

The second factor is construction materials and quality: because marsh gas is produced under anaerobic conditions, the tank must be tightly sealed and well insulated. A survey revealed that 60% of marsh gas tanks in Manas County are made of brick and concrete, which are relatively low cost. Glass-reinforced plastics are good materials for such tanks, but only 11.43% of tanks in the project area are made of such materials because of high costs and low quality.

The third factor is capacity: family-use marsh gas tanks should not be too large, because the amount of material available for fermentation is limited. Most peasant households build $8 \sim 10$ m^3 tanks, to ensure energy efficiency.

Because the tanks require a big up-front investment and pose other challenges, just 13% of households in Manas County are participating in the project. And even households that do participate often use marsh gas for cooking just two to three months a year.

However, despite these barriers, marsh gas program has had a significant impact on coal consumption among peasant households in Xinjiang and Sichuan (Figure 7.4).

In Sichuan districts, marsh gas now accounts for about 16% of household energy use, mainly replacing direct burning of straw and coal (Figure 7.5). Much of the straw formerly used as fuel is now returned to the soil, increasing its organic content and improving its quality.

As noted, marsh gas fermentation produces liquid methane, which contains elements such as nitrogen, phosphorus, and calcium, as well as many bioactive substances, including rich amino acids, micronutrients, plant growth hormones, B vitamins, organic acids, and some antibiotics. If farmers apply these organic residues to farmland, they can prevent crop diseases and pests and reduce their use of chemical fertilizers and pesticides. This approach also reduces nitrous oxide emissions from animal waste, helping to mitigate climate change.

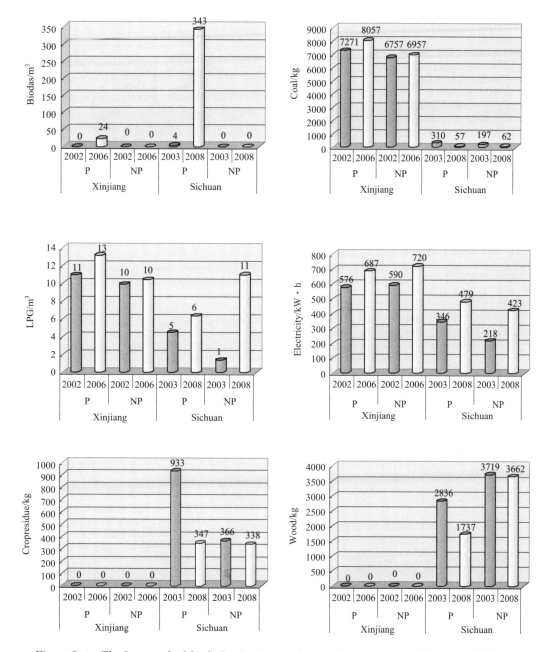

Figure 7. 4　The Impact of a Marsh Gas Project on Energy Consumption in Xinjiang and Sichuan
Source: Door-to-door survey by faculty of Environment Department, Peking University, 2007 and 2009.

In the sample villages, farmers mainly used nitrogen and phosphate fertilizer as well as some potash for planting rice, corn, and wheat. Participants in the marsh gas project, in contrast, replaced these with organic fertilizers, including not only dregs and slurries from marsh gas tanks but also plant ash, oil cake, and cake-shaped rapeseed dregs (Figure 7. 6).

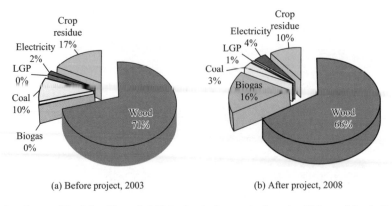

(a) Before project, 2003   (b) After project, 2008

Figure 7. 5   Energy Used for Household Needs, before and after the Sichuan Marsh Gas Project
Source: Door-to-door survey by faculty of Environment Department, Peking University, 2007 and 2009.

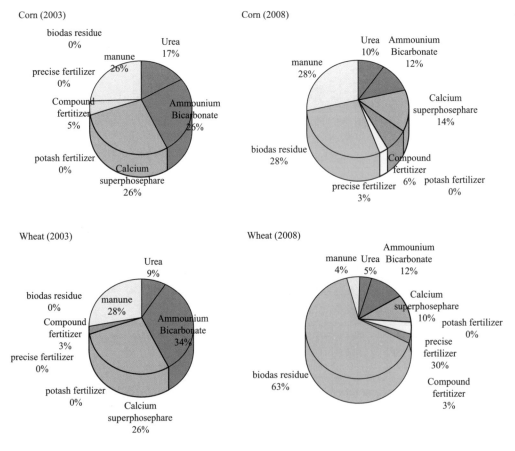

Figure 7. 6   Fertilizer Input for Staple Crops before and after the Marsh Gas Project
Source: Door-to-door survey by faculty of Environment Department, Peking University, 2007 and 2009.

7.3.4 Case Study: Soil Testing and Formulated Fertilization Project in Sichuan

Farmers growing wheat, rice, corn, and rapeseed have traditionally applied a base layer of fertilizer such as carbamide, ammonium hydrogen carbonate, and ordinary superphosphate, and then used more during the growing season. Jian'ge County is one of more than 200 counties that have encouraged farmers to test their soils and then apply fertilizer specially formulated to provide the precise amount of nitrogen, phosphate, calcium, and trace elements that the soil and crops need. The goal is to increase the percentage of the fertilizer that plants absorb while reducing the overall need for fertilizer.

To pursue the project, the county has built 5000 soil-monitoring stations, as well as a soil-monitoring laboratory and two fertilizer manufacturing plants. The county now appropriates 30 million Yuan for the project, mainly for operating the soil-testing points and managing test fields.

Both project and non-project farmers have reduced the amount of single-element fertilizers they apply. For example, in the case of rice paddies, project farmers reduced their use of carbamide, ammonium hydrogen carbonate, and ordinary superphosphate by 44.4%, 92.1%, and 98.39%, respectively, from 2003 to 2008. Non-project farmers also cut their use of those fertilizers by 20%, 51.8%, and 62.3%, respectively, during that period.

Compound fertilizer as well as formulated fertilizer replaced a significant amount of traditional single-element fertilizers (Figure 7.7). (Households that did not participate in the project could apply compound fertilizer as a partial substitute for single-element fertilizer.) However, project farmers found that they needed to apply little additional fertilizer, saving labor, and they also reported higher crop yields.

The project therefore had a remarkably positive impact on the gross and net income of participating farmers, although it had an insignificant effect on income from animal husbandry and non-farm employment.

Peasants receive no government subsidies for using the new approach. To encourage more farmers to test their soil and use specially formulated fertilizer, the state should provide direct subsidies for the practice, and also grant marketable credits for reducing GHG emissions. The government can phase out these direct subsidies as peasants see the benefits of adopting these practices.

7.3.5 Case Study: Drip Irrigation Project in Xinjiang

From 2003 to 2005, a pilot project promoted the use of drip irrigation to apply water-soluble fertilizer to farmland in a village of Manas County, in Xinjiang prefecture.

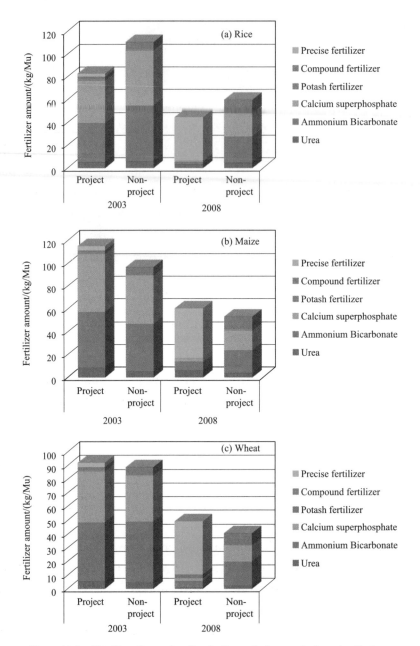

Figure 7. 7   Fertilizer Input for Staple Crops before and after the Project

During drip irrigation, water seeps into soil slowly and distributes the fertilizer evenly around plant roots, so they can absorb it more efficiently. This approach, designed to reduce fertilizer use, is used mainly to fertilize short-stalked plants such as cotton and tomatoes.

At first the project promoted the installation of a drip irrigation system near the soil surface (a technique sometimes known as "little white dragon"). Such a system initially costs less than a deeper drip irrigation system, but the pipes need more maintenance, and must be replaced every year or two. The project therefore later promoted the use of deep-buried drip irrigation, in which the main pipe sits $80 \sim 150$ cm below the soil surface, and lasts 10 years. Some 73% of peasants participating in the project have adopted deep-buried drip irrigation, while the 27% are using the surface method. The system is therefore not yet perfect, as discarded pipes can cause new forms of pollution.

Investments in drip irrigation vary with the needed equipment. Building a deep-buried drip irrigation system costs $900 \sim 1300$ Yuan per mu. The project relies on government subsidies as the main source of construction funds, supplemented by investments from the village committee and loans from peasant households. Peasant households maintain the system.

In 2007 and 2009, researchers at Peking University conducted a door-to-door survey of participants in the project to evaluate its impact on cotton, one of the most important crops in Xinjiang. The study team actually found a slight increase in the amount of fertilizer applied in sample drip irrigation plots, compared with plots with other kinds of irrigation (Figure 7.8).

For example, in 2002 the average input of carbamide in drip irrigation plots was 26.55 kg/mu. By 2006 that amount had risen by 11.26%, to 29.54 kg. The amount of carbamide applied in non-drip irrigation plots fell slightly during the same period. Thus the fertilizer application rate was higher in the drip irrigation plots.

However, the researchers also found that crop yields in the drip irrigation plots rose from 211 kg in 2002 to 261 kg in 2006——a 26% increase. That means that drip irrigation decreased the amount of fertilizer needed per unit of yield, so it was somewhat more efficient.

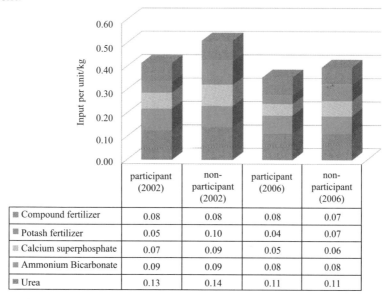

	participant (2002)	non-participant (2002)	participant (2006)	non-participant (2006)
■ Compound fertilizer	0.08	0.08	0.08	0.07
■ Potash fertilizer	0.05	0.10	0.04	0.07
■ Calcium superphosphate	0.07	0.09	0.05	0.06
■ Ammonium Bicarbonate	0.09	0.09	0.08	0.08
■ Urea	0.13	0.14	0.11	0.11

Figure 7.8   Fertilizer Use before and after the Drip Irrigation Project

Source: Door-to-door survey by faculty of Environment Department, Peking University, 2007 and 2009.

The study team also found a marked change in the amount of water used for irrigation. Water volume used by project participants fell from 639 m³ in 2002 to 564 m³ in 2006—or 12%—while water use among non-project users fell by 3.05%.

During irrigation seasons, peasants participating in the project must go to their plots to turn pipeline valves on or off, to ensure a uniform supply of water and fertilizer in each plot. Thus the technology requires somewhat more labor than other forms of irrigation, and raises the amount of diesel fuel used by agricultural machinery slightly.

7.4   Cases on Post-Disaster Revegetation and Economic Development

On May 12, 2008, a massive earthquake of magnitude 8.0 occurred in Wenchuan, Sichuan Province. This quake and its accompanying landslides—the most destructive since the founding of new China—caused enormous casualties and huge property losses, destroying farmland, clogging rivers, and disrupting the ecology. According to preliminary calculations, the region lost 122 136 hectares, accounting for 3.4% of the region's ecological system (Ouyang et al, 2008).

The earthquake's major impact occurred at the west rim of Szechwan Basin, the transitional belt to the Qinghai-Tibet Plateau. This region has complex geological features, including high mountains and deep valleys, and provides key ecological services, although it is ecologically fragile[1]. Extensive destruction of mountain and gorge areas in the earthquake have worsened local conflicts between residents of these areas and the land.

For example, The government also needs to prevent large-scale land clearance of sloping fields for agriculture during post-disaster reconstruction, as such a use could lead to water loss and soil erosion. In fact, the government needs to ensure restoration of sloping fields damaged by the earthquake by encouraging the planting of pasture and shrub, which can provide both ecological and economic benefits.

Communities also need local forest resources to rebuild village houses after earthquakes, and that need is unavoidable. However, after reconstruction is complete, pressure on forests from peasant households stems mainly from the need for energy. If fuel wood continues to serve as an important energy resource, it will prevent revegetation of forests affected by the earthquake and restoration of biodiversity.

To allow forests to rebound, households could move toward the use of other renewable resources, such as marsh gas. However, the cost of building materials and

---

① According to one analysis, Sichuan Province lost 781 000 tons of reserve capacity for sequestering carbon in forests, valued at 250 million Yuan. The release of oxygen from the forest declined by 673 800 tons annually, valued at 270 million Yuan. In all, the province lost 105.588 billion Yuan in ecosystem services, while economic losses totaled 252 731 billion Yuan.

labor in the disaster area soared as a result of post-disaster reconstruction of infrastructure and homes, and a survey found that most peasant households could not afford to install renewable energy facilities such as marsh gas tanks (Table 7.5). The government therefore needs to increase its support for the transition to sustainable energy use, which would not only speed post-disaster reconstruction but also accelerate ecological restoration in the seismic region.

Table 7.5 The Cost of Constructing Sustainable Energy Facilities in Rural Households

Project	Before earthquake/Yuan	After earthquake/Yuan
Marsh gas tank	2200	3500
Fuel-wood-saving stove	400	600
Solar water heater	1900	2500
Multipurpose heating stove	1300	2000
Toilet and livestock house	2600	4000
Total	8400	12 600

The government can also develop a forest economy by encouraging the reasonable use of forestry resources not destroyed by the earthquake. They can do that by creating an agroforestry system based on an ecological model, which connects fruit trees, bees, pasture, livestock, marsh gas, and organic fertilizer, taking into account landforms, climate, and vegetation (Figure 7.9). An agroforestry system could test the effectiveness of a recycling economy, which minimizes waste by creating a virtuous cycle of energy and production.

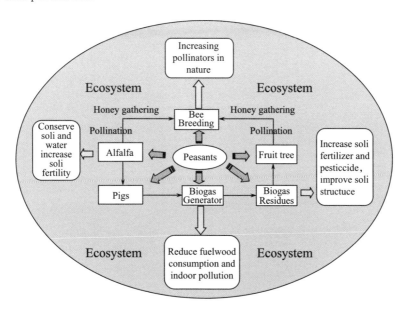

Figure 7.9 Agroforestry Circulation System

The ecological benefits of an agroforestry system include a reduction in water loss and soil erosion, an increase in soil fertility, more natural enemies and fewer plant diseases and insect pests, and more efficient use of land. The economic benefits of such a system include higher-quality fruit, higher output, stronger channels between bee products, livestock, and pasture, and lower production costs owing to reduced use of fertilizers and farm chemicals.

Fortunately, recent projects have aimed to return land severely damaged by the earthquake to forestry, restoring natural forest cover and sheltering the Yangtze River. Before the quake, regulations and efforts to protect local ecology were often feeble, as peasants living in poverty devoted their attention to short-term economic needs. The result was a vicious cycle of ecological damage and poverty. Ecological restoration is now aiming to break this cycle and establish a sustainable economy.

One example is the Integrated Conservation and Development Project, which has sought to reduce human pressure on the ecological system in Pingwu County in Sichuan Province. By helping poor Tibetan households living near the habitat of giant pandas develop a sustainable livelihood, the project provides a model for post-quake restoration—although it actually began before the earthquake hit.

7.4.1　Case Study: Integrated Conservation and Development Project in Pingwu County

Pingwu County is in northwestern Szechwan Basin, along the upper reaches of Fujiang River, a branch of the Yangtze River. The county encompasses 5974 km² and a population of more than 180 000, including 12 nationalities, of which Hans account for 97%, Tibetans 1.38%, Hui 0.64%, and Qiang 0.09%. The mountainous region, which has a mean annual temperature of 14.7℃, average annual precipitation of 866.5 mm, and forest cover of 72%, offers habitat for rare wild animals such as giant panda and golden monkey.

Pingwu County is one of 12 seriously earthquake-stricken counties, and thus a good candidate for research on post-disaster revegetation. The government also chose the county for a reconstruction project because a team has conducted more than 10 years of research on the country's society, economy, and environment. For example, the research team conducted a three-year study of 120 farm households from 2005 to 2008, to evaluate the impact of the Integrated Conservation and Development Project (Figure 7.10).

The project provided equipment such as marsh gas tanks, solar water heaters, and multipurpose stoves to peasant households, with the goal of reducing pressure on forests by cutting the use of firewood. The project also aimed to encourage peasant households to move from stocking beef cattle to breeding them, and to pursue more sustainable

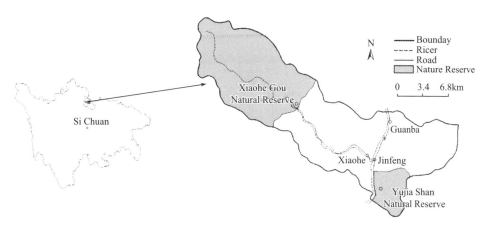

Figure 7.10　Geographical Position of the Survey Region

livelihoods such as bee feeding, which could also raise family income (Figure 7.11).
Some 24 towns, 165 villages, and 22 829 households were involved in the project.

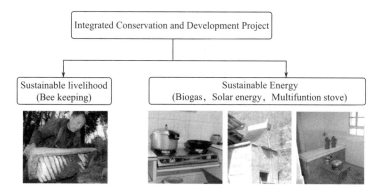

Figure 7.11　Integrating Ecological Protection and Economic Development in Pingwu County

According to the research team, the project has had several notable impacts. It has: Reduced the ecological footprint of farm households. The per capita ecological footprint of 12 investigated families dropped from 2.7 hectares of forest and pasture in 2005 to 1.6 hectares in 2007. Meanwhile per capita reliance on fossil energy land, arable land, build-up land, and sea area rose slightly (Figure 7.12).

The consumption of fuel wood dropped dramatically. In 2005, peasant households consumed an average of 6920 kg of fuel wood each year, but by 2007 that amount had dropped by 23%, to 1570 kg.

The use of marsh gas tanks, solar water heaters, and multipurpose stoves has also greatly reduced the harmful gas and smoke produced from the burning of fuel wood, protecting peasants' health and reducing fire hazards.

Raised the income of peasant households. From 2006 to 2009, family income and the structure of peasant households changed significantly (Figure 7.14). In 2006, average family

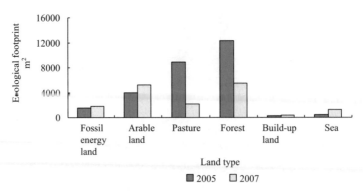

Figure 7. 12   Changes in the Ecological Footprint of Pingwu County Households in Various Land-Use Modes

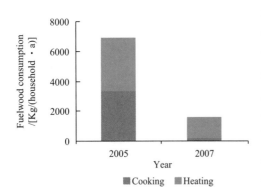

Figure 7. 13   Change in Fuel Wood Consumption among Pingwu County Households

income—mainly from beekeeping and paid employment—was 13 900 Yuan. In2007, that figure rose to 21 600 Yuan—a 55% increase. In 2008, family income fell to 16 200, because a financial crisis prompted former residents to return to the region, and because of a decrease in income from apiculture and animal husbandry after the earthquake.

However, analysts expected average household income to reach 27 000 in 2009—an increase of 25% over that before the earthquake—even though government subsidies for returning farmland to forestry have dropped 60%. Incomes are rising because revenue from beekeeping is growing as the scale of those operations expands, the product becomes more popular, and beekeepers receive higher prices because of production standards created by a professional beekeeping cooperative.

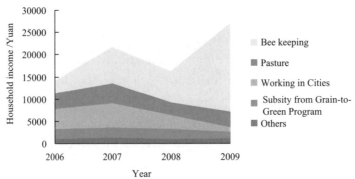

Figure 7. 14   Change in Income Structure of Peasant Households, 2006~2009

Improved the indoor environment in peasant households. Before the project, peasant households relied on traditional methods for cooking and heating with poor combustion efficiency, which caused serious air pollution. Livestock houses and toilets were also breeding grounds for harmful organisms such as flies and germs, threatening residents' health (Figure 7. 15).

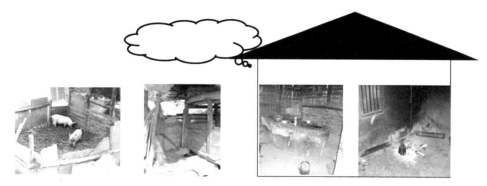

Figure 7. 15　Domestic Hygiene in Peasant Households before the Project

Because it greatly reduced the amount of smoke and harmful gas produced from burning fuel wood, the project brought widespread improvements in household hygiene as well as animal welfare (Figure 7. 16).

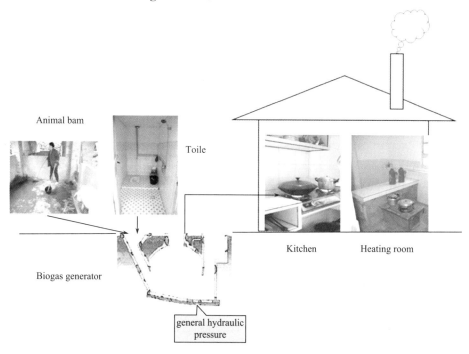

Figure 7. 16　Domestic Hygiene in Peasant Households after the Project

By 2006, Pingwu County had also converted 123 000 mu of cultivated land to forests, including 80 000 mu of forest that serves solely to preserve the local ecology, and 53 000 mu of forest used for production.

Post-disaster reconstruction efforts can rely on lessons from the project to consolidate ecological forests and ensure sustainable use of forest products. For example, if 25 000 formerly farmed mu in Pingwu County—48% of the area now devoted to economic forestry—were planted with walnut trees, those resources could become a key financial resource for local households.

China's many rural enterprises are operating below capacity, as a result of the global financial crisis, so their capacity to absorb surplus rural labor has fallen sharply. At the same time, numerous migrant peasants are returning to home to help with post-disaster reconstruction. Many of these migrants have the knowledge and skills to help develop local natural resources. However, they need guidance in developing sustainable livelihoods. Such guidance could greatly aid post-disaster reconstruction while expanding jobs and providing opportunities for scientific research.

7.4.2 Promoting Rural Electrification and Hydropower

As part of its effort to rebuild communities devastated by the earthquake while promoting the efficient use of clean energy, the government also needs to help households tap into local hydroelectric resources. The earthquake zone in Southwest China is rich in such resources, and already has numerous hydropower stations. However, few local residents enjoy access to cheap electrical power.

For example, Pingwu County has one large-scale and three medium-scale hydropower stations. But the price of electricity for peasant households near hydropower stations is 0.55 Yuan/kW · h—12% higher than the price of electricity for Beijing households.

A December 2008 survey of 200 peasant households in Pingwu County found that an extremely low proportion of peasant households used electrical power for cooking and heating, and that high prices are the major obstacle to rural electrification (Table 7.6).

Table 7.6 Service Conditions for Electricity in Mupi Township, 2008 Survey

Peasant households using electricity for cooking and heating	2% used an induction cooker 1% used an electric pad
Peasant households that would like to use electricity to cook	44%
Peasant households that would like to use electricity for heat	90%
Reasons for not using electrical appliances for cooking and heating	High price of electrical appliances: 45% High price of electrical power: 95%
Desired price of electrical appliances	160 Yuan for induction cooker 200 Yuan for electric pad
Desired price of electrical power	0.13 Yuan/kW · h—22% of the current price

Some 44% households would like to use electricity to cook, and 90% would like to use electricity for heat, to lighten the burden using of labor-intensive fuel wood.

In the survey, only 45% of households considered the price of home appliances too high, given an existing government program that helps rural households buy such appliances. However, 95% of households considered the high price of electricity as the major obstacle to the use of home appliances. The average price these households prefer to pay is 0.13 Yuan/kW · h—just 22% of the current price of electricity. Some households argue that electricity should be free for residents of districts with large-scale hydropower stations, as they can undermine the local environment, such as by reducing income from fisheries.

To encourage a shift to cleaner energy sources during post-disaster reconstruction, the government should subsidize electricity use by peasant households while helping them purchase induction cookers and electric radiators. Enabling peasant households to enjoy clean, convenient, and efficient electrical power will protect forest resources while increasing consumption of goods among rural households, accelerating the pace of post-disaster reconstruction and the move to a new socialist countryside.

8 Policy Recommendations

To fulfill farmers' demands for high-quality energy, China needs to make full use of renewable resources throughout the countryside. The government can also comprehensively address rural energy and environmental needs by fully enlisting government entities, enterprises, and farmers. Our recommendations include:

Modernize the traditional use of biomass. Modern gasification and carbonization technologies can convert straw and firewood into high-quality energy sources. Such systems can create a more intensive and efficient energy supply while reducing waste disposal costs.

However, up-front costs now restrain this development. The initial investment needed to build a straw gasification station averages 1. 2 million Yuan, for example. If each biogas station serves 200 rural households, that means each household must contribute 6000 Yuan in construction expenses. Similarly, stations that press straw into blocks are difficult to organize, operate, and market. Thus governments will need to promote these technologies to bring them into widespread use.

All districts and government sectors should establish strategic objectives and specific policies to spur the shift from traditional to modern forms of biomass-based energy. Existing government subsidies for developing modern facilities for gasifying and using rural biomass need to be expanded, and new incentives added. Policies to accelerate the use of modern forms of biomass should require farmers to maintain soil quality by leaving some crop residues on the land.

Develop biomass resources in line with local conditions and resources. Local economic development and residents' living habits can drive development of modern forms of biomass energy. In the southwest, for example, a vast population has limited farmland, the climate is hot and damp, and farmers rely on livestock breeding. This region is suitable for developing small marsh gas tanks that rely on human and animal excreta, as well as straw and other organic wastes, to meet local energy demand.

In the plains of north China, crop straw resources are abundant, so this region can use large-scale treatment to process straw as a renewable energy source. For example, crop straw can be made into briquette fuels. The region can also rely on new solar-powered marsh gas tanks to popularize biogas production while keeping residents warm in winter—reversing the notion that north China is not an appropriate area for developing marsh gas. Other rural settlements and agricultural areas can rely on medium-sized biomass gasification systems to convert agricultural wastes into energy resources.

Government agencies need to provide region-specific technical guidance on appropriate biomass energy technologies and practices. First, agencies should create guidelines on developing biomass energy projects, and on their possible impacts on soil and the environment. Field advisors should then help villages, farms, and enterprises evaluate and use modern techniques for producing biomass energy based on those guidelines. Projects that meet the guidelines should receive loans and grants, as well as credits for creating renewable energy and reducing GHG emissions.

Strengthen the rural development and use of small hydropower, small wind-powered electricity plants, solar energy, and geothermal energy, and accelerate R&D on clean, high-quality coal. The resources available for renewable energy vary from region to region. Mountainous areas of the southwest have abundant hydropower resources, while northwest China, Inner Mongolia, and coastal areas have strong winds. Solar resources are widely distributed in every region except the Szechwan basin, including rainless regions of north and northwest China. Thus most parts of China can rely on solar energy.

In fact, China's rural regions are crying out for renewable energy sources to spur economic development. However, the use of renewable energy does not always reflect its economic and environmental benefits, and social and financial capital is often unwilling to pursue research and development. At present, the problems lie in immature technology, high cost, and unstable energy supply. These problems can be addressed by government policies that reduce the cost, increase the reliability, and stimulate the commercialization of the technology. Such policies should aim to make renewable energy sources more competitive with fossil fuels.

Direct subsidies, low-interest loans, and tax credits can provide important incentives, as can the granting of saleable credits for reducing greenhouse gas emissions and developing renewable energy. The government should also expand its own investment in energy infrastructure, to encourage more enterprises to participate in the research, development, and production of renewable energy. We also recommend pilot projects for developing efficient gaseous fuels such as coal gas and natural gas in some regions.

To increase the effective energy supply and ensure sustainable growth in rural energy demand, strengthen energy conservation and improve the efficiency of energy end-use. China can develop and encourage the use of efficient cooking technologies such as gas ovens and straw-saving ovens; improve the energy efficiency of agricultural machinery, especially irrigation and drainage equipment; and make township enterprises more efficient by adjusting their structure and systematically eliminating energy-intensive equipment.

All these technologies require financing, and government needs to expand the economic incentives for households and township enterprises to adopt them. Agencies also need to develop and apply energy-efficiency standards for new buildings and equipment.

Enhance the statistical analysis of rural energy use. To lay a solid foundation for these public policies, authorities need to strengthen their statistical analysis of rural energy end-use by both households and producers. First, these authorities must unify the definition of rural production, to ensure that statistics reflect the actual energy use of township enterprises.

Second, national officials need to bolster the ability of county governments to organize and manage energy statistics. As our survey revealed, county-level accounting is a weak link in the creation of national energy statistics, as county statistical departments are unable to present systematic and accurate data on rural energy use.

Agricultural Bureaus, Forestry Bureaus, and other industry bureaus should then calculate and report statistics on local energy consumption under the guidance and organization of local statistics bureaus. The national statistics bureau can collect, check, and issue the overall results, to ensure authority and authenticity in the nation's energy statistics.

Popularize low-carbon, high-efficiency agriculture. Farmers, foresters, and pastoralists have an important role to play in reducing greenhouse gas emissions, by planting trees, reducing tillage, expanding the use of cover crops, improving grassland management, relying on farmyard manure and biological pest control to reduce the use of fertilizers and pesticides, and switching to breeds of animals that emit less methane. An agricultural system that combines farming and forestry can also reduce the need for artificial fertilizers and pesticides while also curbing the erosion of fertile soil and water loss and. increasing rural household income.

These techniques reduce greenhouse gas emissions and spur carbon sequestration—the process of storing more carbon in soil and biomass—which can reduce atmospheric carbon dioxide levels while enabling soil to recover its fertility more quickly and increasing crop yields.

Such a low-carbon agricultural economy would improve both the rural environment and peasants' quality of life by cutting energy consumption and thus air pollution, and disposing of wastes from animal husbandry.

The popularization of energy-saving technology has already cut energy consumption throughout the agricultural system, including farm machinery and livestock breeding. Agricultural sectors now test soil and create balanced approaches to fertilization. High-efficiency spatial planting and breeding and the efficient use of land, sunshine, air, and water have expanded the amount of growing space, increased agricultural output, and improved efficiency. The development of water-saving irrigation modes and drainage facilities has cut the use of water resources.

However, given recent policies that aim to spur rural construction and balance development between urban and rural areas, the national government needs to pay more attention to promoting such energy-conserving, low-carbon, high-efficiency agricultural technologies. Education, technical guidance, and accelerated economic incentives for adoption of these technologies are essential. That, in turn, will stimulate economic development, prevent financial crisis, and alleviate poverty through "green" techniques.

Use comprehensive planning and local circumstances to develop low-carbon agriculture. The government and farmers should work together to establish long-term policies and subsidies to reform the agricultural structure, improve production technologies, and improve farmland management. These efforts can include:

- Awarding financial aid to farmers to adopt low-carbon agricultural practices.
- Establishing multilevel intermediaries and consulting services to popularize low-carbon agriculture and clean production techniques.
- Funding R&D on more efficient agricultural machinery.
- Regulating agricultural markets to promote low-carbon products.
- Creating procedures for granting saleable greenhouse gas emission credits for low-carbon rural production.
- Relying on low-energy, low-carbon agriculture to reconstruct the earthquake-prone Sichuan region.
- Importing agricultural products whose energy efficiency is low.
- Strengthening macro-level guidance to ensure that small projects move forward even if big market players jump on the low-carbon bandwagon.

Analyze the biodiversity of the nation's crops, assess their vulnerability to climate change, and use biodiversity to cope with climate change. China needs to store the resulting information on biological diversity in national and international gene banks. The nation should also use technical guidance and education to help farmers use biological diversity to cope with climate change, and provide information on adaptive methods to farmers, pastoralists, and fishermen and their local institutions.

Spur the use of renewable energy to provide heat and electricity for rural buildings. Rural buildings already account for a large proportion of the nation's energy use. In particular, the amount of energy used to heat buildings during the winter in north China is remarkable. With the nation's rapid urbanization and rising standard of living, the amount of energy used in rural buildings will grow rapidly.

Especially in north China, energy for heating rural buildings has gradually moved from biomass to fossil fuel. Our research shows that further rural construction and development of the nation's agricultural economy will worsen environmental problems. However, as noted, vast rural areas are rich in renewable energy sources such as solar and shallow geothermal. These regions have superior conditions and enormous spaces for applying these technologies.

The Central Committee already introduced financial subsidies for energy conservation based on renewable energy in rural buildings in demonstration areas. In 2009, ground source heat pumps can receive 60 Yuan/m^2, integrated photovoltaic-solar thermal applications can receive 15 Yuan/m^2, and solar-powered bathrooms can receive 60% of the new investment. No county can receive more than 18 million Yuan. The Central Committee will adjust these annual subsidies based on the cost of applying renewable energy in rural buildings.

A multi-pronged approach to spurring energy conservation in rural buildings, expanding the use of new technologies, and maximizing end-use efficiency should include:

- Strengthening construction standards while considering regional constraints.
- Providing technical guidance to projects.
- Training designers, builders, and supervisors to ensure project quality and safety.
- Creating specialized agencies and mechanisms to evaluate projects and analyze project experiences in a timely manner.
- Ensuring that new systems run safely and efficiently long after new facilities are complete.
- Integrating the strengths of manufacturers, scientific research institutes, reconnaissance and design institutes, and construction enterprises, and promoting connections among production, survey, design, and construction teams.
- Improving policies to lay a foundation for further promoting energy conservation, including grants, loans, and efficiency standards.
- Breaking down regional monopolistic barriers to developing an environmental protection industry.
- Granting marketable credits for reductions in GHG emissions resulting from energy conservation projects.

These efforts can improve people's lives by providing heat to rural homes, schools, health centers, and other places; drive the growth of clean energy and related industries; boost household demand for clean energy; replace a great deal of conventional fossil fuel; and promote structural adjustment.

Systematically analyze experience with natural disasters, to better predict them and help the agricultural system adapt to climate change. The nation needs to evaluate the speed and scale of disasters that climate change could cause while also bolstering community-based disaster prevention and training. For example, the government could strengthen rural organizations such as farmer field schools to help growers and local agencies understand the potential local impact of severe weather related to climate change. The government should also develop systems for monitoring regional climate change and providing early warning of disasters.

The government must give subsidies, insurance, and credits to all rural populations to advance these goals—especially in areas with fragile ecosystems and large numbers of farmers. However, the nation should adopt flexible approaches that reflect the needs of each area.

Spur harmonious economic, social, and environmental development while relieving poverty. In areas where the local ecology has been seriously disrupted, life conditions are odious, or natural resources are so poor that they are "natural obstacle zones," China needs to compensate farmers for property losses. The nation also needs to plan for immigration and development while respecting the wishes of farmers, lest local environments worsen because of population pressures.

Sustainable development requires the creation of "green jobs." The government should create economic incentives for creating green jobs by encouraging development of renewable energy, energy conservation, and low-carbon agriculture projects. Those projects can succeed only if financing and workers with "green" skills are available. The government therefore needs to provide guidelines defining green jobs and skills, and offer programs, grants, and loans for training workers.

Ensure the nation's food security. Both facts and models convince us that climate change will have a profound impact on the nation's food security. The international community has focused on addressing this challenge by both mitigating and adapting to climate change. The ultimate goal is to prepare public and private entities, communities, the infrastructure, and the economy for a changing climate while encouraging them to adjust their behavior and participate in campaigns to reduce greenhouse gas emissions.

Critical steps for China include:

- Ensuring that relevant departments formulate policies spurring energy conservation and emissions reductions in agriculture.
- Devoting more funds to developing and testing innovative policies, institutional solutions, and energy-saving and emission-reduction projects in agriculture, land use, and forestry.
- Creating comprehensive rural cooperatives by integrating rural credit cooperatives, supply and marketing cooperatives, and farmers' professional cooperatives.
- Promoting cooperation between guiding township enterprises, enterprises that process agricultural products, rural cooperative organizations, and social intermediaries, and encouraging them to participate in R&D and implementation projects.
- Strengthening rural financial and credit policies, loans, and services, and promoting grassroots financial reforms.

- Linking rural credit systems with existing banking systems to transform social capital into economic capital for developing clean rural energy.
- Tapping funding for mitigating and adapting to climate change, including the United Nations Framework Convention on Climate Change, and mandatory and voluntary carbon markets created by public and private partners.
- Promoting international cooperation on low-carbon agriculture and energy sources, and urge international organizations and developed countries to share advanced technologies and successful experiences.
- Liberalizing agricultural trade polices, by removing subsidies and border taxes.

Create a program to produce credits for reducing GHG emissions, and to market and trade those credits. The scientific community recognizes that climate change—caused at least partly by rising levels of greenhouse gas emissions from human activities—is a threat to global sustainability. Cuts in GHG emissions by all major emitting nations are essential to addressing climate change.

Greater energy efficiency and reliance on renewable energy are essential to tackling this challenge. Carbon sequestration—storing more carbon in soil and biomass—can also help cut GHG emissions and remove carbon dioxide from the atmosphere.

These activities can also provide new income for farmers, herdsmen, foresters, and other workers and managers in rural China. Farmers can remove carbon dioxide from the atmosphere and sequester carbon in soil by changing tillage practices and vegetation management. Farmers can also reduce GHG emissions such as methane by changing the way they manage livestock and rice production, and reduce nitrous oxide emissions by changing the way they manage soil.

Afforestation—the planting of trees on nonforested lands—can remove large amounts of carbon dioxide from the atmosphere by storing carbon in biomass, soils, and harvested products.

Together, these changes in agricultural and forestry practices can significantly affect the GHG balance while also compensating farmers and foresters.

Credible production of GHG credits requires a system for accurately measuring and accounting for cuts in greenhouse gas emissions from China's agriculture and forests. That system must provide a comprehensive yet practical approach that encompasses the nation's numerous and dispersed land-use activities.

The system must specify:
- The types of activities that can meet criteria for high-quality projects.
- Methods for quantifying GHG credits for activities that increase carbon sequestration and reduce or avoid GHG emissions.
- Techniques for assessing the "additionality" and "leakage" of project activities—as defined in GHG policies throughout the world.
- Techniques for measuring and verifying project results with enough scientific

integrity to meet the objectives of the program.

- Methods for accounting for uncertainty in producing GHG credits, as well as insurance and options for addressing risk for each type of project and its conditions.

References

Alexandrov V, Eitzinger J, Cajic V et al. 2002. Potential impact of climate change on selected agricultural crops in north-eastern Austria. Global Change Biology, 8: 372~389

Barnes D. 2007. The Challenge of Rural Electrification, Strategies for Developing Countries. Resources for the Future, (1): 1-18.

Barnes D, Foley G. 2004. Rural Electrification in the Developing World: A Summary of Lessons from Successful Programs. Energy Sector Management Assistance Program. Washington D. C.

Bian Y S. 2005. The Disposal and Recycling of Waster from eco-Agriculture System. Beijing: Chemical Industry Press

Cai C Z, Liang Y, Li X L. 2008. The analysis of Chinese future food security based on the AEZ model prediction. Bulletin of Agricultural Science and Technology, 2: 15~17

Cai Z C, Xie D T, Xu H et al. 2003. Factors influencing CH_4 emissions from permanently flooded rice field during rice growing period. Journal of Applied Ecology, 14 (5): 705~709

Cao G L, Zhang X Y, Wang D. 2005. Inventory of atmospheric pollutants discharged from biomass burning in China continent. China Environmental Science, 25 (4): 389~393

Chen F J, Wu G, Ge F et al. 2004. Impacts of elevated CO_2 on the population abundance and reproductive activity of aphid Sitobionavenae Fabricius feeding on spring wheat. J. Env. Nutr, 128 (9-10): 723~730

Deng G Y, Yu H N. 1992. The impact of the greenhouse gas increment on climate and agriculture. *In*: Deng G Y eds. The influence of Climate Change on Agriculture in China. Beijing: Science and Technology Press, 3~18

Deng K Y, He L. 2000. Forecast study on medium and long term energy demand in rural area of China. Engineering Science, 2 (6): 16~21

Department of General Affair of National Energy Board. 2009. China Energy Statistics Yearbook 1996 ~ 2008. Beijing: China Statistics Press

Department of Science, Technology and Education of the Ministry of Agriculture, Center for Energy and Environmental Technology Development of the Ministry of Agriculture. 2008. National Rural Renewable Energy Statistics. Beijing: Science and Technology Education Department of the Ministry of Agriculture

Department of Science, Technology and Education of the Ministry of Agriculture. 2008. China Rural Energy Yearbook 2000~2008. Beijing: China Agriculture Press

Dong B C, Ju X F, Gan J et al. 2006. Feasibility study of family heating with biogas in Northeast rural area. Chinese Society of Agricultural Engineering, 22 (1): 101~103

Dong H M. 2008. Case study of biogas CDM project in Enshi, Hubei Province. Agriculture Engineering Technology (New Energy Industry), 5: 23~26

Duan M S, Wang G H. 2003. Greenhouse Gas Mitigation Benefits of Biogas Project in Livestock Farms. Acta Energiae Solaris Sinica, 24 (3): 386~389

Editorial Board of China Agriculture Yearbook. 2008. China Agriculture Yearbook 1996 ~ 2007. Beijing: China Agriculture Press

Editorial Board of China Rural Energy Yearbook. 1999. China Rural Energy Yearbook 1998~1999. Beijing: China Agriculture Press

Ferraro P, Kiss A. 2002. Direct payments to conserve biodiversity. Science, 298 (29): 1718~1719

Fischer G, Van Velthuizen H T. 1996. Climate change and global agricultural potential project L A case study of Kenya. International Institute of Applied System Analysis, Lazenburg, Austria

Fuhrer J. 2003. Agroecosystem responses to combination of elevated CO_2, ozone, climate change. Agriculture, Ecosystems and Environment, 97: 1~20

Gao C Y, Bi Y Y, Zhao S M et al. 2008. Economic benefit of pentad-ecological homestead patterns — A case study of "fruit-livestock-biogas pit-water cellar-grass" pattern in Luochuan County, Shaanxi Province. Chinese Journal of Eco-Agriculture, 16 (5): 1287~1292

Gunasekera D, et al. 2007. Climate change: impacts on Australian Agriculture. Australian Commodities: Forecasts and Issues, 14 (4): 657-676

Han G X, Zhu B, Jiang C S. 2005. Methane emission from paddy fields and its affecting factors in hills of the central Sichuan Basin. Rural Eco-environment, 21 (1): 1~6

Hector A, Schmid B, Beierkuhnlein C et al. 1999. Plant diversity and productivity experiments in European grasslands. Science, 286: 1123~1127

Hirano T. 2007. Biofuel Resources in Asia, Presentation to the International Biofuel Conference, Tokyo.

Hitz S, Smith J. 2004. Estimating global impacts from climate change. Global Environmental Change, 14: 201~218

Huang B Q, Tian M. 2008. Helpful attempt for minority areas to construct socialistic new village-an investigation of ecological home and civilized new village in Enshi State. Nationalities Research in Qinghai, 19 (2): 125~132

Huang Y, Zhang W, Zheng X H et al. 2006. Estimates of methane emission from Chinese rice paddies by linking a model to GIS database. Acta Ecologica Sinica, 6 (4): 980~988

Huang Y. 2006. Emissions of greenhouse gases in China and its reduction strategy. Quaternary Sciences, 26 (5): 722~732

Hulme M. 1996. Climate Change and Southern Africa. Norwich, United Kingdom: Climatic Research Unit. University of East Anglia. 104~115.

IPCC. 2007. Summary for Policymakers. In: Metz B, Davidson O R, Bosch P R et al. Climate Change 2007: Mitigation. Contribution of Working Group III to the Fourth Assessment Report of the Intergovernmental Panel on Climate Change. Cambridge: Cambridge University Press

Javier Blas, Geoff Dyer. 2009. China sows seeds of food self-sufficiency, Financial Times

Ju H, et al. 2008. Adaptation Framework and Strategy Part 1: A Framework for Adaptation. AEA Group, UK

Ju H, Xiong W, Ma S M et al. 2008. Climate Change and Chinese food security. Beijing: Academy Press

Kevan P G, Clark E A, Thomas V G et al. 1990. Insect pollinators and sustainable agriculture. American Journal of Alternative Agriculture, 5: 13~22

Kong X Z, Pang X P, Zhang Y H et al. 2004. An empirical study on input and causal factors of wheat production in the North China. China Rural Survey, 4: 2~7

Li C S. 2001. Biogeochemical concepts and methodologies: Development of the DNDC model. Quaternary Sciences, 21: 89~99

Li C S, Aber J, Stange F et al. 2000, A process-oriented model of N_2O and NO emissions from forest soils: 1. Model development. Journal of Geophysical Research, 105 (4): 4369~4384

Li C S, Frolking S, Frolking T A. 1992a. A model of nitrous oxide evolution from soil driven by rainfall events: 1. Model structure and sensitivity. Journal of Geophysical Research, 97: 9759~9776

Li C S, Frolking S, Frolking T A. 1992b. A model of nitrous oxide evolution from soil driven by rainfall events: 2. Applications. Journal of Geophysical Research, 97: 9777~9783

Li C S, Narayanan V, Harriss C R. 1996. Model estimates of nitrous oxide emissions from agricultural lands in the United States. Global Biogeochemical Cycles, 10: 297~306

Li X F, Chen M X. 2008. Impact of global warming on Chinnese stock raising. Chinese Journal of Animal Science, 44 (4): 50~53

Li Y H, Wang W Y, Yang L S et al. 2002. Study on the environmental epidemic characteristics and the safety threshold of fluoride of coal-burning fluorosis. Chinese Jouranl of Endemiology, 2002, 20 (1): 41~43

Li Z W, Ren A G, Guan L X et al. 2006. Investigation on indoor air pollution from coal burning in rural area of Shanxi Province. Chinese Journal of Public Health, 22 (6): 728~729

Lin E D. 1997. Climate change and agriculture research findings and policy consideration. Earth Science Frontiers,

4 (1~2): 221~226

Lin E D, Xiong W, Ju H et al. 2005. Climate change impacts on crop yield and quality with CO_2 fertilization in China. Philos. T. Roy. Soc. B, 360: 2149~2154

Liu Y, Kuang Y Q, Huang N S et al. 2008. Rural Biogas Development and Greenhouse Gas Emission Mitigation. China Population Resources and Environment, 18 (3): 84~89

Liu Y, Zhang Y X, Wei Y J et al. 2007. Measurement of emission factors of carbonaceous aerosols from residential coal combustion. Acta Scientiae Circumstantiae, 27 (9): 1409~1416

Lu H, Lu L. 2006. An empirical analysis of the impact of farmers' income level on the household energy consumption structure in the countryside. Finance and Trade Research, 3: 28~34

Lu X Z, Qiu L, Wang L Y. 2003. The contribution of developing biogas on environmental protection and ecology. Renewable Energy, 6: 50~52

Luo G L, Zhang Y M. 2008. Analysis on rural energy consumption of China. Chinese Agricultural Science Bulletin, 24 (12): 535~540

Ma S et al. 2008. "Efficient System Design and Sustainable Finance for China's Village Electrification Program". Midwest Research Institute, Batelle. Available on: http: //www. osti. gov/bridge [2006-12-4]

Markandya A. 2008. Rural Electrification and Rural Energy in China. Paper prepared for the 2nd Meeting of the Task Force on Rural Development and its Energy, Environment and Climate Change Adaptation Policy, CCICED, Beijing, China

McCarthy J J, Canziani O F, Leary N A. 2001. Climate Change 2001: Impacts, Adaptation, and Vulnerability. Cambridge: Cambridge University Press, 235~342

Mirza M Q. 2003. Climate change and extreme weather events: can developing countries adapt. Integrated assessment, 1: 37~48

Nakicenovic N, Alcamo J, Davis G et al. 2000. Special Report on Emissions Scenarios. A Special Report of Working Group III of the Intergovernmental Panel on Climate Change. Cambridge: Cambridge University Press

National Development and Reform Commission. 2007. China's National Climate Change Programme

Nearing M A, Pruski F F, O'Neal M R et al. 2004. Expected climate change impacts on soil erosion rates: A review. Journal of Soil and Water Conservation, 59: 43~50

Niesten E, Rice R. 2004. Sustainable forest management and conservation incentive agreements. International Forestry Review, 6: 56~60

Ouyang Z Y, Xu W H, Wang X Z et al. 2008. Impact assessment of Wenchuan Earthquake on ecosystems. Acta Ecologica Sinica, 28: 5801~5809

Parry L M, Carter R T, Knoijin T N. 1998. The Impact of Climatic Variations on Agriculture. Dordrecht: Kluwer Academic Publisher

Peng S B, Huang J L, Sheehy E J et al. 2004. Rice yields decline with higher night temperature from global warming. Proceedings of the National Academy of Sciences of the United States of America, 101 (27): 9971~9975

Qin X B, Li Y E, Liu K Y. 2006a. The effect of lone-term fertilization treatment on methane emission from rice fields in hunan. Chinese Journal of Agrometeorology, 27 (1): 19~22

Qin X B, Li Y E, Liu K Y. 2006b. Methane and nitrous oxide emission from paddy field under different fertilization treatments. Transactions of the Chinese Society of Agricultural Engineering, 22 (7): 143~148

Reiche K, Covarrubias A, Martinot E. 2000. Expanding Electricity Access to Remote Areas: Off Grid Rural Electrification in Developing Countries. World Power, 52~60

Ringius L, et al. 1996. Climate change in Africa: Issues and challenges in agriculture and water for sustainable development. Report 1996: 8, Oslo: University of Oslo, Center for International Climate and Environmental Research, 128~136

Rosenweig G E, Parry M I. 1994. Potential impact of climate change on food supply. Nature, 367: 133~138

Scherr S, et al. 2004. Tropical forest provides the planet with many valuable services. Are beneficiaries prepared to pay for them? ITTO Tropical Forest Update, 14 (2): 11~14

Shiel M J. 2007. Electricity for Social Development in Ireland. *In*: Barnes D eds. The Challenge of Rural Electrification: Strategies for Developing Countries. Resources for the Future, Washington D. C. and Energy Sector Management Assistance Program, Washington D. C.

Stern N. 2006. The Economics of Climate Change: The Stern Review. Cambridge: Cambridge University Press

Strzepek K, Simth J B. 1995. As climate changes: International impacts and implications. Amsterdam: Springer

Sun F, Yang X, Lin E D et al. 2005. Study on the sensitivity and vulnerability of wheat to climate change in China. Scientia Agricultura Sinica, 38 (4): 692~696

Sun Y M, Li G X, Zhang F D et al. 2005. Status quo and developmental strategy of agricultural residues resources in China. Chinese Society of Agricultural Engineering, 21 (8): 169~173

Sun Z J. 2004. Biomass industry and its developmental trends in China. Transactions of the Chinese Society of Agricultural Engineering, 20 (5): 1~5

Sun Z J, Yuan Z H, Zhang F D et al. 2004. Research Report on Strategy of Utilizing Agricultural Residues as Energy Resource and Biomass Resource in Rural Areas. Strategic research on national medium and long term science and technology development

Tan X C, Liu L W. 2008. Study on the mode of ecological construction in the national minority area. Journal of Anhui Agricultural Sciences, 36 (8): 3337~3338

Tian Y S. 2009. Analysis on the biomass solid fuel industry development in China. Agriculture Engineering Technology (New Energy Industry), 2: 13~17

Van Ittersum M K, Howden M S, Asseng S. 2003. Sensitivity of productivity and deep drainage of wheat cropping systems in a Mediterranean environment to changes in CO_2, temperature and precipitation. Agriculture Ecosystems and Environment, 97: 255~273

Wang F, Wang G H. 2006. Econometric analysis of the impacts of "Four-in-One" household biogas construction on farmers' planting behaviors. Chinese Society of Agricultural Engineering, 22 (3): 116~120

Wang J, et al. 2008. Can China Continue Feeding Itself? —The Impact of Climate Change on Agriculture. Policy research working paper 4470, The World Bank

Wang X H, Feng Z M. 1996. Survey of rural household energy consumption in China. Energy, 21 (7~8): 703~705

Wang X H, Feng Z M. 1997. A survey of rural energy consumption in the developed regions of China. Energy, 22 (5): 511~514

Wang X H, Feng Z M. 2004. Biofuel use and its environmental problems in rural areas of China. Journal of Nanjing Agricultural University, 27 (1): 108~110

Wang X H, Gao S M. 2003. Sustainable Development of Rural Energy in China: Status, Challenger and Countermeasure. China Biogas, 21 (4): 41~43

Wang X H, Wu Z M. 1999. Research on forecast method of rural household energy demand in China. Rural Energy, 5: 1~3

Wang X H. 1994. Situations and trends of China's rural household energy consumption. Journal of Nanjing Agricultural University, 17 (3): 134~141

Wang Z, Zheng Y P, Feng H J. 2001. Simulation of environment and economy security of China under global change with complexity. Journal of Safety and Environment, 1 (4): 19~23

Willey Z, Chameides B. 2007. Harnessing Farms and Forests in the Low-Carbon Economy: How to Create, Measure, and Verify Greenhouse Gas Offsets. Durham: Duke University Press

Xie L Y, Hou L B, Gao X N et al. 2002. Suitable planting regions of winter wheat M808 in Liaoning Province. Journal of Shenyang Agricultural University, 33 (1): 6~10

Xiong W, Lin E D, Ju H et al. 2007. Climate change and critical thresholds in China's food security. Climatic Change, 81: 205~221.

Xiong W, Xu Y L, Lin E D et al. 2005a. Regional simulation of maize yield under IPCC SRES A2 and B2 scenarios. Chinese Journal of Agrometeorology, 2 (1): 11~15

Xiong Wei, Xu Y L, Lin E D et al. 2005b. Regional simulation of rice yield change under two emission scenarios of greenhouse gases. Chinese Journal of Applied Ecology, 16 (1): 65~69

Xiong Wei, Xu Y L, Lin E D et al. 2005c. The simulation of yield variability of winter wheat and its corresponding adaptation options under climate change. Chinese Agricultural Science Bulletin, 21 (5): 380~385

Xu L, Jia J. 2003. The analysis on the contribution rate of fertilizer use to grain production. Science and Technology of Sichuan Grain and Oil, 1: 58~62

Xu X H. 2006. Experimental Studies on Chopping Cotton Stalk When Compressed to High Densities. Shihezi University Master's degree thesis

Yang Xiu, Sun F, Lin E D et al. 2004. Sensitivity and vulnerability analysis of rice to climate change in China. Journal of Natural Disasters, 13 (5): 85~89

Yang Xiu, Sun F, Lin E D et al. 2005. Study on the Sensitivity and Vulnerability of Maize to Climate Change in China. Areal Research and Development, 24 (4): 54~57

Yu H N. 1993. The Impact of Climate Change to Food Production in China. Beijing: The Science and Technology Publish of Beijing, 118~127

Yu J P, Cui P, Wang W Y. 2008. Estimation on SO_2, NO_x and TSP emissions from energy consumption for non-production purpose in rural areas of China. Geographical Research, 27 (3): 547~555

Yu K Z. 2009. Economic situation of livestock feed in 2008 and forecast analysis in 2009. http://www. feedtrade. com. cn/news [2009-1-19]

Yu W J. 2008. The harm and loss of ecosystem assessment of earthquake disaster in Sichuan Province. Acta Ecologica Sinica, 28: 5785~5794

Zhang G W, He W Q. 1998. Arid region flood basic characteristics in China: the case of Xinjiang. Arid Land Geography, 21 (1): 40~48

Zhang P D, Wang G. 2005. Contribution to reduction of CO_2 and SO_2 emission by household biogas construction in rural China: analysis and prediction. Chinese Society of Agricultural Engineering, 21 (12): 147~151

Zhang W X, Sun G. 2008. Potential of CDM project on agriculture and stockbreeding. Jiangxi Energy, 1: 21~23

Zhao X S. 2003. The trends and challenges of rural energy consumption in China. http: //www. ccchina. gov. cn/cn/NewsInfo. asp? NewsId=3957 [2003-3-21]

Zhao Z C. 2006. Latest Advances in Global Climate Projections. Advances in Climate Change Research, 2 (2): 68~70

Zhu S H. 2007. Sustainable development of rural energy in China policy: review and prospect. Issues in Agricultural Economy, 9: 20~25

Zhu Z L, Sun B. 2008. Agricultural non-point source pollution control strategies in China. Environmental Protection, 8: 4~6

85-913-04-05 Key Project Task group. 1994. Forecasting the change trend of N_2O emission from agricultural nitrogen fertilization (1990~2020). Agricultural Environmental Protection, 13 (6): 259~261

Acknowledgements

We would like to thank the China Council for International Cooperation on Environment and Development (CCICED) of the Ministry of Environmental Protection, the Department of Climate Change of the National Development and Reform Commission, and the U. N. -China Climate Change Partnership Framework for leadership and guidance on this research. We would also like to thank the U. N. Development Program, CCICED, and the Environmental Defense Fund for generous financial support, and the China International Center for Economic and Technical Exchanges of the Ministry of Commerce for management support. We also give special thanks to Mr. Zhu Guangyao, Mr. Shen Guofang, Dr. Art Hanson, Mr. Li Yonghong, Ms. Lu Xueyun, Ms. Zhang Ou from CCICED, Mr. Zhang Weidong and Ms. Zhang Yu from UNDP, Ms. Li Liyan, Mr. Wu Jianmin and Ms. Li Yan from NDRC, Ms. Zhu Duanni, Mr. Libin, Ms. Tian Yuanshi and Ms. Gao Jing from CCICED, your tireless work ensured the success of this project.